Friends and Lovers

Mary Bernard has written one previous novel,
Truth and Consequences,
published by Secker & Warburg in 1983.
Born in Canada, she has lived
in England for the past thirty years.

MARY BERNARD

Friends and Lovers

Mandarin

A Mandarin Paperback
FRIENDS AND LOVERS

First published in Great Britain 1994
by Mandarin Paperbacks
and William Heinemann Ltd
imprints of Reed Consumer Books Ltd
Michelin House, 81 Fulham Road, London SW3 6RB
and Auckland, Melbourne, Singapore and Toronto

Copyright © Mary Bernard 1994
The author has asserted her moral rights

A CIP catalogue record for this title
is available from the British Library
ISBN 0 7493 1599 7

Printed and bound in Great Britain
by Cox & Wyman Ltd, Reading, Berks

ONE

Chapter 1

Feminism solves nothing, she had thought around five in the morning. Nothing, nothing in the world of love and partings. But she suppressed that bit of the story—she would never hear the end of it from Maggie if she admitted it. 'You had his number all along,' she said instead; that much she was willing to grant.

'You could tell?' said Maggie. 'And I thought I'd been so diplomatic.'

Elinor looked at her askance. 'Diplomatic, fiddlesticks. You said he was another of my brilliant loonies, remember?'

Maggie's lips twitched. 'I did? Well...it's true. He's the cream of the crop, too—wanting you to want it even though he didn't.'

'He wanted me to grieve for it,' Elinor said ruefully.

'But—your period was late, that's all. How could you grieve for a baby that never even existed?'

'He said if I loved him I'd be grieving because I *wasn't* pregnant.'

'Crumbs. Nuttier than a fruitcake.'

'The rest is just a blur.' Elinor shook her head. 'It's sunk without trace, and no wonder. I was brain-dead by dawn, but John was still going strong—and on and on all morning, right through till midday, when I said I had to go to work. "You're walking out on me just to open that *fleapit*?" he said. "Don't bother coming back, then—that's *it*." He was *apoplectic*.'

Maggie snorted. 'Graduate students! He'd sing a different tune if he had a job himself.'

'Anyhow, something snapped, I'd had enough. I said, "That's fine by me—but let's at least be friends." But John said: "I'd as soon be friends with a cobra. And you're not leaving—*I* am;" and slammed down the stairs ahead of me.'

'But you were at *his* place—where did he think he was going?'

'God knows. It struck me as so funny that I let out a shriek of laughter, even though I felt like the wreck of the Hesperus. Maybe he heard me, because when I rang yesterday to tell him to fetch his things that were at my flat, he just shouted—'

'Chuck it all out?'

'Bull's-eye,' said Elinor, surprised. The men she got involved with—'your boy-men', Maggie called them—were forever making melodramatic gestures, but surely Maggie's grown-up Clive never did. 'Anyhow, I took the stuff over to his place, but he wouldn't come down—I had to leave it by the door. I could see him peering through the window, though, like Mrs Danvers.'

Maggie burst into laughter; after a moment, so did Elinor. They were best friends, enjoyed each other, laughed at the same jokes, and told each other as much of everything as anyone ever does; their friendship felt like one of the primary bonds that last a lifetime. In ways they were a lot alike, but sometimes all they noticed were the differences: they belonged to different genera- tions, though Maggie was only a year older. Elinor was optimistic and vaguely radical—straight out of the seventies. Maggie was a throwback to the nineteen fifties, pessimistic and conservative. What she wanted more than anything was to marry Clive and have children. But he was married already, with children he adored; and though he talked about leaving, he never did.

'Have a baby on your own,' Elinor sometimes suggested. 'Have two. Leave them with nannies. On your salary you could afford it.'

'Children need both parents, and their mother at home,' Maggie always said—and she lived by what she believed. So did Elinor, but for her it was easier: she rolled with the punches. Maggie took things hard; and wore her exasperating offhand gallantry like a badge of style: like Marlene Dietrich in *Dishonoured*, playing the piano in front of the firing squad.

Maggie refilled their glasses, and Elinor gave her a wry toast. 'I feel better now—you've laughed me into it,' she said. 'But I was *miserable*. Another man I've walked out on—you can imagine. John, Adam, Ludovic, Martin—ten years of men so fine-tuned that the least hint of common sense drives them wild—men so unhappy they infect me with it—it's exhausting.'

4

'Your counterculture dafties—you know I've never seen the attraction.' Maggie hardly thought of them as men at all; they were weedy poetic boys, who tended to look through her, not at her. She was used to having an effect on men. When she didn't, she unconsciously assumed it was because their sexual appetites weren't very strong. Secretly she had always been a little sorry for Elinor.

'But what is it about me?' said Elinor, who was badly shaken by her string of failures. 'Why can't I make anybody happy, or be happy with anybody—'

'Nonsense, Nell, it's not you, it's them. They're as convoluted as corkscrews, and you're the opposite—'

'Simple-minded?' Elinor said drily.

'Straightforward was what I was *going* to say. That's what attracts them to you in the first place, but then they're too screwed up to take advantage of it.'

'Bored to tears, no doubt, so they pick fights for diversion.'

'Ninny. They pick fights because it's their nature. They'd do it with anyone.'

'They say it's me.'

'They'd *say* that to anyone. Look, the only thing I think you should ask yourself is why you go for these cross-grained types instead of somebody more solid—'

'Stockbrokers?' Elinor suggested. 'Accountants?...Civil servants?'

'Don't sink *that* low.' Maggie was a civil servant.

'What I think—I should take a break. Steer clear of men for a while, think things over, work out what keeps going wrong. A year of celibacy.'

'A year? You? You haven't been celibate for six weeks since the age of eighteen.'

'I have too.'

'When?'

'There was ... No, that was only... But there must...' Elinor laughed and gave in. 'Still, you're never too old to start. A year—or at least six months.'

'That's the quickest climb-down I've ever seen. You won't last a month.'

'A bet—loser does the New Year's meal?' They always had dinner together on New Year's day.

'You're on.'

Elinor lasted a month, but not six, so they both lost the bet, or won. One bought the wine and the other the food, and they cooked it together at Maggie's flat in Great James Street—three light, airy rooms furnished with what Maggie called her Maples' heirlooms. Her formidably modern kitchen was too narrow for table and chairs; they ate in the sitting room, at a table set with candles and sprigged china.

'To happiness,' Elinor said, lifting her glass and leaning across to kiss Maggie.

'To yours, anyhow,' Maggie said with a grimace.

'Things no different, then?'

'Not a scrap. I know he won't leave, I *know* he won't. But I have fantasies. I miss him. Seeing him at work isn't enough; having lunch together isn't enough. Nothing is. Not the odd hours after work when he rings his wife and says he's missed his train; and not our Wednesday evenings'—which Clive regularly spent with Maggie under pretence of a weekly bridge game. 'I probably see almost as much of him as she does, but it's not the same. And Christmas is the worst—going to parties alone; fending off the hordes.' She shrugged. 'Your turn. Tell me about this young man you met at the NFT.'

Elinor grinned. 'You'd have loved it. I'd put next month's programmes in the foyer and stopped for coffee, and he sat down across from me and did a sort of double-take and said, "Aren't you an usherette at that cinema in Bloomsbury?" "I'm the manager," I said. "And it's usher, not usherette." '

Maggie groaned. 'Nell, Nell, you don't deserve—'

'Yeah, not very tactful. But he saw the point.'

'Oh-oh, another daftie.'

'No, he's different. That is, he's got the same sort of politics as me; but he *seems* much more conservative. More solid—remember? His clothes, for instance. Not just the evening dress—he can't help that, he wears it for a living, like a headwaiter. But even in the daytime he always wears a jacket and tie.'

6

Maggie whooped. She was an elegant creature, petite and composed, with small pointy features, short silky mouse-brown hair and amused light brown eyes. But she wasn't composed when she laughed; she rocked back and forth and snorted and gasped and crowed. It was irresistible.

Elinor usually stifled her laugh behind her hand—she was self-conscious about her front teeth, which were slightly crooked, though less so than she imagined. She was tall and thin, with olive skin and dark brown eyes and hair. She wore shirts and jeans or loose skirts where Maggie wore suits; but even in smart clothes she soon looked untidy: she had utterly uncooperative hair that slithered out of the slides she pinned it back with or the knots she wound it up in. She had cut it short once, but with her small head and long neck she had looked as if she came to a point.

'Well, none of my other men did,' she said defensively. 'And if you want solid—Tim's got a decent-sized house in Islington all to himself; he bought it with a legacy, before prices went sky high. He makes wonderful furniture in his spare time—he's got dining chairs sort of like those ladder-back Mackintosh ones—'

'An owner-occupier into DIY—promising. More solid than bedsits, anyhow.'

'Not necessarily. Chris is an owner-occupier—I bet you wouldn't call her solid.' Elinor and Chris Haldane had lived in the same squat when Elinor was an undergraduate. Chris had been a medical student with a husband and three children. Since then she had become a medical sociologist, got divorced, joined a collective household that broke up, founded another that still survived, had affairs with a couple of women and several men, and written the timely books that were starting to make her something of a media star, always living vividly in a welter of crossed love and booze.

Maggie and Chris were the only friends from student days whom Elinor still saw much of. The rest had moved away from Bloomsbury, and she, who worked afternoons and evenings, couldn't easily keep up with people who had regular daytime jobs and lived halfway across London. Chris, too, had moved, out to Dulwich—ditchwater Dulwich, she called it—after years of seedy inner-city squats and flats. But she worked a stone's throw away from the cinema, leading a research group in University College, and stopped by Elinor's office now and then. Elinor was always glad to see her, though she was never sure how much she liked her.

Maggie snorted. 'I know what I'd call her—the witch of Endor.'

'Come on, she's entertaining in small doses—admit.'

'Hmph. Her and that rackety commune—they'll drum them out of Dulwich one of these days. Anyhow. Tim's spare time, you were saying. He makes furniture.'

'And music—that's how musicians relax, it seems. He's got a string quartet on Sunday mornings with some friends; and after concerts he winds down by playing the piano. He's asked me along to the quartet, but I need to sleep in after the Saturday late show. I'm fed up with a sixty-hour week—I'm going to get a co-manager.'

'You've been saying that for the past five years.'

'But now I mean it. Stanley's less willing to sub for me these days.' Stanley was the former manager of the Cromer; he had hired Elinor as a part-time usher when she was a student, then as assistant manager until he retired. 'He gets ill, too, and then I don't even get a day off. Enough's enough. I'll advertise in the trade press—I've already cleared it with the Wellesfords.'

'Sounds to me as if you're in love with him.'

'Nah—too old for me.'

'Not Stanley, dope—Tim.'

It felt like pushing her luck to admit it. 'Um...I don't know. For one thing I hardly ever *see* him, except last thing at night—he's always working. After his last involvement broke up, he said yes to all the engagements he was offered—'

'Drowning his sorrows in work, I know the feeling—'

'But now he's stuck with them—and he keeps making new ones. He's single, so he's the first person the fixers ring for a last-minute substitute; and he doesn't know how to say no. Like this week—we were going to have lunch together tomorrow, but now he can't make it all week: he's got recording sessions, subbing for someone who's ill. He's not easy to get to know, either—he doesn't talk about himself much. Maybe that's what I mean by more conservative. It's the first time I've begun an affair without *discussions*—you know, the ethics of sexuality under late capitalism, sort of thing. This just...started.'

They had been standing in her office. She couldn't remember what she'd said, only the emphatic, suddenly personal tone of his reply: 'I don't think you could ever say anything that would offend me.' His mouth wasn't smiling, but his whole face seemed to be, ardour on offer beneath his frank jovial surface.

They were hardly a foot apart. She was stifling with impatience. He just stood there, looking at her. She tried to make herself do something, but couldn't break through all that conditioning. He reached for her shoulder. The rest of her came with it—how, she could hardly tell in her violent triumph—and they were touching from head to knee, moving hands to small of back, to arse, to hip, in a hot exploratory silence that bypassed high-souled explanations and declarations.

'I don't know,' she said again. 'He likes movies, I like music, we both like walking everywhere...'

Maggie, who didn't, made a face.

'And I'm comfortable with him, and he's entertaining; and reasonably sane—at least he doesn't visibly *twitch*, like the others. And...but...I don't know. Sometimes I'm sure—like the first time I heard him play—in my office: a few bars of something he'd just performed—very quietly, like whispering, so it wouldn't carry to the auditorium. His face...'

It had shone with secret joy. Usually he looked both cheerful and inwardly perturbed; she was startled to see him so transformed. 'Or sometimes when I see him unexpectedly'—meeting him for dinner after work; her eye finding him immediately in the buzzing after-concert crowd: alone, in white tie, tall, bulky, downy of countenance; the shock that ran through her at the entire filling-in of the blurred image that was all her memory had retained. 'But...I need to know him better. It was easier with the boy-men—these solid types take more digging.'

You're in love with him, all right, Maggie thought. She felt like a tug bringing Elinor in to dock. Nearly there, nearly safe. Don't rock the boat—let her find it out for herself.

9

Chapter 2

Before drafting an advertisement Elinor rang round the other reps to say there was a job going. That night a young woman came to the office. She had blue eyes, short curly brown hair, chipmunk cheeks and an animated face, pale with high colour that came and went.

'It's about the job,' she said in a high, clear voice. 'Peter Howden—I work at the Electric—he says you want an assistant manager. I'm Rose, Rose Quinlan. I think he'll give me a good reference, but I expect you need to interview me, right?' She plumped herself down comfortably. 'Though it'd be less hierarchical if I interviewed you at the same time—you know, check out your qualifications as an employer.'

'It might get a bit confusing'—drily. 'Perhaps we can take turns.'

Rose didn't notice the irony. 'Okay, you first,' she said, taking off her duffle coat. She was wearing faded purple cords and several jerseys with wavy stretched hems.

'To start with, I don't just want an assistant,' Elinor explained. 'I'm looking for someone to train as a co-manager—same pay, same responsibilities, equal say in everything.'

'Oh wow. I'd like to manage a cinema myself someday, sort of political and avant-garde, like The Other Cinema. Not that it's likely, they're folding all the time; but being co-manager here—I'd have more credibility if a screen ever does come up.'

Political, avant-garde—it went with the clothes and the non-hierarchical kick-off. What would Rose want to show—*Salt of the Earth*? *Nightcleaners*? 'Um, well, to put it bluntly, I keep my politics and my programming in separate compartments. The Cromer's a mainstream rep—and it's got to stay solvent, which it wouldn't with that kind of programming. Besides'—showing her colours—'mainstream movies are what I *like*.'

'Me too, isn't it awful,' Rose agreed, as if admitting to an illicit addiction.

Elinor couldn't help grinning. 'Another point—I try to keep things non-hierarchical, but I'll be training a co-manager in *my* methods. I'm open to suggestion, but the final decisions are mine. Once the trainee is ready to become a co-manager, it changes to equal say and all that...' It was surprisingly hard to say it. Equal say—share her cinema—*her* cinema, all its successes hers? 'But in the meantime—maybe you'd be uncomfortable; or frustrated with the programming.'

'You lay it right on the line, don't you?' Rose said admiringly. 'No problem—you've got to please the bosses. And the Cromer's the wrong venue for a political cinema anyhow. Too many seats; too many apolitical me-generation students in the audience.'

That was astute. 'Well then, what about a quick canter through your c.v.?'

Rose looked mutinous—did she expect Elinor to check out her theory of cinema, not her background?—then yielded. 'I'm twenty-three'—a surprise, her fluting voice and self-confidence made her seem older, in spite of her round youthful face. 'I'm against labelling people by educational qualifications, but if you really want to know—You do? Right. Two years at Essex—sociology. But I split before the second-year exams and came and lived in a squat in Notting Hill.'

Her accent was ripe and fruity underneath her carefully flattened vowels. Elinor was amused to catch herself bridling at it—she hadn't known she had such a chip on her shoulder.

'I was working in a wholefoods collective—all the comrades with that hangdog vegetarian look. I *approve* of the wholefoods principle, but I've got this degenerate craving for crisps and sugar-coated cereals. I used to sneak out and buy sweets with the petty cash. So I quit—it was too *low*, ripping off one's own collective. And I was afraid they'd smell Smarties on my breath.'

Elinor laughed and began to enjoy Rose, accent and jargon and all. Maybe having a colleague could be fun—and she'd rather share the Cromer, after all, than work sixty hours a week for the rest of her life.

11

'Then I started ushering at the Electric—strictly temporary till I found something more political. But I'm a film freak. I like seeing movies three or four times, even bad ones; and manning, I mean womanning, the ticket office; and hanging out in the projection booth picking up tricks of the trade; and getting Peter to teach me how to do accounts—I'm not bad with figures—and how to programme one film against another so they'll both take money; and rushing off to Wardour Street for an armload of cans the distributors forgot to send; and working on programme layouts; and—and—everything about working in a cinema. So I deserted the revolution—and here I am. What else do you want to know?'

Elinor had a pricking in her thumbs. Most film buffs thought of a rep job as a way of getting paid to see all the films they themselves were interested in, and no others. What this unlikely young woman enjoyed was the multitude of odd jobs that were the real work of running a cinema. 'I think we've about covered it. If I decide...'

She'd already decided; why not say so? 'I'll have to check your references, and get the Wellesfords' agreement,' she said. 'They're the owners. They'll want you on probation for a while—I was at first. Other than that, the job's yours—depending on what you decide after interviewing *me*. I believe you wanted to? Fire away.'

Rose looked startled but recovered fast. 'Oh, I have been, all along as we talked. Now all I need to know'—briskly—'is sordid details like hours and job description and pay.'

Ah. She'd wondered if Rose would get round to basics. Full marks, feet on the ground. 'Okay, let's get down to brass tacks.' They gave each other a friendly look, as if something had been settled.

'No frills, as you can see,' Elinor said the day Rose started work. They were in the outer office, a big room with a smaller room off it, both rooms furnished with battered desks and old green filing cabinets. The outer office also held several lumpy armchairs. 'Stanley liked this room, so he put me in the inner office—which I quite like; I hung on to it when he retired. So I'll keep it, if that's okay with you—unless company bothers you: this is where the cashier and the ushers sit in their breaks.'

'Hang loose,' said Rose. 'This is great—I like the eye of the storm.' She brightened the walls with a poster of Janis Joplin, and the grey cord carpeting with a red dhurrie rug. She also brought an electric kettle and a packet of tisanes. The stand in the foyer sold coffee, fruit juice, carrot cake and all-dairy ice cream, but Rose was watching her weight, so fruit juice was out; and she had not so completely abandoned the wholefoods principle as to drink coffee.

Rose and Elinor were comfortable together right away. 'It's great having somebody to talk shop with,' Elinor told her after a week. 'There's been nobody since Stanley retired. Mrs Ekins'—the full-time usher—'isn't interested in movies at all; and Margaret stays up in the projection booth between films—shy, I suppose.'

'Yeah, I went up to get acquainted, and she could hardly wait till I split. But what about the UCL kids'—the part-time ushers, who were mostly students at University College. 'Aren't they movie freaks?'

'Sure, but they don't give a damn about the problems of running a rep—as you'll find out when you try to explain why you can't mount seasons of Telugu documentaries or...'

'Japanese silents: that's what Marcus hopes we'll do a season of. I told him no way.'

Marcus was the man Rose was semi-living with, a moody, brown-bearded, don't-care-how-I-look ex-schoolmaster too distraught by unemployment to decide between her and her rival, a woman in Brighton. 'He goes to her whenever he's fed up with me,' she had explained. 'Or maybe he comes to me when he's pissed off with her. It's dire, whichever.' Her bright composure wavered. 'What about you and Tim, or shouldn't I ask? He's très Cary Grant in white tie, I must say.'

'Ask away, but I haven't got much of an answer. He's such heaven, compared to the people I've been with before—I keep pinching myself, wondering when the trouble will start.'

'Maybe it won't.'

'Maybe.' Safe haven at last? Tim was less buoyant than Elinor, but he didn't keep veering to extremes: he was stable—solid, in Maggie's word. They'd been involved for a couple of months now,

13

and he hadn't started making wild accusations or falling into suicidal depressions; they hadn't even had a quarrel.

Chris breezed in one day, her irregular face witchy above a potpourri of loose black clothes. She had been signing copies in Foyle's. 'Too incredibly tedious,' she said with satisfaction. 'Why people want autographed copies I don't know. I've brought you one, Nell, d'you want it signing?'

'Oh please,' Elinor said with a straight face. 'And this is Rose, our new co-manager.'

Rose, beet-pink, said, 'Hi, I'm a great fan of yours.'

Chris dug in her bag, produced another copy, inscribed it to Rose with a flourish, caught Elinor's eye and grinned and shrugged, then zipped off with a quick, 'Ta-ra.'

'Mindblowing,' said Rose. 'Your friend Chris, you didn't say she was Chris *Haldane*. She's one of my heroines. *Demystifying Medicine*, *Childbirth and After*, *Quest*—they're terrific!'

'Yes, well, she's quite something,' Elinor said vaguely. Let her make up her own mind about Chris.

Rose gave her a shrewd look. 'But...?'

'Um, I suppose just that we're friends for old times' sake as much as having a lot in common. But she's full of life.'

'There's still stuff to learn, but you know the routine,' Elinor said three weeks later. 'The rest is just details. Ready to be left on your own?'

Rose looked pleased, but apprehensive. 'Uhhh...can I ring you if disaster strikes?'

'Sure. Now, what about days off? I expect we'd both like Sunday and Monday—maybe we should alternate?' They would both have to work on Saturday; it was the Cromer's busiest day.

'Uh, Sunday's the day Marcus has his brother out of the home, the one with Down's—'

'Then you must—I wouldn't want—'

'No, what I mean...A whole day of Buffy—working Sunday is the perfect letout,' Rose blurted. 'If it's okay by you, I mean.' She looked terribly embarrassed.

14

Elinor touched her shoulder. 'I'd feel exactly the same, don't worry. And it's incredibly convenient for me—I'll have more time with Tim. He tries to keep Sundays and Mondays free.'

'Great, then what if I take Thursday and Friday off—oh no, you'll need me for the late on Friday—you say they're sometimes rowdy.'

'Nah, that's okay, I'll do it alone. I always have, after all; it's not so bad.'

'Then I'll do the late show Saturday,' said Rose.

It was just what Elinor had been hoping for. 'Terrific. I won't be zonked on Sunday mornings, I can take in Tim's quartet.'

'Good,' said Tim when she told him. 'That is, if you'd like to. Chives ready?' They were at her flat. His place was much bigger and more comfortable, but Elinor didn't want him to think she was moving in on him unasked, so she made sure they took turns.

She passed him the chopping board. 'Like to? I'm *dying* to.'

'We're just amateurs,' Tim said with sudden diffidence. 'That is, I'm not, and Sheila's almost not, but Thoby and Alan are. And it's not like a concert, we do bits over and over, dead slow sometimes. You might not—'

'That won't matter, you'll be playing real music. It whets my appetite hearing you practise.'

'It's boring, I know—just exercises,' he said, flicking the chives into the soup and ladling it out. He thought she was just being polite. He hated practising with anyone else around—it was like being a child again, steeling himself to practise, sure that his parents hated the noise. He could hardly ask her to go back to her flat after spending the night with him, but he sometimes wished she had to leave for work after breakfast, like other women he had been involved with.

'Boring—are you crazy? It's *wonderful*, like—like—I don't know. Skeletons.'

'Deathly, you mean?' he said drily.

'You know I don't. Like drawings where you still see the construction lines, that sort of thing.'

15

He had never imagined that a non-musician could feel the way he did about exercises. He flushed; the warmth was soothing, like putting a hot flannel to his face. 'You're more musical than you think,' he said.

She started her soup. 'Mmm, delicious. But I don't *know* anything about music, I just...respond.'

'That's all most people do, even musicians. You don't need to know a...a rondo from a fugue, any more than I need to know about...editing films, say. What matters is *listening*. To the whole thing, not just the juicy bits and the rest as background for your thoughts.'

'Oh.' She was pleased—flattered. 'Well, I do tend to get sidetracked when I'm listening, but I'll try.'

Music wasn't the chief reason for hoping Tim would ask her to live with him, but it was one of them. She had hardly come across classical music at all until the age of fifteen, when a teacher played Beethoven's Ninth in class. It had been love at first earful; and she had started buying records—but not going to concerts. They were for people who understood music, not people like her. It was years before she realised she was wrong, and by then she was working nights and could hardly ever get to concerts. So until now she had heard very little live music. It was a wonderful luxury, after their nights at Ockendon Road, to sit in the front room with the double doors to the music room open, while Tim practised and she read the paper over a second cup of coffee and now and then glanced up to see him sitting askew on a straight chair, with his music stand angled to catch the light from the back window and his left profile in silhouette—beak nose, backlit fuzz of hair, lips thin with concentration, jowl creased into a lopsided double chin from pressing the violin—unfurling scales, arpeggios, and études in smooth glowing tones: the raw materials of music, like rich bolts of silk in Liberty's.

A peaceful time, in a peaceful house. Tim hadn't done much to it, but he had overpainted 1950s cream with 1970s white and papered the basement dining room with fine-striped summer-woods green—'It's like an aquarium,' he said deprecatingly. He had also had bottle-green carpet laid throughout the ground floor, and put up heavy bottle-green velvet curtains, floor to ceiling on mahogany poles. For the acoustics, he said, but that explained only the fabric, not the colour. On sunny days it was like being in a pergola; on dark days, in a wood.

He didn't have much furniture: a few pieces that he'd made himself, and some Edwardian hand-me-downs from his parents, the varnish honey-thick. 'I don't like buying things,' he had told her: 'I've got this fantasy of making it all myself in my spare time, though I never will—just those dining chairs took a couple of months each.' Only the music room was fully furnished. What with his practice chair and music stand, his grand piano, chairs for the quartet, and shelves full of music, records and hi-fi equipment, it was even crowded. The drawing room next door was almost bare by comparison: big speakers, a small sofa, bookcases, a twisty standard lamp, and armchairs with caved-in seats. The rest of the house was like the drawing room—a bare minimum in each room. Maybe that was why it was peaceful. Elinor loved the sense of space, the high ceilings, the deep green and white. She'd never lived in a place with lots of room round the furniture; it was very easy to get used to. Ockendon Road was beginning to feel like home, and her own flat was becoming just somewhere to store her things while...until...

Chapter 3

Once in rare exasperation Sheila Canterbury asked Thoby if he believed in *anything*. 'Oh yes,' he had replied. 'The good, the true and the beautiful. In other words'—more lightly—'you.'

Sheila had been born happy. In all her baby snaps she was...not sunny; hers was a more delicate light. Moonly; beaming moon-beams—as she still did, in spite of all that had clouded her life. The trusting warmth of her smile was unchanged, and the caution in her eyes seemed no more than an endearing shyness. Everybody who met her warmed to her; everybody who knew her loved her—her old people, the whole Debec clan, Thoby himself. Her veiled moonliness made him want to snatch away the cobwebs.

Her trust moved him, and her need for him: fragmentary things she sometimes let fall: 'You hold me together,' 'You make me possible;' as if he were a knight in shining armour—which he guessed wasn't the way the rest of the world saw him. He was volatile and fantastical, with a zany manner which he had put on as self-protection so long ago that it was nearly second nature.

She had seemed so much better last summer, nearly the way she'd been when he met her—happy on holiday with his cousins and their babies, and so wistful, parting from the babies when the holiday ended, that he'd said, 'Shall we?' They were both thirty: time to start if they were ever going to—and he passionately wanted children, but hadn't dared say so till Sheila regained the ground she'd lost.

She had looked panicky, then said, 'If you want...if you think...yes, let's.'

Three months later she was pregnant—and all right, at first: almost her old giggly self. Then she went quiet, and he had begun worrying; but hadn't known what to say, or how, or when; or

18

whether saying something wouldn't make it worse. She hated him to ask if she was okay: 'As if I'm in remission and you're waiting for an outbreak,' she'd once put it.

That other time, a few years back, her retreat had been abrupt and drastic: she had scarcely been able to speak. This time it was slower, more practised. She pretended nothing was wrong, putting a smooth blank surface up between them like a wall; but behind it she was just as remote. During the week she stayed late at work, practised when she got home, then watched television till bedtime; at the weekend she immersed herself in writing letters and reports. She listened politely if he spoke, but replied in monosyllables, or nothing. If he asked what was wrong, she pretended not to understand him, or else said something about problems at work. If he tried to hug her, she went limp as a rag doll. Every few days she did turn to him to make love—but not lovingly: as neutrally and impersonally as you could do such a thing. Sometimes she said, 'I will make love to you, I will make love to you,' as if steeling herself to it, which made him not want to go on; but he did, because she wanted him to—the absurd gentlemanliness of it made him want to laugh in the midst of his miserable desire—and because it was the only time he got to touch her. His need to hold her and be held was even greater than his need for sex.

His need to talk and listen—tell her what was on his mind, learn what was on hers—was perhaps greater still.

If he'd known what he was in for, would he ever have got involved with her? Maybe, maybe not. But life didn't work that way; you fell in love, and that was that: in one moment—her face turned up to his with snowflakes landing on it and melting, and then one that didn't melt. He'd brushed it off and kissed her, and her whole body had reached up with neediness.

Her hands were cold. 'Put them in my pockets,' he had said, and she did, and stood there looking at him with delight, and the wariness of an animal surprised in the undergrowth.

Thoby Debec was business manager of the Haydn Chamber Orchestra—he had become an accountant in a fit of late-adolescent rebellion against his bohemian clan, but ended up in their world

19

anyhow, by the back door. By the time he'd guessed that his mother might have put the conductor up to hiring him, the job had him hooked, and she could say, 'Thoby manages the Haydn—he always was musical,' so vaguely that anyone who didn't know better would think that managing was like conducting, only more so.

Tim was leader of the Haydn—it was one of his most regular engagements. He saw Thoby at a rehearsal the day after Elinor said she could come to the quartet, but forgot to mention it. He had to ring on Saturday night to ask, 'Mind if I bring someone tomorrow?'

Thoby answered—Sheila was practising. 'Fine,' he replied. 'Lunch, too, of course.' After ringing off he told Sheila, 'He's bringing "someone"—sex unspecified. Woman? New romance? Must be, don't you think?'

She had rested her bow hand on her knee while he was on the telephone. She waited a moment longer, in case he had more to say. He didn't, so she found her place and went on with the movement.

Was her need for silence so absolute that they couldn't even have a moment's gossip? His patience was fraying. God, her tone was wonderful, even now, even on a workaday instrument. She should have a Ruggieri, an Amati—might have had, if...

Sometimes her music made him forget his longings, but not tonight. When she reached the end of the movement, he said, 'We've got to talk *sometimes*.'

She laid the cello in its case and clipped the bow inside the lid, saying, 'I've got to wash my hair.'

She hadn't said she wouldn't talk. Maybe she was ready to?

First she squirted herself in the face with the shower-hose, then she spilt most of the shampoo. There was enough left for her hair— which didn't actually need washing. Anything to get away. Why couldn't he leave her in peace?

When he suggested having children, she had said yes, trusting him to know what she could cope with. But he hadn't. She was so angry it frightened her, and so frightened she could hardly breathe.

Her body was hardly changed yet; but her life was changed. When babies screamed, she was sure they were about to die. Would her baby die? Hate her? How could she teach it how to cope with life when she didn't know how herself?

People who didn't live in fear couldn't imagine what it was like—Thoby couldn't. The only time she was free of it was when she was playing, or when someone scared and helpless needed her.

The cello made her whole. Playing, she was hidden in it, enclosed. She became the instrument, or maybe the music—like a singer singing: giving voice to herself: to the thread of herself that was powerful, eloquent, possessed of desire.

She had had to give it up, had to. To this day she didn't fully know why, but fear wasn't the reason—or not fear of playing.

Thoby was so happy; she fed on it—she couldn't imagine life without him. People relied on her at work, and she was terrified of failing them—not her old people, all the rest: the finance committee; the Council; her secretary; the alcoholics' group; the uncontrollably ever-expanding women's support group, thirty-five of them turning to her—her of all people!—for words of wisdom. She got through her fits of terror by pretending she was him: doing what he would do, saying what he would say.

It worked—her colleagues at the Falcon thought she was fearless. 'Give Sheila the tough jobs,' they said—and did; and she did them, and well: got her old people what they needed—a new set of teeth, somewhere to live—pestered people, barged into consulting rooms, staged sit-down strikes in social security offices: *got it done*, and easily, because in those situations she didn't exist. She disappeared into the problem, as into the cello; became the diplomacy, the bullying, the stratagems; wasn't herself, but inside the role—like the singer and her song.

She had imagined disappearing inside the role of mother, too. A pregnant woman, content. Then a mother, smiling at a child. By the time she saw how wrong she was, she was pregnant.

She should have known better. Thoby should have. Now it was too late. Not technically—the information was on cards at the Falcon; she'd looked it up. But week followed week and she just got frozen deeper into silence. It seemed to be easier to have a baby than say she couldn't.

— * —

21

Thoby heard the hair dryer stop whining, but she didn't come back. He found her in bed in a drift of black hair, asleep. Genuinely asleep, sound asleep: she could fall asleep anytime. 'I used to sleep a lot, it made time pass,' she had said once.

Used to—and now again. Sleeping Beauty. That other time, he had once shaken her awake and said, 'You've got to *talk* to me.'

'What about?'

'You. Me. Us.'

'What about us?'

She sounded so cooperative, echoing him in that soft voice, and her courtesy never broke. He had eventually given up.

This time he didn't try. He let himself out of the flat, stumped down the stairs, and took a turn round the square. The houses, once rather imposing, were on the way back up after sinking to multiple-occupancy slums; there were always skips in the road. In one of them he spied a set of panelled shutters. Builders asleep at the wheel—they could flog them down the architectural salvage. He hauled them out, shook off the plaster and carted them upstairs; they were just the thing for the bathroom.

Sheila practised every day, even when she wasn't hiding. Thoby was forever meaning to and putting it off until Sunday morning, when he leapt up from breakfast and hurried through the music they were about to play.

Today was no exception. He was still trying to master a tricky bit in the minuet of the Dissonance quartet when the doorbell rang.

A flurry of hellos; everybody assessing everybody; Tim hoping Thoby and Sheila would think well of Elinor and she of them; Elinor expecting frightfully superior beings, and almost afraid to look at Sheila. On the walk up to Hackney she had asked Tim about them.

'They're nice, you'll like them,' he had unilluminatingly said.

She pressed him for more, but he was at a loss until she got specific: 'Okay, Sheila. What does she look like?'

'Beautiful,' he said definitely. 'Big eyes; very thin—skin and bones; very feminine in manner—'

'Meaning...?' she had said challengingly, feeling attacked.

'Er...a mysterious air. Malleable, soft, willing, all the feminine things. No threat to men.'

Unlike me? she had thought, convinced she would hate her. Feminine, malleable—yuck.

The doorbell again: Alan Golde, the second violin, a stout, turnip-faced man in his late forties, wearing a V-necked jersey, a brown wool tie and Hush Puppies.

Sheila showed Elinor to an armchair in the bay window at the front of the long sitting room, and the players set four kitchen chairs in a semicircle, put up their stands and got out their music— Tim very quickly: he did it every day; Alan slow and businesslike; Thoby darting and bobbing: raising his stand and lowering it again; switching a light on and then off.

Before tuning up, Sheila tied back her smooth black hair. It was thickly streaked with white at the sides, though she was only thirty. She was as thin as Tim had said, and as beautiful—waifish, with a wide delicate face, large, almost protruding blue eyes, a soft appealing voice and a hesitant manner. But Elinor didn't hate her— surely no one could. She was lovable, the way children are—and painfully shy; far from flaunting her beauty, she seemed to shrink from observation.

Elinor had never heard two good musicians playing in an ordinary room in a house, let alone four. She wasn't prepared for the rich piercing sweet vibrant rush of harmony, melody, undertone, overtone. It filled the room from top to bottom, side to side, front to back, vibrating the very floorboards beneath her feet. It was physical, sensual, like walking head first into a high wind. Impossible to float along easily with the tune; she was in at the deep end, overwhelmed; yet for the first time in her life could easily follow all the parts as they came simultaneously and equally to her ravished attention.

Tim was the first violin, the one professional player, his tone richer, his notes true, his line carrying them triumphant over moments when Alan or Thoby fumbled—though they were much more competent, especially Sheila, than the word amateur had led her to expect.

23

'I try to hold back and play somewhere near their level,' he had said. If *this* was holding himself back, this clear soaring line that bound them together and led them forward, what was he like at full stretch? His face was shining. In love with him—of course she was. It was a wonder that every woman at his concerts didn't succumb. Maybe they did—maybe he had groupies. Mozart swept in and around her, she shut her eyes. When she opened them, she saw Tim leaning into a phrase.

The minuet was new ground. They went slowly, but began having problems. Tim began looking alert rather than absorbed—interrupting to suggest a bowing or make them repeat a ragged phrase; getting them to go slower, slower—mechanically, expressionlessly. Elinor opened her eyes again and watched them. Alan and Sheila played with the same sort of manner—concentrated, withdrawn into themselves. Thoby was all expressions and black eyebrows that frowned when he couldn't get a phrase to come right, and flew up with surprise when he finally did. He had luminous blue-green eyes, short dark hair, a long mobile face, and an alert, enquiring air—a good-looking man in his way; thin but not weedy, with high square shoulders. Either his arms were very long or they seemed so; his jacket was slightly short at the wrists, like a boy's in the midst of a growth spurt. His voice was light and clipped, and his accent almost as fruity as Rose's; he spoke with an elaborately tentative diffidence.

A boy-man, Maggie would call him. Tim had a thick neck and a jutting brow-ridge, and his head and trunk were too massive. He was less conventionally handsome, perhaps; but to Elinor he was more attractive—stunningly so. Très Cary Grant—she could see what Rose meant—but he reminded her more of Marlon Brando: taller, less electric; but with something of the same sensuous bloom; the same surprising light-footedness; the same impression of classical features thickened away from beauty towards pure sensuality: a Roman, not a Greek.

She was comfortable in the bay window, looking out at the world or in at the quartet. There were bare trees in the square; behind them a disc of sun slid in and out of shifting layers of cloud.

24

It was brighter indoors than out, an Aladdin's cave of colour—worn red turkey rugs, an irregular glaze of buttercup yellow on the walls, faded blue silk curtains, a Georgian chesterfield covered in flaking green leather, blue and crimson Victorian armchairs crowned with fat mahogany curlicues, lots of pictures, books and knick-knacks: an effect of luxurious profusion.

Funny how different friends' places could be. Tim's house was cool; Thoby and Sheila's flat glowed. Then there was Maggie's pretty flat, all of a piece with its Liberty prints in soft apricot hues, its beds with bedskirts and white counterpanes; Chris's stripped pine and tubular metal; and Rose and Marcus's glorified bedsit with its third-hand bamboo table and chairs, its beanbag seats and posters—and its one arresting Augustus John drawing.

Elinor's own small flat was furnished in the same pinched fashion; she didn't have enough money to buy what she really liked, or enough time to ferret through junkshops—though like Rose she had one good picture, a small Ravilious engraving, in a cheap frame, of a girl enfolding herself in a towel in a chequer-tiled bathroom. She had fallen for it at a jumble sale when she was eighteen, without knowing who Ravilious was. The jumble organisers hadn't known either—she'd got it for a quid. It was a sort of mascot; she even took it with her on holiday.

'No, look, if you slur from the semiquaver...'

'It's not marked...'

She was warm and sleepy with the sun on her head. Tim's was the only voice she heard—light, unhesitant: the same voice exactly, even the same tone, in which two hours ago he had said, 'Come this way, yes,' then, coming into her, 'Oh,' in a different voice and tone—a groan flung out of him as if against his will. She, pierced, penetrated, had groaned herself, repeatedly.

A spasm like a jolt of current stopped her breath, shut her eyes. Did other women—did men—again and again con their memories of making love, as if learning each detail by heart? Did Tim?

She hadn't herself, all that much, before meeting him; but she did now—catching her breath; circling round and round questions she had no answers to; pondering the moral and emotional issues raised by gestures, requests, compliances—less in words than in a jumble of physical details that recaptured the sense of being emotionally shaken. There were limits to what you could think without words—and their lovemaking pressed against and through frontiers of areas there were no words for; no ways of thinking about.

A faint, sweetish sexual aroma lingered on her palm. Her senses flooded with the memory of Tim's head curled into the pillow, eyes shut, mouth curved in what could have been a smile but was a wince of ecstasy.

'You make me so happy,' she had whispered.

'I hope to make you happier,' he replied in a comically matter-of-fact daylight voice. 'We've only begun exploring...'

Exploring, not experimenting. She had once been briefly involved with a man who went in for experiments with sensations and 'positions'. The nadir was when he said, 'Let's try it standing up.' Oh the misery, they were the wrong heights, find something to stand on, it's cold out of bed, now at this implausible angle try to get cock into cunt; try keeping it there, grope to retrieve it, oh dear, try again, grab grope, no it doesn't seem to work does it; and back to bed and a glum end. She'd fled back to the gentle, democratic embraces of the boy-men, and not known she wanted anything else.

She hadn't guessed it with Tim, either, at first. He'd been even gentler than her former lovers: careful not to force anything on her, especially penetration; and very restrained once he was in her—even when coming. Was he governing himself by an effort of will? Finally she had worked up her courage and whispered, 'You don't need to be so restrained, you know.'

'I don't want to hurt you.'

'You won't.'

'Or make you feel I'm...being violent.'

'You won't.'

The next time was different. Waking up the morning after, she'd looked at his big head on the pillow—light wiry hair, heavy stubbly curve of cheek, the bony ridge above his eyebrows, his full mouth drawn close and small in sleep—and caught herself thinking vaguely: If this is the best life has to offer, it's enough. Absurd

26

words, extravagant to match her happiness. Such engrossing union, body suffused with soul, soul with body, must signify...something: oneness...likeness. Where had it come from, that ease and flow? Never like this before. Sexual happiness, yes, but this was more—more—she didn't know what. His face had shone with a magnification of the light that touched it when he played.

No violence had replaced his vanished tentativeness: only an ardent vehemence—pulling away this morning with that, 'Come this way, yes;' heaving himself round and onto her in his rush to be inside her again—that sparked a matching vehemence in her. She liked being the object of such urgency—felt it herself, an edge to her greed—wanted to obliterate the hiatus between intensities: if they must stop doing *that*, then quick, start this—*Yes*.

It was Thoby who was having trouble with the tricky bits. Suddenly he got it, and they were off, cantering through the allegro and sailing smoothly across to the last movement. It seemed to be easier: they took it at a rollicking pace.

Drawing his bow off the final note, Tim looked cheerfully across at Elinor before signalling one last run-through. Just so he had looked the other day, arriving at her flat for lunch before a rehearsal, burly, his face happy. 'Well, which way shall we go?'—pointing at the two doors off her sitting room: kitchen and bedroom.

He had only an hour. The bedroom, she had wanted to say, but that wouldn't leave him time to eat. 'How much do you want lunch?' she asked.

'How much do you want to make love?' His eyes were bright, friendly; his smile showed what he wanted, but left the choice to her.

A lot, she thought. She wanted to match his boldness—why did her tongue cleave to the roof of her mouth? 'More than lunch,' was all she could manage. 'But I've got time to eat after; you don't.'

'Let's see if there's time for both, shall we?'

All day the memory had kept rooting her to the spot: the bright-eyed look; the words, bold because not murmured. 'How much do

27

you want to make love?' As much as you do; as often as we can; as soon as possible, now.

Another memory had kept teasing her, making her want to laugh, though she couldn't see why: a memory of kneeling above him, hands planted on his chest, calves splayed out on either side of him, like...like...The image was on the periphery of her vision, but she couldn't focus it.

In the evening, standing at the back of the cinema, torch in hand, ready to light the way for latecomers, she got it, and nearly burst out laughing. They had stuck out, her calves, like a chicken's wings before trussing.

Chapter 4

'We have lunch together afterwards,' Tim had said, but 'we' didn't seem to include Alan, who left soon after they stopped playing. Two minutes later Elinor couldn't quite remember what he looked like.

Sheila made salad, Thoby heated soup, and Tim set the table. 'That's new,' he said, looking at a pretty tapestry-covered chair.

'Dreadful, isn't it?' Thoby clutched his head.

'No, rather beautiful.'

'But utterly useless. Visited the ancestors last week—Maidie thrust it on us. The tapestry's Burne-Jones—he designed it for my great-great aunt to work—for a chair that was *already* falling apart at the joints.'

Tim got up and turned it upside down. 'It only wants knocking apart and glueing—I'll do it for you.'

'But even then—how can we sit on a Burne-Jones tapestry?'

Thoby caught Elinor's eye; it looked distinctly beady. He'd forgotten she was a stranger; did she think he was dropping names?

He began rattling. 'Tried to leave it—Maidie wouldn't let me. And us trying to live sparsely. They think that's what they do up in the ancestral halls, but, my God, the clutter. Bore it back—tube packed with football fans wriggling like sardines. Hoped they'd shiver its t-timbers. But they parted like the Red Sea.' He fluttered one long lean hand dramatically across his forehead.

The flat was hardly Elinor's idea of living sparsely. They had shabby things, but no ugly ones. That took more than good taste: either money, or a family with nice things to give away. There was a silence, and she found herself saying, 'You could have refused it.'

'Ah.' He frowned at her intently. 'The voice of reason. Perfectly right. I could have—I should have. But'—he clutched the middle of

29

his frown with thumb and forefinger, as if pulling the thought out from between his eyebrows—'But one's so inconsistent. With family one becomes all psychologies, don't you think?'

'I'm not sure I understand.' She didn't understand his first stab at explanation, either; it involved Hegel. Eventually she made out his meaning, more or less.

'You mean people tend to act like children around their families?'

He bobbed his head vigorously. 'Just so, Elinor, just so.'

Why didn't you say so in the first place? she thought.

Sheila showed them a dead dragonfly she had found, dry, fragile and sinister, with a shiny brown carapace and ribbed transparent wings. She rested it on the yoke of her blouse. 'Like an Art Nouveau brooch.'

'They only live forty-eight hours,' Tim said.

'One crowded hour of glorious life,' Thoby said.

'Poor thing,' Sheila said.

Elinor felt outside a charmed circle. Did Alan, too—was that why he had left? 'But before that they have a much longer life as grubs,' she said flatly, wanting them to feel guilty for only caring about the dragonfly once it became beautiful. They didn't, of course. They made noises of polite agreement, and Thoby changed the subject.

'Went to Wiltshire on Friday,' he said. 'Casing a joint for Prosser. My boss—conducts the Haydn—wants to start a festival,' he added for Elinor's benefit. 'Had a quick trot along the Ridgeway—same place I once saw a puddle full of tiny f-frogs. Dozens of them, absolutely chock-a-block.' He had a staccato stammer that never got stuck.

'I've seen that,' said Tim. 'In Yorkshire—huddled together all over each other. For protection from late frosts, maybe.'

'Or a frog bacchanalia.' Thoby's hooting laugh sputtered in between the words.

'But what if the water freezes?' said Elinor. But the men were getting up to clear away the main course; her question got lost— just as well, it was so plodding and literal-minded. She couldn't get on their wave-length.

They moved into the front room for coffee. Elinor found a book about the geology of England, and began flipping through it for something to do.

'We're going to Shropshire at Easter,' said Thoby. 'I want to understand its geology by then. Such a nuisance not knowing what one's looking at—limits what you see. I've never found it easy to understand calcareous rock, have you?'

'Calcareous rock?'

'Limestone.'

'Oh. Why should it be harder to understand than—sandstone?'

'Its relation to life. After all, chalk is just compacted fossils, isn't it?'

Elinor nodded blankly. What made him think she would know anything about rocks?

'Life dying out and springing up again, and on such a large scale—unimaginable, both processes, don't you find?'

This time she did understand. 'Yes,' she said reluctantly. She wanted to say she didn't waste time worrying about it.

A door slammed upstairs; heavy footsteps; a thud. Tim raised his eyebrows. 'The phantom pacer still here?'

'The who?' Elinor asked.

'Our upstairs neighbour,' said Sheila. 'We never see him, only hear him—mostly at night.'

'*Late* at night,' said Thoby. He had a suspicion he'd somehow got off on the wrong foot with Elinor, and started rattling again, in a frenzy of determination to please. 'He starts pacing at one or two a.m. Throws himself on the bed now and then—*thwang*—leaps up, pace, pace, thwang.' He paced about to demonstrate, his angular, high-shouldered body bent in a Groucho glide. 'About three, he decides the bed's in the wrong place, drags it to the other end of the room. That's no good. Drags it back. Paces some more—knocks over a bookshelf or two.' His hand fluttering across his brow sketched Sheila and him at the end of their tether. 'At four or five he gives up all hope of sleep—spins a disc. Heavy metal.' He brought out his handkerchief and mopped his forehead.

'What does he do in the daytime?'

31

'He's a mole. A Socialist Worker mole. Posters in his window, fellow moles creeping up to conspire about undermining the fabric of society. In fact,' lapsing briefly out of fantasy, 'he comes down to tea now and then—spills the beans. He's a proxy mole, an SWP theoretician. Writes pamphlets.'

'Curious mixed metaphor,' Tim said. 'Moles undermining fabrics.'

Elinor almost said no, not mixed at all, if the fabric in question was the fabric of a building, but Thoby was already launched on an extravagance about society as a fabric, spread on the lawn to dry, falling into caved-in mole tunnels. She didn't think it very funny, but Sheila and Tim did.

She ventured her own variation. 'Maybe it started as moths—moths eating up the fabric of society. But moths got misprinted as moles, and then an editor changed "eating up" to "undermining" because that's what moles do.' God, would they think she meant it seriously?

But Thoby capped her with, 'Three moths taken on by Doncaster Colliery,' and Tim tried, 'Socialist moths infiltrate British Steel.' She felt as if she had managed a small contribution to the general gaiety.

'Tell me more about them,' she said on the way home. Tim was carrying Thoby's chair. 'The quartet, I mean.'

'What do you want to know?' he said dubiously.

'Alan, for a start. Do you like him?'

He glanced at her uncertainly. 'I suppose so—I've never thought. I don't know him as well as Thoby and Sheila.'

'Why didn't he stay for lunch?'

'He never does.'

'How come? Haven't you asked him?'

Tim got the implication. 'Repeatedly. His wife wants him home for lunch.'

'And he's so much older and straighter, he wouldn't fit in anyhow?'

Yes; but he thought it better left unsaid.

'What about Thoby? Does he always talk like that?'

32

'Like what?'

'About things I don't know anything about.'

Tim laughed. 'Rum chap, isn't he? He gets interested in things and goes into them in depth, then talks about them as if you know as much as he does. He went to Rome a few years ago, said he'd spent his time "trying to understand the relation between Borromini and Bernini." I didn't even know who they were.'

'That's what I mean. He's terrifying.'

'But you were talking about the difference between Hawks and Huston just the other day. I didn't know who *they* were.'

'But they're, everybody knows...' She laughed. 'Oh, I suppose you're right.'

'Thoby just comes at things from odd angles. Like his thing about geology. Alan went to Jerusalem last Passover, and the first thing Thoby asked when he got back was, "What kind of rock is it made of?" Of course Alan didn't know. Recently it's been the "desert daddies"—the Church Fathers, would you believe it—Origen and Augustine.'

'He's Christian?'

'No, just reads strange things. Hegel, as you heard. I like it—he keeps conversations going.'

'I keep thinking I know his name from somewhere.'

'Maidie, probably—his mother. She paints people—royalty, that sort of thing.'

'His mother is Maida *Debec*? But she's *famous*.'

'To Thoby's annoyance—he's always being quizzed about royals. There are other Debecs you might have come across, too— it's a clan that keeps on producing people you've half heard of. I once found a travel book by his great-grandmother; she went to Tibet in the 1890s. There's a Debec who's a novelist of sorts today. Also a BBC administrator—Thoby's father—and several musicians. They're a very musical lot; we usually have our do at Maidie's.' He upended the chair and balanced it on his head with its feet in the air and its back bumping into his.

'Your do—what's that? I must say, you look like one of those statues that hold up roofs.'

'Caryatids? We have a do every June to play the quartets we've been working on. Very informal, just families and a few friends.' He grinned under the chair-seat. 'One time I was up at Maidie's, Dora Russell came to dinner, and—'

'Really?' That was much more impressive than Maida Debec. 'What was she like?'

'Nice enough. But the other guest was a woman from Bletchley, who said, "I'm just up to see my banker, Mr Coutts," and glared at Dora Russell the whole time as if she were some sort of communist plot—while Dora Russell either didn't notice, or pretended not to.'

'With that background, why isn't Thoby a'—she didn't trust herself to pronounce 'violist' right—'a musician?'

'Not good enough. Same as Alan, but Alan really wanted to play professionally; Thoby didn't.'

'And Sheila—you said she was good, and I could tell. Couldn't she have been a professional?'

'It's a criminal waste,' he burst out. 'She could have been *really* good—she threw it away.'

'But why? Didn't she want to?'

'I've never asked.' Tim liked to hear other people gossiping, but hated doing it himself. It was invasion of privacy—and he didn't know how to express the things he saw in people.

'Then how do you know she threw it away?'

'All I know is what Thoby once told me.'

'Which was?' It was like pulling teeth.

'She started the cello in school—God knows how, from the secretarial stream in a Limehouse comprehensive: she's a working-class girl—all right, woman. Maybe a teacher got her interested. Anyhow, she was phenomenal—got a full scholarship to the Menuhin School. The chance of a lifetime. I'd have given my eye teeth—but she dropped out.' His voice shot up with bafflement.

'But why?'

'Thoby said something about social conscience—feeling she had to do something useful.'

'I can understand that.' Elinor had started university full of lofty ideas, and still got guilty twinges about enjoying herself running a cinema.

'Well, but—someone with her talent,' said Tim, the more grudgingly because he understood it too.

'She doesn't have an East End accent at all—it must have been a job losing it,' said Elinor with some fellow-feeling for Sheila: losing her own suburban twang had been hard work.

'Maybe, maybe not. With an ear like hers, she probably speaks like whoever she's around without even thinking about it. I know a bassoonist who's a vocal chameleon—you listen to him talk to five different people, he's got five different accents.'

'Wow. So she went into this Southwark charity instead?'

'Not directly. I gather she had different jobs, then took A-levels at a tech and started university, but had a breakdown or something. Then she was a secretary in a wholesale place in the City and ended up pretty much running it—found she was good at management: though what that has to do with social conscience I don't know.'

'Getting herself back together, maybe, after her breakdown; or just earning a living—it's not easy to get paid for doing, um, socially useful work, especially without a degree.'

'Maybe,' Tim said shortly. This was what talking behind people's backs led to—being unfair to them. He was glad they were nearly home.

'You forgot to show Tim your shutters,' Sheila said that evening. 'To ask what kind of hinges.'

'Next time,' Thoby said absently; then realised that she'd said something, if not quite started a conversation. Keep it up; say something harmless. 'What d'you make of Tim's young lady?'

'She's nice,' Sheila said. She wished she'd known how to put Elinor more at her ease.

'Three of us, one of her: not easy. Carried it off well, don't you think?'

It made her claustrophobic when they thought alike. She nodded and turned on the telly.

Thoby ran out of patience. 'We've *got* to talk sometime,' he said desperately; 'I can't stand it.'

She turned down the sound, and went and sat down with her hands folded in her lap. 'What about?'

35

'I don't know. About what's in your mind. Anything's better than silence.'

She looked down at her hands for so long he thought she wasn't going to answer, then said, 'What if there's nothing there?'

'That's nonsense,' he said, shaken with pity.

'But it's how I feel.'

'But why?'

The silence lengthened. Her eyes strayed to the set. 'For God's sake, Sheila!' he said.

She stood up. 'It's a middle-class obsession, wanting to talk all the time—working-class people don't need it,' she said sharply, going over to the television. 'Why do you want me to change—why can't you?' She turned up the volume and sat down to watch.

Yet at bedtime she wanted to make love—and after coming said furiously, 'You beast,' as if he'd forced her to.

Chapter 5

Tim stopped short at the door of the inner office. An attractive woman, very attractive, was sitting on Elinor's desk, swinging one elegant leg idly against the other with a silken swish, turning an unlit cigarette round and round between her fingers, and inspecting him sidelong out of quizzical round brown eyes.

'Hullo, I'm Maggie McAdam. You're Tim, I take it. Nell's up with the projectionist. I was just going outside for a fag—she won't even let *me* smoke in here; *too* tedious. Keep me company while we wait?'

Maggie's allure did not depend upon her lively but nondescript features, or upon her figure, which except for her long legs was ordinary enough, or upon what she wore: her deliberate elegance was severe, almost Parisian in its strictness; and she could, and did, have the same effect in sweatshirt and jeans. What riveted men's attention was her pert, amused, inviting stare; at once open and defensive, it implied inordinate satisfaction of sexual demands and safety from emotional ones. She was not overtly seductive; her surface was all amusement. But the erotic challenge was there, and no mistake: she projected it, out of a desperation long antedating her liaison with Clive, towards every personable man she met.

As she slid off the desk and stooped for her coat, the neckline of her blouse fell away from her throat, and Tim caught a glimpse of lacy bra. Elinor was the first woman in his life who did not wear alluring underthings; he missed the look of them, and the slide of flesh under silky fabric. He could tell, as surely as if he were to lift Maggie's skirt, that beneath it were lacy-silky briefs that matched her bra. Elinor wore colourful cotton ones, jaunty rather than seductive. 'D'you ever wear the silky kind?' he had asked with a good imitation of mere idle curiosity, running his forefinger under the edge of a snappy red pair.

'Nylon, you mean? Nope, they don't breathe, so you get a hot steamy environment,' she had revoltingly replied, 'and things like thrush can multiply like mad.'

Maggie met his eyes as she straightened up, and from their quick flicker guessed that he had been eying her lustfully. Ah. She was utterly faithful to Clive, but her effect on him would be less electric if she did not, every day, allure men by the dozen. He liked knowing that many men wanted her and only he had her; and that under her sober business clothes she wore, to please him, underthings that were not merely silky but—Tim's imagination had not gone far enough—silk from Janet Reger: not only bra and pants, but also suspender belt and stockings.

'How *can* you?' Elinor had once protested. 'Suspender belts are a symbol of—of—and they're so uncomfortable.'

'So are tights, just differently. And if a man likes something there's no harm in, why not go along with it?'

Tim knew that Maggie had seen the direction of his gaze, and read disapproval into her amused, complicit stare. It wasn't my fault, he thought resentfully, following her outside.

She leaned back against a poster for *Bound for Glory*, dragging deep on her cigarette, then directing her slow exhalation considerately away from him. Two images came to him simultaneously: Vivian breathing smoke straight at him, silently defying him to turn away, willing him to breathe it as the price of touching her; and Elinor pushing herself down on his cock, loath to stop even when he said he was in danger of coming. Tortuousness; simplicity.

'That's better,' Maggie said. 'Now tell me about fixers.'

'What?'

'They keep nabbing you for engagements.'

'Oh, them. They're—you know I'm a free-lance player?'

'Vaguely.' She raised an enquiring eyebrow.

Tim began to relax—he loved talking about his work—and described how a few of the big orchestras, like the Philharmonia or the RPO, consisted of full-time members under contract; while all the other London orchestras—the Academy of Ancient Music, the

Haydn Chamber Orchestra, and thirty or forty more—were made up afresh for each concert or recording from a pool of about two hundred free-lance orchestral musicians. 'I'm one of them.' He had a surprisingly light voice for such a big barrel-chested man.

'But all those orchestras—on the radio they sound so different from each other.'

'It's the conductor that counts—they know how to get the sound they want.'

'Don't you get dizzy, being in one orchestra one night and another the next?'

'Oh, I don't have many one-night stands.' Noticing the *double entendre* he added quickly, 'It's usually three or four days with one band—up to a fortnight for recording sessions. But you asked about fixers. They're the middlemen—middlewomen; they're women, all two or three of them. Amazing, really—all those orchestras and all their engagements, and halls, and musicians, booked two, three, four years ahead—'

'You get bookings for two *years* from now?'

'I'm full up for the next six months—pretty much the whole year, in fact—and part of next—and I already know I won't starve the year after.'

Elinor was in the office when they got back. 'I've got to go,' he told her. 'I'm on in the Purcell Room—I just stopped in to say hullo.'

She beamed with pleasure and walked out with him as far as the street. 'Well, how did you like her?'

'Very much.' With sudden fellow-feeling for Maggie he added, 'She's sad underneath, isn't she?' Her allure, so like Vivian's, still disturbed him, but he could, just, disentangle her from Vivian.

'Oh yes, immensely.' So there, she told someone in her head— Maggie or herself? He was the only one of her men who had seen Maggie's vulnerability. She went to kiss him, but at that very moment he turned his head, and her kiss landed on his neck, just below his ear.

'He's utterly charming,' Maggie said when she returned. 'That combination of diffidence and social ease. And you're definitely in love with him.'

39

Knowing it herself in that rush of delight at the quartet was one thing; admitting it out loud was another. 'I...I don't...' she began.

'Come off it, I saw your face. All lit up, it was.'

Elinor laughed and gave in. 'Well, yes. But I *still* don't feel as if I know him—we *still* never get enough time. After the quartet we go walking on the Heath or Hackney Marshes—he gets stir-crazy in London—and you can't really walk seriously and talk—'

'I'll say.'

'And he keeps taking things on. Repairing a chair for Thoby. Making a side table for Sheila's birthday. Teaching—he's got three violin students. Practising, rehearsing, performing, cooking—'

'*Cooking?*'

'He loves it, and you know how I hate it. So we split the work. I shop for food in the morning, and when we get back at night, he cooks it.'

'Nell Benton, d'you mean to say you never cook for that man?'

'What's wrong with that?' said Elinor. 'He's a good cook, I'm a lousy one—'

'If it were *me*, I'd be cooking for *him*—or at least sharing it fifty-fifty.'

That got her. 'I do the shopping,' she pointed out defensively. 'That takes as much time as cooking it. Anyhow, as I was saying, what Tim *does* with little bits of spare time is go into his workroom and work on Sheila's table. So we don't get to talk—and how can I be in love with him if I don't know him?'

But she was in love, brimful and overflowing: with his ponderous good-natured sense of humour, so different—oh, the relief—from the irony with which John and the others had zapped her optimism; with his seriousness, his solidity, his music; with his lovemaking—the measure of everything.

Had she thought that before Tim? Surely not. She wasn't sure she really thought it now—or should.

But this. She was living in a glow of astonished sexual delight: the flow of things, the harmony of movement and stillness, of what was wanted when. Melting under his tongue this morning; trying hard to keep from coming; touching his head to stop him when she got close. Twice he stopped; the third time he didn't. She pulled back; he followed greedily. She moved back again; he hunted after her like a truffle hound. She felt a dangerous joy in the idea of being forced to come; yet managed not to.

Finally she hauled him up by the hair, saying, 'Don't want to come yet.'

'All right,' he replied, but almost immediately gave a chuckle and began to lick again.

'Please stop,' she said, 'please,' but he did not hear her, or ignored her. She felt...ravished, like Io by Jove, yet still held on, possessed by the delight of being treated so, her plea ignored.

The nearest she'd ever come to living out a fantasy, she mused now; but quickly stepped back from the idea. It was indecent to associate those dark imagined enactments with even the thought of Tim.

Jove and Io, she thought firmly instead: that was innocent enough. Ludovic had once sent her a postcard from Vienna: Io with her plump pretty back to the viewer, her head thrown back in sensuous abandon, one arm clasping the compact cloud that billowed between her opened thighs. It looked like a big woolly head—like Tim's. Had Correggio or Caravaggio—how did anyone remember which was which?—meant it to, or would that inter-pretation occur only to a woman?

There were things that perplexed her, though—limits, within the tender burning intimacy of his lovemaking, on what he would do or let her do. Not for him a fond murmurous transition between the daylight world and the sexual; no cuddling, no twining of limbs, no kissing and gazing into each other's eyes—he went straight in at the deep end, pulling her with him. He lavished caresses on her cunt, and a few on her belly, arse and thighs, but hardly touched her anywhere else, not even her breasts; and didn't respond when she touched him anywhere but his cock. Nothing like that had ever happened with the boy-men. How could such truncation and such ardour coexist?

Out of bed there were limits too. He smiled at her warmly and regarded her intently while they talked—but at arm's length or more. He held her hand if she put it in his when they were out

41

walking, but never reached for it himself. He didn't put his arms round her of his own accord, either; and when she put hers round him, he gave her a quick one-armed squeeze in return—stiff, not moulding his body to hers. If she said, 'No, a real hug,' all she got was another quick squeeze.

What really floored her was that he only kissed her if she kissed him first—and only with a pebbly pursed peck that seemed to bounce her own kisses back to her. Yet very occasionally his mouth melted when she kissed it, soft, soft, and opened at the touch of her tongue.

She couldn't go on making all the running herself; it made her imagine crazy things—that he didn't *want* her to hug him, kiss him, pat him in passing. But that was impossible.

She'd have to say something, she wasn't sure what. Soon.

She woke up feeling amorous, rolled close to Tim, who was already awake, rubbed her hand across his furry belly, and lifted up on one elbow to look at him in the half-light sifting through the white curtains. His eyes slid away; when she bent to kiss him, his head rolled smoothly aside—a movement that might have been chance, but that it happened so often. It was as if his features had been rubbed out, left off the drawing.

Say something, she remembered; and was still looking for words when with his fingertips he brushed her hip, her belly, then her cunt; delving, sliding, spreading; his face rapt—too rapt to notice a minor detail like her face close to his. But she no longer wanted to say anything.

He came down onto her, into her, gathering her to him, fastening her down in place: the warm fleecy flesh of his trunk all along hers; a rapturous mutter in her ear, 'Oh Elinor, oh Elinor.' She gave herself up to a trance of pure penetration, pure passivity, down into the underworld, out of reach of daylight and consciousness; a long drift of nearly coming, holding off, holding off, till she couldn't— liquid rolling to the boil, one moment a smooth twitching surface, the next a seethe of bubbles. Another rapturous, 'Oh Elinor,' and he came too, with slow deep thrusts as if to the centre of everything.

42

Triumph; loss. Sometimes she had momentary fantasies of twenty men entering her, quickly one after another, each coming instantly, so that she could feel it again and again. When he made to move off her, she tightened her hands on his arse, whispering, 'No, stay like this,' and they fell into a drowse punctuated by twitches, one of which woke them by popping his cock out of her with slippery finality.

'Where am I?' he said in a dazed voice; then, shaking himself: 'Time to get up, Elinor. I've got a rehearsal.'

Had she imagined his rapturous whispers? She found herself unaccountably testy. 'My friends call me Nell.'

'Nell?' He frowned. 'I like Elinor better.' Then he repeated, 'Got to get up,' and jumped up, neither kissing her nor looking at her.

No question, she had to do something about this. Next time she'd stop him before she got too caught up to want to. Promise.

Chapter 6

Her flat was dark—Tim had let himself in and gone to bed. But he sat up and turned on the light when she tiptoed in.

'Oh good, you're awake,' she said, hurtling out of her clothes and into her nightgown. 'The most fantastic movie—I had to work to get a print, and I'm so glad I did, it's on tomorrow afternoon too, you've *got* to see it, are you free, you'll love it—'

'Whoa, calm down. I thought you didn't like *Novecento*.'

She perched on the edge of the bed. 'That was the second evening performance. I mean the late show—*The Sweet Smell of Success*. The Mackendrick season.'

'But you don't like British cinema, either—'

'Only most of it, not all—'

'But he's British; didn't he do *Whisky Galore*?'

Elinor groaned. 'God yes, and the pensioners love it; and *The Man in the White Suit*, though that's okay for a British movie. But *Success* is in a different league—he made it in America, that's why. Brassy, sassy; mile-a-minute script—by Odets, but doctored by Ernest Lehman, you know, who wrote *North by Northwest*—and *wonderful* cinematography, crisp black and white, by James Wong Howe—he's the greatest. There's something he does in this movie—Burt Lancaster is a columnist who uses his power to destroy people; and Howe photographs him without any catchlight in his eyes, so they look dead, except in the one scene where he's vulnerable for a moment. It's brilliant, but it doesn't call attention to itself, it just *works*; and ninety-nine people in a hundred won't guess that that menacing look isn't just acting, it's Howe.'

Tim laughed. 'Nine hundred and ninety-nine out of a thousand, more like. Anyhow, yes, I'll take a couple of hours off Sheila's table and see dead-eye Burt.'

44

'Ah.' She smiled at him happily.

He smiled back, his clear brown eyes gazing directly into hers. There was a pause. He touched her knee with a half smile of invitation, and his eyes unfocussed, then, as his hand slid along her thigh, closed.

Her eyes closed too, and her thighs opened; then she had an unwelcome memory-flash. She shook herself. Something to say: say it. 'Tim, I've been wondering.'

His eyes met hers directly again, intent, querying. 'Wondering what?'

She had a speech all worked out. 'Um, wondering...about things I'd like to happen when we make love, that don't—things it almost sort of seems as if you avoid, like when I kiss you, or looking at me, or...' He wasn't making it easy for her, just listening in silence. 'I'm used to...I like...starting more slowly, with, you know, a bit of cuddling and...well, I'm wondering if we could include some of that. Out of bed, too.'

He was quite silent. At last he said, 'I've got—difficulties with that.'

Difficulties! With hugs and kisses? She had thought he would agree as soon as she mentioned it. Her turn to wait in silence. But he didn't go on. 'What kind of difficulties?' she had to ask.

'The last person I was involved with, Vivian, I told you it was...fraught...and—traumatic. I can't even...' He looked utterly miserable.

Her optimism curdled. If Vivian still upset him so much—'Are you still in love with her?'

'Good God, no.'

The conviction in his voice cheered her up. 'Then the question is, what are we going to do?'

'What about?'

'About me wanting more kissing and cuddling,' she said with a touch of exasperation.

'I—I can't just—you don't—I'll try, but you'll have to give me—*time.*'

'But you'll try to meet me halfway?'

He nodded.

45

'Okay, then—and I'll try not to jump you so much.' She meant it as a joke. He didn't laugh, but when she put her mouth close, he gave her a little darting kiss and then a softer, longer one.

'Tell me about the cinema, Elinor,' Thoby said, over Sunday lunch in Tim's dim green basement dining room, leaning his elbows on the table—which was a flush-core door on trestles: Tim hadn't yet made a proper table to go with his elegant chairs.

'You mean my cinema, or The Cinema?'

'Both. Eady levy, for instance, what does that do to your profit margins?'

Her answer set him sucking information out of her like a Hoover, about distribution, international markets, barring, profits, grosses, changing audience profiles, the market for art cinema, the relationship of the reps to first-run cinemas. If most of the new independent cinemas were owner-managed, how did the owners capitalise them—private money? Limited companies? Loans? Mortgages? How many employee-managers were there in London besides her? What kind of control did her employers exert?

'Hardly any—we're terribly lucky. They're a farming family, and not interested in movies. Old Mr Wellesford was the film fan. He bought the Cromer in the forties, then made it into a trust in his will. I'm sure his children could break it if they wanted, but they're well off—they seem to see the Cromer as their contribution to the arts. They don't subsidise it, though. We make a profit—almost as much as a rep could on that site—and anything over upkeep goes to them. But they could get far more by selling for development. They're always getting offers—I just keep my fingers crossed.'

'And hope they don't develop expensive tastes, and the price of sugar beet stays up,' said Tim.

'You make *almost* as much as you could?' Thoby asked.

'Well, a first-run house could make more—the Renoir does, round the corner. A nuisance, too—it gets some of the student impulse trade that we used to get all of. Besides, a rep with a conscience doesn't only show what will take the most money. Part of the fun is making sure we screen a wide range of films and still stay solvent. That's why I started the Friday and Saturday late shows. They're usually full, and they give us the margin to show films that only a few people come to.'

'Part of the fun—what's the most fun?'

'Elinor's job is filling houses,' Tim said; 'but her passion is getting people to see good films. She jumps up and down if she pulls it off with one nobody knows about—and she's grouchy when they flock to films she doesn't like.'

'Or when we show a movie I believe in, and nobody comes, like *Bound for Glory* recently—a beautiful movie: good script and direction, great songs, David Carradine as Woody Guthrie, photography by Haskell Wexler—ravishing pale dusty colours. But could I make anyone come? No, they wanted to see Klaus Kinski overacting on the Amazon. *Aguirre, Wrath of God*. Wrath of Nell Benton. I never want to see that popeyed ham again, but I'll have to—people keep *asking* for it.'

'So how *do* you entice people in—when it works?'

'Programme notes in the foyer; and we go and put them in the racks of theatres and left-wing bookshops and other reps.' Elinor glanced at Tim in case he remembered that that was how they'd met; but he wasn't looking. 'But *Time Out*'s the most important. The reviewers are adventurous, so they'll often give a splash to movies that would otherwise play to a house of three—the ushers and projectionist.'

'But Elinor, tell me—'

'Elinor, could you pass the—'

Sheila and Thoby had spoken together and stopped together.

'Do call me Nell,' she said impulsively. 'My friends mostly do.'

'Which do you like better?' Sheila asked.

'Both. I think of myself as Elinor; but it sounds so formal.'

'Nell it is, then,' Thoby said.

Tim sat silent. He should have told her how much he disliked Nell; then she might not have asked his friends to use it. It was vulgar. It was Nell Gwynne and Eskimo Nell and Nelly put your belly close to mine. He would never use it himself.

'Tim—a Beecham quote for you,' Thoby said over pudding. 'He once called von Karajan "a sort of musical Malcolm Sargent." '

47

Tim cracked up. When he got his breath back, he said, 'And I've got a story for you—about a time André Previn was in the practice rooms in Maida Vale, working on Rachmaninov for a concert the next day. Someone in the next room was practising the most elementary stuff over and over—C major scales and arpeggios—and driving Previn crazy. He thought he'd ask him to lay off for a while; but the person who answered his knock was...Rubinstein.'

Elinor laughed at that more confidently than at Thoby's Beecham quote—she knew who Beecham and von Karajan and Sargent were, but wasn't sure what she was supposed to think about them. But she was less intimidated by Thoby this week. He still struck her as a flyaway quicksilver creature darting across conversations like a pond-skater skittering across the water; but she liked the sweetness in his eyes—rather haunted eyes, sometimes—and was beginning to warm to his throttled staccato stammer punctuated by hoots of laughter.

Sheila said very little, though she laughed and smiled as the stories went back and forth. Elinor was alone in the hall with her for a moment at the end, and took the chance to say, 'Tim tells me you're pregnant—congratulations.'

'Oh—yes.' Sheila looked aside. She'd forgotten it for the past hour or two.

'Lucky you. I wish—'

But Elinor didn't know what she wished—or couldn't tell Tim's friend what had flashed through her like a shooting star that vanishes in the seeing, but stays imprinted on the eye.

Sheila looked beseechingly at her, wanting to say, Help me, I feel like an animal in a trap, tell me how not to be terrified. I live a split life, I help other people all day, I'm efficient, I run things. But nobody helps me; nobody knows—Thoby does, but he—See it, please see it, then *make* me talk. You're new—see through to me.

But Elinor only saw shy friendliness.

Tim and Thoby came through from the kitchen. 'Can I pick my fiddle up later?—we're off to the Marshes,' said Tim. 'Interested in a walk?'

'Thanks, but I've got a report to finish,' Sheila said.

'You, Thoby?'

48

If Sheila was going to shut herself off for the rest of the day—
Thoby opened his mouth to say yes; then thought: Gooseberry, and
shook his head.

'Too bad,' said Elinor—rather insincerely. She wanted Tim to
herself this afternoon; she wanted to get him talking. She had
already told him lots about herself—her childhood, her lovers, her
friends; some of her secret hopes and fears—but while he seemed to
enjoy listening, he didn't say much about himself in return.

He didn't today either. The subject on his mind was orchestral
politics, and he kept reverting to it without seeming to notice her
openings—and she got interested and kept saying, 'Then why
didn't he...' and, 'But that's crazy...' and only remembered her
project when it was time to start for home.

Plenty of time, she thought. Probably not during the week: they
were so often in a hurry. Next Sunday.

Sheila's mind kept sliding out of its groove; she couldn't concentrate on her report. Unhappiness is *boring*, she thought. She'd
known that well enough before Thoby, but then—with him,
because of him—she'd come to be happy, some of the time, at least.

The best thing about happiness—you could think about all sorts
of things, flick flick flick like a swallow. When she was unhappy she
had to watch what she thought, or flatten her mind and think about
absolutely nothing, otherwise—

But it got you in the end. A stray word, a case at work, and you
were sucked into the vortex. Da. Giving up the cello. What Da did;
what I did. Loss, loss, loss. And now the new fear.

No, don't think about that, she told herself. Think about Thoby,
have faith in Thoby. He would be there, he would make it work.
She had got out of the pit before, with his help. She still had her
secrets, she'd survive.

She put down her work and went and stood by his chair. He was
reading with headphones on. When he looked up and took them
off, hope irradiating his face, the Elgar cello concerto tinkled thinly
from them. Jacqueline du Pré. Sheila took a step back.

49

Idiot, he told himself. He knew not to play du Pré through the speakers; why take the risk at all? He'd blown it for today. He pulled the jack out anyhow, cutting off the cello in mid-soar.

Sheila's eyelids flickered with—fear? horror?...Fear of him?

Grasp the bull by the horns, he thought. 'What this is all about...is it that you're afraid I'll be like your father—history repeating itself?'

She looked stunned, and in a little constipated burst said, 'No, no, I never thought that, or I couldn't have...I wouldn't be...'

He'd been so sure it was that. His heart swelled with relief. What *was* going on, then? Could it be...My blood is bad, she'd said, telling him about the past in that incoherent outburst before her first long silence. He jumped up and tried to fold her in his arms, whispering, 'Oh my sweet, it's *not* hereditary, you *don't* need to worry, *please*.'

She stood absolutely passive; he stopped. Don't rush it, he told himself. Teach her to trust you; you've done it before.

Sheila knew what he was thinking: she studied his reactions minutely, as if they were a survival manual. 'Poor wounded damaged Sheila,' was in his mind whenever he suddenly laid off the pressure to talk or hug him or whatever. I can't *bear* it, she thought: being defined by one thing from my past. She wished she'd never told him. But it had been like quitting the cello—she'd had to, without knowing why.

A long haul, Thoby thought, hating the idea of living through it all over, slowly drawing her out. But he was full of hope. She was coming back—he could wait.

Chapter 7

The following Sunday Tim started off on subsidies the moment he set foot on the Heath; but Elinor was ready for him. 'It's not that I'm not interested, but could we discuss it some other time? Right now it's *you* I want to hear about.'

He took a deep breath—he could hardly hope to avoid talking about himself forever. 'Like what?'

Your lovers, she thought, but started with: 'Like...oh...how you got started on the violin.'

An easy one. 'Well, my parents let us play their old 78s when we were very small, and there was one violin record, I'd put it on and go under the piano and cry. The Haydn serenade it was called—it's the andante of one of his early quartets.' He sang her the sweet, slow tune, but had to break off. 'Damn it, it still brings tears to my eyes.'

Seeing tears in hers, too, he was intensely touched, but embarrassed, and started talking again to cover his confusion. 'Besides howling *under* the piano, I was always messing about *on* it, so when I was five they sent me for lessons. One day there was a violin on my teacher's piano. I asked to try it, and she let me. It made the most godawful squawk, but I knew it was what I wanted to play, not the piano.'

'So your parents got you one?'

'Not straightaway.'

'How come?'

'They tried to discourage me.'

'Then how...?'

'I was stubborn, so they gave in. Then I worked and worked. Learning to make notes, not noise—that's my first memory of pure happiness.'

51

'But you were five—you must have earlier ones.'

'No.'

'Maybe you were too young to remember them.'

'Maybe.' Then, less disbelievingly, 'Maybe. I've got memories of Swarthgill that must date from before that—walking through the hayfield down to the beck with the sun on my head and haystalks tickling my ears; jumping up like a beagle to see if I was still headed right. But that's a place-memory—it kept getting reinforced. I meant memories of moments.'

'But why did they try to stop you?'

Don't make me dredge it up, he wanted to say. The terror of standing up to them—he had no words for that. His past must seem so harmless in the telling, as if his childhood had been happy. Yet what he remembered was anxiety like an endless plain. Only growing up had released him.

'Noise,' he answered briefly. 'And I was too...serious about it.'

'But they had records and a grand piano—they must have liked music.'

'Oh, yes, but—'

'In its place?' she guessed. 'Not to make a career of?'

'That's right. They were kind about it—came to recitals, congratulated me if I did well in the Royal College exams. But they were happier when I became a passable bowler.'

'Yes, you'd be good'—imagining his big well-coordinated body, elegant in whites, moving in an instant from lazy repose to action.

'They're connected, bowling well and playing well—they didn't see that.'

Neither did Elinor. 'How do you mean?'

'It's...it's...' He knew it in his bones, but could not articulate it: something about following through with the whole body: the swoop of the bowling arm and of the bow arm flowing up smoothly from thigh muscles through belly, chest and shoulders.

They were by a clump of woods. Far off on Parliament Hill there were families with dogs, but no one anywhere close. 'It's like this,' he said, and moved off and hurled an imaginary ball; then changed stance only slightly and drew a bow across an imaginary violin.

52

The grace of his empty-handed gestures was absurd and moving. 'It comes right up from the soles of your feet,' she said.

He was going to marry her. He nearly told her so then and there. He started walking again, glancing at her sidelong as she walked beside him, tall and thin, head down against the raw breeze, hands stuffed in her jacket pockets. Little dark hairs were wisping across her forehead. Her nose was red, her cheeks sallow brown. The sight of her filled him with pleasure, contentment, passion.

'What sort of thing did they say, that made you realize how they felt?'

He tried to remember, and couldn't. 'They wanted me to be—somebody else,' he finally blurted, and felt the ground rock under him.

'Like, an engineer?'—Tim's father's profession.

'Probably.'

She waited, but he didn't enlarge on his reply, so she thought up something else to ask. It was hard going. He answered the literal sense of her questions, not the implications, which were often more important. When she asked if his parents had known any professional musicians, he just said, 'No,' not seeing that she wanted to know whether they'd had any picture of a musician's life and earning power. When she asked that, explicitly, he said, 'I don't think so,' and nothing else, so that she again had to ask the implicit question: whether they had tried to push him towards other careers because they wanted him to be secure.

'They didn't push me towards anything else.'

That was a surprise. 'Then what made you feel as if they wanted you to be different?'

To that she didn't get even a monosyllabic reply, just a headshake.

'You just felt it?' she asked.

'Yes'—violently.

She went on dragging answers out of him, and gradually saw that he'd always been afraid of his parents. Poor Tim, she thought; poor baby. But the more she got out of him, the more she wondered whether the Scotts had really been such dragons. They sounded much like her own parents—ordinarily imperceptive, ordinarily kind. Had they had a hard time, trying to do their perplexed best for a son born without a skin?

He had felt isolated at school, too, she discovered as, out of his stingy answers, she pieced together a picture of a solitary, acutely sensitive boy, not teased much, but raw with expecting it—until, when he was thirteen, he went to a school with an orchestra, where for the first time he met people who wanted to spend their spare time playing or talking music, and made friends, or at least companions, and felt his real life beginning.

It was getting dark. 'Did you have girlfriends at school?' she asked as they turned for home.

'Er, a couple.'

'Tell me about them.'

He gave a resigned sigh and let her quiz him about his far-off adolescent passions, then about his attachments at university and after.

'You haven't said anything about the last one,' she observed. She couldn't just not know about Vivian Roberts for ever.

He walked along in silence until she thought he was never going to answer. At the edge of the Heath he stopped and said, 'I don't want to talk about Vivian, but I suppose you've got to know; so I'll tell you. Once.' He started walking again. 'She was married. She wouldn't sleep with me—in either sense. She *certainly* wouldn't spend the night with me in a bed—wouldn't go near a bed—and she wouldn't...whatever the word is—wouldn't have intercourse with me, except twice. She was guilty about her husband, and afraid of pregnancy; but it wasn't just that. She was mixed up about sex. She wanted it—teased me with it—but she was afraid of it. Afraid of men's violence. I had to be very gentle with her, so she wouldn't feel I was forcing her.'

'How long did this go on, then?'

'Three years.' Three years and two months, to be precise, but it would be tactless to show how well he remembered the exact length.

'Three years, and you weren't lovers except *twice*?' Elinor said in astonishment.

54

'It depends what you mean by lovers. She almost didn't want me to touch her, but she did like, er...oral sex. But only one-way.'

Elinor was too fascinated to restrain herself. 'Which way?'

She sucked me off, he thought. 'Me...coming in her mouth,' he said hesitantly. He had never spoken of such things to anyone before.

'And Vivian?' She wondered why he looked so blank. 'How did *she* come?'

'Sometimes she...rubbed herself against me; or let me, er, bring her with my finger. But usually she didn't want to come at all—she wanted to stay detached.'

'Sounds like a lot of men's dream woman.'

'What do you mean? It was *awful*.'

'But you were involved with her all that time—you must have been getting something out of it.'

'I kept hoping. She had something, a quality...she was fragile. Like a bird you hold in your hands. Alluring—like your friend Maggie. But I nearly went crazy. She was so elusive. She'd make dates and not show up—not ring—nothing. Twice she agreed to go away for a weekend, but come the day she was ill, or her little boy was. The third time I said, "If you don't show, that's the end." She got as far as Ockendon Road, and sat there in a panic, and said, "I can't."'

'But you didn't end it.'

'No.' He tried to think how to explain. But you couldn't explain obsession. 'She did. I came back from a week on tour and rang her at work—and she'd left her job. No forwarding address, or so they said. It was how we'd got in touch—I'd never rung her at home, obviously. I didn't even know her number—she just disappeared.'

'What about the telephone book?'

'I couldn't ring every Roberts in the directory! Anyhow, a few months later, just when I was starting to feel a little less awful, she rang—said she'd been scared. So it all started again—and then she disappeared *again*. This time she didn't come back. I got a postcard from her a few months ago—nearly a year after she vanished— saying she'd moved to Leicester. And that's Vivian. Any more questions?'

'Uh...not that I can—'

'Good. I don't want to talk about her again.' Or about anything else so personal—it made him sick with apprehension. 'It was a bad time—no point raking over the ashes.'

'Okay.' She wasn't sure she trusted herself to say anything much, anyhow.

'Want to hear the opus 3 quartet?' Tim asked when they got in.

'The...oh, the Haydn. Sure.' She sat down on the sofa, hoping he would join her. He sat in an armchair.

'This is it,' he said at the andante—'the serenade.' Tears came to his eyes.

They came to hers, too, but not in response to the sweet melody. Hearing about Vivian had rowelled her up. Fragile. Elusive. Alluring. He'd used words like that about Sheila, too. He never would about her, though—no one would. It was the way women were supposed to be. Tease men, tantalise them; keep them interested.

She could do it a little, for fun: what was known as harmless flirtation. But systematically, deliberately?—no, impossible. But if she did, would Tim feel about her as he had about Vivian?

He made an omelette for dinner, but she was so tense that it seemed like a three-course meal. She pushed it aside, put her forehead on the table and started to cry in the middle of what he was saying about Bartók.

'What's wrong?' he asked in dismay.

'I can't tell you, you said not to.'

He sighed. 'Vivian.'

'I'll never interest you as much as her.'

'You're out of your mind.'

'But the things you said—you'll never care as much about me as—'

'Where did you get that idea? You're *much* better for me. You're—you're health.' He sputtered the words out with such angry forcefulness that she was somehow convinced.

'Like Doris Day,' she said, her spirits returning.

56

'*Not* like Doris Day. Like fresh air after a smoky room'—
thinking of Vivian and her incessant smoking.

She blew her nose and decided to believe him.

She was still feeling raw when they went up to bed, but wanted to
make love. She needed to obliterate the thought of Vivian and the
fear that what Tim most wanted was something she hadn't got.

She reached for him, and was gradually reassured. Whatever
Vivian had meant to him, sexually it didn't sound like much—
certainly less urgent and intense than this. He was barely moving
inside her, but the lightest glide of his cock made reverberations far
down that built up and built up like...like...

She nearly laughed—so much for urgent intensity. What she'd
remembered was a concert recently where she'd seen the percussionist
touch-touch-touch a padded mallet to one spot on a Chinese gong—
slowly, delicately, secretively, until it was quivering with a whisper of
resonance — then stand back and wait for it to erupt all on its own,
untouched by human hand, in an enormous crash-boom that
shuddered on and on. Mind you, there were differences. The Chinese
gong, once primed, would sound on its own; she, to come, needed the
unstopped touch of a human body or tongue or hand.

Tim was very close, she could tell; but she was on a plateau. She
tried to come; couldn't; thought she was there for a moment;
wasn't. 'You first,' she said.

'All right,' Tim said cooperatively; and came.

He lay dazed for a while, then, reminded by her slow stirring
above him, said in her ear, 'How do you want to come?'

Tongue or finger, he meant. She knew which she wanted—but
dared she say? He *seemed* to like licking her, greedily returning and
returning even after she tried to make him stop. But maybe he only
liked it before he came himself. She lay on him in silence, weighed
down by everything she had read or heard about men's secret
disgust for women's bodies.

But but. Sometimes he came in her mouth after she'd come, and
she liked it. Justice. Equal treatment. Claim the same for yourself.

'I want you to lick me,' she said.

57

But she didn't dissolve in bliss under his tongue. Was he valiantly forcing himself to the task? She wanted to come fast and release him, but she was stuck.

Vivian. Elusive. Fragile. Vivian wanting him to come in her mouth but not letting him lick her—or do anything else, either. 'It was *awful*,' he had said. But had he unconsciously *liked* not having to reciprocate?

She tried tensing her thigh muscles; no good. She was tempted to open her bad-fantasy box for an image that would bring her in a flash. Instead, she opened her eyes and saw: his fuzzy head between her thighs, his heavy brow-ridge, her pubic hair brushing his cheeks and nose. She couldn't see his mouth and tongue, only feel them. When she shut her eyes again, the image of his head stayed on her eyelids, blocking out bad images and inciting her towards the brink...but not over.

Eventually, tired of trying, she stopped him and said, 'I can't.'

'Why not?'

'Nervousness, I suppose.'

'What about?'

'Whether I'd come—' in some surprise.

'Oh, is that important to you?'

'Yes—very'—bridling automatically. Was he one of those men who thought coming mattered less to women?

'Oh, it's not to me. It's the whole thing that matters, not just that.'

Oh. She sighed with pleasure and went to sleep.

But the same fear still blocked her the next time they made love. She managed not to open her box of bad images; and managed to come—but it was an effort.

Afterwards Tim lay breathing quietly; before long he would shake himself and get up. Suddenly she had to know. Now.

She opened her mouth, shut it; opened it and said quickly: 'Tim, you awake?'

'Mmph...'

'I need to ask you some things.'

He sat up. 'Ouf. Time to get up. What?'

58

'I want to know—do you like...licking me?'

'Would I do it if I didn't like it?'

Was he being evasive? 'You might do it to please me but not like it for yourself,' she pointed out.

'True.' He scrunched up his face, thinking it through. 'No, that's not why. I like doing it, because—' All he could think was a jumble: because of what you are, what you become, and the intimacy: something to do with speech, and what's beyond speech. Helplessly he said, 'Because it—feels nice. And because I'm giving you pleasure. I wouldn't like it if you didn't.'

'Lots of men don't like it at all.'

'I'm not lots of men'—impatiently.

'I know—I've just wondered...'

'Why didn't you ask before?'

'Um, you didn't seem to want to talk about sex.'

'That's right.'

'You mean—never? But I *need* to sometimes.'

'I don't mean never'—though in effect he did. 'It's just...I've got a dual sense. It's dangerous, talking about sex; but it's sometimes necessary.'

'Dangerous—how do you mean?'

'This depth of...of intensity that I have with you—you've probably had it all your life, but it's—'

'No—'

'But it's new to me, and I'm afraid of losing it by talking about it.'

'It's new to me, too,' she said. 'It's never been like this before.'

He looked at her as if he hardly believed her. 'Besides, it's hard talking like this; I feel—nervous.'

'Me too.' It *was* unsettling, trying to talk about things there were no words for. Daunted by his warning, she fell silent.

Get it over with, he thought, and said resolutely, 'What else do you need to talk about?'

She seized on the invitation. 'Well, I was wondering...you don't look at me when we're making love. Do you...' She wanted to know if he closed his eyes to concentrate upon fantasies, as she'd done herself with other lovers; but that was too hard to ask. 'Are you...trying to forget it's me you're making love to?'

59

He shook his head. 'I don't *think* so. Except insofar as making love always involves something...something in sex that's not about either of us.'

Something in sex that's not about either of us? Yes. She stored it away in her mind.

'What else?'

'Nothing, not right now.' Let him learn in slow stages that it's safe to talk; don't force too much on him at once.

The talk seemed to release something in Tim. In the midst of making love a few days later he muttered something into her shoulder.

'What?' she said.

'I said, Why is it so wonderful?'

The next time they made love he whispered, 'Sometimes it's almost too intense.'

'What do you mean?'

'A combination of pleasure and pain, it's...at the limits of what's possible.'

And the next time, in the same impassioned whisper: 'You don't *know* how much pleasure you give me.'

'I do—from how much you give *me*.'

'No, you *can't* know.'

You don't know, she thought; you don't know, you don't know. Not a contest, an oblique agreement. This was so much the absolute edge of bliss that no one else, not even he, could ever have felt anything like it.

'You're so open to me,' he said with astonishment one morning, moving deep inside her.

It was exactly how *she* felt: open to him everywhere; open to his will. He led her in places she wanted to go, away from the over-considerate alternations of sexual democracy, which had some-times reminded her of people giving way to one another on a footpath. He filled her new-found craving to comply—a deep passivity which before him she had been unaware of, so little had it been met; and still hardly dared acknowledge; but luxuriated in: a

60

sense of utter dependence, the illusion of yielding over reciprocity, of submitting—

She shied away from that word; shut it out—quite successfully: her sexual happiness had its own resonance. She was drifting in a bemused sensual dream, content—almost—to ignore contradictions between what she thought she ought to feel and what she really felt.

Yet she couldn't altogether duck them. It was alarming, after years of gentle, personal, equal sex, permeated with tenderness, to find that she also wanted fierceness, greed: wanted to sink into a well of pure sensation; wanted to be penetrated to the core with no thought but yes, yes, yes; wanted to be compliant, passive to his will: a fantasy of endless consent.

At least it was only a fantasy—when actually making love she wasn't tempted to consent to anything she didn't want. But reciprocity was fundamental to humane and equal sexual relations, so wasn't it deeply suspect—reactionary, she told herself with rueful self-mockery—to want even the illusion of compliance?

'I don't know him,' she had protested to Maggie; but she was coming closer—by being with him; by thinking about him all the time. Everything about him was touching. She read his soul in his expressions, his furniture, his friends, his lovemaking, their fragmentary talks, his music.

When he played the violin he was entirely absorbed and forgot she existed, but after practising or performing he often unwound by playing the piano; and there he could afford to be more nonchalant, smiling at her over the music rack, pausing to say something about the piece, rambling from Schoenberg to Brahms as the mood took him, not fussed about his limitations as a pianist, playing with an openness of feeling, a mixture of musical understanding and technical limitations, that made the music amazingly poignant— his body quivering with the effort to play well and expressively; his face opening into a rapt gravity that was like his expression when making love.

That look, when he lifted his head from his music, or from her shoulder in bed, made her think he must love her. But they spent

61

almost every night together, and he said nothing about his feelings—not a word of love, or even any pet names. Nor, in his silence, did she. Silly babbling endearments thronged to her tongue and died there. She couldn't say 'my pet' or 'my sweet' to a man whose exclamation in the extreme of bliss was, 'Oh Elinor.'

Chapter 8

'Let's go to the Heath this Sunday,' Elinor said. 'We haven't been since...' since the day he told her about Vivian. 'For ages,' she substituted; Vivian was still a sore point with her. One week he had been performing; twice they had gone to concerts. 'We should walk this week, or we'll be stiff as boards in Yorkshire.' They would have four days there: Tim always kept time free at Easter to go to Swarthgill and walk.

'Er, I'm squeezed pretty tight, finishing Sheila's table.'

'You've been wasting so much time seeing me,' she said jokingly.

Tim did not contradict her; he had been getting up his courage to say something. 'Actually, I've been thinking...' He got up from her sofa and started pacing to and fro in the small open space. 'The point is, we both want to be together; why postpone it?'

She sat there gaping, trying to keep her legs out of his way. What, no tender words, no hesitancy; straight out with it, cool as could be?

'It would be more convenient,' he added, turning about and about in a slow methodical walk.

'That's not enough reason,' she snapped. She loved him, wanted to live with him, had been waiting for him to ask her to—but for the sake of love, not convenience. 'Live with you, so you'll have more time for your furniture? You must be joking.'

He stopped pacing. 'It's not a matter of furniture. It's a matter of committing ourselves.'

It was an oblique declaration, but she was still narked. *She* wasn't oblique. 'Do you mean you love me?' she asked bluntly. There was no light in his sensual features; maybe love was irrelevant to what they shared. But she had to know.

63

How could she come straight out with such a question?—how could he answer? He needed her. Her practical vitality had become his food, the air he breathed. But he could not say he loved her. What did people mean by the word? He loved music—was it like that? Perhaps, then, he did love her, for his feeling for music was very like what he felt when they made love. In his former involvements lovemaking had had a solitariness that had reminded him uneasily of masturbation. With her it was union, dissolution of self; freedom to follow impulse without fear of upsetting her; depth upon depth of physical sounding of her; a richness like some resonances of the cello.

But outside bed she did not, thank God, rouse him to the erotic tumult he had felt with Vivian—and wasn't that love? He never wanted to feel it again in his life.

'Not exactly,' he replied carefully, 'I'm in love with you. But the other—that takes time.' A form of words, with perhaps a germ of truth.

She winced with pain at the slap of, 'Not exactly;' but got a jolt of pleasure from hearing, 'I'm in love with you,' even in that measured tone. If only he would stop prowling and sit down.

'I don't see the difference,' she said.

He took another turn or two, eyes down. All he saw of her was her thin legs and long narrow feet tucked sideways against the armchair. Her legs moved him. 'Skinny', she had once called them, comparing them with Maggie's—which were as supple as a swan's neck, it was true. But he distrusted Maggie's allure. 'Your legs are just fine,' he had said. 'A little thin, that's all, not skinny.' He had not known how to tell her that he found them touching, eloquent, unselfconsciously sure of themselves.

Suitable words would not come; he would have to try anything. 'I'm not sure what it means, "loving someone". A *grande passion*—the world well lost for love? I'm not capable of that—and it's juvenile. I've got a different idea of love.' The effort made him weak on his feet. He sat down. 'Being in love,' he went on heavily, 'is only a beginning. Real love grows slowly, knowing someone, living with them. Building something solid together. Not just a bolt

64

out of the blue.' He hoped it made more sense to her than it did to him.

She looked at him doubtfully. He was in love with her but didn't love her. Why was that so hard to grasp? 'It's—I don't work that way myself, so it's a new idea to me. And...but I'm glad you told me.'

'You asked.'

'You could have said things you didn't mean.'

That was just what he had done. The undeserved gratitude penetrated his guard. He said forlornly, 'I just *need* you, I haven't got much to offer you.' There was truth for her.

'That's not true, how can you think it?' She put her hand caressingly on his thigh. He was so vulnerable to unhappiness: she could, she would, make him happy.

He carefully did not shrink from her hand. After a moment he took it and held it, a trophy, and fixed her with his eye and said something he did believe. 'We're right for each other, you know that.'

His face drew her like a magnet; she wanted to cover it with kisses. Right for her—a man who often barely responded if she kissed him? Who didn't love her? Yet—a man who was in love with her, and to whom she was sexually in thrall. 'I didn't expect—' she cried, pulling her hand out from under—but didn't know what she didn't expect. 'It's just...I'm afraid of everything going wrong.'

'I didn't know you thought so little of me,' he said with a pathos that was no less genuine for being deliberate.

What had she said that made him say that? The whole conversation was like walking in fog: she couldn't see backwards or forwards. But Tim was sitting with his shoulders tight, as if he were chilly—she shouldn't sulk because he was honest about his confusion. She said helplessly, 'I need to think about it.'

'All right, then, you should take your time. Would a month be enough?'

It was more than enough, but right now she didn't feel like dickering. 'I—yes.'

'Fine. I'll ask you again in a month.' Tim was tired and hurt and wanted to lick his wounds in private. He stood up. 'I think I'll go home, if you don't mind.'

She jumped up. 'But you were *staying*!'

'I wouldn't be much company.'

'Oh—please stay, and we can try to get comfortable together again.' What she meant was, 'Stay so that I can comfort you.' His pinched loneliness was unbearable.

He shook his head. His need to get out of sight was overwhelming. 'I thought I knew how you felt. It's been a shock, I need to sleep it off. Don't worry,' with a small smile, 'I'll get over it. I'm at the QEH tomorrow, shall we go to my place after?—Good, I'll come by the office for you.'

Opening the door, he added: 'By the way, I'm talking about marriage, not living with,' and shut it behind him.

She blinked. He wanted to marry her, so he must love her—so why did he split verbal hairs about it? Turning back into the room, she barked her shin on the coffee table and sat down, rubbing the sore spot. Marry him? Awfully formal—why didn't they simply live together? But he was emotionally conservative; she could see he would want marriage. Okay—she wouldn't make an issue of it.

Their first quarrel. On the boy-men Richter scale it hardly registered, but if he hadn't mentioned marriage on his way out, she'd have been afraid he was gone for good.

Tim had a great capacity for putting problems out of his mind until it was time to deal with them. The next night he was easy and friendly, as if there had been no discussion, no quarrel. If anything, he was a little warmer than usual, to show he had no hard feelings.

For Elinor it was harder to act as if nothing had happened. She was used to talking things out—immediately; exhaustively. But that had its costs. She decided to try following Tim's lead; and after a couple of days it was hard to remember that anything had changed.

But something had changed—he wanted to marry her—and she wanted...

66

But what about meeting her halfway about kissing and hugging? 'Give me time,' he had said, and she'd given him weeks and weeks of it, but he was no different. What did he mean, 'I've got difficulties'? Were they connected with Vivian?

No, it's me, she thought in discouragement one day. She was too robust—too straightforward, as Maggie put it: not fragile or alluring like Vivian or Sheila, or for that matter Maggie. Not his emotional type.

Or was it—

Did he look away, did he not want to kiss her because...

That night at Ockendon Road she ate, got ready for bed in silence, then lay down with her back to Tim, wishing she were alone so she could cry.

He was utterly bewildered. He had obviously offended her—but how? He was tempted to turn out the light and hope she liked him better in the morning, but she had never been like this before; he could not bear feeling alienated from her. 'What's wrong, Elinor?' he said at last.

A big sob. 'Nothing.'

'What have I done?'

A heave; a wriggle; dark wet eyes above the sheet; a sheet-muffled voice saying: 'It's not you—I'm not...'

He waited; she welled a silent tear. 'Come on,' he said.

She muttered into the sheet: 'Not kissing me—is it because—is it my teeth?'

'Your *what*?'

'My *teeth*,' she said angrily; then in a wail: 'They're so *crooked*.'

He looked at her with horror and in a rush of fellow-feeling said what he had never thought to say aloud. 'No no how could you think, it's not you, it's me, I'm—'

The eyes blinked, widened. 'You're what?'

The face Tim saw in the shaving mirror was coarse-featured, heavy-jowled, sullen. His first girlfriend had once said, seeing him shamble in half asleep from the bathroom, 'My God, you look like Frankenstein;' and though she was only teasing, he had believed

67

her. Then his last lover before Vivian had said the same thing—in the same circumstances. The comparison was irresistible: hunched in his dressing gown, stiff-gaited with sleep, he did move just like Boris Karloff. Elinor thought so too, but, older and more tactful, hadn't said so.

'You're what?' she repeated.

Ugly, he thought. He translated the naked word into: 'Not exactly how women want men to look.'

'*What*?' She let the sheet drop.

'You heard me.'

She sat up. 'But—you mean you think you're—not good-looking?'

'Obviously.'

'But that's—that's as weird as Audrey Hepburn growing up thinking she was ugly.' She noticed him quiver at the word. '*You're* not ugly, you're one of the handsomest men I've ever seen.'

He shook his head as if shaking off words in a foreign language. 'It's not just me that thinks so. Maggie thinks you're good-looking; Rose says you're like Cary Grant. You've told me yourself, women in audiences giving you the eye—what do you think that's about?'

'My music—or I'm so often the leader, and they think that's glamorous.'

'You nitwit. You come onstage by yourself—they see you better than anyone else. If you were ugly, they'd stop looking right away.' She felt a lot better. Of course her teeth weren't crooked—only a little. 'But what connection—' She got it. 'Not kissing me, turning away—do you think if I see you, I'll be put off?'

It was like talking to a doorpost, but his eyes flickered.

She got up on her knees. 'Tim, *I'm* not ugly, I'm perfectly presentable. Lots of men are attracted to me—at the cinema...mind you half of them would make a pass at any female under eighty— but still, it's not for want of other opportunities that I'm with you. And I wouldn't be if I didn't like the way you look—*love* the way you look. You're not some Frankenstein's monster...'

He stopped hearing her. She could not have hit on that particular comparison unless it was what she at least unconsciously thought.

68

'...not just handsome—beautiful,' she was saying. 'You don't need to turn away. Turn towards me. Please.'

He said nothing.

'Please,' she said again; and then, in exasperation: 'Tim—*everybody* wants to be kissed. If we're to live...I can't do without that for the rest of my *life*!' Her voice ran up on the word.

He knew it was halfway to an ultimatum. He was shivering all up and down his body, deep inside where she couldn't see. 'I—I—I said before, I need—more time.'

'I know, but—' Poor love. It must be Vivian—whatever she'd said or done had gone deep.

'I don't mean a few days, I mean—I don't know when.'

'Okay'—doubtfully. 'If you'll promise to try.'

'I'll...if you're sure you can put up with...'

'Sure I'm sure.' His face was thick with misery. She wanted to kiss it better, but remembered what she'd just agreed to, and didn't.

Chapter 9

The Cromer had a Billy Wilder season in Easter week. Chris and Maggie both came to *Kiss Me, Stupid* on her recommendation, and stopped by the office afterwards. Elinor got out the office whisky bottle, and Rose fetched paper cups from the coffee stand.

The movie had made them mellow. ' "Detour by way of Warm Springs, Paradise Valley and Climax—it's the only way to go," ' Chris quoted reminiscently. 'I do hate that word, though—climax.'

Maggie agreed. 'Orgasm's worse, though.'

'Orgasm's a *thing*,' said Rose. 'Good, better, best: something you can give Michelin stars to.'

'And it sounds like organ—"his enormous organ" sort of thing,' said Chris.

'And orgy, and gasp and spasm,' said Maggie. 'Why are all the words for sex so awful?'

'They aren't all,' said Elinor.

'Almost all,' said Maggie.

'The polite ones are worst,' said Chris.

'Like wee-wee for piss and willie for cock?'

'I meant the medical kind, like genitals and vagina.'

'No worse than the slang ones,' said Rose. 'Tits, jerk off, wank.'

'Yes but think of prepuce,' said Maggie. 'Think of *glans*.'

They all laughed nervously and inspected their paper cups. Rose broke the silence, her voice higher than usual. 'I think the worst polite words are...flaccid and turgid!'

Everybody laughed. 'You're right about glans,' said Chris. 'It's a cross between gland and slippery.'

'Like vulva,' Elinor said. 'A cross between Volvo and vulgar.'

'Pudenda,' said Maggie as if holding up a dead fish.

'Pubes,' said Rose, and they all said, 'Ugh.'

'Penis. It rhymes with obscene.'

'And mean.'

'And teeny weeny.'

'It sounds *flaccid*,' said Maggie definitively.

'Erection is okay.'

'His erection, Was perfection,' Rose sang. 'Better than hard-on, anyhow—'

'Or horny. Or stones.'

'Or rocks. Getting your rocks off.'

'Yuck. Never heard that one.'

'Balls.'

'I sort of like balls,' said Chris.

Maggie hooted. 'Me too. And, dare I say it, cock.'

'But not prick,' said Chris. 'Prick's sharp—they want to hurt you with it.'

Maggie and Elinor agreed, Rose made an 'Oh...' of dissent.

Elinor topped up the paper cups, and they got onto words for—for—for what each of them had different words for. Chris called it fucking or having sex; Maggie, making love *to*; Rose, making love *with*; Elinor, fucking or making love—to or with, depending. None of them was entirely happy with any of the words, including her own.

'But the alternatives are even worse,' said Rose. 'Think of ball, screw, score—'

'Shaft.'

'Shag. Poke. Have it off with. Get a leg over.'

'Hump. Bonk—'

'Really?' said Elinor. 'As in bonk over the head?'

'Haven't you heard that?'

'Never.'

'Such hard ramming words,' Chris said. 'You wonder why men want to do it at all, if that's what they think of it.'

'Or why they want to do it with women, from the things they call us,' Rose said. 'Slag, slut, dog—'

'Piece of ass, piece of snatch.'

'Tight bitch—or else you're an easy lay; you can't win.'

'Ballbreaker.'

71

'Cunt.'

'Awful for a woman,' said Maggie, 'but okay for genitals. Otherwise you're back to pudenda.'

Elinor agreed, but not Rose: 'The sissiest master at my school was called Cuntface Crockford, so I always think of him.'

'Twat is worse,' said Chris. 'As bad as wank. Equal first.'

'Aren't there any nice words?' Rose asked plaintively. 'What do *women* say?'

'His thing,' said Maggie drily. 'And down there for their, er, cunts.'

'We must say *something*,' Chris said. 'Or *think* something.'

'Clitoris isn't too bad,' said Maggie. 'Clinical, but flirty, too—like frilly underwear.'

The others murmured agreement. 'That's because men don't use it as a swear word,' said Rose.

'How can they—half of them have never seen it.'

'Or found it.'

'Or heard of it.'

'I use one set of words thinking about sex and another when I speak,' said Elinor.

'Me too. What ones do *you* think with?—No, I asked first.'

'Uh, somebody's already objected to every one of them while we've been talking. Cunt, cock, fucking, sucking—' She hadn't quite meant to say that one.

There was a little silence, then Chris said, 'Cunnilingus is sort of cute.'

'Eating pussy?' Maggie offered.

'Oh no,' Rose wailed. 'It makes me think of pussycat stew!'

'*Soixante-neuf*, then. Not the same thing, but...'

'That's okay because it's French.'

Everyone laughed, everyone agreed. Elinor said, 'But why does that save it?'

'Same as clitoris—it's not used for swearing. You can say, "You cocksucker"—but imagine, "You soixante-neufer"!'

'Cocksucker—yuck,' said Rose. Nobody asked if she meant the word or the deed.

'And a blow job is something you have at the hairdresser's,' said Chris.

They all laughed, and Maggie murmured, 'You must give me the name of your hairdresser,' causing a fresh burst—but with a nervous edge. Rose hitched off the stool. Everyone stretched; Chris said she must be going, and left; Rose drifted out to her desk.

'That was sticky at the end,' said Maggie, putting on her coat. 'Actually, I think the worst word connected with sex is thank you. Men who say, "Thank you" after making love. I mean, what do you say back?'

' "My pleasure"?' Elinor suggested.

'No—I've got it.' Maggie cackled. 'You say, "So glad you enjoyed it. *Do* come again."'

'God it was funny,' Elinor said, telling Tim about the conversation. 'Flaccid and turgid! But you could have cut the air with a knife. Why? I mean, all the basic body words are short—arm, leg, toe, belly, spit, chew. So why the problem with'—her voice tightened in spite of herself—'with cock and balls and fuck and cunt? Just that they're swear words?'

'Partly squeamishness—lots of people do say abdomen and saliva, after all, rather than belly and spit. And words like...fuck'— he too hesitated before saying it—'they're more explosive; they're about the parts we keep covered. Private words for private parts. Long words cover them up.' He chuckled. 'Like the story about the man who tells the cops, "I went down the fucking pub and had a fucking drink and went home and opened the fucking door and found the fucking neighbour having fucking sexual intercourse with my wife."'

That night in bed he whispered, 'I want to fuck you.'

She was shocked, yet transfixed; she felt as if her eyes wouldn't focus properly. Her mind formed the sentence: I want you to fuck me, but all she got out was: 'Me too.'

Chris stopped by the office, wearing something shapeless and black as usual. 'Apropos of what we were talking about the other day,' she said, perching on a stool, 'you'll never guess what I found in Daniel's room—porn mags.'

73

'Good Lord—he's only twelve.'

'Thirteen. They're absolutely disgusting—close-ups of fucking and fellatio, full frontals of women opening their legs. I took them right out to the rubbish and told him to keep that sort of thing in his school locker, not in a house with young kids. I don't want James and Kate getting their first images of sex from pictures of women doing everything men dream about. I rang his father, but he just said it's inevitable. Half pleased, if you ask me. Anyhow, I've decided to write a book about it. Now—what about you? You look flourishing, I must say.'

'Well, I—'

'Right, love, must run—ta-ra.'

Elinor put on her overall and went to let out the first house. Chris always stayed long enough to say what she wanted to, and no longer. You couldn't be annoyed, she was so transparent.

After letting the second house in, she went back to her office and started counting the take. 'Pictures of women doing everything men dream about.' She was glad she hadn't been the one to find them. She owned nothing more pornographic than *Lady Chatterley*; she was afraid to—she read the porn she came across on friends' bookshelves so avidly that she wondered if her appetite for it was insatiable. She hated it; yet it was what fuelled some of her own fantasies.

Not all; some of them were innocent enough—lust working upon memories of making love; images of excitement, intimacy, exploration. But there were also her bad fantasies, which were of dominance, submission; unwilling assent followed by entire willing submission of the whole being: being used for his own pleasure by a man who was entirely indifferent to hers (but whose needs happened to match hers; even in fantasy she saw to that)—a man who wanted her to have pleasure, but only in order to make her dependent upon him, who was master of his own desires, but made her the slave of her most secret ones, using not physical coercion, but a blurrily conceived psychological equivalent.

What stung her imagination was psychic enthralment, not brute force; her fantasies were never of rape. But that repeated image of

74

compelled desire was frighteningly close to the idea that women always 'want it' even when they say no.

In those fantasies she wasn't even herself, Nell Benton, 'I'; she was a doe-eyed, docile stranger, 'she', someone with whom she temporarily identified, as if watching a movie. 'She spread her legs wide,' she would think, or, 'She let him...' The man wasn't anyone she knew, either, but a novelette hero, saturnine, contemptuous. Yuck. She hated having stuff like that inside her head.

At least it had surfaced less in recent months—the erotic force of lovemaking with Tim pushed it into the background. With him the images that flickered across her mind seemed different in kind— momentary wishes for the impossible, like wishing she could come ten times, or that he could; for boundless giving and receiving; yielding to pure impulse, oceanic desires, the unconscious.

Men had fantasies, but she'd read somewhere that most women didn't. Was she a freak? If only she could talk to another woman about it.

But look how tense she, Chris, Rose and Maggie had got, just lightly discussing words for sex. No one seemed to talk about such things—and no wonder; her ponderings took place somewhere at the edge of language, where she fumbled for words to think with, far less speak.

Chapter 10

On Good Friday Elinor went to Camden Passage and bought a blue crêpe thirties frock to wear to the concert, then on to the office to clear her desk and welcome the locum assistant manager, a fat man with a Sidney Greenstreet paunch and a vast tired air of having seen and heard too much of everything, especially from a snippety girl who insisted on explaining her titchy little cinema's routine when he'd been running the big ones before she was born.

What with one thing and another it was late afternoon when she got away from the office, bought a pair of high-heeled scarlet shoes and went home to bath and change. Frock, shoes, a smudge of grey eyeshadow, a twirl of mascara, stand back and inspect. Oh God, the blue frock made her look narrow and weedy. She pulled a couple of things out of the wardrobe—no—no. And it was time; she had to wear it anyhow.

Thoby and Sheila were waiting in the foyer. Sheila had come straight from work and was wearing a nondescript black skirt with a jacket that no longer fastened over her belly. Her dark hair was swept back with combs into wide, white-streaked wings; she looked delicate, lovely.

Thoby handed Elinor a score. 'Thought you mightn't have one.'

'I can't read music,' she said irritably, flipping through it. 'Or German. I should have brought the libretto from my records. Maybe there's one for sale.'

'No need—let's switch. This one's from ours—it's got English.'

'Oh—oh thanks,' she said in some confusion. Really, he was kind: he had clearly brought his own score for her, intending to make do with a small-print four-language libretto himself.

'It'll be hot,' he warned her—'all that fervent humanity. Let me put your mac in the cloakroom.'

76

She wanted to clutch it to her, but obediently took it off, feeling like a scarecrow.

'Dashing frock,' he said. 'Let's see the back. Nice swirl.'

'And lovely shoes,' Sheila said.

Elinor flushed with pleasure. Nice Thoby and Sheila, she caught herself thinking in gratified vanity as they found their places.

The two small orchestras filed in and started tuning up, then the choruses, the soloists and the leader—Tim, looming large, to a smattering of applause. She wasn't sure, with Thoby and Sheila beside her, whether or not to clap. Sheila did, Thoby didn't. Finally Horniman, bowing; more applause. Dimmed lights; silence. A woman's head was blocking her view of Tim; but he leaned forward into sight when Horniman's baton came up and the great first chorus surged out.

While it lasted she was full up with music and forgot about Tim, but her eyes found him again when it was over, and the music blurred in and out of focus as she looked at him and away, back and away.

She should be listening, not gazing at him lovestruck. She dropped her eyes to the libretto.

She had a recording of the *St Matthew Passion* and had thought she knew it well; but she had never followed the words. Now she discovered that she had only ever half listened to it, tuning in for arias and choruses, but out for the tenor and baritone recitatives: the Evangelist, narrating the events of the last supper, and Jesus, whose every utterance resonated with the pain of all the world's sadness. How was that spiritual intensity achieved? A minor key, presumably, and something in the contrast between the two voices. The question wouldn't have occurred to her before Tim.

She looked up, as if the answer might be written in the singers' faces. 'Er sprach zu ihm,' the Evangelist sang. The harpsichord and cello continuo ceased; the strings poised their bows; and Jesus replied, 'Du sagest's.' Of course—how better to freight his words than by underscoring them, and them only, with an unearthly shimmer of strings?

Suddenly an extraordinary passage was upon her. 'Nehmet, esset, das ist mein Leib,' said Jesus. Take, eat, she read, this is my

77

body. And: Drink all of this; this is my blood of the New Testament. Oh. That. The heart of the faith she had been baptised into but not brought up in. Her parents hid from their dread of extinction by trying to believe in something out there, because there had to be more than just this, didn't there, but they had never been churchgoers. At school she had daydreamed through RI. Tears rose to her eyes and slid down her cheeks; she needed to blow her nose. Would Bach be happy or angry to know that his expression of faith was moving her to tears, but not to belief, more than two centuries after his death?

Her thoughts went out towards Tim, there at the centre of it all, making it happen. She felt closer to him than ever before, though probably he hardly remembered her existence just now.

Her handkerchief was in her bag on the floor. She fumbled for it and glanced at Thoby on her way up, expecting him to look superior if he had noticed her tears. There was a shiny runnel on his cheek.

After the interval her mind wandered for a while. She began paying attention again during the recitative in which, after denying Jesus thrice, Peter remembered his prophecy when the cock crew and went out and wept bitterly. Marvellous, the small-scale human drama within the immense framework of divine tragedy.

In the silence after 'bitterlich' there was a stir. She looked up idly. It was the contralto standing for her aria—and Tim, standing up too. He racked up his music stand, tucked the violin under his chin, glanced up with bow ready, and at Horniman's nod launched into a melody she had heard him run through quickly that morning. But he hadn't told her he would stand up, drawing every eye towards him, and play it alone, pure note upon pure note with only a light under-thread of strings, before the singer joined him with, 'Erbarme Dich, mein Gott,' then paused after two lines of aria while Tim continued alone; and again; and again; voice and violin interresponding, one rich and liquid, the other sharper and piercingly sweet. Elinor, transfixed, blinked away tears to keep him in sight: heavy curve of cheek distorted by the instrument, look of entire concentration clamped masklike over a rapture that he could

78

not completely conceal, body pliant, leaning into the music. He and she were alone in the hall. Did he know she was there, was he at all privately dedicating his solo to her, or was she forgotten with the rest of the audience in his effort to let grace speak through him unimpeded? Her whole body remembered its knowledge of him—with incredulity, not desire. The man now drawing meaning from the violin before hundreds of people had this morning been a naked body fronting hers, moving with, within, upon; coming. A different order of knowledge; a different rapture. With other lovers, at parties or meetings, she had felt that abrupt giddying awareness of her carnal relation to a social being just then moving and talking in a room; but never had the disjunction between public and private seemed so absolute. Tim wasn't just in public, he was on show. Absurd, the sense of privileged access. Most people in this hall, in the world, had just such private knowledge of another person. Oh but that was unbelievable. True but unbelievable. Was someone looking at the black-haired contralto with startled secret pride? At stick-thin Horniman? At the violinist whose music stand Tim had just brushed with his elbow as he lowered his own stand and sat down? At the tubby beak-nosed harpsichordist? Did Sheila, two seats away, quiver with the untellable secret of her relation to Thoby? Did practically everyone vibrate from time to time with this absurdity?

She was dizzy with imagining the web of sexual relations invisibly interwoven with the social fabric. A chorale and some recitative passed her by. A violinist from the second orchestra came forward to accompany a bass aria. She wished it were Tim, then didn't; she was wrung as much as she could bear. She half listened, half drifted. After quite a while they crucified Jesus and cast lots for his clothes—'That it might be fulfilled which was spoken by the prophet,' the translation said. Good Lord. She flipped back. Yes—in using Judas's thirty pieces of silver to buy the potter's field, the high priests were fulfilling a prophecy of Jeremiah. Were all those cross-references to the Old Testament the tip of the iceberg, was the shape of the narrative purely accidental—each incident dictated not by the writer's sense of tragic inevitability, but by the need to bear out obscure Messianic prophecies? How disillusioning—the

79

way she'd felt when she learned that the laws of gravity were only by-products of Newton's search for a mystical numbers system.

'Did you ever think of being a soloist?' she asked Tim afterwards.

'Good heavens, no. It's an awful life—always on the road, and the tension: the audience waiting for the matador to slip. Even a short solo like tonight—I want to do it—but I still feel all churned up.'

'Not even when you were little?'

He considered. 'I don't remember. Maybe. But by the time I was old enough to think about it seriously, I knew about the life. Also, I guessed I'd be about as good as I am—good, but not a virtuoso. A first violinist—which is what I wanted.'

A happy man, then, she thought as she fell asleep.

'Blimey,' said Elinor when she saw Tim's parents' house on the outskirts of Harrogate. It was a big Victorian stone semi, exuberant with battlements and barge boards—the other half of the semi had turrets. 'It's like a set for a thirties horror movie—*The Old Dark House*, maybe.'

'Observe the fenestration,' Tim said in tour-guide tones. 'On this facade alone there are bay, dormer, oriel, mullioned, leaded, round, sash, casement and Romanesque windows.' In his own voice he added: 'Round the back there's also french, Early English and Venetian Gothic.'

Christopher Scott, Tim's father, was a tall, thin, abstracted man with a Tati lope, nearly-white hair, a youthful high-coloured face, and an air of absent-minded boyishness which he seemed to believe would charm Elinor to pieces. Muriel Scott was big-boned like Tim, and almost as tall as her husband—and far more vigorous, rushing in at the end of the day saying sorry, she'd been held up at the office. She wore her fair wiry hair compressed into a French roll with discreet hairpins; her clothes looked as if they came from Burberry's.

'Oh, that's not *work*,' she said when Elinor asked about her job. 'I haven't worked since the children were born. That's just the Citizens' Advice Bureau. I got involved once they were in school;

that and the Samaritans. It keeps me busy.' Her voice was carefully modulated to filter out excessive enthusiasm—excessive anything—as if good breeding consisted of moderation in all things. Elinor guessed she was on guard against overpowering people with her energy; but it bristled through anyhow. Just sitting back in her armchair after dinner she looked like Napoleon considering his next move.

Elinor could see why Tim had trouble interpreting his mother's smothered staccato energy, but felt at more ease with the Scotts than she ever did with her own parents—good-natured, humorously self-deprecating people whom she couldn't stand being with for long, and wasn't very nice to when she was. She went home as little as she decently could, chiefly at Christmas, and thanked God for having to leave after Boxing Day to open up the Cromer. If she relaxed with Mavis and Walter she would become like them—like her sister Marion—timid, accepting, unvehement. She didn't see into her own fear, but knew she behaved badly to them, and might have melted into decency if they had ever protested. But they never did.

'Tim, get out the albums and show Nell,' his mother commanded. He fetched them, and they sat on the sofa looking at family photographs.

'Is that you?' Elinor asked him uncertainly, pointing. The clothes were wrong, but the face was his.

'No, that's—'

'Tim's grandfather Scott,' said Mrs Scott, leaning forward. 'Tim looks like his father's great aunt Jane, too.'

Exactly like: Tim's features, slightly finer of cheek and brow, under an upswept roll of hair. 'Amazing,' Elinor exclaimed. 'There's nothing like this in my family. My sister and I are a ragbag of bits from both sides.'

'Eerie, isn't it?' Mrs Scott said. 'What I always wonder—how many generations could you go back and still find that face, if there'd only been photography to record it?'

They slept in twin beds in his old bedroom. In the morning Elinor crept into his bed, hoping to make love; but his parents' room was

81

next door, and he said, 'It, er, them so close, it's a bit...uncomfortable.'

Oh yes?...Well...she'd feel the same way if they were in *her* parents' house, she supposed, so she shouldn't mind it in Tim. But she did. She made no reply. They lay awkwardly, trying not to touch: not easy in a single bed.

Their silence was broken by little high squeaks coming through the wall. 'Do you hear that?' she whispered.

'That's Mother. My father tickles her to wake her up.'

Elinor went into fits. 'Tickles her?' she gasped. 'She wasn't *laughing*; she was *coming*.'

'But—she—I heard that *every morning* all my—' Tim stopped, feeling sickish, as if he had blurted a family secret. 'They'll be down soon, we'd better get dressed.' He climbed out of bed over her and went to take his shower.

Prudish man, she thought irritably. Perhaps it was inherently embarrassing to recognise that your parents made love, but she'd managed it—she'd had to. Mavis and Walter were forever touching each other in little ways—a hand on the shoulder and a chaste peck when Elinor and her sister were around; a pat on the bottom and an amorous kiss when they thought themselves unobserved.

Mind you, she'd never actually heard them making love. Living in a small semi they were probably more careful to keep the volume down than the Scotts in their big soundproof-seeming house.

Going out into the garden after breakfast she found Mrs Scott on her knees digging with a fork, with the pale April sun behind her. Little wiry hairs, touchingly like Tim's, sprang up back-lit from her tight roll of hair. She glanced up, her expression alert, enjoying. Her polite-lady mask was off; for a moment Elinor saw her not as Tim's mother, but as a strongly sensual woman—rooting out weeds for all she was worth; basking in sun and exercise. That's where Tim gets it, she thought—his woolly hair, his sensuality.

Chapter 11

They left Harrogate on a narrow road that ran absolutely straight between strips of plantation, with a blur of blue hills through the tree trunks. Usually Tim read it as a promise; today he hardly glanced aside from the road. He was wondering whether Elinor would like the moors.

Then they were climbing out of the plain onto Blubberhouses Moor. His heart swelled; he forgot everything else. In the distance ahead and all round were steep-sided hills with long flat purple tops, contour shading into contour, depth into depth. On either side of the road rose stone-walled, sheep-cropped fields, brilliant green, with rusty patches of fern higher up; then nothing but ferns, moss, and the deep purplish brown of heather. Home. Heart's country, all the way to Oughtershaw and beyond. He did not need to ask Elinor if she liked it; he could tell—he usually could. But since he never thought to make the most minimal noises of fellow-feeling or dissent, she had no idea how acutely he sensed the flux and flow of her moods.

Elinor sat bolt upright, looking and looking and looking. Something had clicked into place in her mind as soon as they were on Blubberhouses. Home, she thought with astonished recognition, as if all her life she had unknowingly carried in her imagination an ideal landscape to which, ever more exactly as they went deeper into the distance, this corresponded.

The hills got higher, and even higher. Whale-back hills, dolphin-back hills, alive with the slow unfussed life of trees: deep-rooted, greying in winter but not dying, enduring. Tim turned up a narrow road studded with cattle-grids, and climbed steadily through villages with names of a fitting harsh wild beauty—Hubberholme, Yockenthwaite, Beckermonds. Higher, barer, wilder: they were on

Langstrothdale Chase. There were sheep dotted everywhere; wobbly newborn lambs; older ones frisking.

He turned off the road onto a track running beside a wide, tumultuous stream. 'Oughtershaw Beck.' His voice was calm, but his belly was knotted with happiness. 'Nearly there. That's Oughtershaw Moss'—waving towards the hill beyond the beck.

An old farmhouse came into view. 'Is this it?' she asked.

'This is only Maresgill. The Lands live here—they farm all these fields.'

'Your landlords?'

'No, they're tenants too.'

The track got rougher, bump, bump, thwack. Elinor got out twice to open gates. A narrow strip of wood; then a solid stone cottage facing south onto fields with a steep hill behind it—Oughtershaw Side. The grass was high in the low-walled front garden; the windows had a glassy uncurtained stare.

'Swarthgill,' Tim said in a coming-home voice.

Indoors it was bitterly cold and smelt dank and mouldy; the faded floral wallpaper in the dark little parlour was clammy to the touch. The lean-to kitchen had a cold tap but no running hot water, only a boiler in the coal range. The three tiny bedrooms upstairs were lighter, but just as cold, with lumpy mattresses on iron bedsteads. Elinor shivered at the thought of the next three nights.

Tim laughed at her expression. 'Don't worry, it'll be warmer by this evening. Come on, let's get walking.'

They made up a bed, used the smelly whitewashed-stone privy outside the kitchen door, lit fires, filled the boiler with water and packed a knapsack with sandwiches and flasks. Outdoors the air was chilly, but felt warmer. Here were the fields Tim had walked through eye-high with the corn, and beyond them the beck, a few scotch pines and the pure rise of Oughtershaw Moss—a long steady ridge as far as the eye could see. Filmy indeterminate clouds were thinning and thickening overhead. Cloud-shadows slid across the piebald moor; the Moss brightened to dark richness and faded, brightened and faded.

'Can we go up it?' she asked.

84

'It's hard going—soggy and tussocky. The Side is better for walking.'

'Oh, okay.'

He led the way up Oughtershaw Side, opened up the 2½-inch map to let Elinor get her bearings, discovered she didn't know how to read it—and gave her a crash course in map-reading on the spot. Then he said, 'Okay, you lead. Get us to Jam Sike, then due north up Snaizeholme at 810 834.'

She set out, squinting at the map. After a few hundred yards she said, 'I can't see that barn on the map.'

'That's because the map's thirty years old, and the barn is new—can't you see?'

In a little while she stopped again, swivelling the map round to orient herself. 'It doesn't look right. We should be at Cold Keld Gate by now, I've been counting becks. We've crossed seven, but—'

'Most of those are only runoffs. We're not there yet. Look at the map—you can tell by the contours. And keep it right way up—you should never need to turn it upside down.'

A few minutes later she got confused because there were two paths on the ground and only one on the map; then because a stile took them out of their way; then because she read the contours the wrong way round.

'But I've already explained...' Tim would say patiently; or: 'If you'll just look at the contours...'

At Jam Sike she headed south instead of north. Tim followed, waiting for her to notice the discrepancy between map and terrain.

It was several hundred rock-strewn yards before she stopped and said, 'It doesn't make sense. Something's wrong.'

'Can you show me where we are on the map?'

She pointed.

'We're going uphill, not down; and where's the plantation?'

She took a long time, turning the map this way and that. 'Not...here?'—pointing to approximately the right spot.

'Mmm-hmm.'

She looked up sharply. 'You mean you just *let* me go wrong?'

'You saw for yourself in the end—it's best to learn by—'

'*On purpose*? Jesus Christ! Here, take your fucking map and get lost with it.' She sat down on a clump of moss and burst into tears.

Tim folded up the map and stood in dismayed silence. 'I've been expecting too much of you,' he said when she subsided. 'You'll learn in time. Let's just walk for now, shall we?'

Elinor stayed where she was, feeling chastised and mutinous, and wishing she were in London. They were both so still that a nearby sheep came closer and closer, chewing, until it was only a yard away.

A hair tickled her cheek. Raising a hand to scratch, she startled the sheep. It scampered to a safe distance, stared her straight in the eye and showed its indignation by raising its tail and shitting little hard round black turds. She forgot she was cross and laughed; so did Tim. She got up, and they started north, with Tim leading. Not a word more was said about maps.

The clouds thickened and rode low, sidling along great half-visible swoops of hill and valley with folds like the curves of a sleeping cat. The light was luminous and pearly, with infinite gradations of grey; layers of cloud were blowing across one another as close as kites and sliding down the flank of Pen-y-Ghent like water. The world was only moor and sky, simplified and abstracted by cloud, but thick with detail—tiny white and rosy flowers starring the sheep-cropped turf; tight-furled new fronds of bracken springing up from rusty clumps. Tim and Elinor were both completely happy, walking at the same pace, in unison, side by side, or with Tim ahead, or Elinor, eyes peeled, at ease with each other and the day. There were bird cries in their ears, and a perpetual small noise of wind. Lapwings started up, baring their white underwings; meadow pippits fluttered and glided straight out from the ridge, as if they could get no higher.

'Like the aeroplanes just clearing the treetops in *Only Angels Have Wings*,' she said.

'Or novice kites on Parliament Hill.'

There were ewes and newborn lambs everywhere. Down at the bottom of Dodd Fell they hitched themselves up over a high wall and landed close by a ewe who huddled away from them in fright, her lamb rickety and glistening wet beside her, and the bag of waters still hanging, translucent, from her vagina.

'Poor thing,' Tim said. 'She's used to being able to run from danger.'

Elinor had a clutching sensation in her womb—identification; rebellion. She wanted children; but to get them she would have to live through this utter helplessness, and she was afraid—less of pain than of being so entirely given over to biology.

The ewe was still straining. Her flanks shuddered, and she expelled the afterbirth, dark liver-red, in a gush of brighter blood that sprayed the lamb. Tim was fascinated and revolted. Revulsion was stronger; he turned away and set off. It was hateful, the whole business. He hated to think that he himself had ever been subjected to it: trapped in his mother's womb, without a separate existence, then emerging bloody and slippery, in anonymous animal indignity. It was horrible to think that his children would have to take this passage through dark red and slime; horrible to imagine Elinor trapped in labour like the ewe, gushing blood and waters and afterbirth. How did women stand it? He shuddered and squeezed himself tight against the thought.

It was nearly dark when they got home, stiff in every limb. The house was now warmer than the outdoors, but not much. They ate hugely, and took turns soaping up crouched in a tin tub in front of the range, and rinsing each other off with pans of hot water—which chilled them off, and did nothing for aching muscles.

In bed they clung to each other, footing the hot-water bottle and complaining about cold hands, and gradually warmed up, and gradually felt amorous. Elinor managed to get her diaphragm loaded with jelly and into her cunt without gumming up the bed; and they pulled the duvet over their heads to keep out the staring forty-watt bulb, and made love with a singleminded concentration that held, as in suspension, their uncertainty about their future; her rapture at the *St Matthew Passion*; his embarrassment about his mother's early-morning squeals; her new-born allegiance to Yorkshire; his sense of being at home; their quarrel about maps; their delight at striding in unison across the moors; the birthing ewe. The womb-dusk under the duvet was like the streaked burgundy behind eyelids closed in daylight, their eyes seemed trained inwards upon red pulsating vitals—dark and not-dark; seen and not-seen; interior. Unfocussed images of the ewe played across their minds, along with a sense of their lovemaking as an act of union with nature, and an indistinct fantasy of her diaphragm not being there at all, of her being entirely open, without barriers, ready to conceive the instant he came—not, as science had it, after the lapse of some symbolically quite inappropriate interval.

With one accord they began moving as slowly as it was possible to move without stopping altogether, then stopped, with him deep inside her, stopped everything but her half-involuntary tightening round his cock, and his half-involuntary pulse of response; then for a long moment stopped even that, in an impulse towards just-being, stasis; until in one or the other of them the capacity to hold back the body's sexual momentum broke, and they started moving, barely moving, with an effect almost of vehemence after that halcyon instant.

With his coming as the focus of their vague imaginings, they didn't try very hard to hold back. Getting close, she could feel he was closer still. She nearly signalled to slow him up, but didn't want to break their seamless rhythm. He could bring her after. She relaxed—and in a sudden surge was nearly as close as he.

He started to come; his vehement push brought her to the very edge. She gave an involuntary twist—which forced his pace: which forced hers. Not two simultaneous arrivals—she was a short pulse-beat behind, and came in an implosion that seemed entirely caused by the shock waves of his coming.

Had the same things been in both their minds—the ewe; conceiving a child? She wanted to ask, but he got up to put out the light. The silent country darkness pressed down on her, forbidding noise, and pulled her into sleep.

They had beautiful weather the next two days, but the last morning was grey. 'Where to?' Elinor asked at breakfast. They had to be back in London by evening, but didn't have to set off till afternoon.

Tim was easy; he had shown her his favourite places. 'Your turn to choose. There were a dozen places you wanted to go, only I was dragging you off somewhere else. One of them.'

She couldn't remember where any of them was; and she wouldn't look at the map. 'Oughtershaw Moss,' she said finally. 'It's such a pity not to, when it's right in front of our eyes.'

Tim groaned. 'All right—but don't say I didn't warn you.'

The low land by the beck was a marshy slog, and the footing got no better higher up. The Moss was full of moss. It held water like a sponge and formed treacherous slippery tussocks hidden by dwarf bilberry. They couldn't see where to put their feet, and kept falling to their knees into bristling bilberry bushes and squelchy moss. They were both cross; Elinor felt guilty. At intervals she suggested turning back, but Tim only said in a long-suffering voice, 'Now that we've got this far, we might as well finish.'

But the view from the top was wonderful. One way lay Swarthgill, tiny, with the Side sweeping up behind it. The other way lay a valley full of conifers in rows; but the ridges beyond it were bare, and in the far distance the rocky summit of Ingleborough towered sheer-sided like a fortified castle.

'Impressive, but sort of uninviting,' Elinor said. By now she knew without asking that Tim would feel the same. 'The nearest ridge is more my style. What's it called?'

'Cosh, I think.' He fished out the map. 'Yes, Cosh.'

She peered over his shoulder. 'Cosh Inside. What a funny name. Inside what? Have you been there? You must have, it's so close.'

'No, there's all that plantation in between—not to mention the Moss.'

'Could we go there?'

'It's a long walk.'

'Not from here. Go back, pack up, then get closer by car. Here, let me look.' She took the map from him and frowned over it for a few minutes. 'Look, there's a road to Foxup. We could park there and walk in. There's a footpath, I mean a bridle path—'

'An unfenced unmetalled track, actually.'

'Oh—yes—and it follows the contours, so we wouldn't be climbing much. We could get all the way in and back before it's time to go.'

' "In" to what?'

'Into Inside. It's such a nice shape on the map.'

'Then let's do it.' Since her outburst he had not mentioned maps, just silently used them. He had simply been avoiding conflict, but felt as gleeful as if his silence had been a ploy to get her interested. 'If the weather holds,' he added. The sky had been getting darker all morning.

Foxup wasn't a village, only a seedy farm with rabbits and lean yappy dogs in pens. The sky was getting lower by the minute. 'I don't think we'll make it,' Tim said.

'Let's at least try.'

They went through a gate and crossed a muddy field with cows. Beyond it was moorland. The unfenced unmetalled track was a wide ledge of flat rock beside a pounding beck. A hundred yards upstream a little humpbacked stone bridge spanned the beck, with bare trees arching over it. Still further upstream was one more clump of trees, then a great worn naked hillside, curving round, on, out of sight, with the track hugging its base. The one perfect place. Elinor looked at the map, and the strength of her desire to guess what lay beyond the curve made her see how the contour markings worked. Yes. This was only the beginning, it would get better and better. But the sullen sky was scarcely higher than the hillside, and the air was getting raw. She walked faster and faster to outrace the rain.

What started to fall was not rain, but soft fat snowflakes, whirling down as thick and fast as if somebody in the sky had upturned a big basket of feathers.

'The compass is in the car,' said Tim. 'Time to turn back.'

She slowed up. 'Can't we just get to the curve?'

'Quickly, while we can see the track.' It was a voice of command such as she had never heard from him. 'Next time,' he added with a faint smile, understanding how she felt.

She grinned, feeling silly. 'Next time.'

'We're right for each other,' he said suddenly, and Elinor almost melted like the snowflakes on her cheeks. Then he turned up his collar and headed back.

Chapter 12

The quartet resumed, and the leisurely Sunday lunches. 'I know you work with old people, but what exactly do you do?' Elinor asked Sheila. She wanted to know her better, and work made a good starting point.

'Oh, the Falcon's not just old people; we've got a shelter for the homeless—adult literacy classes—youth training—a drug outreach project...'

We—she sounded like a brochure. 'You're involved in all that?'

'Yes, to some extent—but I mostly work with over-sixties.'

'Doing what?'

'Bringing people and resources together.'

'Which means?'

Sheila gave in—she wanted to reach Nell and make friends. If only that didn't mean talking. But it did. But at least talking about work was easier than talking about herself. 'A lot of over-sixties don't know their entitlements, for one thing, or what's available from the services—and such little things can keep them in their own homes for years. Railings for the front steps so they can get out to the shops; someone to cut their toenails; groups so they're less isolated. We've got a daycare centre, a health project, a carers' support group...'

'Group-therapy group,' Thoby reminded her.

'Oh Linchpin, yes. It's huge, more than thirty women; but some of them get a lot from it.'

'Crumbs,' Elinor said admiringly. 'I didn't know social workers did therapy.'

'I'm *not* a social worker.'

'Oh.' She had never heard Sheila being so emphatic about anything.

Thoby said, 'Get Sheila going, she'll say training in social work's about *not* making bonds with the customers.'

'Oh Thoby,' Sheila said faintly.

Let her speak for herself, Elinor thought, and asked, 'What *are* you, then?'

'My job title is "community worker with the elderly", but I don't like the word "elderly". I say I'm a worker with over-sixties.'

Full stop, end of para. Elinor cast about for a way to keep her going. 'It must be rewarding, doing something so useful,' she came up with. Lame. 'Tim says that's why you didn't go on with the cello.' Oops, Sheila looked stricken. She reeled in her fishing line and shut up.

End of para, end of topic. Nobody said anything; Elinor and Thoby both scurried about their heads for a new subject to paper over the silence.

Thoby got there first. 'Meaning to say, Nell: theme for a season— the Kennedy assassination. It sneaks into a lot of films.'

'Oh, like *Night Moves*—that's where I first heard the question: "Where were you when Kennedy was shot?"—"Which Kennedy?"—"Any Kennedy." '

Sheila, safe on the sidelines, crept into her shell and curled up. Doing something useful—the official version of why she'd given up a life in music. She was ashamed of hiding behind a story so flattering to her social conscience. But she could hardly say: I stopped as penance; or: it was getting harder to hide in the cello; the better I played, the more it dragged me out to the surface.

After lunch she went up to the music room to put her cello away, sat down for a moment, hugging it, and without exactly meaning to picked up the bow and began playing the Bach D minor cello suite. Things she couldn't say to Elinor were coursing through her head.

Where had she been when Kennedy was shot? She didn't know. She'd been in an orchestration class when she heard that Jacqueline du Pré's nervous breakdown was multiple sclerosis. At the Menuhin School that was the Kennedy moment. For everyone, not just her, but perhaps she was the only one whose life it had changed.

Sitting there that day thinking: If that happened to me. Not that she could have been a du Pré. But someone. Cellist in a string quartet; maybe even a soloist: a Steven Isserlis. But she'd have had to let the cello bring her right out. There would have been no going back if it had failed her the way it failed Jackie. Naked for always.

It was her only friend, she couldn't let it become an enemy. Scouring London for a room and a job; leaving. Nothing to admire in that.

Thoby kept telling her not to feel guilty. She *knew* it wasn't her fault, she *knew* that was the hook her Da had got into her—but knowing didn't help.

The others came up and sat in the front room to listen. Sheila went on to the end, impassioned, fumbling now and then, Jackie, Sheila, Casals, herself, nobody. Why did playing such sad music make her happy—and why, knowing it would, didn't she always rush to the cello when her devils started gnawing? It's easy, really, she thought, snapping the case shut, and did a little jiggle of pleasure by Thoby's side on the way out.

'Hop you,' he said, catching her mood, and jumped her down Tim's front steps, his hands on her waist, hers on his shoulders.

She loved it, especially pregnant, the sense of floating, the mock-dangerous lift and fall, the way Thoby's eyes crinkled up with glee. 'We're *silly*,' she said breathlessly. 'Look, someone's coming.'

'Let them.' He swung her off the bottom step and went back up for their instruments.

They were still angling the cello into the Renault when the passer-by stopped and spoke. 'Sheila Canterbury, isn't it—remember me? Bob Mears, three houses down from you in Limehouse, then you got that scholarship. Still playing that big thing, I see, and as pretty as ever. How are you these days?'—with a glance at her belly. 'And how's your Da? Great fella—great fella.'

Sheila managed a smile and a few words. Thoby said rudely, 'Can't stop, we're in a hurry, sorry,' bundled her into the car and set off with a lurch. 'Idiot,' he fulminated, wondering how much damage had been done. 'How could he say such a stupid thing?'

He didn't expect an answer, but for a miracle she gave one. 'He doesn't know, nobody did. And Da's not a monster, everybody liked him.' Oh yes, the life of the road, always a joke and a friendly word for everyone, laughing and chatting behind his barrow;

mending people's appliances in the evening, toasters, Hoovers, clocks—for free, till the developers closed the market and he was out of a job; then people would say, 'Hard times, Jimmy, take a fiver, do,' and he'd hum and haw and take it. The time he tried mending a pocket watch—stooping over it, carefully loosening screws. It burst all over the parlour. Bits in Mum's hair; his great laugh roaring out.

The neighbourhood children were in and out, clambering all over him—it was him they came for, not Mum. They'd envied Sheila her Da.

'Are you yer Da's little girl? Come sit on our lap, then.'

No, don't think about that, Sheila told herself. Unhappiness is boring, remember? Say something to Thoby—*pretend* to say something. What would get him going?

'Nell's so nice,' she tried. 'Don't you think they make a good couple.'

It worked—Thoby chattered happily all the way home about what fun Nell was, and how much happier Tim seemed; and she sheltered in his shade.

That night when they made love Thoby opened his eyes and saw her mouth stretched wide in a silent scream, but when he tried to stop, she wouldn't let him. 'No, go on, go on,' she said angrily. 'Nothing's wrong.' But after she came she burst into tears.

'What's wrong?' he said again.

She only shook her head. 'It's too hard,' she whispered when he asked again. Too hard to keep trying to be happy. He thought she meant it was too hard to explain her tears.

'I do hope you like it,' Elinor said as the four of them filed into the Everyman for a Sunday matinée of *The Awful Truth*. 'You never know with old comedies. I once had a boyfriend who hated it—he said it endorsed the double standard, which I suppose is true, but that's not what it's *about*. And I warn you, there's a dog.' She rather liked the dog, but she wasn't going to confess *that*.

They liked it, all right; they were beaming as they came out into an April drizzle and headed for coffee at Louis's.

'That was wonderful, Nell, thank you,' Sheila said.

'Perfectly spiffing,' said Thoby. 'But the cinema—half empty—why wasn't all of L-London there?'

'People want colour movies—young people, anyhow, and they're the main customers. And the art-house audience want significance with a capital S; they undervalue what they simply *enjoy*.'

'Nothing simple about great comedy, Nell. Hardest thing in the world, writing funny lines, putting them across.'

'Sure—I think the best sophisticated comedies of the thirties and forties are the greatest thing since—since—'

'Since *The Importance of Being Earnest*. Since Jane Austen. Since Restoration comedy.'

Elinor bounced in her seat and nearly spilt her tea. About Restoration comedy she didn't know, but about *Earnest* she did: she'd seen the movie. 'Hey—that's great. Can I use it in programme notes? It'll fill some seats.'

'Be my guest. But won't it put people off—whiffs of set texts?'

'Nah—they like to feel they're improving themselves.'

'But *Earnest* isn't one bit improving,' said Sheila. 'It's just *fun*.'

'I won't tell anybody if you don't,' Elinor said.

Afterwards they went for a walk on the Heath. Sheila's baby was kicking hard; now and then she had to stop. 'I can't help trying to walk in step,' she explained, 'But it's too irregular—I get confused.'

'Still, lucky you,' Elinor said, more wistfully than she knew.

Sheila heard the undertone. 'Feel,' she said impulsively, and put Elinor's hand on her belly. She couldn't give Elinor intimate talk, but she could give this wordless gesture of friendship.

The memory stayed on Elinor's palm: muffled thumping beneath a belly drumskin-taut. What would it be like to press her own belly and feel a baby kick—the voluptuous thickening of pregnancy; the drumbeat on the palm; the sense of being given over?

'You've got to see this,' Maggie said, stopping in late one evening when Elinor was closing up. 'Graffiti from the National Theatre ladies'. Here, I copied it. Every line was in a different hand, I should say. *Art trouvé*.' Scrawled on her programme was:

Clapton

ISN'T THERE A POND?

Clapton is god

But not with a capital G.

Of course not, 'God is dead' (Nietzsche)

GOD IS NOT DEAD, SHE'S LIVING IN CLAPTON!

In a pond

'It's a better class of graffiti in the National,' Elinor said. 'All we ever get here is A loves B in the women's, and obscenities and pickup numbers in the men's; not to mention our row with the contract cleaners.'

Maggie pricked up her ears. 'What row?'

Elinor groaned. 'One of those petty wars that's *too* boring but still churns you up. You know those Rape Crisis and Lesbian Line stickers on the cubicle doors in the women's loo? We ask the cleaners to leave them; but they think they're filth, so they scrape them off; and their boss takes their side. We've got a supply of the stickers, and it's got so we're putting up new ones nearly every day.'

'Put perspex up,' Maggie said.

'Hunh?'

'Over the stickers, fixed with those Modric screws that you need a special tool for, so they can't just unscrew them.'

'Maggie, you're a genius.'

She preened herself. 'Oh—Slingsby's cut perspex to size, and Romany's have the screws.'

Elinor laughed admiringly. 'Is there anything you *don't* know?'

Maggie grinned and shook her head.

'Stay while I check round?'

'Sure.'

No one in the auditorium—the ladies—the gents—the cashier's booth—the projection booth; the emergency exits were locked and chained. Elinor went back to the office.

'Here, you look as if you could do with this.' Maggie handed her a glass of the office whisky. 'Cheers. What's eating you?'

97

'Oh...it's so...formless. I told you about Tim saying we're right for each other...'

'In the raging gale, very touching. You agree with him, I take it?' Don't bugger it up, Nell, she told her silently.

'Well...yes.' Yes. 'But still I wonder—where do I come on his list of priorities? He's always rushing from one thing to another. A student wants an extra lesson, a fixer needs a last-minute substitute—so he cancels time with *me*.'

'But you have lots of time together. Films, concerts, those ghastly long walks—'

'But it's not time to *talk*. No, that's not true, we do talk, especially after concerts. He's on a performance high, and talks a blue streak about music, or pumps me about movies—and listens hard, I'll give him that. But if I start on something more personal, suddenly it's bedtime.'

'So be more assertive. Say, "Wait, I've got things I want to talk about." '

'But I can't keep him awake just to discuss...I don't know...the small change of life? Like: doesn't he wonder why I didn't say yes straight off? Not that I know the answer, but—'

'And I *certainly* don't—if I were you I'd marry him like a shot.'

'A man who says he's not capable of a *grande passion*?'

'Maybe he thinks you want one of those tidal waves that hit adolescents, and adults grow out of.'

In the face of such self-possessed grownupness Elinor wasn't going to admit that she still wanted that tidal roar and swirl. She wanted to be seized by absolute conviction, not to inch into love by rational stages; she wanted Tim to be so seized himself.

'You know how you ask someone what they're thinking—a lover, I mean—and they're supposed to tell the truth?' she said. 'Well, if I ask Tim, he's never thinking about us, or him, or me; it's always music or joinery or what to have for dinner.'

'No different from most men.'

'Not the ones I—'

Maggie pounced. 'So why aren't you with them, if they're such hot stuff?'

Elinor had to laugh. 'But still—saying he doesn't love me—'

98

'Maybe he's afraid of the word because of that last woman, the one that wouldn't more than half sleep with him. Vera, no, Vivian. I bet she drove him mad with frustration, so he thinks *that* was love.' Drawing a bow at a venture she added: 'Besides, he's someone who'll ripen slowly. You won't see the best of Tim till he's forty.'

'Maybe,' Elinor said musingly. She was always so impatient; now was her chance to rise above it. He was trying to show more affection: turning away less often, letting her kiss him, giving her an occasional peck on the cheek. And think of their lovemaking— every gesture transfused with passion and tenderness. He might be too traumatized by Vivian to say he loved her, but his body proclaimed it. Give him time.

Maggie came back after work the next day. 'Hullo, I didn't expect you,' Elinor said, looking with concern at her pinched little face. 'Isn't it your evening with Clive?'

'Open night for parents at Emma's school.' Maggie sat down, crossed her legs, fidgeted, opened her bag, snapped it shut, stood up. 'I'm dying for a smoke, I'll be back.'

'Let's take a walk—there's half an hour till the house lets out.'

The sun had set, but a few yellow rays were still glinting off television masts. Elinor shortened her pace to Maggie's small high-heeled steps, and they wandered into Queen Square, while Maggie smoked one cigarette and got out another.

'And two between my office and yours,' she said ruefully, lighting it. 'That man will be the death of me.' Then, sharply: 'No, I can't. Give them up—or him.'

'I didn't say anything.'

'But you were thinking it, admit.'

'Not just—'

'You don't know how often I'm tempted.' Puff, puff, savagely. She stopped in front of the Mary Ward Centre and looked unseeingly at the statue in the window. 'Break it off, be sensible, look around. The world's full of men. Handsome men, eligible men.' Her voice lacked its usual gurgling undercurrent of pessimistic amusement. 'Half the ones I know are after me, too, so what am I *doing* with a married one? I can never even say, "Let's go to the flicks"—he can't take the risk of being seen with me. I just go on from week to week—there's no future in it. He'll never leave her, only talk about it. Every little crisis in the children's lives, he says, "If I'd left, this would be worse for them." And he's *right*. Children get messed up by divorce. But it's so sad, Nell. It's *me* he talks to about the children, not his wife. As for sex—he can hardly bear to touch her, poor man.'

'Poor her too,' Elinor said tartly, and looked at her watch. 'House out in ten minutes.'

Maggie ground out her second stub, and they started back. 'Do you think he's just using me?' she suddenly asked.

'In what sense, using you?'

'Maybe he's not unhappy with her at all; maybe he just says that to keep me on the hook.'

'I don't know,' Elinor said slowly; it seemed perfectly possible. She had never seen the attraction of Clive, an aloof pale-lashed man given to cynical insider's remarks. 'But from what you've said...' Should she say something comforting, or what she really thought?

Maggie saved her from either by saying, 'Shit, misery's such a bore. I spend half my time wrestling with bitterness—making it dissolve so I won't spit it out at Clive. There's no time for the luxury of quarrel, work it all out, make up. He *always* has to leave. Do you know how lucky you are to have a personable, intelligent, decent man who's free to marry you?'

Elinor had been involved with unattached men before Tim, but Maggie hadn't thought enough of them to envy her. Their relation registered a slight shift.

'I'm a fool to hope,' Maggie went on, 'but I do. I have fantasies of writing an anonymous letter to tip her off, and she'd divorce him. But it might backfire—he'd promise to give *me* up; because children need a father, and he's theirs, so that's his place, and he knows it, and it's so admirable, it's one of the things I love about him, but I can't stand it.'

They were back at the Cromer. 'Oh Maggie,' Elinor said, hugging her.

100

'Oh Nell.' She put her head on Elinor's shoulder for a moment, then stepped back. 'Don't look so worried,' she said, touching her arm. 'I'll survive. One always does.'

'I want more than that for you, dear—I want you to be happy.'

'Happy—that's a lot to ask.' Maggie shrugged. 'Don't know why this is *such* a bad day. Pre-menstrual tension, maybe. Who'd be a woman?'

'Me,' Elinor said firmly.

'Hah. Got your goat.' She grinned, kissed her darling Nell—for whom she wanted the happiness she didn't expect for herself—and clickety-clicked away home.

Chapter 13

The month was up; time to speak. Tim was already in the music room opening his violin case when he remembered. He stood with his hands on the catches, steeling himself, then went through to the front room. Elinor looked up from the paper, and he sat down, cleared his throat and launched into his speech.

'Remember before Easter, you said you needed to think, and we agreed to wait a month?'

We didn't *agree*, you decided, Elinor thought, but didn't say—she had been half wondering if he'd thought better of the whole thing. She couldn't bear to lose him—his solidity, his heavy frankness, his odd mixtures of sexual warmth and emotional reserve. Yes, she would say, to whatever he asked—live with him, marry him.

'Swarthgill—being together all the time—you should have a better idea now of what I'm like in day-to-day living—'

She quite forgot to let him finish so that she could say yes in reply. 'Day to day isn't us together all the time,' she said testily. 'It's you up to your ears in so many things that there's hardly *any* time for us—and never saying no to other people; so we arrange something, and you arrive late, or leave early, or put me off altogether. I seem to be the only person you don't mind disappointing.'

He led a busy life; she would have to get used to it. But this was not the time to say so. 'It's not as if it's for other pleasures. I take on obligations at the expense of pleasure.'

'At the expense of my pleasure too.'

'The thing is, I grew up thinking life was stern stuff—duty, not pleasure. I could *make* myself take more time off—but then it's just another obligation. I don't want to think of *you* as an obligation, Elinor.'

102

How could she resist? Yet—rebelliously: 'You don't even call me Nell, and I've *asked*.'

This time he was ready. 'Everyone calls you Nell. I think of Elinor as my private name for you.'

'Oh Tim'—melting. She jumped up and bent over to kiss his cheek. It was like kissing an idol; his face was inert. 'But we don't *talk*!' she said in sharp reaction, returning to her chair. 'Not about anything real.'

'I don't want to burden you with my problems.'

She shook her head.

'It's *hard* for me,' he said. 'You put too much weight on words. You can't trust anyone unless they spell everything out.'

'But...' Was he right?

She looked away, and he added, with some change of tone: 'Sometimes I want to come in your mouth, you know that—that's something to do with words.'

How could such a reticent man say that so boldly? The words, the tone transfixed her. He said something she missed; she had to say, 'I'm sorry, I didn't catch that.'

'Maybe this isn't the right time to talk?'

'Maybe not.'

'What now, then?' He was looking at her alertly.

Let's make love, she thought; but couldn't make herself say it. 'Whatever you'd like.'

'I'd like to make love.'

'Me too.'

They came down and made coffee. 'So,' Tim said, sitting down at the kitchen table. 'We were talking about whether you'll marry me.'

Such a practical voice, as if the question had nothing to do with his passion a few minutes ago. Again Elinor forgot to say yes as soon as he asked. 'But you don't even love me!'

'What?'

'You said in March. You're in love with me but you don't love me.' It still hurt; the words were lodged in her mind like a splinter.

'Would I ask you to marry me if I didn't love you?' he asked brusquely, hoping she would not hear the evasion.

Joy flooded her. She nearly got up to kiss him—surely at such a moment they should kiss—but remembered his inertness when she kissed him earlier, and stayed where she was. His face was heavy with depression and antagonism—why? Was he still afraid she would say no?

'Okay,' she said, reaching across to touch his hand.

'Okay what?'

'Getting married.'

'Oh. Good.'

'But I'll keep my own name.'

'Of course.' He smiled, quietly triumphant.

It was a slow afternoon—a good time for doing the books. Rose and Elinor usually shared the job, but Rose was out watching the house—Mrs Ekins was off with flu, and the student usher hadn't showed. Elinor's desk was heaped—calculator, ledger, audience figures, wage slips, figures for the week's take, film rentals, gas bill, printer's bill for the May programme, overtime to Margaret for the crisis with the dud projector lamp. Out to the cashier's booth to check the float. Note for Rose—A4 envelopes; second-class stamps, and oh yes, 'We're low on tickets, could you ring tomorrow?'

Happy, happy. Would I ask you to marry me if I didn't love you? A declaration. Funny oblique man.

The buzzer. Trouble at the front of house—where Rose was alone—

Elinor dashed out and flung open one of the auditorium doors, and Rose came through it holding a big drunk in a solid armlock.

'If you'd just get ready to woman the barricades...' she said breathlessly as she frog-marched him through the outer doors and let go with a push. The cashier and the woman from the coffee stand ran to help; they had all six doors locked by the time the man staggered back and started kicking and shouting, 'Fuckin' cunts, fuckin'—'

In a loud voice Elinor told the cashier, 'Annie, ring the police.'

104

'Fuckin' cops;' kick, punch.

'How hard *is* toughened glass?' Rose muttered. But his eye was on Annie. He stopped kicking as soon as she reached the telephone, and trailed off towards Gower Street.

They watched him round the corner, then unlocked the doors. 'I didn't know you did karate,' Elinor said admiringly.

'Ages back. I'm into Tai Chi now.' Rose struck a pose, dusted her hands smartly, and went back inside.

Elinor returned to the books, smiling fondly at the image of Tai Chi Rose, who with her plump cuddly body, round face and clear fine skin sometimes seemed no more than fifteen. She was far less naive than she looked—not naive at all, in fact; her head was screwed all the way on. But she *was* ingenuous—guileless, candid, affectionate, with a basic simplicity that came from being happy. It made her extraordinarily easy to be with. She had no chip on her shoulder, no hidden agenda; she said what she meant and meant what she said, and judged people charitably but not foolishly— with the possible exception of Marcus. She was not at all cross-grained or difficult herself, but was for some reason drawn to complication and ambivalence in art and other people: in the films of Rivette, Fassbinder, Straub/Huillet; in contradictory Chris; in Marcus, whose turbulence grieved but didn't undermine her; and in Maggie, whose irony she relished.

Maggie liked her, too—all but her sixties' jargon. 'Where *did* she pick it up?' she had grumbled the other night. 'And when? She was still in pigtails when that stuff was current.'

'She's keeping alive traditions that were dead long before she was born,' Elinor had replied. 'That's how the valet describes Walter Matthau in *A New Leaf*.'

Crash clunk of film cans in the outer office. The nine-o'clock film, good. She always fretted when the distributors didn't send it till the same day. She went out to check that there were no reels missing, said hi to the courier, returned to her pencilled subtotals; then stopped, remembering Tim this morning.

Sometimes she felt as if he entered her everywhere, as if he pervaded her, as if she were entirely in his hands. She became—only this: his desire; entirely open to what he wanted to do; wanting to

105

be what he wanted her to be. Sometimes the feeling of being possessed by him rushed right out to the ends of her fingers.

You weren't *supposed* to think things like that, but she did. Never had the profound asymmetry between women's and men's experience of sex been so borne in upon her. To pretend it didn't exist was to fly in the face of her own desires, which weren't for amicable democracy or perfect reciprocity, but for being plumbed, known, possessed.

Why no reciprocal desire to know, to possess—what monsters lurked in her depths? Men entered, women were entered, true; but Tim didn't literally plumb or possess or know her. Sometimes she tried to imagine she was possessing Tim; taking him into herself. But there was a cheery falsity to the idea—and it didn't touch her erotically; the idea of being possessed did.

The violence of her desire for Tim mounted into her throat. It was like being seized by a huge hand and shaken.

Tim Tim I think of you fucking me—

The memory of last time, the thought of next. Opening her legs to him; the gasping almost painful almost masochistic moment when, as he started to enter, her cunt involuntarily tightened, then yielded enough, just enough, to let him push in: always that absolutely non-reciprocal sense of seizure—rapture, in its root sense. A country open to the conqueror, a furrow to the plough: all the metaphors were true.

She went to the tiny glass over the washbasin in the corner to see if her face was a mask of desire. It looked disappointingly ordinary, but she smiled at herself secretly, a conspirator.

'I went to the registry office,' Tim said at bedtime. 'We have to wait three weeks—shall we make it three weeks tomorrow?'

Elinor laughed and threw herself across the bed. 'Whew, you're a man in a hurry. Okay, why not? I'll ask Rose to mind the shop.'

'I've got the day free, though I've a concert that evening. But if you don't mind—'

'Oh no.' *She* wasn't going to make a fetish of a marriage ceremony.

'Or if you'd rather another day...'

106

'Oh no.'

'Or place...'

'Oh no.'

She was laughing again. He looked down at her, drinking up her liveliness, feeding on it. She was not often witty, but she could turn the smallest things into play, even saying 'No' three times running. 'I thought, very simple,' he said. 'Just us, and Thoby and Sheila for witnesses. An ordinary day. What do you think?'

'Sounds fine.' A touch unceremonious—she had imagined he would want something more formal. He never stopped surprising her.

Chapter 14

The quartet's do was in Highgate, one Sunday morning in the middle of June. 'Only just in time,' Elinor heard a Debec murmur near her. 'Another week and Sheila will be too big to get at the business side of that cello.'

'Study in round forms, what?' another Debec replied. There were at least a dozen Debecs in Maidie and Lionel's drawing room, along with Alan's wife and adolescent daughter; Rose and Marcus; Maggie; a few musician friends of Tim's and Thoby's; two of Sheila's co-workers; Sheila's mother, a stout, sharp-nosed, sweet-faced woman, who gave no impression of feeling out of place in Highgate; and Elinor's parents, who did. Tim had insisted on inviting them.

Walter and Mavis were easily impressed by large houses and cultured accents, but they were no fools. They knew, piercingly, that the distance Elinor kept them at was not one they'd made themselves. With insight she didn't know them capable of—and wouldn't have thanked them for—they dimly guessed her fear of becoming like them, and knew, though they had no language for saying so, that her frightened disdain was not to her credit. The knowledge was submerged—the wound in the heart borne stoically like chronic arthritis. 'She's gone beyond us,' they told each other; 'It's only natural.'

That was just what she couldn't bear—the way they put up with things. 'Best not make a fuss,' she'd heard them tell each other all her life. Why not, damn it?

She sat with them on one side and Maggie on the other, quite far back in the Debecs' tall-windowed drawing room. Just families and a very few friends, Tim had said, but they were behind what seemed like three dozen people. She could hardly see him through the thicket of heads, and was cross, as if it were somehow her parents' fault.

The quartet sounded much better than last week at Ockendon Road. Elinor was impressed, though she preferred the privileged intimacy of being their sole audience, with a torrent of sound rushing round her and an unimpeded view of Tim—and of the others, too: Alan sober in face and compressed in movement; Thoby perpetually expressive, angular to the last crook of elbow and drop of wrist; Sheila, her lovely face blurred by pregnancy, frowning at the score and pressing the cello to her belly.

Afterwards people stood around saying, 'That was *wonderful*.' Debec women and children glided among them offering wine and plates of mushrooms fried in this and bacon wrapped round that—water chestnuts, as it turned out.

Somebody said something about lunch. A number of people said, 'We really must leave'—Walter and Mavis among them, and Sheila's mother, and Maggie. Thoby pressed her to stay—he had taken a fancy to her during an improbable dialogue about constitutional freedoms and Middle Lias marlstones.

Maggie looked round at who was left and remembered an afternoon engagement. 'Too dispiriting,' she muttered to Elinor. 'It's all *couples*.'

Lunch was in the garden—between fifteen and twenty people, depending on how many children were in sight, sitting on garden chairs or blankets spread on the grass. There were high mature trees, and a long bright border waving loosely with day lilies and delphiniums and century-old varieties of rose. The midsummer sky was soft blue. People were good-humoured; on a day like this it was hard to remember winter.

Tim, Thoby and Elinor sat on a blanket, Sheila and Maidie on lawn chairs beside them. Tim stretched out in his shirtsleeves and in the course of lunch happily made his way through half a bottle of white wine—a rare indulgence. On days when he was playing— which was most days—he seldom drank at all until late in the evening, for fear of fuzzing his fingertips.

The third glass made him expansive. 'I was talking to a homeless man on the South Bank yesterday who wanted money for new shoes; his have got holes in the soles. "I have to wear them to bed, or the men in my hostel would steal them," he said. "They never get a chance to rest—they're worn out, poor soles."'

'S-o-l-e-s or s-o-u-l-s?' Maidie asked.

'Both, I think. But not joking. He'd have been hurt if I laughed.'

Lionel, Thoby's father, was an administrator at the BBC, tall and imposing and well able to hold his own in the world, though Maidie's fame gave him a few secret pangs. People he met could seldom resist telling him what was wrong with their favourite programmes and the BBC in general; Elinor won his heart by plying him instead with questions about his particular job and how he did it. 'Interesting wife you've got,' he congratulated Tim a little later.

The redoubtable Maidie, whom Elinor had pictured from Thoby's hyperbole as a cross between Medusa and Catherine the Great, was an engaging little pouter-pigeon with sharp eyes, a booming voice, a half-veiled habit of command, the little caressing mannerisms of professional charm, and a fund of stories about everyone from David Hockney to her aunt Bet and uncle Ezra. 'They're sister and brother, and they've lived together ever since their spouses died. Bet's fast, Ezra's slow. I was there once when he set off in the car, and Bet noticed that he'd left a letter behind. She was ninety at the time, but she grabbed it and ran after him, lickety-split up that steep Brighton street—and caught him, that's how slowly he drove.'

The Debecs corresponded better than Tim's family to Elinor's preconceived ideas about the upper middle class; they were shabby abstracted distinguished-looking people, unconcerned with appearances—within limits; they'd have sat on the floor rather than give house-room to her parents' furniture. At twenty-one she would have been bowled over. At twenty-nine she could see the tinge of snobbery in their shabbiness, of ambition in their abstraction. For all their leftish eccentricity they were firmly knitted into the journalistic, artistic and administrative establishments; their stake was in things as they were. They knew, or were themselves, editors of the New This, drama critics of the Sunday

110

That, Presidents of the Royal What-have-you, painters of royalty, playwrights whose plays got produced in warehouses or the West End, members of the governing bodies of the ICA, the Arts Council, the Tate, the BBC, the World Wildlife Fund, Oxfam, the Georgian Society, Amnesty, the National Trust.

Their political opinions were 'advanced' in a dated way. Thoby's aunt was a founding member of the Abortion Law Reform Association; two of his great-grandmothers had been women's suffragists—but certain questions were not asked. Daughters and nieces and wives and female cousins and friends unobtrusively made lunch, brought it to the garden, offered seconds, topped up glasses, kept an eye on children, cleared away, handed round fruit, made and served coffee. Sons and nephews and husbands and male cousins and friends sat and talked and accepted it all as the natural order of things, or carried a plate or two into the kitchen and felt a glow of virtue. Only Thoby and Tim did anything like their share. Elinor could see why Thoby was uncomfortable with the cushioned ancestral bohemianism, and why he tried to live more marginally, and more sincerely.

The Debecs were interested in cinema; they were interested in all the arts. But their haunts were the Curzon, the Academy, and sometimes the ICA; not the Electric, the Cromer or the NFT. They preferred well-intentioned humanist directors to wild geniuses: Wim Wenders to Fassbinder, Satyajit Ray to Benegal, Rohmer to Godard, Tati to Billy Wilder—indeed, any European movie to any American.

'The Cromer, oh yes, I'm not sure we've been to it,' a Debec cousin said. 'We've so little time for films, and we really prefer European cinema—and of course Japanese. Tell me, why do you show so many American films?'

Elinor tried not to mind that she pronounced it 'cine*mah*'. She found herself replying unguardedly, 'Because American cinema *is* cinema. It's Cukor and Hawks and Hitchcock and Wilder and Huston and Welles and Woody Allen and Altman and De Palma; it's *Ninotchka*, *North by Northwest*, *The Big Sleep*, *Laura*, *The Philadelphia Story*; it's *Double Indemnity*, *The Godfather*, *Casablanca*, *A Star is Born*, *To Be or Not to Be*, *The Awful Truth*,

111

Some Like it Hot, *The Manchurian Candidate*, *Swingtime*—it's Astaire-Rogers, Garbo, Cary Grant, Gary Cooper, Brando, Barbra Streisand. It's screenwriters, cameramen—this incredible cornucopia of talent and genius all making something—a corpus—a...It's *different* from European cinema. Like classical music and jazz—the way Kiri te Kanawa couldn't sing "Stars fell on Alabama" as well as Billie Holiday. And, yes, most of the very greatest films are European—there's no one in American films to compare with Bresson, or Godard or Fassbinder—or Ichikawa'—with a nod to the woman who liked Japanese cinema, but who looked bewildered: probably she'd only seen Kurosawa. 'But they're isolated peaks—Everests—and most of the rest of the mountains in the range are American. Most of the foothills, too. There's not an immense *body* of high-quality work in any other country's cinema that provides a base for people of talent to find themselves. Except France, to some extent.'

She ran out of steam and sputtered to a stop. Everyone was looking at her. 'Dear me,' she said in dismay—'I got carried away.'

'Not at all,' said Lionel. 'Quite fascinating.'

There was a silence; then attention turned away from her. 'Whew.' Her face was hot. 'I suppose one has to make a fool of oneself every few years, but I could have chosen a less public occasion.'

'Wrong end of the stick, Nell,' said Thoby. 'Wonderful speech. Explained a lot of things I've been meaning to ask.'

'But ranting at your poor family—'

'They love it. Rant at one another at least once a day. They understand vehemence. Your stock's soared.'

He was right. People came over to ask her about this film and that—what about Truffaut—Herzog—Renoir—Visconti—Pasolini—Bergman—Carné—what about new Senegalese cinema?

'I'm afraid I haven't seen any,' she said politely. When the person who had asked about it went off, she said, 'The trouble with most new anything cinema is that you give credit to good intentions and overlook the form. Form *counts*. A film without it is a time-filler, like TV; or else propaganda—which can be very useful; but in the

112

end you don't take it seriously. Nobody tries to tell you poems are good just because they're about oppression.'

'Just so,' Thoby said. ' "Jenny kissed me when we met"—much better than, "Work, work, work, She sang the song of the shirt." '

Elinor didn't need to know the poems to agree. 'But hardly anyone sees that about movies,' she said eagerly. 'Oh—I'm ranting *again*. Too much wine, I suppose.'

'Must ply you with it more often.'

Someone brought out a tea-tray. The far end of the garden had grown shady; people carried their chairs closer to the house. Instead of scattered groups, there was a gathering.

The conversation turned to children, then to childbirth. Every-one in the clan had ideas about how Sheila should conduct hers. A woman in her forties recommended epidurals, and got a chorus of disagreement. 'All those so-called pain-killers cross the placental barrier—infants born dozy—possible neonatal damage.'

'It can't be that bad,' said Maidie, remembering the bliss of Pethidine. 'Virtually everyone here over the age of twenty was born with anaesthetics—it doesn't seem to have done much harm.'

She might as well not have spoken. All the younger adults believed in 'natural childbirth', and only disagreed on the finer points. You should go to hospital, you should stay at home. You should deep-breathe according to this system; or that one. Stand up and walk about as long as possible. Have your belly massaged during contractions—which only people of Maidie's age called pains. Give birth sitting up, lying on your side, squatting, in an accoucheur's chair. Tim found himself under pressure to make one for Sheila, until she said she intended to squat. At home—she had found a midwife who believed in home births even for first babies.

Elinor pricked up her ears—Tim was trying to stop his. Breech deliveries, flying squads, emergency Caesareans, placenta praevia; it belonged in the surgery between a woman and her doctor, not at afternoon tea. He managed to change the subject to the question of whether post-Baroque music should be performed on authentic instruments. Several Debecs had strong views on fortepianos and gut strings; childbirth was forgotten.

The last guests left after tea, except Tim and Elinor, who tried to go, but let Maidie persuade them to stay. Tim, Sheila and Lionel—who played the piano—sight-read their way through a Haydn piano trio; then it was seven o'clock and Maidie was saying, 'Stay to dinner, do.'

Thoby muttered, 'Yes—do. We've got to—royal command—you'll make it b-bearable.' So they stayed.

They got back to Ockendon Road late, in a state of stunned languor from sun and wine. They thought of making love; then thought no, too sleepy, and turned out the light; then did anyhow. The dark was very intimate, and his cock in her, and his weight on top of her. Silence, darkness, sleep, and that burning movement at the centre. Then really sleep.

The next day it was as if their intimate carnality hadn't happened; he was brisk and friendly, nothing more, and didn't respond when she kissed him. 'You won't see the best of Tim till he's forty.' It had better be sooner than that.

Yet yet yet. Utter carnal satisfaction; an almost abstract fierceness and concentration; wants slaked without concession to good manners and democracy.

'I don't have to *think*, making love to you'—one of Tim's delirious mutters.

'What do you mean?' she'd whispered.

'Don't know—just...never having to worry that I'm not pleasing you—just following...' He made a gesture meaning: whatever occurred to him.

She didn't have to worry what would please him, either; she just did what she wanted, knowing he would want it too. She sank out of thought; all that was left was rudimentary images, little chunters of amusement, momentary intrusions of practicalities like: 'Remember to buy lettuce'.

Sometimes his breath juddered when she was sucking him, and he had to pull back suddenly to keep from coming. Glancing up, seeing his eyes squeezed shut and lips parted, his barrel-chested long woolly torso, and his cock, leaping with life, with maleness, she could understand why Priapus had been a god, and for a

114

moment feel herself a worshipper in the cult and Tim hardly a particular person, but representative—the most alive thing about him not his face but his cock.

An inward snort at her extravagant solemnity—a flash of alarm at her reactionary imagination.

She needed to believe that her sexuality and her feminism, both of them so deep-felt and so central to her being, were mutually consistent. How could she square Priapic worship with the current sexual orthodoxy of only-gentleness, only-tenderness? Was she colluding with male images of power? She didn't think so: her instincts felt right, the theory wrong. Sex wasn't only tenderness and gentleness, but passion, phantasy and insolent wild greed. It was the body, full, weighty, earthy, carnal, suffused by soul; it was the soul, which flooded in when thought fled. Tim was a gentle man—pain was no part of their relation. But neither was gentleness, except incidentally. Even pleasure wasn't at the centre of it, but more imperious, less biddable feelings, so extreme they were frightening: passion, identity, bliss, depth, simultaneity, communion, craving, ecstasy, greed, penetration, trance, rapture, permeation, reverie, interfusion, slaking, union, intentness, transfixion, binding the whole world to yourself, opening yourself to the whole world.

That understanding was Tim's gift to her. Before him it had been invisible behind the tender, reasonable, equal alertness her lovers had given her and asked in return. They had also given her the kissing and fondling she never stopped wanting from Tim: but with them she had never had what she had with him.

Chapter 15

Sheila sieved the pasta, Thoby poured the sauce. A grate of Parmesan, sit down, twirl up the first mouthful—telephone. Thoby answered, listened, said a resigned, 'Okay,' hung up, re-twirled.

'Prosser,' he said, between mouthfuls. 'Tomorrow's soloist—French horn—Customs—Gatwick—outraged—terrified. Rescue her instantly. Royal command.'

'Selfish old bugger. Finish your dinner first—you'll need it.'

'You too—you've scarcely touched it.'

Sheila giggled. 'It's too much fun watching you Hoover it up.' She didn't finish after he left, either; she was restless, and not a bit hungry. She got out the cello.

After a while she was aware of discomfort: more than discomfort, the familiar low grinding pain of...Not period pains. Labour.

Pretend it's not happening. She worked through another few pages, watching the clock. It was happening. She laid the cello to rest, went to the telephone; stopped. She didn't want to face that formidable woman alone. The phantom pacer was moving about upstairs. She toiled up and asked him to come down, and only then rang the midwife.

Thoby got home to find Sheila squatting mother-naked on the bed, smiling seraphically and holding on hard to the pacer. 'We're doing fine,' the midwife said. 'Six centimetres dilated already, wonderful for a first baby.' Her tone suggested that this was a special cleverness of her own. 'But...'

'But what?' Thoby instantly envisaged a stillbirth.

'She won't have a stitch of clothing on.'

'It's a hot night.'

'But that—that *man*'—the pacer—'It's not decent. And she doesn't know who I am. I'd say she's delirious, only she's not got a fever. Now you're here, I'll go ring for doctor.'

Thoby knelt by Sheila, who kept on smiling and stared straight through him. 'Sheila.'

No answer.

'My love.' It felt all wrong, beseeching her while she gripped another man's hands. 'D'you suppose you could...'

'Over to you, mate.' The phantom pacer transferred her hands to Thoby's and stood up.

Still no recognition. Every three minutes, with the contractions, she gave a baritone wail; then a smile re-wreathed her face.

Thoby said in despair, 'It's affecting her brain.'

'Hang loose, old chap' the pacer said comfortingly. 'Nothing wrong with her brain. She was pretty uncool when I came down, so I put a little acid in her tea.'

After a while she stopped smiling: the trip was turning bad. Throughout her son's birth and for hours afterwards she was back in Limehouse—hiding behind the cello with her father glaring in the doorway; cowering in the coalshed while he searched the house—the yard—opened the shed door. When Thoby tried giving her the baby to hold, her arms were limp; he had to hold him up to her breast himself.

'Then she fell asleep,' he told Tim and Elinor, calling round two days later, 'and it wore off. When she woke up she knew how to hold him, all right—but she doesn't remember *having* him. Bastard took it away from her.' He turned his head away; there were tears in his eyes.

Elinor looked at Tim; Tim looked away. He's your friend, she thought, but went and knelt by Thoby's chair and touched his arm.

Tears coursed down his face. In a whisper he said, 'It was awful, Nell—wondering if she'd *ever* come back—and when she wouldn't *hold* him...looking at her sleeping...and Euan—not knowing whether to be glad about him—would he have a mother or...remembering everything I ever heard about LSD psychosis— oh God it's a wonder I didn't kill him—'

117

'The baby?' Elinor said involuntarily, then saw what he meant.

'No, the pacer,' they said together, and Thoby gulped with out-of-place laughter and wiped his eyes.

'But she's all right now, you said, no after-effects.'

'Better than she's ever been. Radiant. But...' But he was still afraid—she was so fragile. He mustn't say that, though—Sheila didn't want anyone knowing about her father. The only person he'd ever told was Maidie, during Sheila's first long silence: hoping for some miracle of maternal understanding; getting a few flints of worldly wisdom. But she'd taken Sheila on those healing trips: give Maidie her due.

Tim saved him from temptation by growling, 'It was bloody dangerous. I would have torn him apart.'

'I nearly did. Went up, started to shake him—stopped. Small fellow, afraid. Told him to find another flat fast or I'd tell the cops he had dope. It was us or him—Sheila was talking about moving out—didn't want to meet him on the stairs. Disgusting feeling, Tim, coming over the bully. Sickened me.'

He got up to go, and Elinor said, 'Can we come see her tomorrow—her and Euan? It's a nice name, Euan.'

'Isn't it, Nell? Anytime—we'll be there.'

Tim winced privately. He liked straightforward English names.

'It's raining.' Tim shut the front door and came back for his mac.

Elinor was feeling in her bag. 'Damn, where's...I know, down on the kitchen table—my present for Sheila. Be right back.' She started down the stairs in a rush.

On the second-to-last step she slipped, overshot the bottom step and hit the quarry-tiled floor with her right foot. She gave a hoarse shout—overbalanced—sat down hard. Waves of hot pain pumped out of her ankle.

Slowly dragging herself into a sitting position, she hauled her leg up with both hands and felt her foot. No bones poking out—it was probably just sprained. She shut her eyes and rocked to and fro, panting from shock.

Where was Tim—out in the car? No—she heard movement in the hall, then: 'Elinor?' and his footsteps on the stairs.

Why hadn't he come sooner?—it must have been a minute or more since she fell. Or did pain make time go slower?

'You all right?'

'I think so. It just *hurts*.' Her voice sounded either too loud or too soft.

'Can I do anything?'

She opened her eyes. He was standing beside her. 'You could hold me,' she said. It sounded like a line from a bad old movie—'Hold me, darling, hold me close.' She didn't care: she needed him to hug her and pat her and murmur, 'There, there.'

Squatting, Tim felt her ankle gingerly between thumb and forefinger. 'Nothing seems to be out of place.'

She closed her eyes again, waiting for his arms to go round her, then leaned towards him to remind him. Her cheek met, not his shoulder or chest or embracing arms, but two hard tweedy shins. She opened her eyes in shock. Yes—while she was waiting for him to hug her, he'd stood up.

She wasn't going to fawn at his shins, damn it. She hitched across to the newel post and leaned against that instead. Tim just stood looking down at her, like a post himself. The pain was waning. How could he ignore a plea for the most elementary kind of comforting? She had to get out from under that cold gaze.

He held out his hand when she started struggling to get up. She took it—she needed it. He hauled her up carefully and helped her to a chair in the kitchen. Maybe he hadn't heard her ask him to hold her. She had felt half blind with pain; maybe she'd been half mute as well.

In the ears of memory it was loud enough. The humiliation—abasing herself at his shins—undeserved; unforgivable.

'Back there in the hall,' she said, 'I asked you to...to hold me. Didn't you hear me?'

'I...' He stumbled out with the implausible truth. 'I didn't hear you *then*, but a moment ago I heard it in my head like an echo. Why the delay I don't know.'

'Oh.' She believed him, and was appeased; yet felt befogged.

— ✳ —

119

Sheila looked happier than Elinor had ever seen her, and utterly beautiful. Radiant, as Thoby had said: a full moon in a clear sky. She was a bit tired, she said, but not very; she wanted to resume the quartet next week, and go back to work within a month. She had piles of papers beside her chair—her secretary had brought her some work to do at home.

'Crumbs, that's real dedication,' said Elinor.

'Oh—not really—we're so short-handed, I can't leave them in the lurch.'

When Euan cried, Sheila opened her smock, unhooked her nursing bra and put him to the breast. She was happy, happy. It'll all be different from now on, she kept telling herself in amazement. He didn't hate her, she could tell; and feeding him, satisfying his needs, was everything her first fantasies of motherhood had been, before fear struck. She wasn't herself, she was Euan's mother, inside the role.

Tim had never desired Sheila—she, like Maggie, reminded him of Vivian. Once burned, twice shy. But her full moon-breasts, half glimpsed in the folds of her open smock, roused him to an abstract lust—to hold them, bury his face in them, lick and suck the hard nipples that looked as if a man had already sucked them erect. When she moved Euan to her other breast, the nipple he had already fed at was elongated and shiny with milk; for a hallucinatory moment Tim thought it was his own spit.

The fantasy was like defiling a shrine. Suckling was what breasts were for, he should be able to take the sight for granted—but there was a lot to be said for the taboo on breast-feeding in public. Images of Elinor pregnant, then suckling, flashed into his mind. With her he would have licence to gaze, touch, suck—no, not suck, milk would come out into his mouth—horrible—like that painting, was it Daumier, that both excited and revolted him, of a French peasant woman suckling a starving man.

Elinor was also, if less guiltily, fascinated. She wanted to stare and stare, not sneak glances while pretending to give full attention to Sheila's face, as if nothing remarkable were going on below. Her own breasts felt small and purposeless. She wanted them full, and a mottled red baby sucking, while Tim watched with the half-jealous

120

desire that she thought most men must feel who didn't transform it into disgust. Did women feel it? Did she? Was that part of why she wanted to stare so? Or did women sublimate their lust to suckle into a desire to give suck themselves? Perhaps. Or perhaps you didn't need another woman's breasts when you had breasts yourself, part of your body and being, that you could hold absentmindedly, comfortingly, when no one was looking.

He should have hugged me anyhow, she thought suddenly—whether he heard me or not. He shouldn't need prompting to hold someone in pain.

Even when she asked, he had ignored her. 'I didn't hear you *then*. Why the delay I don't know.'

Because you didn't *want* to hear, she told him hotly in her head.

No kisses but the ones she took from him; no embraces except in bed; cold assistance when she was in pain, but no comfort. 'I need time,' he'd said. How much, for God's sake? What had she let herself in for?

Just then he looked across at her and smiled—clear, direct, warm. She wasn't mistaken about his warmth; it was real.

And his coldness?

But she'd get angry if she spoke of what had happened. She didn't want to risk starting the downward spiral of quarrels that she'd got into with other men. Everybody had faults.

It was raining in a thick drizzle when they left. Halfway down the front steps Tim suddenly said, 'We should have children ourselves.'

Elinor stopped in panic with her sore foot just touching the pavement. The square was lush in the wet warmth. She stared at long-legged weeds until the world came back into focus, and managed to say in a normal voice, 'Not for a year or two, surely—we're so busy.'

Tim was relieved; he had spoken almost unconsciously. But he wanted children. People who did not were selfish. And Elinor would give his children the unconditional love he felt his mother had never given him. 'We mustn't put it off forever, though.'

Again a deep pulse of fear. She stared at the dripping toadflax, then found her voice. 'I know,' she said, and stepped down onto the pavement.

TWO

Chapter 16

'It's positive.'

She'd expected it, but was still stunned. Caught: a gate clanging shut. It was too *soon*.

'Would you like to talk about it?'

'I...thanks, but I'm okay.' She stood up and propelled herself outdoors and back through the airless summer afternoon to the cinema, where, in a daze, she chatted with the part-time ushers and the latest locum assistant manager, let in the first evening house, and sat down in her office to do the books.

She couldn't concentrate. Talk to somebody—but who? Tim was on tour till tomorrow. She rang Maggie. No reply. Everyone else was on holiday—Rose in Yugoslavia with Marcus; Chris in the Dordogne; Sheila and Thoby in Tuscany with Euan, who was two now, and their new baby, Fergus—Tim had growled at the name— who was already six months old.

Pregnant. Impossible: that's other people, not me. The books kept blurring before her eyes. The end of July now. By the end of next March she would...

Think about it tomorrow like Scarlett O'Hara. Tim would be home, they could talk. She punched a column of figures into the calculator; double checked; entered them in the ledger.

Talk? Fat chance. Two years they'd been married, and nothing had changed. He was almost as undemonstrative as ever, and as for talk...Well, he did talk: but about subjects, topics. Music; films; things he read about in the lulls of work—endangered species; the causes of famine; the misuse of IQ tests; the French revolution— anything on earth as long as it wasn't personal.

If it was, he wriggled out of it—week to week, month to month, ignoring her openings while he got on with something, then

125

something else, seamlessly; or else he listened for a little, then said, 'Look, I'm busy right now, can we talk about this some other time? Sometime soon.' But 'soon' came, and something else cropped up— something worthy, damn it. Some men watched football on telly or went out boozing; Tim typed up the CND newsletter...made furniture...took on a violin student who was too poor to pay.

Maybe she was too tentative. But he'd been wounded, and his pain went deep; she didn't want to do more damage. 'You think I *want* to be like this?' he'd said once.

And when she asked for more affection...He tried, give him credit; but then he lapsed back—and she *hated* asking for it: she wanted him to want it himself.

Patience, patience. But the goal was no closer.

Intimacy; soul to naked soul, a voice sometimes whispered subliminally.

Yet her hope was perpetually fed. Every two or three months they spent a long weekend at Swarthgill; and walking there was like having one mind, one breath. So was listening to music, and they did that almost every day. Think of the way his face shone with music; the intensity of his lovemaking. 'Why is it so wonderful?' he'd whispered the last time. His impassioned mutterings touched her inordinately because of the silence out of which they emerged.

Time to let out the house. As she passed the coffee stand a slight nausea fluttered behind her ribcage.

She finished the books and tackled a pile of letters. May we enquire whether. Enclosed is a cheque for. Thank you for your information on. We shall be mounting the season in the spring, and—

In the spring.

She picked up the telephone. This time Maggie was in. Elinor invited herself round, left the cinema in the locum's hands and set off for Great James Street.

Once there she was shy. Before her marriage they had talked about everything under the sun, including themselves and their lives. But now there were limits. Maggie seldom talked about herself and Clive any more, and didn't want to be told about Elinor and Tim.

But she had heard the urgency in Elinor's voice on the telephone. She poured drinks, sat down in one of her comfortable apricot chintz armchairs, crossed her ankles on a footstool, smoothed her straight black skirt, lit a cigarette and said, 'How are things with you? You look...funny.'

Elinor put down her whisky without tasting it and looked up with a queer smile. 'I'm...I'm...I've got some news, actually. I'm, uh...pregnant.'

'You don't exactly sound overjoyed,' Maggie said, carefully showing nothing but interest. Elinor had got there; she herself was still as far off as ever. She would lose her, too—women with children didn't need friends.

'I...actually, I'm terrified,' Elinor confessed. 'Not so much about pregnancy or labour; it's more...'

'Bringing up children? Responsibility?'

'No, they're scary, but...all sorts of things. The cinema, for one. Remember the plan to hire an assistant manager and show four or five films a day instead of three, only we've had to shelve it because of the joists?'

'Speaking of which—any luck finding a builder who'll do it in bits so you can stay open?'

'Yes, thanks to you—Rowntree Stearn. They'll even stop at two so we can have an afternoon show. But they'll be all winter—parts of the auditorium roped off—it's no time to change to five a day. We'd thought—next spring. But it'll be so much work at first...'

'Oh, and with a newborn baby. Pity—you'll have to postpone it again. But surely that's not enough to make you—terrified?'

'No, it's that—that—it's too *soon*. I'm not *ready*. Tim and I aren't ready. Even now we never find time to talk and...work things out: so how will we ever do it with a baby?'

Maggie felt a stab of hatred so strong it frightened her. How dare Elinor have everything and not even want it? She swallowed, looking at the friend who was so dear to her. 'Are you thinking of an abortion?' she said neutrally.

'Um, it crossed my mind; but no. It'll probably always seem like the wrong time for children; and I'm thirty-one: just as well to have my mind made up for me.' Maybe even something of a relief.

127

Maybe she was even...could she possibly be...pleased?

'That sounds pretty negative.'

'Oh, but I *want* children. Minding Euan and Fergus at the quartet every week, I've been so envious of Sheila. Only I hope I have a girl.'

'Do you really?' said Maggie in surprise. 'I want—I *would* want—boys.'

'How strange.' They stared at each other across a fundamental divide. 'Of course you take what you get, but most of the women I know would prefer girls—though I've never asked Sheila: somehow you can't ask her such personal things.'

'You know where you are with boys,' said Maggie.

'That's what *I* think about girls. They'd be more like me, we'd get along, we'd keep on wanting to talk about the same things as they grew up, whereas boys—'

'But you're the one that thinks the sexes are the same.'

'Never. Just that they're not inherently different—except physically; you can save the ribald laughter.'

Elinor glanced down, and felt giddy. This wasn't just some abstraction they were discussing, it was her future child, who was in there somewhere, behind the flat plane of her jeans, with its sex already determined—a daughter, or a son: a secret of her body, secret even from her. If it did turn out to be a boy, Maggie mustn't think she didn't want it.

'It's only a marginal preference,' she said, stretching the truth. 'And I *do* want it.' That at least was true, after these panicky and rebellious hours.

The conviction in her voice dissolved Maggie's bile. 'Then I'm happy for you. Of course I envy you like crazy'—lightly acknowledging a fraction of what she felt. 'But I'll exercise my full rights as fairy godmother—the wicked one. What about Tim—how will he react?'

'Oh he's wanted a baby for ages. Sheila having Euan set him off, and Fergus even more. Fergus is death to music stands now that he's crawling—if that hasn't put Tim off children, nothing will.'

If he did have doubts, she'd never know: he would keep them to himself, like everything else.

— ✳ —

She couldn't sleep. She'd been using her diaphragm religiously; how had it happened?

Maybe a child would release Tim's dammed warmth—maybe this was the turning point.

What sort of tone could she tell him in? Brisk: I've got some good news...Diffident: I, uh, hope you'll be pleased...Breathless: you'll never guess—the most amazing thing...

Three o'clock came and she hadn't slept. She dozed a little, but by four she was wide awake again, and sweaty. She got up and ran a bath, and lay in it drowsily musing about the spring, babies at her breast, the gulf of childbirth...

Better get up, before she fell asleep and drowned. She stepped out of the bath, giggling—really, she felt drunk—reached for the towel; froze. Furtive noises downstairs? Imagination; not surprising at this time of—

Not imagination. Footsteps on the stairs. Not Tim—he wouldn't be back till morning. She wrapped the towel tight round her, tipped dried flowers out of a china ewer and stood ready to smash it down on the intruder's head.

Fortunately as Tim opened the door he said enquiringly, 'You there?'

'*Tim*?'

'Did I startle you? John Boynson was coming back tonight—I got a lift.'

Her towel came untucked and slowly slid off. Her dripping bath-flushed body and pallid face seemed to belong to two different people. She let him put the ewer down, then flung her arms round him.

Overreacting as usual; and getting his jacket wet. He pushed her gently away. 'Now, then. Dry yourself—you'll catch your death.'

In the bedroom she wriggled under the covers and said, 'I thought you were—'

'A burglar, I guessed. But what made you have a bath at this time of night?'

She was too tired to embark on it. 'I—uh...tell you tomorrow.'

— * —

129

She woke up feeling sick, and sat up in bed, hugging her knees, watching light and the shadows of glazing bars waver through the long white curtains. Tim stirred, groaned, and opened his eyes. Without giving herself time to rehearse she said, 'I went to the Women's Centre yesterday for a test. I'm pregnant.'

'Good heavens.' He sat up. 'When—how long—when is it due?'

'The end of March.' Quite far off; only a few months. 'I'm six weeks now.'

'But you had a period a fortnight ago.'

'Apparently it was a sort of sham bleed. I guessed because I've felt sick in the mornings this week while you were away.'

'But you were using your diaphragm.'

'They've got a failure rate, and I'm part of it.' Why didn't he tell her how he felt, for God's sake? Irritably she asked, 'Are you pleased?'

'Yes,' he said simply. 'It's wonderful.' Why did she ask?—she knew how much he wanted it. 'But you—how are you feeling?'

'A mixture. Frightened—it'll be such a change...' But for him it was, in that voice of simplicity, wonderful. She should meet him on that ground. 'But mostly happy.' It was the truth; she was beginning to be very happy.

'What I meant—do you feel sick right now?' He reached out a hand to her shoulder. She looked blank, then nodded. His poor Elinor. He pulled her down into the cradle of his arm and stroked her back gently. 'Does it go away later in the day?'

'A little. Not quite. And I'm tired all the time—dazed, not quite wide awake.'

'Don't work so hard, then—don't fight nature. We'll have to make sure you get enough rest.'

She was entertained by his calm royal we. At another time she might have made fun of it, but not today, secure in his arms, getting the comfort she'd missed for the past two years—though she was still startled by the way he had focussed on her health and ignored what she said about her feelings. Maybe he hadn't heard her say she was frightened.

— ✳ —

130

Her morning sickness got worse all week, and lasted all day, every day. Even the smell of cooking sickened her. She drank nothing but water and ate nothing but Bath Olivers and cold boiled potatoes.

'You've got to see your doctor,' Tim said. 'This can't be normal.'

But morning sickness was all it was. '*Do* try not to let your husband fuss you—men get pregnancy out of proportion so,' her GP said with an oddly complicit smile, as if inviting Elinor into a freemasonry of motherhood.

'I'll be over it by twelve weeks, when the baby switches to the placenta,' she told Tim that night in bed, letting him force-feed her with Bath Olivers. 'Why I'm nauseated now is because it's feeding on a yolky thing that raises the level of some hormone. It's in *Our Bodies, Ourselves* if you want to look it up.'

'Mmm.' He had heard quite enough already, thank you.

Seeing the doctor had cheered her up. 'Funny to think it's developing like crazy, right now—right here.' She put his hand on her belly.

To her astonishment he kept it there. He was flooded with tenderness for all three of them. Before long he withdrew his hand; the emotion had frightened him back into himself. But it left a residue in his mind.

Chapter 17

'Stay home in bed—relax,' Tim said on Sunday. Elinor had been retching; her skin had a waxen yellow cast.

'No, you need me to mind the boys, and besides—'

'Don't be silly—we'll survive.'

'But I *want* to come,' she protested. 'It'll distract me, and—'

'But—'

'Look, I'm coming—the quartet's almost as important to me as it is to you.'

'Oh Elinor.' He touched her cheek lovingly—it was so easy, so natural—why hadn't he started doing it long ago?—and went for his fiddle. As important to me as it is to you. Those words meant more to him than when she said she loved him, which he both took for granted and could not really believe.

Elinor sat in the bay window with sunburned Fergus squirming on her lap. Tim's notes were bounding strong and sweet above the others', as usual. Half the time she listened to all four of them; half the time only to him, as if he were the soloist in a violin concerto. A secret vice: he would scold her if he knew. Euan was at her feet, beating the carpet with a wooden spoon in time to Beethoven's opus 95. He had Sheila's wide-apart china-blue eyes; he was a serious child, thin and delicate like a flower on a long stalk—a white rose flushed with pink, after their fortnight in the Dordogne. The only flower Fergus was like was a zinnia.

Fergus grunted, then let out a yell. Sheila took a break to feed him. Thoby picked Euan up; Alan rubbed his bow with rosin. Tim played a few bars of the next section, then wandered into a Brahms violin sonata so sad, so sweet that it pulled Elinor's heart right out of her.

Clink-clink. 'Tim said you'd like these.' It was Sheila with Fergus and a bowl of ice cubes.

Elinor made a face. 'Yes, I chew them—gives me an illusion of eating something solid.'

Sheila looked down at her with concern. 'You're so pale. I was a bit seedy a few mornings, but nothing like you.' Having got that far, she didn't know how to go on; she never did. 'How are you otherwise?' she ventured.

It was a question about her general health, but Elinor thought it was about her feelings. 'Happy and scared, both,' she began.

Scared—how brave to confess it. 'I was scared too, before—I...' Sheila longed to share with her—meet her—tell the submerged panic she had been living in ever since her first pregnancy, except for a few weeks after each baby's birth. But the effort brought her up against her furthest limit. Prickled all over from self-exposure, she retreated. 'It's better once they arrive, though. You'll be the same, don't worry—it comes instinctively.' It was true as far as it went—and for Nell it would probably go on being true. She settled Fergus on her hip, rubbing her nose on his brick-red cheek and smiling shyly.

'Yes, I'm sure,' Elinor said without quite meaning it. Who else had said that recently, or something in that tone of voice?

Her GP. Pregnancy seemed to admit you to a bond of solidarity with all mothers. Attractive, alluring; she could feel the pull.

Rose bounced in to work on Tuesday, red all over from the Yugoslavian sun, hugged Elinor; did a double-take. 'You got flu or something? You've got circles under your eyes like a panda.'

'No, I'm not ill, just...' she tried for an offhand tone: 'just pregnant.'

She'd overdone the nonchalance; Rose's, 'Oh,' was worried.

'No—I mean, it wasn't on purpose, but I'm happy—except for having morning sickness *all* the time.'

'How dire. Poor Nell—why not go home? I can manage.'

'God no. This weekend—feeling sick with nothing to do—it's ten times worse than working, really it is.'

'Okay. And you're really happy?'

'Really and truly.' Elinor crossed her heart.

Rose's face cleared. 'Hey, me too, then. Unless—you won't do anything awful like chucking your job, will you?'

'You *are* funny'—affectionately. 'You'd have your dream if I did—sole manager of a rep.'

'Nah, that'd be like climbing up over your body, you know? Besides, what I've got in mind is a smaller house. My kind of programme, a hundred and fifty seats is all I could fill. So—what kind of childcare are you thinking of? I do hope it's a girl, don't you? And what are you going to call it? Is Tim pleased? Your surname or his?'

'Mine, of course,' Elinor said, answering the only simple question in the excited rush.

'Goody. Hey, this will be such fun, once you're past the sickness stage. When's that? We'll have to line up locums for while you're away—when's the baby due? If only there were any women locums—those guys are such total and universal creeps. Will it be a home birth or hospital? With pain-killers or not? Have you thought of a birth bath?'

'A *what*?'

'They've got them in California. Like a tepid hot tub. You sort of float through labour and give birth under water.'

Rose's straightforward enthusiasm was refreshing after her GP's and Sheila's coded smiles. Their secret society of mothers had its allure, but she wouldn't join it just because she was eligible: not if it put her on the opposite side of a fence from Maggie and Rose.

'This can't go on,' Tim kept saying—Elinor felt sick all day, every day, and stunned with lethargy.

'It won't, I told you—my pregnancy books say it stops at twelve weeks, fourteen at the worst.' August crept by. Eight weeks, nine, ten, eleven. Work was the only distraction.

September—twelve weeks—time for their week at Swarthgill. The lethargy lifted overnight, but not the nausea—long walks were the last thing she wanted.

'You go, though,' she urged Tim. 'I'll be fine.' But he wouldn't leave her.

She spent the week working. Tim could not so easily find last-minute work, but he got a few stand-in jobs, gave a few extra lessons, practised a lot; and started, at last, on the dining table.

Her nausea hung over everything; even so, she was very happy. Tim was more than solicitous; he was tender: stroking her cheek, cradling her in bed morning and night—and kissing her gently, to her astonished joy. Silly man, why had he been so stubborn? They could have been like this all along. The only fly in the ointment was that she had lost all interest in making love. *All* interest—desire wasn't just muted; it was blanked out. Even in childhood she'd had more sexual feeling, drifting to sleep in a wash of warm sensation with her hand tucked comfortingly along her cunt. For herself she didn't mind—you don't miss what you don't feel—but for Tim she did. He said he didn't mind, either, but that was hard to believe.

'Mrs Benton, a few questions...' The ante-natal nurse opened a file and took Elinor's medical history. 'Now some questions about Mr Benton, if you don't mind.'

'Sure, only his name's Scott—Timothy Scott.'

She went back over the forms, making changes; asked her questions; then said, 'If you'll just wait over there for the doctor, Mrs Scott.'

'It's not Scott, it's Benton—I haven't taken my husband's name.'

'We like to use the father's name—it's simpler for our records.'

'I'm sorry, but my name is Benton,' said Elinor.

'It can't be *that* important.'

Don't lose your temper, polite but firm, count to ten. 'I'm afraid it is.'

The nurse sighed and changed the forms back. 'Very well, Mrs Benton, if you'll just wait—'

'I'm actually Ms not Mrs.'

'We call all our mums Mrs, not to embarrass the single ones. It's policy.' Try getting round *that*, her smile said.

Fourteen weeks. No change. Fifteen—no change. Elinor combed her books and found a footnote. A small minority of women were nauseated throughout pregnancy. Jesus.

135

She still wasn't interested in making love, but it seemed so hard on Tim that one morning she snuggled up to him invitingly anyhow. Maybe something would kindle once they got going.

No fire; not a spark. Eventually she had to say, 'Sorry, it's no use,' then, with a giggle: 'I'm like Tony Curtis not responding to Marilyn on the yacht; except he was only pretending, and I'm not.'

'Poor Elinor.'

'Poor Tim.'

'Don't worry about me, I'm all right.'

It was the simple truth. His sexual fires were banked low; his being was concentrated in a tranquil tenderness that surprised him as much as her. He was used to Elinor strong and independent. Elinor in need of him, carrying his child, called up an emotion more like what he conceived love to be than anything he had ever felt before. Her sickness overrode his fear of being rejected if he showed affection. Her tired face resting on his chest, his arms round her—he felt strong, necessary, plenteous. It seemed like a foretaste of fatherhood. Instead of being just two people, they were a family.

Bang, buzz, scrape, thud; the basement was full of builders. Dust billowed up into the auditorium; Rose and Elinor had to rush up and down before the matinée flicking dust off the seats nearest the stairs.

Then it was just Ron and Daz, the carpenters. Ron called them Miss Quinlan and Miss Benton, Daz called them Rose and Nell. Ron didn't say much, Daz talked for two. But it was Ron who came up and said he smelt dry rot.

'Oh God, more bills for the Wellesfords,' said Rose.

But Andrew Wellesford only said, 'Don't worry, it happens. Our fault—we've neglected the fabric.'

Elinor was alone in the office when the first rep arrived from a rot-control firm. She showed him downstairs, where he said with relish, 'Dry rot all right—that fruity smell—' then was suddenly talking to blank air as Elinor rushed to the ladies' and retched.

'Sorry,' she said, returning along the passage. 'Morning sickness.'

He looked flustered. 'But it's afternoon.'

'Better late than never?'

He didn't think it was funny. After that they left the rot reps to Rose.

'You'd better do something about the damp,' the dry-rot operative said. 'Next time the rot could get your nice new joists.'

Rose rang Andrew Wellesford to report. 'Obviously we can't afford it this year, though—with two big repairs we'll be lucky to break even.'

'Do it right away is my philosophy. The Cromer's been doing well—we can carry a small loss. I'm sure Sefton and Ginny will agree.'

'Look, the meter's almost off the scale, this pier's so wet. Now the Gardiner process—I invented it—is like the way insects make their skins waterproof—I did a doctorate in insect physiology. It permeates the masonry by capillary action—but I won't bother your pretty heads with technical detail. Your basement will be as waterproof as Wellingtons—I guarantee it.'

'Yes, well if you'll give us a quotation and a starting date, Mr Gardiner, we'll—'

'*Doctor* Gardiner.' He was a short, stocky bald man in a tight double-breasted grey pinstripe suit and black patent leather shoes.

'And your guarantee'—Rose's voice went very posh—'it says here water-resistant, but you were talking about watertight.'

He snatched it and peered. 'An oversight—a first draft.'

'You'll amend it before we sign?'

He said yes with a bad grace and went away.

'Pompous prick,' said Rose. 'Let's not use *him*.'

But his bid was lowest and his amended guarantee so ironclad— 'Watertight,' Rose said with a cackle—that Andrew Wellesford instructed them to accept.

Nineteen weeks. No change. Twenty, twenty-one, twenty-two, no change. Tim cradled her asleep every night; brought her biscuits in bed every morning and sponged her face with a cool cloth; rang her at work two or three times a day to see how she was. By twenty-

137

three weeks the baby was drumming on her thick belly. Her palm still remembered Euan thumping inside Sheila. She'd wanted it for herself; and here it was—but muffled by sickness. She wasn't revelling in pregnancy, just waiting it out. She felt cheated, but for the change in Tim. His tenderness, his arms enfolding her, his mouth soft on hers—that was worth anything.

By the middle of December they had been expecting Gardiner's men for a month. 'Let me guess,' said Elinor after Rose's latest telephone call.

'Yeah—the beginning of next week.' Rose spoke listlessly, for her—Marcus was giving her a hard time.

'Huh. They won't show till the New Year.'

But a black-bearded man with a potbelly like a lava-slide arrived with a laconic mate and drilled the basement walls full of holes, taking no notice of the line in the contract about stopping at two o'clock: Elinor had to offer the matinée customers their money back on the way out. Most refused; nine took: eight pensioners and a soignée lady trembling with rage—at the film, as it turned out. 'You should warn people. A name like *Lili Marleen*, I expected—but it was *trash*.'

The next day the men pumped the walls full of Gardiner's goop, said, 'Happy Christmas,' and left. Done.

Chapter 18

New Year's dinner was cold beef, garlicky aubergine salad and burgundy for Maggie, Bath Olivers and water for Elinor. They started off gaily enough, swapping stories. Maggie told about a northern mayor who introduced Sir Samuel Hoare and his wife as, 'Sir Samuel and Lady W.'

Elinor looked blank, then said, 'Oh—w for whore!' and broke up. 'Which reminds me—no connection, really—the other day in the foyer I heard a woman asking, "Your new cat, is it male or female?" And the woman she was with said, "Neither, actually—it's been *improved*." '

Maggie whooped.

But things went downhill from there on. The smell of cigarettes made Elinor sick, so Maggie had promised not to smoke, but got edgy and started popping into the lavatory every half hour for a few drags. Smoke seeped under the door; Elinor started feeling very queasy. At her own place she would have said so; at Maggie's she somehow couldn't; and grew a little more polite than usual, and a little stiffer.

Maggie was stiff, too, with jealousy and an intense, complicated curiosity. The details of Elinor's pregnancy were none of her business—but she wanted her to talk about it. Elinor was dying to, but, thought Maggie wanted her not to, and felt awkward every time it came up, as it inevitably did.

'How's Rose?' said Maggie into a silence.

'Pretty miserable. Marcus has a bad case of other-womanitis— how he keeps the two of them on the hook is beyond me—'

'Yeah, those staring wet eyes and the beard that's like pubic hair—yuck.'

Elinor went into fits. 'Oh God, it is, too—I'll never be able to look him in the face again. Anyhow, we're hauling junk back to the glory hole behind the cinema screen—making room in my office for another armchair, a camp bed, a carrycot stand, that sort of thing—and sometimes it just comes over her, and she drips tears onto a pile of old journals, or once it was onto a pre-war Remington; and when I went and hugged her, she started to hug *me*—forgot she was holding the typewriter, that's how far gone she was. Thank God our reflexes worked faster than the law of gravity, or we'd have had two-dimensional toes.'

'A *carrycot* stand? What's *that* in aid of?' Maggie sounded like Lady Bracknell saying, 'A *handbag*?'

'Me and the baby and Helen—she's the mother's help, didn't I tell you? She's working for a friend of Rose's right now, but she'll be free by the time I'm likely to be going back to work. Now all I have to do is find a crèche for after the baby's weaned—they're scarce on the—'

'A *crèche*?' Maggie was still in Lady Bracknell mode. 'What *is* this? You're not meaning to work full time with a baby!'

'Well yes—I thought you'd know that, we've argued about it often enough.'

'But I never thought you'd really *do* it,' Maggie said passionately. 'Don't, Nell; it's not fair on either of you. Babies need their mothers—and what's the point of having one if you don't take time to enjoy it? You've got the chance, don't waste it.'

You've got the chance, I haven't. Whether or not Maggie meant it, Elinor heard it, and replied less hotly than she might have; but though they found their way to another subject, the rest of the evening limped along. The chatter they manufactured to fill up silences was bright and forced. Elinor got up to go as early as she decently could.

At the door Maggie said, 'If you're determined to dump your baby in a crèche, it might as well be a good one. There's one quite near the Cromer—about ten minutes' walk. Wait, I'll get the address. Here'—coming back with it. 'And if your baby grows up to be a mass murderer or a—a—a TV compère, I'll be the first to say I told you so.'

140

'Oh *Maggie*,' Elinor said, laughing too hard, and kissed her goodnight. 'You should open a problem-solving bureau: you'd make millions.'

But Maggie's gesture hadn't really changed the flavour of the evening. 'If me being pregnant is so hard for her, how will it be next year when I've got an actual baby?' Elinor said sadly when she got home.

Tim was not entirely sorry. It had irked him that she celebrated the New Year with Maggie. He was enough of a Northerner to want to celebrate it himself—with Elinor, not alone; and he resented her attempts to escape what she called the tyranny of the couple. He liked Maggie, but a couple, a family, belonged together at the New Year.

'Hot news,' said Rose, shaking her umbrella and shedding her mac. 'Marcus has got a job. In Camberwell—supply teaching till September, then full time, just what he wants. He's...transformed: full of zip, the way he was when we met—I'd forgotten. We went out to celebrate and disco'd till dawn, that's why I look like yesterday's porridge.'

'You look like a new penny,' Elinor said with pleasure. Gone was the droop of recent weeks; Rose's eyes were bright, her very curls crisper. 'But what about the Brighton Belle?'

'Well, he rang her to tell, but he didn't go there, he's been with me, and he says—mind you he's said it before...Come in'—to a knock at the office door.

It was Ron the carpenter. The basement floor was under water.

Rose tore downstairs; unwieldy Elinor followed at a statelier pace. Water an inch deep, trickling out of pinholes in the cement— 'Waterproof cement,' Elinor said bitterly—that filled the drill-holes.

'Not to worry—I'll send an operative tomorrow,' Gardiner said imperiously when Rose got him.

No operative showed; no reply from Gardiner's office for days. 'There will be a short delay,' he said in a peculiar voice when Elinor finally reached him: 'The head operative has had a nervous breakdown.'

141

Something fishy, if you ask me,' Elinor said to Rose.

'Nah—you'd bug out yourself, working for a guy who looks like Akim Tamiroff in *Touch of Evil*.'

The laconic mate showed up a few days later to pump more goop into the walls. 'I dunno nuffink about it,' he said when Rose asked after the black-bearded operative's mental health.

A dry week; a rainstorm. Water up to the bottom of the stairs, where the loos were. They couldn't get hold of Gardiner. They hired duckboarding, and posted apologies in the foyer. The only complaint came from—good Lord, the soignée lady who'd hated *Lili Marleen*, back for, of all things, another Fassbinder.

'Teething problems,' said Dr Gardiner, and sent the laconic mate again.

A few dry days; rain—a wet basement.

The mate came back. 'I don't unnerstand it, there's gallons and gallons in them walls.' He sounded almost tearful.

Rain that night; a sea in the Cromer the next day.

'This cannot be happening,' Dr Gardiner said furiously down the line. 'It must be coming up through the floor.'

'The floor is solid asphalt,' Elinor said. 'The water's coming through the walls—which according to our contract you were to make watertight.'

'Very well, I'll come and see for myself.'

Gardiner parked his Mercedes on the double yellow lines outside the Cromer and scooted in under a big umbrella, wearing a blue double-breasted suit and patent leather shoes as shiny as puddles. The office telephone rang as he arrived. Rose stayed behind to answer; Elinor followed him down the stairs.

Water lapped the duckboards, licking at Gardiner's shoes. He plucked his trouser legs up out of harm's way and tiptoed. Rose, zipping down the stairs, got to the doorway just in time to see a plug of cement pop out of the leaky wall and a fine jet of water hit Gardiner square in the chest. He yelped, teetered, backed up, and mopped himself with his handkerchief, glaring at Rose and Elinor as if it were their fault.

— * —

Up in the foyer he said, 'You've got crumbling brickwork there—the Gardiner process cannot make up for defective materials—'

'Then you shouldn't have quoted for the work,' Elinor said angrily.

'—but as a goodwill gesture I will pump in more—'

With a seraphic smile Rose interrupted: 'Good, and we'll take samples, of course, same as we've done all along—to send for analysis if there's any dispute about the results.'

Elinor stared—they'd done no such thing. But the effect on Gardiner was electric. He glowered wordlessly, stomped out without his umbrella, tore up a parking ticket and drove off.

Rose let out a squeal of glee. 'Totally awesome, Nell: that was his ex-operative on the telephone—black-beard. He's heard what Gardiner's been telling people, and he's ringing customers to say he didn't have a breakdown at all—he *quit*: because Gardiner was diluting the goop so thin it didn't work. Which I don't suppose he'll do with the next lot—not here, anyhow.'

'Thanks to you, Rosykins. Did you see his face when you said we were keeping samples? He looked like Rumpelstiltskin when the miller's daughter tells him his name.' Elinor forgot her size and did a jig; the first customers for the matinée stared up from their coffee and carrot cake.

The next round of pumping dried up the walls dramatically, though a little water still trickled out after a heavy rain. Another round made no difference. Rose wanted to make Gardiner keep going, but Andrew Wellesford came into town to have a look, and said, 'It'll never be perfect—he's right about the masonry. And the walls are bone dry now, all but those few spots. We'll install a sump pump and call it a day. A brilliant bluff, Miss Quinlan. Getting that guarantee, too.'

Rose preened and basked and gazed into Andrew Wellesford's watery blue eyes. He gazed right back, and only with difficulty tore himself away to meet a nephew for lunch.

'I've stopped work,' Elinor told Sheila and Thoby after lunch the next Sunday—it was the middle of February. 'And I'm glad of it, which I never thought I'd be. I'm heavy as lead, and I look like a

143

beached whale. People *stare* when I'm taking tickets—or go all pinched and look the other way—or look me in the eye pretending they haven't noticed. As if it's some sort of deformity.'

'Like me with our piano tuner when I was a child,' Tim said. 'I'd tiptoe across the carpet and watch the way his eyes moved and blinked but weren't focussed on anything. Of course he knew I was there—I had no idea how well blind people can hear. It's one of the worst things I've ever done.'

'If that's your worst—!' said Thoby.

Worse than not holding me when I twisted my ankle? thought Elinor. But she was touched.

'They shouldn't stare, though—pregnancy's not a deformity,' Sheila said.

'Oh-h-h,' said Elinor. 'Sometimes looking at myself in the mirror I'm...horrified. It's not *me*, this balloon-belly.'

'That's why the stares, don't you think?' said Thoby: 'It's you now, but soon it'll be somebody else. Witchcraft.'

'Even pregnant women stare at each other,' Elinor said—'I notice at National Childbirth Trust classes. Maybe that's why.'

'You been to them, Tim?' Thoby asked.

'They're in the evening—I've had concerts.'

'I take notes,' Elinor said, 'then tell him what he's supposed to do—give me water, help me with my breathing.'

Tim looked up, and back at his plate. Childbirth was women's business; he wanted no part of it. But Elinor assumed he did, and from week to week he had not wanted to disturb their equilibrium by telling the truth. Instead, he had crammed the latter half of March with concerts and recording dates, hoping that one would coincide with her confinement and give him an excuse to miss it. He got up and started clearing plates away.

Thoby picked up the serving dishes and followed. 'I was scared too,' he offered. 'Don't worry. Like stage fright. All right on the night. Besides, it's...astonishing. The baby's head coming out—wouldn't have missed it for anything.'

Tim ran a noisy stream of water into the sink. Was his face so transparent? Blast Thoby and his, 'I was scared *too*.' Impossible now to rely on concerts to bail him out—Thoby would guess that he was simply funking it. He would have to ring the fixers and arrange to be stood in for at short notice.

Truth to tell, he wished it need not happen at all. He wanted to go on like this forever, holding Elinor safe, watching the slow changes in her body: the gourd-swell of her belly with its new brown line from navel to pubic hair; the baby thrumming at him from inside. Not making love would become unbearable, he supposed, but so far he did not mind; his desire for her remained in abeyance. Even her breasts did not stir him to lust, though they had become the very stuff of his fantasies, swollen and ripe, with blurred brownish areolas and hard nipples. Abstinence felt like the price of their cocooned world—enter her and he would break the endless hush in which it seemed as if she could slowly, endlessly grow without ever stopping.

Elinor started awake that night from a dream about couples making love—people she knew: Sheila and Thoby, Rose and Marcus, Maggie and Clive. Yuck—nobody should make love but her and Tim.

She grinned at herself in the dark—but that didn't make the feeling disappear altogether. Most people must have it, she guessed. No wonder they got tense seeing her belly: it reminded them of what she'd done to get that way. She might as well be wearing a sandwich board saying, 'I fuck.'

Chapter 19

The dining table was nearly done, and Tim was dying to finish it, but he spent his free time with Elinor. He had never been so happy. When they went for walks, he held her hand; when they sat in the drawing room, he drew her head to rest in his lap, and now and then leant down to kiss her cheek, her forehead, her mouth. At night he helped settle her on her side in bed with pillows supporting her belly, then curled himself into the curve of her back and fell asleep with one arm across her, cradling her belly. He wanted to nurse the bounce back into her. Yet if she were her old self he would not be able to take care of her—unconsciously he was half relieved that her sickness had not lifted at twelve weeks.

'We should think about names for the baby,' he said one afternoon, putting down his book.

'Why not wait and see what it's like?' she said sleepily.

'Because then we'll call it some dreadful nickname till we decide, and it'll stick. Diddums. Poky Pie.'

'Yuck.' She sat up. 'I suppose we'd better—though I'd *never* nickname a child.'

A couple of hours later they had several names for a girl—Lucy, Isobel, Rosalind, Jane—but none for a boy. 'What about Christopher?' said Tim for the third or fourth time.

'Every other baby these days is a Christopher.'

'So what? It's a good solid sensible name.'

'Solid, sensible, and dull, like most boys' names.'

'*I* like it.' It was his father's name, and his grandfather's.

'Christopher,' she said experimentally. 'Christopher Benton.' Not so bad, really. 'Only it'd have to be Christopher, not Chris— Chris is Chris Haldane.'

146

'Christopher Scott,' he said, thinking she had made a slip of the tongue.

'Oh, it's having my name.'

'You can't mean it,' he said slowly, reluctant to enter upon a subject so obviously—now that they were directly before it—dangerous. 'If it doesn't have my name, what part will I have in it? There'll be nothing to show I've got a stake at all.'

'The same's true for me.'

'You bear it and feed it—you don't need a name to show you've got a part in it. And think of the child. If it's got your name, people will think it's illegitimate—'

'Come on, Tim—Euan and Fergus are illegitimate, and so are half the children we know; they don't suffer for it.'

'Benton could be its middle name.'

'So could Scott.'

'What about Benton-Scott, hyphenated?' he suggested. Hyphenated names usually got shortened—to the last half, not the first.

No flies on Elinor. 'What about Scott-Benton?'

'It's our child, not just yours. I've never objected to your keeping your own name, but—'

'*So* grateful—'

Their tones and words got sharper. She was licking her lips with thirst, but felt she would lose ground if she went for ice cubes. They watched each other coldly, angrier than it was safe to show. Eventually she laid her head on the armrest of the sofa and started weeping.

Tim could not bear it. He got up and went down to his workroom, into the world of tangible objects; picked up a curved chisel; remembered her licking her lips. Was she thirsty? He went to the refrigerator, turned some ice cubes into a bowl and went back upstairs.

Elinor, half asleep on the armrest, looked up incredulously. His gaze was trained somewhere just behind her. Would she somehow weaken her stand by accepting the ice cubes? But she was parched. She crunched one gratefully, closing her eyes.

She was tired, his poor Elinor. He was drawn to her across the abyss she had opened up. He stroked her forehead very gently while

147

she chewed two more ice cubes, then returned to his workroom and the curved chisel.

He had a concert in the evening. Afterwards he came home wrapped in a cloud of disapproving unhappiness, got dinner, fetched things for Elinor and helped her settle for sleep, never quite meeting her eyes, never visibly avoiding them, making no tender gestures, then got under the covers and turned out the lights, staying on his own side of the bed for the first time in months.

Elinor was miserable. But she wouldn't give in—wouldn't.

But—his hand on her forehead this morning—the flow of tenderness these past months, cut off—

Tim was miserable too, and angry. Then with sudden clarity he thought: I am being unkind, she needs me. With a resigned sigh he touched her shoulder, preparing to concede that the child could have her name. Anything to restore their peace.

She gulped. Twice today he'd reached out over the gulf of a quarrel—how could she be so stubborn? 'I—all right, if you want Scott, then—'

'Oh Elinor.' Flooded with passionate gratitude, he slid across and wrapped his arm around her. She had made a huge concession; he was touched close to tears.

She woke in the morning with a stirring of desire. Thank goodness—a bit of her had feared it was gone for good.

Catch it while it lasts. Tim was halfway up already, sitting on the edge of the bed shaking his head like a retriever on a riverbank. She hoicked herself closer and put her hand on his back.

He turned round. 'You awake?'

His brown eyes smiling, his face bending to kiss her—hard to remember that it hadn't always been like this. She wound her arms round his neck and kissed him back, with her mouth, then her tongue; and felt a ripple of surprise pass through his body.

'Lie in awhile, why don't you?' he said into her shoulder, making to sit up again.

She held on. 'You too. Let's make love.'

148

'But I thought you didn't—' She would be hurt if he said no. But he did not want...he was not sure what...to harm the baby; to engage in rivalry for her body with the stranger inhabiting her.

'I didn't, but I do right now. God knows for how long, though—let's make hay while the sun shines.'

'You're not feeling sick?'

'Uh...' To find out, she had to cross a line into the rational world. 'Yup—it's just not so noticeable at the moment. Like that thing in the Kinsey Report about not hearing a gun going off if you're about to come.'

That was that, then.

He thought her bulk would make all sorts of things impossible. But his fingers knew their old place in the pleated satiny softness of her cunt; and when he turned to go down on her, it was easy to curl round her belly and fasten on the liquid nub of her clitoris.

She was sliding her fingers over and round his cock, wetting them sometimes by licking them, sometimes with the drops that it exuded one by one. She touched it with her tongue, and he drew back, saying, 'No, or I'll want to come like that, and you'll be sick.' How he knew that, he did not know. They were living in a delicate symbiosis in which for the first time he knew in his own blood what another person felt.

Twice she pulled his head back. The third time he ignored her. She gave another feeble tug, but he only redoubled his efforts, pulling on her clitoris and labia with loud sputtering sucks. Her hand on his head stopped tugging and pressed him closer, and she came with a sharp groan and a yielding shudder. His chin was against her belly; he could feel her womb ripple with orgasm. He was half intending not to come at all, but was so moved and astonished that he came instantly between her feathering fingers.

He was glad it had happened, but made sure it did not happen again—another of those immense womb-spasms would surely start her labour. Yet at a deeper level of fantasy he did not quite believe that anything so uncouth as childbirth would ever arrive to rupture the slow harmony of their life.

— * —

But a fortnight later a noise of whimpering woke him up in the small hours. He turned on his bedside light. She was asleep, fist to her mouth. He waited, watching the clock. Seven minutes passed, then she whimpered again, clenching her fist, and hunched her back in a spasm. Half waking, she stared at him with blank fear, then, as she guessed what was happening, with frightened dependent trust.

It was the look that had bound him to her all these months. He wanted to lay his head beside hers and soothe her back to sleep. But they had been caught up with; their idyll was over.

'It's started,' he said briskly, and got up to take her to hospital.

People kept intruding all night—midwife; nurses; auxiliaries. Tim wanted to order them all out. It was obscene that they should see his wife propped upright on pillows, panting and half naked—her nightdress covered only her breasts and shoulders, because she kept flinging it up to cool off.

At first she still turned towards him with that look of appeal. But by morning she had stopped being completely with him. She gazed through him, beyond, present only to herself. Midwife, nurses, doctor passed in and out, attending her, and she smiled imper-sonally, then returned to her lair, grunting, her mouth pulled back across her teeth in what looked like a repressed scream, though she assured him it was only effort. 'I'll yell if I want to,' she said. He believed her. This concentrated self-willed creature would stop at nothing. She was a Maenad, not his Elinor. He wanted her to let him take care of her. But she was fighting every step of the way—that stare was a frenzy of control.

He got himself through it all by fixing his mind firmly on what she needed. She was hot, so he kept sponging her down; thirsty, so he let her sip through a straw. He rubbed the small of her back, hauled her up on the pillows, gave her his hand to grip.

Around noon she got him to help her squat on her heels. She looked like a frog. With her grunts she almost sounded like one. He avoided looking at her directly. When he had to, he disarticulated her into a set of bodily parts which needed servicing, and made believe they were not her at all. He was calm and efficient, over deep panic; he wanted to utter the screams she refused to—though by

150

now she was moaning, the maenad mask gone and her face given over to pain, eyes squeezed shut, mouth gaping for breath. With horror he saw that it was how she looked when she came. He thought he would never desire her again if he retained any association between this stout, heaving, intent animal and his Elinor.

'The head's descending,' the midwife told him—'Look!'

He glanced obediently between Elinor's legs, but saw nothing, only a gaping blackness inches across—her cunt. It was a picture that must be disjunct from his idea of her; obliterated. That dark palpitating gap could not be the same neat red infolding that pulled tight round his cock when they made love.

'Look!' the midwife said again. He knew better now. To be polite he cast his gaze in the right direction, but made everything a red-dark blur by unfocussing his eyes so hard they almost crossed.

'It's coming,' she cried. 'One more push, Mrs Benton.'

He jumped up and stood behind Elinor, sponging her sweaty forehead and murmuring reassuringly, 'Nearly there, nearly there...' He was staring at the wall. He would have shut his eyes altogether, but that the midwife might notice.

'A boy!'

He could look now. In a daze he watched the midwife start the baby breathing, clean him and hand him to Elinor.

After a few moments' blind snuffling, the baby latched onto Elinor's breast. She stared down at him, then up at Tim, said, 'It's *real*;' and to his amazement giggled.

The third stage took another quarter of an hour. The baby fell asleep, and the midwife put him in his perspex cot. Tim held Elinor's hand. The afterbirth came out. She shut her eyes, forced them open, blinked twice, and fell sound asleep in the gory bed.

'I'll leave you together a while,' the midwife whispered. 'Then somebody will come and give her a nice bath.'

He was alone with his wife and his son. His family. He sat watching Elinor sleep, and now and then got up to look at Christopher. He felt tied in to the universe, infinitely strong. He had helped her; they could depend on him.

151

People came and went, the bed was changed and she was bathed. She hardly stirred. He was alone with her, she was restored to him. The baby woke and wailed. A nurse stopped at the door, told Tim to wake her up, and, when he hesitated, came and prodded her shoulder. 'Mrs Benton, Mrs Benton—your baby.'

Elinor struggled out of sleep, fed him, handed him to Tim, yawned, and fell asleep again. The baby was sound asleep in his hands. He laid him in his cot and returned to his vigil—Joseph in a painting of the holy family: a shelterer.

Eventually he got bored. Nearly concert time. It was too late for him to ring up and say he could play after all—the substitute would already be on her way to the Barbican. But he might go and listen from the wings. He gave the sister an emergency number and went out into the cool air.

When he got back, Elinor was making her way with gusto through an enormous meal of stew and mash, blancmange and Bird's custard. 'My second,' she said happily; 'I'm ravenous. No nausea—I feel so *alive*. Food makes *such* a difference. Have you been ringing people?'

'No, I was backstage at the concert.'

'Funny Tim. You'd better start, though, or they'll be in bed. Our parents, Maggie, Rose, Sheila and Thoby, Chris—I can't remember who else: you've got the list.'

He took it out of his pocket and stood at the foot of the bed watching her eat. The bounce was back in her, he had lost her.

She held out her hand to him. Her face was tired but gleaming with energy. For the first time in months he felt stirrings of desire for her; but he wanted to cry. He gave her hand a cursory squeeze and fled.

Chapter 20

'I'd *never* nickname a child,' Elinor had said—but Christopher was an impossibly formal name for a tiny baby. She called him Kit, and so did the nurses and all her visitors. Tim tried to stop them, but it was hopeless. His son was Kit to everyone but him.

Maggie breezed in to the hospital for about two minutes in a froth of roses and gypsophila and exclamations of, 'Wonderful, so clever of you, and how's the little nipper, what's his name, wish I could stay longer, got to run.' She barely glanced at Kit.

A week later she came to Ockendon Road with another vast bouquet. Kit was at the breast. She kissed Elinor lightly, didn't look at Kit at all, and busied herself filling vases and chattering about work as if he didn't exist. When Elinor's shirt was safely fastened she gave him one quick look, then resumed her airy monologue. She didn't stay long.

Sheila and Thoby came to call with the boys, bringing a natty green jumpsuit for Kit. Euan thought it was a silly present; so Sheila brought them back one rainy Saturday with something they'd chosen themselves—a big pink rattle.

Euan rattled it at Kit, still wrapped up. 'Guess.'

'He can't, he's too young,' Sheila said. 'Better unwrap it for him.'

Fergus grabbed it; Euan grabbed it back. 'No, me.'

'Euan, you untie the ribbon, Fergus, you do the paper.'

They got it undone somehow, and shook it in Kit's face.

'Rattow, rattow.'

'Tow, tow.'

Kit blinked and went back to sleep. The boys got bored and went off to slug it out for possession of the ribbon—Fergus was a born slugger, and Euan had become one in self-defence.

'Pity about the weather,' Elinor said; 'we could have been in the garden—though it's pure jungle.'

'My over-sixties hate rainy summers,' Sheila said. 'We had a coach trip yesterday in the rain, one of my groups, and they were so depressed—one lady said, "Every bad summer, I'm afraid I won't live to see another good one." But then the sun came out, and we all had fun.'

A coachload of old people wasn't Elinor's idea of fun. 'I've always wondered,' she said: 'how did you get into working with old people?' Oh dear—when she asked something like that once, ages ago, it had made Sheila tense.

The meaning behind Elinor's question was the same as last time—'Tell me about yourself'—but the question itself was different: to Sheila, crucially different. You couldn't get through life without answering questions about the past, and she had evolved standard answers to the commonest ones, such as, 'Why did you give up the cello?' 'What was the Menuhin School like?' and, 'How did you end up working with old people?' The cello question always touched a nerve, but the old people one was easy: it was about them, not her.

'I found out I enjoyed it when I was still at school—there was an Age Concern thing: you played for people, painted their walls, listened to them. One old lady wanted me to play bezique and write fan letters to cricketers—who were sweet; they always answered. Then when I left the School I got a job in a home for retired China missionaries—English old ladies in twinsets, but they'd spent their whole lives in China. You'd tiptoe up the stairs and they'd be rabbiting on in Chinese; but they were embarrassed if you caught them at it.' She smiled, remembering. 'There was one woman, Mrs Wainwright—'

Fergus and Euan landed on her, curled up one in her lap, one in the crook of her arm, and went to sleep.

'Mrs Wainwright?'

'She wanted to die—she'd say, "If only I could be taken." But I loved sitting with her, she was peaceful. She'd known Gladys Aylward in China—did you ever see the film about her?'

154

'Oh, *The Inn of the Sixth Happiness*. Pure schmaltz, but very touching—Robert Donat's last film before he died. Remember when he says, "We shall not be seeing one another again, I think"? Even thinking about it makes me cry. As you can see'—Elinor wiped her eyes. 'So. What then?'

'A bit of this, a bit of that'—bad jobs, false starts, unhappy affairs, a breakdown. Not a time she ever talked about. 'Um, I did some drug outreach work, and an adult literacy programme, then got a job with a trust for old people in Bayswater, and realised it was what I wanted to do for good.'

The best time in her life. Seven hundred and eighty people in her patch, and in less than a year she had known them all, and the whole patch: shopkeepers, roadsweepers, cops, men who mended canals. Jumping out of bed in the morning eager to get to work. Using her charm, all the tricks her Da had taught her, for something worthwhile for a change. Finding she could disappear into the work. She'd just met Thoby—anything seemed possible.

'And then?' It was a bit like extracting personal information from Tim: just as you thought the pump was well primed, it dried up again.

'Then I moved to the Falcon—more scope.'

And then, then, she had opened her mouth and told Thoby: 'My Da, he, I, he was a, what they call a, child abuser.'

'You mean—you? He abused *you*? You mean brutality or—?' Or.

She'd left the room, the flat, before he could say the word. But the thing was said. Wishing it unsaid, wishing that giggling larking innocence back, that false innocence. A bus shelter, a faded Rape Crisis sticker. Help me. But it wasn't rape. Creeping back at last, the flat empty, a note, 'Out looking for you, please stay.' Taking the bedroom light bulb out so he couldn't come in and turn it on; pulling the duvet over her head; not letting him pull it off; thrashing furiously when he tried to hug the whole lump.

Wishing the thing unsaid.

The recoil of remembrance—all roads led there. What people did when they talked was tell secrets, and she couldn't tell hers.

155

She shifted Fergus gently from her lap to the sofa, hoping he would wake up and distract Nell from the pursuit. He didn't, but the doorbell rang. Rose Quinlan—good. All three children woke up at once—pandemonium. Perfect.

Rose came almost every day with the latest news: what Mrs Ekins had said when the locum called her an old trout; the take for each show; the distributor who wouldn't rent *La Chambre Verte* for less than a week—'And it's not as if it'll get big houses, though it should.' She was a bit standoffish with Kit, though she brought him a red jumpsuit and a fish mobile for his pram, and sometimes held him for a bit. 'Babies aren't my thing,' she explained cheerfully.

That was a surprise—Rose was such a cuddly and affectionate person. Secretly, Elinor was a little cross; she wanted Rose to dote on her beautiful baby, whom she wore on her heart, her miniature image of Tim...

Who seemed suddenly much busier—was he accepting every request the fixers threw at him?—and less...less...

She couldn't focus the thought—or any other. 'My mind's the texture of mush,' she grumbled one day to Rose. 'Maybe it's postnatal depression starting.'

'Nah—boredom. A few visitors, when you're used to seeing hundreds of people a day at work—it's sensory deprivation, right? Come back—do. We all miss you.' What Rose meant was, *I* miss you. She loved Nell with all her heart.

'I'll try.'

Elinor pushed the pram down to the cinema and put in an hour. The next day, two; the next, three. The more she did, the better she felt—exhausted, but alive. She told Helen she was ready for her and went back full time.

With Rose's help—Rose was a peach. If she wasn't crazy about babies, it didn't show. She did her own job and as much of Elinor's as Elinor let her, and she helped with Kit whenever Helen was out. She even changed his nappies, which was more than Elinor had ever done for another woman.

Babies weren't to Margaret the projectionist's taste at all; she ignored Kit pointedly. 'As if he's a decoration in very bad taste,' Rose commented.

'Or a social disease.'

The rest of the staff petted him incessantly, especially Mrs Ekins, who kept Elinor supplied with items from a comprehensive fund of misinformation. 'He'll catch cold, the way you dress him. He needs a jumper and cap, and little bootees, and blankets. You needn't laugh, dear. There's draughts even in June.' 'A bit dry, aren't they?'—peering avidly into the nappy Elinor was removing. 'It's the way you feed him, dear; bottle milk's not so binding.' 'You won't burp him patting like that. Do more of a thump, like.' For once she was right; Elinor had been afraid of hurting him.

There was no love lost between Mrs Ekins and Helen. 'Babies want to sleep on their tummies,' Mrs Ekins said. 'He'll smother one of these days if she keeps laying him on his back.' As soon as Helen left the office she would come in and turn him over, muttering, 'He'll catch his death, cot death, that's how they catch it.'

'Interfering old cow,' Helen would mutter when she came back, and turn him over again.

Helen was good with Kit. 'He's a lovely baby,' she said. 'So easy.' Every afternoon between feeds she wheeled him off for a long stroll, or sat with him in Coram's Fields: 'Talking to the other mothers,' she once unselfconsciously said—giving Elinor a pang of furious jealousy. But at the cinema she didn't know how to keep herself amused, and hung around talking about auras and experiencing your body.

'God, what a drag,' Rose said. 'She's so *heavy*.'

'Yeah—she's supposed to be giving me time to work, and instead she ties us both up. I keep meaning to say something, but...'

'Me too.'

'Funny—it's easy enough telling the ushers to go away and let us work.'

'That's different,' said Rose. 'With Helen we're on a guilt trip because she's doing domestic work while we hog the cool jobs.'

'Nice of you to say "we"—it's me she's slaving for.'

157

'Oh—it's me that told you about her—I feel, like, responsible.'

Maggie stopped by one day after work to say hello. She ignored Kit, but just touched his cheek on her way out.

A week later she came again. Elinor, alone with Kit in the office, said, 'Oh good—could you just stay while I run down to the loo?'

When she got back, Maggie was hanging over the cot. 'He's a dead ringer for Tim—I don't see you at all,' she said.

'I know.' Elinor gazed down at Kit's small full mouth, heavy brow and deep-set round eyes. Sometimes she shivered, hoping he hadn't inherited Tim's melancholy along with those Scott features. 'It's the hands and feet that get me. I thought they'd be nondescript in babies, like their noses; but Kit's are *exactly* like Tim's, right down to his toes.' She wiggled them.

'I don't have your intimate acquaintance with Tim's toes,' Maggie said sharply, moving away from the cot.

On her next visit she said, 'Mind if I pick him up?'

'Go ahead.'

She gathered him up comfortably. 'Goo,' she said. 'Googly-goo.'

Kit squeaked with pleasure and smiled his enchanting brand-new smile—Tim's smile, though Tim dispensed it sparingly, as if the supply might run out. Maggie froze. Then tension flowed out of her body and she smiled back with a flirtatious tenderness Elinor had never seen.

After that she couldn't keep away. She came every two or three days, sometimes every other day. 'My fairy godson,' she called Kit. She talked to him, dandled him, played with him, took him for walks, or just watched him. 'This is how women feel who snatch babies from prams,' she said. She no longer looked away when Elinor fed him. 'If you disappeared, I'd have milk for him. Women sometimes can.'

No doubt. Elinor was sometimes narked by Maggie's utter engrossment in Kit. She herself wasn't like that—the only time she lost herself so completely was making love to Tim. She was besotted with Kit, but not so rapt that she forgot the adult world, though feeding him she came close: his warm detailed body melting against her, his mouth gripping her nipple, his gaze meeting hers almost combatively. She didn't smile; she looked straight back. She loved him with as much ferocity as tenderness; she had to remind herself not to hug him too hard.

She could feel momentarily jealous of Helen, but not of Maggie's far more serious passion for Kit. 'Do it, do it on your own,' she wanted to cry. 'You want it so much—do it.' But there was no use.

Chapter 21

Somewhere between the hospital and home Tim's calm certainty of fatherhood had vanished. What replaced it was fear—and shame: what kind of man was afraid of a baby? It was the way Christopher looked up at him—looked up without blinking, right into him; then started to wriggle and fret and mewl; and finally howled. For food, said Elinor, but Tim knew better. Christopher read him instinctively, like an animal smelling fear: he saw *through* him.

He was determined not to leave all the work to her, even so. They shared housework; they should share childcare too. He worked out what he should do and doggedly did it. He changed and bathed Kit, fetched him for feeds and put him down again, carried his pram up and down the front steps, shopped for disposable nappies, and did the laundry—all of it: collecting it, loading the washer and dryer, putting it back in place. But by no effort of will could he return Elinor's hugs and loving smiles, or even let her go on holding his hand when she reached for it. It had been so easy while she was pregnant—but she had needed him then: now she only wanted him, which was not the same. And she would see his fright if he let her get that close.

As his tenderness diminished, the desire that had rekindled while he watched her devour the hospital blancmange grew into a fever as hot as the unsatisfied lusts of adolescence. Almost every night, while she lay in bed giving Christopher his midnight feed, he went into the bathroom and masturbated, guiltily, as if committing adultery.

But for some time he made no overtures, even after she stopped feeling sore from the birth. For one thing, she was wearing sanitary pads to catch post-partum discharge, and he was slightly queasy

160

about the discharge, and very queasy about the pads; for another, he had no idea whether she would want him so soon.

Furtively he read what her books on pregnancy said about sex after childbirth. Okay after six weeks said one; after three, said the next. A month or so, said a third. Some women, all the books said, lost interest in sex while breast-feeding.

He waited till Elinor stopped needing to wear pads; then a little longer, and a little longer, patiently-impatiently. He was waiting for her to give a signal. Then one night he thought: Maybe she's waiting for *me*? After the midnight feed he changed Christopher, put him down in his cot in the next room, turned out the hall light, groped his way back to bed in the dark, and found Elinor lying as he had left her, curled on her side, facing away from him. Was she awake? Sliding close, he brushed his fingertips tentatively along her hip.

She woke at his touch, but only just—if Kit was an easy baby, how did women survive demanding ones? But Tim had been so good when she was pregnant—never a murmur of sexual frustration; and she was only sleepy, not, as then, radically incapable of response. I'll try, she thought, and gave a slight welcoming stir.

Hesitantly, then more confidently, he drew her nightgown up and in a remembered ritual skimmed his hand across her hip, belly and pubic hair, slid his middle finger onto her clitoris; further down to wet it; back. Her sharp indrawn breath, her body pivoting on his finger, her long exhalation—it was all so familiar. She tried to turn towards him, but he kept her the way she was, communing with her body in luxurious silence, postponing for a little the complications of mutuality.

Diaphragm, Elinor thought muzzily. Got to get it. She didn't feel one bit like getting up.

It wouldn't fit anyhow; you changed size after childbirth. The clinic had said they'd fit a new one at her six-week checkup—well, she couldn't wait till then.

Wasn't ovulation suppressed while you were breast-feeding? The longer Tim went on uninsistently caressing her, the more she thought so. Trust to luck and old wives' tales?

161

She reached back and found his cock; and with it big in her hand felt happy and at rights with the world. It gave a little jump against her palm; another. She wanted it in her. Now—no more preliminaries; straight in all at once. She crooked a finger to her cunt, found she was wet enough, shifted closer, slid him into position; and felt for the first time in nearly a year the astonishment of being entered.

He moved very gently in her, not going deep, stirring just in the rim of her cunt till it was like a molten pool. His hand rested on her hip, holding them together. He was almost still; she was entirely still. His cock stirred, stirred, with the intimacy of eyes meeting. Stillness; and all the time gentle constant motion.

Eventually he moved his hand to her clitoris and rubbed it in tiny figures of eight, till with a sharp sigh she shuddered round his finger and arched away. The absolute novelty and utter familiarity of making love had wrought him to such a pitch that her contractions took him to the brink, and over, only seconds after her. Neither of them had spoken a word.

All through May, insatiably, they made love almost every night, no matter how tired they were, in the dark, wordlessly, as if it were a secret they were keeping from each other and themselves. Several times a day she was stunned by desire, remembering that vehement quiver reverberating in the soft flesh of her cunt, and wanted it again, nothing but that.

At night she fed Kit with only the hall light on, lying on her side in the shadows, half asleep. Tim, as he sat half up in bed, trying to stay awake until it was time to change him and put him down, could hear his small smacking noises and see him burrow into her breast. By day the sight left him cold—very cold—frozen. In the middle of the night his inhibitions were suspended. Sometimes, instead of waiting till Kit was through, he let his fingers stray across her flank to her cunt. Unless she was nearly asleep, she opened to his hand; and he came in from behind and fucked her quietly, careful not to disturb the baby, in a burning trance.

She would lie still, half awake, half asleep, looking at Kit, excited and disconcerted by his interested, contented eyes meeting hers. He couldn't know what was happening, yet she couldn't escape the

162

illusion that he did; virtually below consciousness there hovered a vague potent fantasy that both Tim and Kit were making love to her.

It was so quiet, so shadowy, so still: the baby's eyes meeting hers; his mouth sucking vigorously, vibrating a nerve somewhere behind her navel; and Tim burning in her, slowly, the flat of his finger resting on her clitoris; a stillness almost like peace, but with all the time at the centre that burning penetration, and his finger's liquid glide; until finally she buried her head in the pillow so that her grimace wouldn't frighten Kit.

The health visitor couldn't find much fault with Elinor's arrangements for Kit at the Cromer, but was uneasy about the whole setup: a baby in an office; an unqualified mother's help; and films. She popped in far oftener than the statutory minimum—trying to catch them out, Elinor suspected.

'Babies take everything in,' she fussed one day in July. 'All the sex and violence on the screen these days, I don't get to the cinema much, but it comes up on the telly soon enough, doesn't it, and not just there, some mums, you wouldn't believe, the poor baby sleeping in the parents' room, and them'—deep whisper, deep flush—'doing *that*, right before its eyes. And there's films where people get cut up with'—shudder—'chain saws: all that screaming. Baby Christopher doesn't get to hear any of that, I hope?'

'Only his own,' Elinor said flippantly.

When she told Tim about the visit, he said, 'I hope you told her Christopher has his own room.'

She fancied he was asking another question as well. 'Don't worry, I didn't tell her that *we*...'

He frowned, embarrassed at the reminder. He had not asked that: why did she bring it up? Out of bed he was astonished at the things he did in it.

'Elinor,' Tim called up the stairs, 'Elinor, Christopher's hungry.'

She could hear Kit howling in the carrycot. 'I fed him twenty minutes ago,' she said, leaning over the banister. 'His nappy okay?'

'I checked.'

163

'Teething pains, then—try picking him up,' she suggested.

'No, best to leave him, he'll soon stop.'

'Not when he sounds like that.' But she could see Tim's mouth set stubbornly; she'd have to go down herself.

'You shouldn't give in, he'll be utterly spoiled,' he said as she gathered Kit up.

'His gums hurt, he needs comforting.' Spoil a baby of five months—ridiculous. 'There there, love—there there.'

Tim was so good about sharing the humdrum drudgery of childcare; it was wonderful not having to wring fair shares out of him. But he was stiff with Kit—formal, if you could be formal with a baby, handling him with a deft, businesslike minimum of physical contact, like a starchy nurse: he didn't talk to him, smile at him, tickle him, hug him, play with him.

Yet twice recently she had come into the drawing room and found him halfway between Kit's carrycot and the door—looking embarrassed, as if he hadn't managed to...escape in time?

Maybe breast-feeding made him feel excluded. The thought helped reconcile her to weaning Kit in time for the crèche. So did the prospect of getting more sleep—Tim had promised to do the four a.m. feed. But she hated to loose that sensual bond with her baby.

Maggie didn't think her fairy godson should be weaned yet, far less sent to a crèche. Finding him furiously pushing aside a bottle one day, she picked him up and murmured, 'Him's miserable, yes, wants Mummy, not a nasty bottle.'

Infuriating. 'Most women wean their babies by six months,' Elinor protested.

'That doesn't mean it's right.'

'But it's getting harder having him here. I'm always on the telephone to distributors, and you can't do business with a baby squalling in the background. Rose helps all she can, but I can't go on letting her do more than her share of the work.'

'So you'll shove him into that hellhole all day.'

'You recommended it, remember? And it's not all day, it's three hours in the afternoon, then two with me—'

'Then all evening alone.'

'Not alone. He'll be with Helen—and at home, not the hellhole—'

'But away from you. I sit at the DHSS reading reports on maternal deprivation, then come here and you're proposing—'

'Jesus Christ, Maggie, he'll be with me seventeen hours out of twenty-four—'

'Less eight for sleep.'

Eight hours' sleep with a baby? Only a woman without children could imagine *that*. Elinor was so annoyed she nearly said so.

Yet she did have doubts. Happiness came easily to her; for Tim it was a struggle. Through music, through her, he managed it some of the time, but it didn't come naturally. Kit was happy and outgoing—'Just like you,' Mavis said when she came to visit at the end of September—but he looked so exactly like Tim. Might weaning tip some inner balance? She would go on with a night feed for a month or two—but she wouldn't tell Maggie.

Kit started at the crèche without visible ill effect. He beamed at the crèche workers when Elinor dropped him there, at Elinor when she carried him off to the Cromer at five-thirty, and at Helen when she came for him at seven-thirty.

But Helen found Ockendon Road dull; she started lingering at the Cromer until eight—half past—quarter to nine. Hints were no good; after a few weeks Elinor had to say, 'You're supposed to take him straight home, you know.'

Helen flushed, said, 'Well—I can tell I'm not wanted round here'—and quit in a peevish flounce. It was a Friday; Rose was off. Elinor let out the next house with Kit on her hip, then rang round frantically for extra ushers.

'I've got cover for the front of house for a few days,' she told Rose the next day, 'but it's stopgap all the way till I find someone for Kit. I'll have to advertise. It'll take *weeks*—and him here all evening in the meantime, just when he's got used to going home.'

'One consolation—we won't have to listen to her nattering on about biorhythms,' said Rose.

'Did she tell you she always sleeps with earplugs in her ears? She likes to hear her blood circulating.'

'Wow, that's *weird*—halfway to Dracula. Probably just as well she's split. You'd *wonder*, wouldn't you—about Kit. Look, I've got you into enough trouble already, recommending her; but why not—'

'No, you only said she was there if I was interested, and I was, and looked no further. It's *my*—'

'Then what I was thinking—you could put up a notice in the foyer, same as we do for ushers.'

'What a good idea. Oh Rose, thank you—for everything. I'm such a nuisance—'

Rose went pink with pleasure and said vigorously, 'Nonsense. It's fun learning about babies. They used to scare me stiff—I hardly even dared hold Kit at first. But now I've had a chance to watch you—and Draculette, for that matter: pick up tips from the pros, sort of thing. I'd never been around a baby before. I bet that never happened till this century—it's the death of the extended family, and advanced capitalism alienating the basic processes of existence, right? I'd like a baby myself, actually—I've begun a propaganda war on Marcus.'

'Oh great. Is he against it?'

'Ambivalent, on account of Buffy.'

'But...'

'Yeah, Down's isn't hereditary, I've sussed it out. But Marcus is still twitchy. He'll come round, though, you wait and see.'

Elinor stuck up a sign: 'Part-time mother's helps needed, evenings. Character references required.' Bright-eyed students of both sexes thronged to her office, and within the day she had two helpers— Lindsay and Roz, both UCL graduate students. Elinor liked them; Kit liked them; Tim liked them: problem solved.

Chapter 22

Thoby sang out, 'Hullo, sorry I'm late,' dropped his briefcase and hung his dripping mac beside Sheila's wet one. The double pushchair was folded against the wall; beneath it were patches of wet.

The hall light was on, and the nightlight in the boys' room; otherwise the flat was dark. Thoby headed for the kitchen and a drink. He took a quick look at his sleeping sons on the way, then glanced into his and Sheila's room, expecting to find her asleep.

She wasn't there. He flipped on the light, looked round, called out, 'Sheila?' Kitchen, bathroom, sitting room, boys' room. She wouldn't leave them alone. Bedroom again, checking behind the door in case she'd...fainted?

Bathroom again. Towels wet—she'd bathed the children. Kitchen: bowls in the drying-up rack. Sitting room. Behind the door, behind the sofa—

Straightening up, he caught a gleam at the far end of the room. She was under the table, watching him, with her knees pulled up to her chest.

Hiding in the coalshed. Oh God, she hadn't done *that* before. How had her father got her out—wheedling, threats, main force? She'd never said—how could he avoid replicating it?

Get in there with her. Her Da was a dandy, he wouldn't have.

He crawled in beside her, careful not to touch. It was a long table, there was room.

'What's wrong?' he said. 'What's happened?'

Nothing. He waited—what else could he do? He wanted to cry.

She'd been so *happy* when they were first together—delighted with everything: her work; meeting Tim and Alan and starting the quartet; lightning raids on the countryside to search out drovers'

167

roads and cruck-truss barns; making love; living together. Her giggles, as if they were playing at life.

Then telling him about her father, and the first silence.

It had ended, but things hadn't gone back to the way they'd been before. She didn't run giggling across the room wrapped in a towel any more and pounce on him, shaking her damp black hair. Lovemaking became fraught—it had hardly happened at all for a while. Then came a stage when she wanted to make him come, but refused to come herself; or else came but didn't want him to.

She had developed a sort of agoraphobia—a dislike of open-endedness. She could go to work, concerts, movies, the quartet—things with a structure; things that were planned ahead—but not for an impromptu walk. They took no more impulsive excursions—holidays had to be prepared in advance. Even then she would use delaying tactics to stay safe in their hotel room. Washing her hair. Naps. Checking something in Pevsner. When they did get going, she walked with her head down to avoid seeing things.

Maidie cured that, at least, by dragging her off alone on visits—once to Ezra and Bet, which was fun, and twice to Paris, where with Sheila in breathless tow she jumped in and out of taxis and rampaged all over the city, rang museum directors and arranged to rummage in their storage, and dropped in on ambassadors and artists and dissected them afterwards with catty shrewdness over tea at the Crillon or dinner at a cous-cous joint, or vice versa. Sheila had only gone with her because you no more said no to Maidie than to a typhoon; but Paris in that forceful company was—wonderful.

Thoby could never have dragged her from pillar to post without regard for her—possibly even Maidie had thought of it as kill or cure. But it worked: Sheila had got back a good deal of her pleasure in the world; and their sexual relation had slowly returned to something like normal.

Then pregnancy, and retreat. Euan's birth, a step forward, then a slow drift back; and the same again with Fergus. There were minor setbacks as well, when Sheila heard about sexual-abuse cases at work, or saw a TV programme on incest, or when Nell mentioned that a friend of hers might write a book about it: 'Trust Chris to pick up the latest thing.'

168

But when he had an affair a year ago, she had shrugged it off. His heart had been in his mouth when he told her, not knowing what would happen, but owing her the truth they'd promised each other when they began.

'Are you going to leave?' she'd asked.

'No, no—it's you I love'—though she hadn't asked that.

She had nodded and asked nothing more. How could *anyone* say nothing, ask nothing, after such a revelation? She hadn't withdrawn, either, she was her normal self, if anything more cheerful than usual.

'Aren't you upset?' he had asked, aware of sounding, and feeling, put out.

'Why should I be? You're here, that's what counts—sex isn't that important.'

Not important—oh Sheila, Sheila, he had thought: the harm your father did, there's no end to it.

Right now he was getting cold and stiff. 'What's wrong, Sheila?' he ventured.

No sound, but she looked at him. Communication.

'Something happen at work?'

Lucky her to be able to nod—the table was pressing on his head.

Euan started to cry. Sheila was up and with him while Thoby was still uncricking his neck. Fergus started screeching too. Thoby came and picked him up, and together they soothed their children back to sleep—a normal evening, except that she kept her head bent and wouldn't meet his eyes. Her hair was greying in thick streaks all over now, not just at the sides, but it made her look no older—younger, if anything.

In bed, in the dark, way over on her own side as always, she finally yielded to his questions. 'The Falcon—they—we...A therapy group for incest survivors...and they think I've done so well with Linchpin...they want...want me to run it.'

'Oh my love—and you can't just say no without saying why, is that it? Can't you tell them you're not qualified?'

'I *did*, but they said they'll send me on a—a counselling course. The kind where you've got to *be* counselled too...and...'

169

'Talk about things?' he guessed. 'Would that be so bad?' These recurrent crises weren't good for her: after each she seemed a shade more withdrawn. He was sceptical about therapy—but what if it made a difference?

A long silence; then she whispered, 'I *couldn't*.'

'Oh my love.'

He reached for her; she went stiff. When would he learn? Remember why she does it, he told himself, as if he didn't know already. But it always hurt. He kept trying to change himself, to want less; he knew he must go on being patient and steadfast if they were ever to have the passionate love he hungered for. But their physical and emotional distance tormented him.

'You awake?' he said in a while. 'I've got an idea. Say you're not the right person; say an incest survivors' group should be run by an incest survivor.'

'But I *am* an...Oh. How clever. Oh Thoby.'

Her hand came looking for his face. He caught her fingers and kissed them; she didn't pull them away.

One December morning when Elinor went to the front door and bent down for the milk, she noticed that her waistband was tight. Must be premenstrual bloating, she thought. She had been expecting her periods back ever since she'd begun tailing off Kit's night feed. Funny, though, she'd never used to swell up this much before her periods.

That afternoon at work, bending over the filing cabinet, she felt like a stuffed sausage and undid the button of her waistband, the way she'd often done when she was—

She dropped the papers, grabbed the telephone and rang her GP.

'So much for being in touch with your body,' she told Tim that night. 'Sixteen weeks pregnant, and I didn't have a clue. I should have guessed, after not using my diaphragm half the time all summer. But after last time I never thought I *could* be pregnant without being sick.'

'You're really not queasy at all?'

'Nope, and she says I won't be, now I've got this far. Isn't that terrific? And, well, I think I'm pretty...pleased—about being

170

pregnant, I mean. If you are, that is,' she added tentatively. She was actually very happy about it; but if he wasn't...

Tim was paying full attention to his meal. Elinor picked up her fork, determined not to say another word until he did.

He went on eating. When her plate was clear, he said, 'More?'

It was impossible to outlast his silences. 'Why don't you *say* something?' she burst out.

Tim looked up in surprise. 'Like what?'

'Like—like—Are you glad?'

'That doesn't need saying.' Of course he was glad, just as he was happy at the *idea* of Christopher: my child, my son. She would need him again, they would find their way back to that idyllic time before Christopher's birth.

'I'm tired of things that don't need saying,' she said crossly.

He didn't reply.

'How will I *cope* with two?' she cried. 'And we were going to speak to the Wellesfords about switching to five films a day—we'll have to put it off *again*!'

Tenderness welled up in him; he briefly covered her hand. 'Start taking it easy right away. You'll have to anyhow, in a few months. Why not stop till Christopher's five or so—be here to give them both their supper, read them bedtime stories—'

'Are you *crazy*? Rose would have to get someone else—I'd never get another screen.'

'I don't mean stop altogether'—he retreated before her anger. 'Work part time, in the afternoons—you say that's when the real work is. Otherwise you won't have enough time for two children. Already Christopher—'

'*I'm* not the one who neglects him. I'm with him all morning, and again after the crèche—and when I *am* with him, he gets lots of attention. When you're with him, you don't even notice him.'

'Babies need their mothers, not their fathers. Let's go up and get some sleep. You're overwrought—you've been looking for trouble ever since we started this.'

Elinor's mouth gaped open. Words tumbled through her mind, but she was dumb with rage. Overwrought—babies need—

But—and—what—how—

171

Looking for trouble—but when we started this I was *happy*.

Why were they quarrelling now of all times? What could she say that wouldn't just prove she was overwrought? She swallowed a furious sob.

He interpreted her paralysed expression as a plea, and put his arm round her to lead her upstairs. He had got her back.

Tim was impossibly busy in the fortnight before Christmas; Elinor hardly saw him except late at night, when he fell into bed and went instantly to sleep. He needed it—he was doing Kit's night feeds, as he had promised, and had a hard time getting back to sleep afterwards. She hoped he at least enjoyed sitting in the half dark with the feeding baby in his arms—but one night she looked in on her way to the loo, and found that he fed Kit in his cot.

She herself was in something of a daze—happy, but stunned. Being plunged willy-nilly into the middle of pregnancy was like coming into a movie three reels late. Her mind was full of the future she had shaped for herself without knowing it.

Then the extraordinary began to seem ordinary. Life came back into focus, and one day she noticed that something was missing. They hadn't made love for ages: since she'd learned she was pregnant, in fact.

Golly, that was *ages*. Where had she been? Well, she was back now.

Let's make love, she thought that night on the way to bed. But Tim turned the light straight out and was asleep in a minute: there was no answer when she whispered, 'Tim?'

Tomorrow morning, then.

But he was up before she was. Oh well—tonight.

It had better be: tomorrow was Harrogate—and no sex in case the Scotts overheard.

But again he turned out the light, rolled over to his side of the bed, and didn't respond to her whisper, or to her fingertips brushing his back.

Why hadn't she said something while he was brushing his teeth or getting undressed or climbing into bed?

172

Because she wanted Tim to make the first move. He'd done so ever since the time after Kit's birth, when she was so tired, and she liked it that way. It satisfied her embarrassing passivity, her wish to do what Tim wanted, follow his lead—and by now it was a habit, and hard to break.

Besides, he'd gone along with it all these months—why had he suddenly changed? Not because he was tired—that had never stopped him before.

In the morning he was again up first. Funny—she was usually faster off the mark.

Was he by any chance *avoiding* making love? Why? Because she was pregnant? But they'd made love when she was pregnant with Kit, the one time she'd felt like it...

Ah. He was holding off because he assumed she'd lost all interest, same as in her first pregnancy, all but that one time.

So tell him—the night we get back. Promise.

She didn't. Come on, Tim, she thought—desire was nagging at her. But she lay in the dark unable to make a move, though she'd done it easily enough in the old days.

Tomorrow night—promise.

But by tomorrow he was coughing with a cold. He moved into the spare room so as not to keep her awake—and stayed there most of January, hacking painfully: she could hear him through the wall.

Then one night she didn't. 'Come back,' she said the next night, and he looked touchingly pleased.

'I've missed you,' she said in bed, putting her head on his shoulder. Tim didn't say anything, or stir, but her courage was up, and in a strangulated voice she went on: 'I, it's different this time...I mean, I'd like to, um, make love—if you would.'

He was silent for a long moment. 'Oh...I thought...'

'Not if you don't—'

'No, I just...' He *had* thought she wouldn't be interested, but it wasn't just that. He had been wrong in thinking he had got her back: she was different this time: energetic, exuberant, giving no purchase to his desire to help and protect her. He did not like to admit to himself that he was disappointed—that was too much like

173

wanting her to be sick. But he was still hoping that she would come to need him, depend on him, as in her first pregnancy, so that he could enfold and cherish her again; and he had an unreasoned feeling that abstinence had somehow been a precondition of their closeness last time—a payment exacted by the gods.

But he could not admit to believing...half-believing...in propitiatory magic. Keeping disappointment out of his voice he said, 'If you're sure you want it yourself—not just for me.'

'Oh, I'm sure. Feel.' Boldly she found his hand and put it on her cunt.

Flooded with desire, Tim hesitated no more. His fingers dipped, slid, stopped momentarily when she touched his cock; started again. Bliss.

But when she started to come on top of him, he impulsively held her back. Her belly was already round and hard—might he not hurt the baby if he entered her? And he had a dim sense that it would be profanity: going where he should not.

Elinor rolled away and lay stiffly in a silence that said as loud as words: I don't want to if *you* don't.

'I didn't mean—I worry...I thought...some other way?' he stammered.

She guessed. 'You won't dislodge it—babies are pretty indestructible.'

Was he grateful or appalled that she read him so easily? He could not say, 'But that's not how I feel'—it was too irrational.

'But if you feel that way, you'll worry anyhow. Okay.'

His hand glided back into place, her legs opened, her breath stopped, then rushed out as he slid down the bed; and she came at the first touch of his tongue—shooting up from underwater to bright sunlight and bursting the surface still sleek and part of the water.

But he pulled back when she tried to do the same to him, and folded her hand firmly round his cock.

Each time they made love it was the same: Tim brought her by hand, or went down on her, but never let her go down on him. Okay, she thought, if that's what you want...

174

It can't be, she decided eventually. I bet he thinks I'll be sick if he comes in my mouth while I'm pregnant. I won't be—next time I'll tell him so. Promise.

But next time she let herself be led—and the next and next and next; and on through February and March and into April, half forgetting her resolution, half remembering it.

Chapter 23

Tim played in a *St Matthew Passion* on Good Friday; then they had four days free—to go north, of course, but not directly. 'We can't keep visiting my parents and never yours,' he'd said: 'It's not right.' Really, he was good. So their first night was to be in Guildford.

They stopped in Highgate on the way, to have lunch with Maidie and Lionel. Thoby and Sheila and their boys were there, of course; and another guest as well: a tiny old grande dame named Geraldine, with a waspish tongue and a limp. She had snapping round eyes in a small wrinkled face, with a scarlet mouth and thin black eyebrows painted in approximately the correct places. Everyone else was in casual clothes; Geraldine wore a brocade caftan.

'Why live in *Hackney*?' she asked Sheila. 'I'd be scared of being murdered in my bed.'

'Cheap housing,' said Thoby.

'It's not so bad, really,' said Sheila. 'People get the wrong idea.'

'Not entirely,' Thoby said. 'I've been mugged twice. Embarrassing. Makes you afraid of being alone on side streets with young males from the oppressed minorities. Principles fly to the winds.'

'And you *stay*?' said Geraldine. 'It can't be *that* cheap.'

Thoby caught his mother's warning look. 'Architecture, too. Spiffy houses.'

'Speaking of which...' Maidie turned the talk to warfare in the Highgate Preservation Society.

Afterwards she came into the kitchen, where the four of them were loading the dishwasher, and told Thoby, 'Sometimes I regret ever teaching you to tell the truth. Geraldine's already a bigot, and you just reinforce it.'

'Then why have her here?'

'Because she's a pathetic old woman who doesn't know what to do with herself,' she snapped, and stalked out.

'She doesn't look pathetic to me,' Elinor commented.

'Fallen glory. Career cut short.'

'Career?'

'Geraldine was a stripper till she got shot in the foot. All downhill after that. Still a beauty, mistress of two or three millionaires. Last one left her well heeled, but she misses the footlights. Sheila, remember the time Maidie was telling about painting Marie Rambert? Geraldine sniffed and said, "Marie Rambert, indeed. *I* knew Marie Rambert. Not her real name at all—she was nothing but a common Polish Jew." My grandmother was there—she's a Polish Jew. Appalled silence. Then Bubba said, "Yes, ballerinas took highfalutin names in those days—Margaret Hookham into Margot Fonteyn. A Shanghai girl. The English couldn't breed good dancers back then, had to import them." Which did for Geraldine; she'd only been a stripper because she wasn't good enough for ballet. Auditioned for Marie Rambert, in fact—didn't get in. As Bubba well knew.'

'Who shot her? And why?'

'Don't know, Nell. She's such a bore—never thought to ask.'

Elinor laughed. 'There are more miles between Highgate and Guildford than show on the map. Your family's got so many stories, you can be blasé about details. Mine's got about three, and they just replay them. There's the time my father pretended to hit me on the head with a hammer, and actually did, "Which explains a lot, ho ho." And there's the time my sister was sent for a white loaf and brought it back with all the inside gone. My mother asked who ate it. "I don't know," Marion said. "Mice?"—Yes, it's funny—once. But it's not in the same league as, "Geraldine was a stripper till she got shot in the foot." And you don't even know who did it!'

But their night with Mavis and Walter wasn't too bad—Kit gave them all something to talk about. He was beginning to talk himself, in a determined babble that contained only one distinct word—'No:' which meant no, and yes, and everything in between.

'It was your first word, too,' said Mavis, patting Kit's leg.

177

'Nelly Quite-Contrary, we called you,' said Walter, who had come home from work calling out, 'Where's my little fellow?' and swung him up to the ceiling, then cuddled and played with him until Kit grew tired, and was now rocking him asleep. Tim watched with a good-natured smile, but seemed a little out of things.

Elinor couldn't penetrate to Tim's feeling about the coming child. He'd said he was glad; and was—she knew the shades of his voice. But was there something else, something he had reservations about? She still lived in the afterglow of his tenderness during her first pregnancy. But it wasn't the same this time. He didn't hold her, kiss her, cherish her; he seemed...tired, as if his January cold had never quite gone away.

Oh but that tenderness couldn't just evaporate. If he seemed less affectionate, it must be because she, with her days fractured into dozens of arbitrary segments, was too distracted to notice his gestures.

The next day they were in Harrogate, listening to Mrs Scott reminisce about *her* children's infancy with a fondness that surprised Tim. He could not picture his barbed-wire mother—the very hairs on her head wiry and upright—writhing in misery because the books told her not to feed her babies oftener than every four hours, or even pick them up when they cried. 'I stuck it with the first two,' she said, 'but with Tim I kicked over the traces and fed him on demand.'

'Same as my mother,' Elinor said. 'She gave me the bottle every four hours, but couldn't bear it with my sister.'

'I fed mine myself,' said Mrs Scott complacently.

'Did the hospital try to stop you? They did Mavis.'

'I had mine here, on our bed upstairs. A good firm Heal's mattress: gives you something solid to bear down on.'

Tim swiftly latched his mind against a flash of his mother squatting in labour like Elinor. Just then Kit woke up with a hungry-sounding, 'No'. Tim gratefully went to get him up, and left the women to it.

In the morning they left Kit with Mrs Scott and went to Swarthgill for twenty-four hours. Elinor, full of ponderous energy, but enormous on the brink of her ninth month, soon found she didn't want to climb any real hills. They walked along the Roman road on the Chase instead. The last bit sloped up, and she was getting tired, so Tim got behind her and pushed.

'You realise I'll roll right back down if you let go?' she said after a few yards, and they dissolved in laughter.

That night he resisted her attempt to wriggle round in the saggy bed—no mean feat at her size—and go down on him; and she suddenly resolved: *Now*—and meant it—yet stopped on the brink of speech.

Shocked, a voice in her head said. He'll be shocked.

What a mad thought. But that voice from the shadowy irrational thickets of taboo spoke the truth of her hesitation—of all her sexual hesitations. If you said what you wanted, men thought you were unfeminine or immodest or insatiable. She'd known that all her life: it was in the air, affected everybody, came from everywhere and nowhere: movies, old wives' tales, tones of voice, atmospheres in rooms, postures, proverbs, expressions.

But other voices spoke in her inward ear. Pleasure was a great good, always under siege. Only one sexual prohibition made sense—you shouldn't force other people to do anything they didn't want. The rest were just weapons in the war of religion against human happiness.

Finally she simply took him in her mouth, and when he tried to resist said, 'No, come like this.'

'But—' stiffening himself against a vehement impulse to yield on the spot.

'I won't be sick.'

'Sure?' They had grown in the same shades, breathed the same air. Mad her thought might be, and yet be true: part of him was shocked.

'Sure. I *want* you to.'

Still he hesitated, against the grain of physical desire. Somewhere below the surface, his fear of making her sick hid something less admissible: a wish for a clear separation between women as mothers and as sexual beings. When he came under her fingers, there was at least a possibility that she might be...not indifferent; he

179

did not want that; but very slightly withheld from complete sexual immersion. If he came in her mouth—the mouth that formed words, within the head that thought—she would be accepting him not in any winking absence of mind, but with entire consciousness: declaring herself from head to foot, outside and in, a carnal being who in no corner of herself kept an altar sacred to an asexual maternity. Not that his own mother had ever bowed at that shrine. Her little high cries of sexual ecstasy had been as constant an early-morning noise as the cawing of rooks in the elm across the road. He wished Elinor had left him in ignorance.

Yet he too had breathed other airs, heard other voices—all around, and in his very home. His mother had been matter-of-fact about sex: one was an animal with lusts which one satisfied. But beneath that dismissiveness she rejoiced in lovemaking, lived for it, got from it glory and meaning enough to sustain a life which, for so vigorous and capable a woman, was otherwise less than satisfying. She had not been able to turn her sensuality off like a tap with her children. Much of what was best in Tim—his music, his feeling for line and form, his impassioned sexual fervour—had been fed at that fountain.

Elinor had often said, 'Come like this.' But only now, hearing her emphatic 'I *want* you to,' did he entirely believe she wanted it herself, not just to please him. Women didn't like it, he had heard at school; that was why prostitutes charged more for a blow job. Vivian had wanted it, but she wasn't the best guide to what most women wanted—and two of his other lovers hadn't liked it at all.

But Elinor did, his amazing...what word was right? 'Wife' did not suit what she was in bed, but 'lover' seemed to deny their marriage bond, their child. His Elinor, his marvel. He was stirred beyond restraint. 'Oh Elinor,' he said, borne down into his body's flame.

A fraction of a second later Elinor felt his cock ripple along her tongue and his come spurt out, as if slightly out of synch with his pleasure. It was an odd taste, but nice in its way: a grown-up taste—she giggled inwardly—like olives or caviar.

He turned and curled into her back. Some cunt-wet ran down her groin towards the sheet. She brushed at it, and he caught her hand, folding it into a fist round his thumb—a gesture of affection so rare it felt more intimate than his coming in her mouth. A few minutes later she loosed his grasp to stop another runnel; and again he enclosed her hand.

She wanted to fall asleep like that, but his come had a pungent after-smell, like having a vinegar bottle open beside her. She had to get up and go down to the kitchen to brush her teeth.

Chapter 24

Maggie opened the windows, and warm May air wafted into the flat, bearing sweet scents from her window box. Down in the side street two women were wheeling prams. She turned away and put her hand out to the receiver—seeing Nell's nine-month belly all evening would be too bloody much. But what excuse could she make? Easier to go through with it. She'd have to face the world sometime; might as well start with Nell. But not tell her, not yet, with the wound so raw. She went to the bedroom to renew her blusher and mascara and experiment with smiles.

At dinner she lit candles—as she did every night, alone or not. It was her version of the dinner jacket in the jungle: a line drawn against despair. Tonight their hazy light veiled her from scrutiny.

Afterwards they took their glasses across to the sitting area. Maggie chose an armchair out of the spill of her well-shaded lamps, and watched Elinor, who was as thin as ever, her belly an excrescence on her long body, lower herself onto the sofa and put her feet up. The thought: I'd carry it off better, rose irresistibly to Maggie's mind.

She was almost silent; Elinor had to make all the running. They had hardly been alone together since that tense New Year's night eighteen months ago. Maggie stopped by the Cromer at least once a week, but on her way home from work, when the children were there—and in any case she came to see Kit as much as Elinor. This year they hadn't even met for New Year's dinner; each of them had been relieved, as well as hurt, when the other failed to suggest it. But they meant a lot to each other; they had both hoped that this unluckily timed evening would bring them closer again.

Instead, it was stiff and chit-chatty. Elinor soldiered on, feeling frivolous, as if Maggie, in finding life hard, had penetrated further into the truth of things.

'Let's see, what else is new—oh, Andrew Wellesford. He's taking two years off. A world tour, he told Rose, but it's more of a busman's holiday—visiting cousins in New Zealand, and his son in Canada, and working on their farms: "So much paperwork here, I never get my hands dirty any more." It's hard to imagine him mucking out a barn—I've only ever seen him in town clothes. Sefton and Ginny will carry on back here.'

'I'd watch it—new brooms sweep clean.'

'They're not new, they've been involved all along. And Andrew told Rose they're all agreed about the Cromer. Rose, I must tell you, has got a new hair-style: gelled into all-over spikes. She looks like one of those spiky balls on the end of chains that knights used to whirl.'

Their wine-glasses were empty. Maggie waggled the bottle at Elinor, who shook her head. 'Anything else? Whisky? Orange juice? Water?'

'Juice, please—I'll get it.'

'No, stay with your feet up.' Maggie fetched the whisky bottle and a glass, and a big tumbler of juice.

'Fresh—yummy. My parents still serve orange squash, would you believe it? I told you we were there at Easter; and it was *much* easier than it used to be—because of Kit. And they're so easygoing with him...'

Unlike Tim, who didn't like to see Kit dribbling food down his chin, or using an outgrown woolly playsuit as a security blanket. 'It's childish,' he said in exasperation. 'And you abet it'—because she wouldn't let him confiscate the playsuit. He was disappointed—more than disappointed: upset—because Kit wasn't more forward in learning to walk and speak; and he got annoyed when he brought home educational toys designed for much older children, and Kit couldn't figure them out.

It bothered Elinor that Tim couldn't see how counterproductive he was being; he got huffy if she tried to say so. But she knew better than to talk to Maggie about it. She said instead, 'My parents still give me the fidgets, though. As Chris says, it's a sign of desperation when all you can find to talk about is children. She's doing well, by the way—breezes through now and then in a trail of media glamour, says she's dying of overwork.'

'Self-induced.'

'Sure—she's been knee-deep in interviews and TV talk shows ever since *Indecent Exposure* came out—the anti-porn one. Now it's the obstetric services, a national survey; she's got a big grant and research assistants. Which reminds me—she took me to a film about childbirth that I think you once saw for your department— primal screams and re-experiencing your birth, and a trendy French obstetrician—'

'Not Leboyer?' Maggie said brightly, with an inward wince at the subject matter. 'A presumptuous man who thinks he knows more about birth than women? Birth in semi-darkness, then dunk the baby in a tepid bath to remind him of the womb?' Her mouth was dry. Everything Elinor talked about had some bearing on her grief—why couldn't they switch to something safe like building-society interest rates? She drained her glass. 'I never do see what you see in Chris,' she said for the dozenth time in a dozen years. 'And these days she must be insufferably full of herself.'

'No more than usual—and you needn't raise your eyebrows like that. I'll say this for Chris: with all the well-known people she knows now, she hasn't dropped me and Rose.'

'All that means is, she can't be more spoiled by success than she already is by nature.'

Elinor gave a guilty snort of laughter, then yawned. Past midnight—time to go. She heaved herself up and went to ring a minicab.

Maggie's will for silence was seeping away. She poured herself another drink and hunched over it grimly. Hold your tongue, she told herself as Elinor came back, but knew she wouldn't.

'What's *wrong*?' Elinor cried at the sight of her ravaged face.

'It's a lousy time of night to tell you, but...I've broken off with Clive.'

'You've—dear God, Maggie. What happened?'

Long pause. 'His wife's pregnant.'

'Oh, my dear.' Elinor leaned over and put her arms round her.

Maggie sat stiffly, then surrendered and started crying quietly. Still crying, she finished her drink, then got up, fetched a tissue, blew her nose, and sat down again, on the other side of the room.

Elinor lowered herself into the chair Maggie had left. 'But I thought they didn't...I thought it was virtually sexless.'

'So he led me to believe—the way he's always talked about her, you'd think the first two happened by artificial insemination.' Maggie felt distant and melancholy. She had an idea she was drunk. 'The worst thing, Nell—he's so pleased with himself—you'd think it took special skills, fucking your wife and conceiving a child. He didn't even guess how I'd feel. He *knows* how much I want a...a baby, his baby—but he thought I'd be *happy* for him. *That's* the man I thought loved me. He's kept trying to corner me at work—thinks I'm completely crazy, ending it. Thank God he's in pensions now; I couldn't stand it if our offices were still on the same floor.' She poured another drink, took a big gulp. 'Do *you* think I'm crazy?'

'Of course not, love.'

Maggie looked up accusingly. 'Then you think it's for the best, because now I can meet someone single. I can see it in your face.'

'No you can't. All I'm thinking is that it must be hard on you, having me here bulging like a fertility goddess.'

'Nah, you're not his goddamned wife.' Maggie yawned. 'I'm tired. Tired and emotional, as *Private Eye* says.'

The doorbell rang. 'I'll send him away,' Elinor said, toiling to her feet.

'Don't bother.'

'I don't want to...' leave you alone, Elinor thought. 'Leave you like this,' she said.

'S'okay. I'd rather...rather be...Please.'

She wanted to crawl to bed and hide, Elinor guessed, and said, reluctantly, 'Okay.' At the door she gave her a fond kiss. 'I'll ring you tomorrow.'

'No need,' said Maggie, trying to fit back into her gallantry. 'Better not, in fact. Better not. I cannot bear it, I cannot *bear* it, you and your husband and your exactly two children.'

185

'I know,' Elinor said helplessly.

Maggie's self-control snapped. 'You know? You *know*?' she said with explosive vehemence. 'You don't know a goddamned thing about it, you fucking self-satisfied bitch. You never have, and you never will—so stop conde-condescending to *me*. I'm sick of it.'

She's drunk, Elinor thought; she doesn't mean it. But she does. 'Of course not,' she replied meaninglessly.

Maggie had already entirely forgotten her outburst. Of course not what? She felt too fuzzy to pursue it. 'See you later this week,' she said, opening the door. 'And Kit, of course. You're only a pretext, my dear.'

'Okay—see you then.' Elinor tried to add, 'My dear,' but couldn't. Their friendship would mend, but not inside five minutes.

Tim had left the hall light on and the bedroom doors ajar in case Kit cried, and was asleep on his belly in the very middle of the bed with his arms and legs flung out. He would groan in his sleep and move over when she came to bed.

She slipped into Kit's room. He was asleep, too, his long limbs sprawled out and his thumb in his mouth. As she touched his shadowed face, so entirely like Tim's, the new baby thumped her hard from inside. He's a terrific thumper, she thought—Kit had been much less lively.

Not he—she or he. Why assume that a vigorous foetus was male?

My daughter, she thought for a longing moment, cradling her belly; then crushed the hope out of thought. Maggie, she remembered. Oh Maggie.

The thumper stopped. Across her blurred one-in-the-morning mind flashed the notion that he—she or he, damn it—had died that very second. She clenched her fist to rap him-her-it awake; then for no obvious reason relaxed and gave it a light pat instead.

Chapter 25

'You're supposed to be resting with your feet up,' Tim scolded, ringing home after an afternoon recording session. Elinor had taken it into her head to re-web the saggy-seated armchairs.

'I know, but I'll go spare. You know me, I need to be *doing* something.'

So different from last time. 'All right,' he said dubiously.

'Don't worry, I'm fine. Full of zip. I'm getting backache peering over my belly to hit the tacks, but that's better than just sitting catching up on the *Monthly Film Bulletin*.'

'Right. Bill's waiting, I've got to go. See you after the concert.'

He rang off as abruptly as usual. Elinor returned to the drawing room and eased herself down beside Kit, who was fast asleep on the dark green carpet. As she threaded the next piece of webbing, her womb tightened in a false-labour contraction—she'd been having them on and off for three days.

The contraction that hit her a quarter of an hour later was so sharp that she winced and sat back on her heels. The real thing? Blast—she wanted to finish the chair. She threaded in the last crosspiece, reached for an upholstery tack—

Another. Much stronger. She checked her watch: hardly a quarter of an hour since the last one.

The next contraction came in twelve minutes; the next, ten. How could the time between pangs shrink so fast? It was supposed to take hours. Better get a message to Tim, so he could get hold of a substitute for the concert—if her labour went on at this rate, he would have to drive her to hospital in an hour or two.

But Tim was goodness knew where, having a snack—he wouldn't get to the South Bank in time to find a substitute.

Damn damn damn. Better book a taxi. No, first ring Roz, or was it Lindsay? Elinor wedged Kit between two sofa-cushions and went to the music room for the list of when the helpers were free to look after him. No, first find a friend to come along to hospital and stay until Tim arrived, so that she wouldn't have to fight any battles on her own. She hadn't been pressured into anything last time, but you never knew.

Not Maggie, after the shock of last week.

Rose? Working.

Sheila? After breathing through another contraction—ten minutes since the last—Elinor rang her.

Sheila said, 'I'd *love* to. Hold on, I'll tell Thoby.' She came back. 'He'll drive us; and the downstairs neighbour says she'll mind the boys.'

'Oh Sheila, wonderful. I'll ring back when the contractions are five minutes apart.'

She checked the mother's helpers' list. Lindsay. Line engaged. Wait, try again. Engaged. Again. Engaged. While listening to the beeps she had another contraction. Nine minutes—had she read her watch wrong? The intervals couldn't close up so fast. She wanted Tim. It wasn't his fault she couldn't reach him, but she felt abandoned.

Through the open door she could see Kit, still sound asleep in his nest of cushions. She resisted an impulse to go and hug him. She couldn't really believe that the baby inside her would soon be a separate being, as separate as Kit.

But she'd better behave as if she did. Upstairs, put last-minute things in the case, carry it down; stand still in the hall, fighting off a contraction. Eight minutes. No mistake this time. She went straight to the music room to try Lindsay again.

Picking up the telephone she glanced in at Kit—and dropped it and ran. He was wide awake in a maze of webbing, and chewing— she got it out of his mouth—my God, an upholstery tack. How many had he swallowed already? Could they perforate his stomach?—his intestine? Get him X-rayed immediately.

Not with labour pains eight minutes apart—get somebody else to take him. Who? She needed Sheila and Thoby herself. Maggie? No time to haver: yes.

She hiked him onto her hip and was halfway across the room when the bag of waters broke. Not dramatically: a steady dribble down her leg like the childhood humiliation of wetting her pants. Everything at once. She groped in a drawer for tissues, breathing through a contraction so strong it puckered her face. Kit looked at her anxiously, his deep brow creased.

Ring Maggie. 'I'll be there,' Maggie said.

Ring Sheila. 'We're coming,' Sheila said.

Elinor went back upstairs, carrying Kit, mopped herself down, changed her pants and tights, went back down again, and settled herself to wait, holding Kit, half fretful, on her lap.

So far the need to act had insulated her; now fear hit her bodily. She squeezed him hard, and his already-shaken composure splintered. He was shrieking at the top of his lungs when Maggie's taxi and Thoby and Sheila's rackety Renault drew up together.

Maggie took charge of Kit, clucking like a nurse in a World War II film, and Thoby drove them all to the hospital, letting Maggie and Kit off at Outpatients. With exaggerated gravity she leaned him down to the car window for a kiss. Elinor clung to his hand; Maggie pulled it away and marched off.

At the main entrance Thoby fetched a wheelchair. 'Have fun,' he said, stooping to kiss Elinor's cheek as Sheila wheeled her off. 'I'll go get a message to Tim.'

'And find out about Kit and come tell me?' she called urgently after him.

'Kit will be all right,' said Sheila in the lift. 'He couldn't have swallowed any tacks in that time.'

'But I should be there.' How could she put her heart into having this baby with Kit in danger?

Don't be melodramatic, she told herself. Her fear was over the top—self-punishment. But she couldn't stop it.

The contractions were getting faster and fiercer. Three minutes. Slow up, she thought for a moment, otherwise Tim would miss it.

Jesus—as the next one ripped through her. No, she didn't wish this a second longer than it had to be.

Sheila sat with her, patient, useful, inhabiting a different universe. The naked violence of Elinor's dark face alarmed her; she was afraid of letting her down emotionally. Otherwise she felt entirely equal to the situation, the way she did at work. She remembered nothing about Euan's birth, but had Fergus's to draw on: she knew how to help Nell—better, she thought with secret jealousy, than Maggie McAdam would. Still, she would be glad when Thoby got back—his darting intuition might fathom Elinor's desperate mood better than she could.

But Thoby was allowed no further than the sister's desk; Sheila had to go out and bring back his messages: 'Kit's fine—no tacks. And Tim will come the instant his concert's over...'

Fear for Kit had kept Elinor obdurately tied to the outer world. The knot slipped. She said, 'Oh, good,' almost absentmindedly, and withdrew, now that he was safe, to hoard herself for the effort in hand. The pain was worse this time; sharper, more sapping, as if she'd been induced. She couldn't breathe through it, there was no controlling it.

Sheila sponged her down, gave her ice cubes to chew, brushed her sweaty hair and held her hand hard during contractions. Elinor clung on for dear life to the primitive human contact—how did women get through labour alone?

Tim rushed to a pay telephone in the interval. He had tried to miss Elinor's first labour—but being together while their son was born had been more important than whether he liked or hated what he saw. This time he wanted passionately to be there.

A chirpy girl went to find out about Mrs Scott. 'Are you sure you've got the right ward? We haven't got a Mrs Scott.—Benton? Why didn't you say so? I'll *see*.' Her tone implied that anyone so careless about names could easily mislay his wife.

'She's doing well, she's accepted some Pethidine.—No, nothing wrong, just a little discomfort.—I really couldn't say how long. She'll be fully dilated soon. An hour? Two?'

190

An hour—the Telemann and Haydn's sixty-first would take nearly that. One of the stagehands promised to have a taxi waiting for him on Waterloo Bridge, and the conductor agreed, none too graciously, to let him slip out as soon as the music ended. 'Afraid you'll start the audience moving, and he'll get less applause,' commented his stand-partner.

Brock was taking the music as slow as Klemperer, without the excuse of genius—Tim almost went crazy with anxiety. He played without seeing the notes, furtively checking his watch at every rest. Why Pethidine?—she had been determined not to have anaesthetics. An hour already; still two movements of the Haydn to go. What had changed her mind—pain, or something worse?

De-de-de, de-de-de, de-de-de *dum*, Dum Dum de Dum; Dum; Dum. Fiddle and bow and chamois cheek-pad into case, slide out, trying to grin at thumbs-up signs from the strings, race up the circular stairs to Waterloo Bridge, leap into the taxi Gerry was holding, more grins, move off. Sometimes the only thing binding him to his assessing-eyed son seemed to be the memory of his birth. If he were late now, there would be nothing whatever to connect him to his second child.

Up in the lift; along three corridors; past the sister unchallenged, since with his evening dress and air of assurance he seemed more like an off-duty doctor than a mere father; open the door; and see, across the room on the bed, with the all-at-once disorientating far-to-near focus of a zoom shot: Elinor, still big-bellied, half squatting, half lying back on the pillows.

'Elinor!' he cried. It sounded silly, like a desperate lover in a costume picture.

Her eyes were closed. She opened them, then her mouth, as if to say, 'Tim,' through her grimace, but it was as if a high wind snatched the sound from her moving lips. Her gaze remained fixed on his. It was the closest moment, that silence in a busy delivery room, of their whole lives together—before that night or after.

He was only just in time. Sheila and the midwife eased her down onto her side. He gave her his hand. She grabbed it and ground his fingers together. He would have been forced to withdraw them, but she loosened her grip and whispered, 'Your bow hand, sorry.' He

191

smiled and gave her his closed fist to cling to instead. Yes, this. Their moment.

Sheila and the midwife said in ragged unison, 'It's a girl.' Sheila added, 'She's fine;' and Elinor fell back with a satisfied groan.

'Isobel.' She shut her eyes.

Isobel? Had that been on their lists? It sounded all right. And it was her turn to choose.

Elinor was snoring. He got up to look at Isobel, just in time for the midwife to turn and place her, dry and wrapped, in his arms. She did not look like Kit, she was red and black and hairy.

The snoring stopped. He swung round, met Elinor's opened eyes, and gave his daughter to his sweaty, smelly, blear-eyed wife.

Chapter 26

'A girl—brilliant,' said Rose. Her hair was back in the old curly crop—'I looked like a hedgehog,' she said ruefully when Elinor asked after the spikes. 'Let's have a cuddle.'

'I thought babies weren't your thing.'

'Ancient history—B.K. Before Kit. Hullo, brown baby. She's exactly like you.'

'Um, not features, I think, just colouring; and not like Tim either'—Isobel had escaped the Scott impress that marked Kit. 'She's my fairy changeling, aren't you, sweet?' Isobel made an indefinite distressed noise, and another. 'Oh-oh, she's off. Here, I'll take her—she'll grizzle now till she falls asleep. Funny, I thought she'd be like Kit, but she's more...sort of *worried*. Sometimes when he'd cry at five in the morning I'd just ignore him, and he'd go back to sleep; but not her, she cries herself into a panic.'

The doorbell. 'I'll get it,' Rose said, and came back with Chris.

'A girl—good work,' said Chris, digging in her bag. 'Looks just like you, too.'

'Not—'

'Somewhere in here I've got...here: for Kit—keep his nose from getting out of joint.' She handed him a pop-up picture book. 'I've got to tell you—you know the Hiram Institute for Social Research—I'm the new director!'

'Terrific,' said Elinor.

'Hey, far out,' said Rose. 'You must be on cloud nine.'

'Well...administration won't be half as interesting as doing my own thing. But it's still a man's world out there—power's where it's at.'

Rose blinked; so did Elinor. They looked at each other, then at Chris. She went on blithely describing the job, and the private secretary—male—who went with it. When she finished she said, 'Got to run, thanks for coffee,' and left.

'Wow,' said Rose. 'You were right.'

'Me? I've never said—'

'You didn't need to.'

'I'm so transparent?'

'Oh, no, I just'—observe you with the eye of love, Rose thought. 'I just know you too well,' she said.

Elinor hugged her. She was very fond of Rose, and these days it was far easier talking to her than to Maggie. But Rose didn't make the very air sparkle for her, even though they had lots in common—movies, work, politics, assumptions about how to live, love of talking about people, a sense of fun: everything but the helpless flow of longing recognition that she and Maggie shared without agreeing on a tenth as much.

Maggie's visits to Ockendon Road were transparently to see Kit as much as Elinor. Her wry face was taut, artificial, as if she'd had a facelift. Suppressed anger—at Clive, at Elinor, at an unjust world—gave her banter a savage edge.

'You save those?' she exclaimed scornfully one day, watching Elinor wash out a plastic food bag. 'Ecology freak or skinflint?'

'Skinflint,' Elinor said lightly, her cheeks burning. No answer was possible that didn't use Maggie's terms.

She wanted Maggie to admire her achievement, her daughter. But Isobel's gender, which roused her to such passionate love and loyalty and identification, only put Maggie off. 'I prefer Kit,' she said, staring down like a bad fairy at Isobel's dark little face. 'Girls are sneaky. If a boy gets angry, it's a shout or a good clean wallop—girls pinch and whine.'

'At three weeks old?' Elinor was inwardly vexed on her daughter's behalf—on her own—but retreated to talking about Kit.

'Busy?'

Good Lord—Clive, of all people.

'As you see'—her desk was piled high. 'I've only been back at work three days.'

'Hard job, juggling work and kids,' he said, closing the door and taking a seat unasked.

'Well, at least two aren't much more trouble than one, and I've got help.'

'Students, I understand?'

'That's right—a rota to help with Isobel here, and a couple of older ones who mind Kit at home in the evenings.'

'And all through notices in the foyer, I believe. Very handy.'

'Very.' An awkward silence fell. It made Elinor itchy. Fill it up, she thought. Tell him about interviewing Hilary yesterday—a graduate student to replace Roz, one of the mother's helps, who had finished her thesis and gone off to a job. But she held her tongue; she didn't want to go on making small talk with Clive.

At last he said, 'You can guess why I'm here.'

'Maggie?'

He nodded. His yellow hair was so thick and well-groomed that it looked like a wig, but his scalp showed pink along his parting. 'She won't talk to me,' he said at last. 'Not a word. As if I don't exist. After all these years—it's horrible. I've never loved anybody as much as her—she *knows* that. It's crazy dropping me just because...It was an accident, that's what she doesn't understand. If she'd let me *explain*.'

His voice was trembling, but his pink secretive face wore its usual look of knowing imperturbability. Elinor didn't know whether to believe voice or face, or a bit of both. 'Mmm, it's difficult,' she said. What did he want of her?

It came out soon enough. If she would just intercede with Maggie, explain that his wife had practically raped him—he hadn't *known* she wasn't using contraception—naturally he was trying to make the best of the situation—but if Maggie only knew how trapped he felt—that he didn't really *want*—that she was the one, the only one...

He didn't seem to doubt that Elinor would speak on his behalf. Would she feel more sympathetic if he were less cocksure? She doubted it. 'I'll tell her what you've told me,' she said uncomfortably. 'But I don't think...'

195

'I've got the greatest confidence in you,' he said, getting up to take his leave. 'Maggie thinks more of you than anyone.'

You prick, she thought.

Isobel chirped in her cot. Clive went over and looked down at her, and in a gentle voice said, 'She's beautiful,' brushing her cheek with his finger. She turned towards it, opening her mouth. 'They all do that, it's a reflex—but it's so sweet.' He put out his hand to shake Elinor's. His composure broke for a moment; a look of utter misery passed over his bland features like a ripple in water. 'You don't know what Maggie means to me,' he said, and left.

Elinor hadn't said she would speak for him, just about him. She didn't even want to do that; but she couldn't receive a visit from Maggie's ex-lover without informing her, whatever ghosts it raised. 'I was pretty narked,' she told her. 'How could he think I'd turn into an agent for him—Mr Eat-Your-Cake-and-Have-It-Too?'

Maggie, with Kit in her lap, was taking it well. 'He's such a hot-shot negotiator, he thinks he can make anybody do anything if he can only talk to them.'

'But I'm *your* friend, he must know that.'

'That's why he wants you on his side; he thinks you're an enormous influence on me.'

'*Me?*'

'The first thing he said when I said I was through was, "It's that Nell Benton putting ideas in your head." '

'*Me!*' Elinor sputtered again. 'You influence *me*—I don't influence *you.*'

'Don't underestimate yourself.'

'But you disagree with everything I—and I disagree with everything you—'

'Yes, pet, and you say, "I'm *your* friend" as if everyone takes it for granted that that comes before everything else; and call Clive Mr Eat-Your-Cake-and-Have-It-Too, which is just what I've felt without realising it—that has an influence. A good influence— don't look so worried. I influence *you* after all—you just said. It's two-way.'

196

'But only when we're not trying,' Elinor said ruefully, thinking of wanting Maggie to have a child on her own.

This time Tim and Elinor took no chances; they didn't make love till she got her new diaphragm and said, 'Let's celebrate.'

'Okay?' he said, coming into her. 'Sure? Don't want to hurt you.'

'You're not'—gritting her teeth in triumph. He was, but she wanted this this this, so she didn't say so: pushing down round him, feeling pummelled but who cared.

Tim cared: momentarily opening his eyes, catching her in a wince of pain not ecstasy, pulling her off; letting her back only when she said, almost crying, 'I *need* it.'

All the next day she went about in a daze of happiness, remembering his fingers, his murmurs, all eloquent of tenderness. But they didn't make love that night, or the next morning, or the next night. The memory faded, and she was left longing for non-sexual affection as well, and for talk—real talk, not just cultural chit-chat. His distance prickled like Shetland wool.

Patience; patience. Hold on. It was like taming a wild animal. Startle it, and your work was for nothing.

Tim prised one eye open. What was that squalling? Crack of dawn. Isobel. Hungry. He squinted at the clock: 8:57 in large red stick numbers. Alarm set for nine. All right, all right. He hit the plunger, staggered up, fetched Isobel to bright-eyed Elinor—lucky woman, wide awake from a standing start in two seconds flat—and lay down again...just for a moment...recover from the shock... propping himself on the headboard to stay awake.

Elinor lifted her nightgown and put Isobel to her breast, nestling into a cocoon, sheet and warm skin and August sunbeams wavering through the curtains, smell of warm milk and baby who needs a bath. My brown darling, squeezing your eyes shut to suck, funny, Kit opened his. By the time she turned to give her the other breast Tim had fallen asleep, snoring slightly, his wsssh-shsssh blending with Isobel's suck-sputter-smack.

She slid out of bed without waking him, changed Isobel and put her back in her cot, already asleep. Kit was talking to his plush lamb. She rubbed his cheek and left before he could decide he wanted to get up.

Tim was awake again, blinking sleepily. He was very attractive; she had an impulse to lean down and kiss his ruddy cheek. But he would only turn aside. Patience—but she'd held on so long. Sitting on the edge of the bed, she said without any forethought, 'Remember on the Heath, long ago, we used to talk about...oh, about me, about you. We don't do that any more.'

'There's something you want to ask,' he said, resigning himself. 'Go on.'

Something! Where could she begin? 'No, nothing specific; I'd just like...to start talking.'

'*Start* talking? We do talk.' He was offended. He prided himself on always having subjects for conversation.

'Yes, but only about...' She couldn't think how to put it. He was regarding her challengingly. Lord, why hadn't she thought it out? She couldn't think of a single thing she wanted to say. She gave up with a shrug and a smile and said—she was a little intoxicated from looking into his wine-brown eyes—'I love you.'

If he had smiled back or held her gaze, it would have been enough, but he looked away.

Say it, damn you, she thought. 'Do you?' she asked.

'Do I what?'

'Love me.'

'That's obvious.'

'Not if you never say so.'

'It's obvious because that's why people get married. Be your age; only adolescents need daily bulletins.'

Why was it that he would do anything to avoid saying he loved her? If she asked that, her voice would shake with rage.

'What's on your mind must be more important than this,' he said.

What could be more important? She swallowed, cast about and said, 'Remember when I was pregnant with Kit—I wish we could be like that again.'

So did he, so did he. He shook his head with pain.

She thought he hadn't understood. 'I mean, with more affection...'

198

'If you can't feel my affection when we make love—'

'I don't just mean in bed, I mean in life. It's—' It's outrageous that you can lick my cunt but not kiss my mouth. But that was a thought too sharp to say.

Tim sighed. 'We've been here before.' It made him desolate to find that she was still dissatisfied with what he gave.

'Yes, and you always say you'll try, but you don't.'

'I do.' It was true—he tried.

'Well it doesn't show, that's what counts. I know you've been hurt and it's hard, but not kissing—and the rest—that hurts *me*.' She was fierce, to make up for begging so abjectly.

He wanted to please her, not hurt her; if he could have done as she wanted, he would have. But he could not, could not; it was not in his control—more than ever since the children, he did not know why. Vivian refusing to kiss him—begging her—begging—needing it like an addict for the first and only time in his life: he could not risk his whole being like that again. Vivian saying: 'What I feel for you, it's a mixture of revulsion and attraction, and kissing you tips it towards revulsion.' One time he had kissed her anyhow—the nearest he had ever come to rape—and she had retched.

Slowly he said, 'Kissing makes me...I can make some gestures, but not others.'

'It makes you what? Sick?'

'Vulnerable,' he said flatly, meeting her eyes and looking away. 'So does talking about it. Concentrate on what I can give, Elinor, don't make yourself unhappy about what I can't.' He got up and stalked off to the bathroom.

She followed. 'No, it's not good enough. Vulnerable—that's something to do with Vivian, isn't it. Aren't you over her *yet*?'

Once he had had a friendly shaving glass that showed only his chin. Elinor had put up the big looking glass that confronted him now. 'Look,' he said, stabbing his finger at his reflection—small deepset eyes, big nose, heavy stubble-fuzzed jowls. 'That is *not* Cary Grant. Or Marlon Brando. Or Spencer Tracy. Or any of those stars you say I look like. That's—Wallace Beery. Anthony Quinn. Jack Carson.'

199

Elinor let out a shriek. 'My God, Tim,' she gasped, 'I shouldn't laugh, but—Wallace Beery! You've got a bad case of...I think it's called inappropriate body image. They're big fat men—you're not a bit fat—look at you.' She patted his thick flat belly.

He looked, remembering Vivian retching, and the two women before her, years apart, who had said he looked like Frankenstein's monster; remembering the time during puberty when he had been plump. 'Timmy's got titties,' a boy had giggled at the pool, and other boys took it up. By the next year they had forgotten, but it was in him still. With his rational mind he could tell that his body in the glass was entirely masculine, but he wished he had the kind of figure where chest and ribcage made one long line without a heavy pectoral bulge. Timmy's got titties.

Nothing in the world could have made him tell Elinor that. But her incredulous laughter had half opened for a moment the shutters over his mind. He said, 'Do you remember in *Dr Zhivago*, Lara being...not exactly raped, but at first she doesn't want it, and then she does? I was very angry when I saw that, because I'm not...attractive enough—dominant enough—to convince a woman like that.'

That scene had made Elinor angry too—on Lara's behalf. He'd been on the other side, the man's side. Did he want to rape women? No, he hadn't said that. He wanted to make them want what they didn't want—like the men in her fantasies. It made her blood run cold; but her cunt was tingling.

But he had offered her something: a fragment of serious talk. Reassure him—quick. She said with perfect truth: 'But you're the most sexually dominant man I've ever known. And you convince *me* easily enough—as you must have noticed.'

Turning on the taps he gave her a strange half-smile. 'Once with Vivian—we were stuck in a traffic jam, and I started to pull her skirt up. It was down to her ankles, so it took time, but eventually I got my hand on her thigh, and then...and managed to...give her pleasure. Afterwards she said: "That was some seduction scene." I was—astounded. Seduction? Every second I'd been expecting punishment.'

There must be more point to the story than just making her jealous. She got it. 'You mean you feel like that with *me*?'

He nodded, swirling the shaving brush on the soap.

'But you don't *need* to!' she cried as the lower half of his face vanished beneath foam. 'Look, Vivian was—bananas, to put it mildly. Don't base your whole life on what happened with her.'

He gestured with the razor. If I open my mouth I'll get soap in it, that meant. She kissed his shoulder and went over to fill the bidet.

Lara—Vivian in the traffic jam—the images ran through her head all day. Poor lamb, thinking he's not attractive. Crazy. She would just have to show him.

The thought was with her when he turned to her that night. She wanted to give him...herself...everything...more than everything; and slid down the bed to go down on him—far down—as far as she dared—further—

Blast: the gag reflex. She heaved dangerously; retreated.

Try again, slower. Still too fast.

Very slowly, very slowly; a little further and further down; until finally she had him touching her soft palate.

Her mouth filled with spit; her throat palpated round him. She pulled back to swallow, went down again. Easier this time: she slowly slid him into place as if he belonged there—as if there were in truth a receptive hollow at the back of her mouth, predestined for the head of his cock. Maybe the soft palate was an erogenous zone, she thought with an inward chuckle; but the notion reminded her uncomfortably of *Deep Throat*, and she brushed it away.

It became easier and easier to hold him deep in, move round him, let him move, slowly, delicately, from far back to farther back: a slow-motion intensity of communication, both of them entirely still except for their tiny reciprocal movements deep in her mouth. Several times her throat closed convulsively and her stomach heaved, but at last she had his cock half blocking her windpipe and was drawing ragged breaths round it. The sense of not setting limits was overwhelming: putting both her hands on his arse and pushing him bodily in past the point where she had any defence: offering him boundless openness.

201

She wished she hadn't thought of *Deep Throat*. Who was she kidding—the soft palate an erogenous zone? Her fantasy of openness wasn't innocently self-explanatory. Where was the line between openness and submission?

Drawing back a little, she said, 'Come like this?'—Tim was trembling with the effort not to come.

'All right.'

'If it's what you want'—meaning: not just to please me.

'Oh, what I want...I want to fuck you, I want to come in your mouth, I want to fill you,' he said in a whisper.

'The things you say to me drive me out of my mind,' she whispered back.

'Then suck me, Elinor, suck me and I'll fill you.' He held her face in his hands and came even as he spoke: movingly, her mouth filled with his cock, with his semen, salty-sweet like *lassi*.

When she woke in the morning, a shadowy memory fell across her mind, barring it. Barring...writing...lines...

She opened her eyes with surprise. It seemed quite mad. Her memory of Tim's coming included a sense of being barred, lightly marked, with blurry diagonal lines like the ash stripes some American Indians drew across their foreheads—but these were across her tongue, not on her skin; or perhaps hovering between tongue and palate.

The physical detail had faded; her memory was of an emotion. It was as if he'd been...writing on her? Daft. Did such ghost images play across the mind all the time, so irrational that you only occasionally, on the shores of sleep, got even a squint at them?

Chapter 27

In September the Cromer held a Bresson season. It was Elinor's doing—she considered him the greatest of living directors. Secretly she was mounting it for Tim, who had never seen any Bresson.

The retrospective just missed being complete. Three of the films weren't in British distribution, and though she had managed to get copies of two of them, Gaumont wanted a flat fee of a thousand francs per showing for *A Man Escapes*, plus transport and handling from Paris. But the film was virtually unknown in England, and the copy wasn't even subtitled. Box-office suicide: the take wouldn't begin to cover the flat fee. The French embassy tried to persuade Gaumont, in vain. Tim helped Elinor to write to Bresson in French, and Bresson himself asked them. No dice. They would rather leave the film on the shelf than lower the fee: typical distributor mentality.

Otherwise the season was a hit, to Elinor's delight, with warm reviews in the national press as well as the listings magazines. The Cromer's enterprise was commended; one paper praised her by name.

She and Tim and Thoby and Sheila saw *Diary of a Country Priest* one Saturday evening—they in the audience, she perched on the usher's jump seat—and after lunch the next day Thoby waxed rhapsodical while Euan, Fergus and Kit clambered all over him— not, Elinor noticed, over Tim, though he was sitting on the same sofa.

'Saw two films of Bresson's years ago. At school. Here, Kit, if I just lift you—Enterprising chap put on *Le Procès de Jeanne d'Arc* and one about a donkey—*Balthasar*, thank you, Nell—showed it first: disaster. Not on his face, Fergus. Holy donkeys not Stowe style. Nearly finished off the film society. Nobody saw *Jeanne d'Arc* but the organiser and me. This one beats them both. "*Je vous répondrai, âme pour âme*"—searing stuff, Nell, don't you think?'

His impeccable French accent set Elinor's teeth on edge. Searing stuff? Not in the usual sense—the young priest said it to a girl tempted by despair. Was he making fun of the film? of her?

'Sickly clericalism,' Tim said with unusual vehemence. ' "The soul"—there's no such thing.'

'But—' said Thoby and Elinor together.

Thoby bowed. '*Après toi.*'

'You first.'

'Not a soul separate from the body—eternal life and all,' Thoby said. 'But it's the only word for the mind and feelings together.'

'The thing that responds to art—to music,' Elinor added.

Tim's obstinate expression did not change. 'Call it the mind,' he said. 'But not the soul—ugh.'

A curtain wavered; Elinor glimpsed something she usually kept hidden from herself. Soul to naked soul—the words she sometimes longingly said to herself: not only wouldn't he know what she meant; he would scorn the idea.

Euan, trying to hit Fergus, knocked Kit off Thoby's knee. Tim caught him, but Kit burst into tears anyhow. Tim handed him back. Thoby whispered, 'There, there, billy-o,' into his ear, and over his head said, 'Word's been misused, Tim—picked up overtones of excessive vibrato—but—'

'It's not just the word that's sickly, it's the film,' Tim said crossly. '*Because* it's about "the soul".'

Elinor said, 'But you're reading the meaning just from the words. It's in the images too, and how they fit together—a sort of vehemence—and heroism—and austerity. It's the opposite of sickly: it's like the C sharp minor quartet.'

'Exactly, Nell. The Busch version—pushing right beyond beautiful tone into that unearthly intensity. Music of the spheres.'

Tim closed his lips. Bresson was not a bit like Beethoven, but he was not going to argue. It made him uneasy to differ with Thoby.

In the next fortnight Tim sat doggedly through every film in the season. Only the Joan of Arc one was tolerable; the rest were wilfully obscure and tedious.

'That *Mouchette* of yours is *Cold Comfort Farm*, only not funny,' he grumbled.

'Tim, it's hopeless—I told you to stop seeing them.'

'Then in a year or two you'll be telling me the best Bressons are the ones I missed.' Know your enemy, he told himself obscurely: the soul. 'Just don't start modelling yourself on his characters, though—they're the gloomiest lot I've ever seen.'

'But they've got such an immense capacity for happiness, it's just—'

'Adults in the real world have got to compromise. I don't suppose *you'll* kill yourself because seals are slaughtered in Greenland'—this being the moral he perversely insisted upon drawing from one of the films—'or because I don't "understand" you, like that sulky girl in *Une Femme Douce*. It's bloody childish.'

'No,' she said slowly, bewildered by his sarcastic tone. Childish... like Kit and his security blanket. Maybe she shouldn't be, but how could Kit be anything else?

'How's your father?' Elinor asked. Maggie was just back from visiting him.

'Not so hot. He's been hobbling to court with that gouty leg for years—I never thought it was something that could kill him. But it's not gout, it's arteriosclerosis, and no wonder—he drinks like a fish and smokes like a chimney and doesn't walk ten feet if he can drive. Like father, like daughter. He's having an arterial bypass operation next month—no picnic.'

He had several—they all failed. Maggie went up to Leicestershire every weekend to see him: 'No one else will, my mother says good riddance.' Her parents were long divorced.

'They're sending him home,' she reported at the end of October. 'They'll have another go in the spring "when he's built up his strength"—though Lord knows he's still strong as an ox: wants to discuss his last briefs; growls if I don't bring fags and booze. Funny—I never did like him, and I don't now; but it turns me inside out to think of him dying.'

205

'All this travelling—have you had any time with Robin?' He was Maggie's new man, good-looking, intelligent and divorced: Mr Perfect, she called him.

'Enough.' Maggie made a face. 'He wants me to marry him, is the latest.'

'You going to?'

'Um...' She grinned and shook her head. 'But he's so goddamn eligible—*why* do I resist? Maybe it's Freudian—if they're available, I don't want them.'

'You're probably not over Clive. It's only five months—they say it takes two years.'

'Ye gods, it had better not. I'm past it already—in two years nobody will look at me.'

Elinor laughed. 'You've been saying that ever since we met. I was twenty, you were twenty-one, and you were *already* past it.'

'You know what? I was right. Look at me now: thirty-five, single, no children, and wrinkles.'

'*Wrinkles?*'

'Here, see? Crowsfeet.'

Elinor saw them, but said, 'Only through a microscope, sweetie.' She and Maggie were easy together again. Maggie seemed less bitter since meeting the too-eligible Robin—not bitter at all, really; her old ironically pessimistic self. She came every week or so to talk to Elinor and play with Kit—Kit, not Isobel, though she scrupulously brought them both presents. It was almost like the old days: although back then they had talked about both of them, and now only about Maggie. But back then they'd both had worries to air, whereas now...

They still both did. But if Elinor talked about hers, Maggie might still bite her head off. Besides, what would she say? The things that slid in and out of her mind were so vague. I live in hope, she would think; then wonder what she meant.

'Complications,' Maggie said on her next visit. She looked very cheerful. 'The romantic front, not Dad; he's okay for the time being. I've met someone.'

'Ah. As well as Mr Perfect, or instead of?'

206

'The trouble with Mr P—he's so nice he bores me. No spice. The best thing about visiting Dad is not seeing Robin.'

'Whereas the new one—what's his name?'

'Promise you won't laugh?'

'Promise.'

'Albericht Gerlach.'

Elinor broke up. So did Maggie, sputtering till tears stood in her eyes and Kit woke up in her lap. 'There, there, love, sandman's coming, back to sleep. He's in the Danish embassy. Unpompous, clever, funny—outrageous puns in a thick accent; cuddly-looking like Tim, only bald on top and thicker through the middle—ample, you might say.'

'Albericht the Ample?'

'I just hope it doesn't become Albericht the Adipose. But there's a fly in the ointment.'

'Oh no.'

'Oh yes. Three children and a wife he's crazy about. She's a professor in Copenhagen—won't leave her job.'

'Sensible woman,' Elinor said.

'A fool, if you ask me—does she expect him to sit alone over here for months on end? Oh my, though—I do pick them. Still, it's better than Clive—he's alone in London, at least, so I can see him as much as I want. We've gone to a jazz club—and one of Tim's concerts, last Tuesday in the Purcell Room. But—I don't know. What do you think, Nell?'

'I don't know, either. It could be worse than Clive in the long run—if he's so available, you might get the idea that he's freer than he is. But you sound so...so bubbly about him.'

'That's it in a nutshell—I should run a mile, but I won't. Nuts reminds me: my new boss, the compulsive eater—he told me today he always walks through the Ritz on the way to his club and helps himself to the nuts in the bar. Which I can believe—the other day he even helped himself to my lunch. I'd got my secretary to fetch in a sandwich. It was out on my desk, and he stopped by—on his way to a fancy lunch, mind—and absentmindedly just picked it up and *ate* it!'

— ✳ —

Sefton Wellesford was younger and handsomer than Andrew. His trouser creases were sharp, his shoes gleamed. 'Ginny and I have been looking at our position,' he said, leaning back comfortably in an armchair in Rose's office, 'and frankly we're a little worried. The Cromer's something of a drain at the moment—the recession hitting us, not to mention school fees, new piggery, tractors...It's hard times for farmers.'

Rose and Elinor nodded, hypnotised.

'To be frank, we wonder how long the trust can go on carrying the Cromer.'

Elinor found her voice. 'We made a small loss last financial year, but it's the first ever, and *very* small—after exceptional outlays on urgent repairs.'

Rose chipped in. 'This year looks like being the best of the last ten; we're getting better known; mentions in the quality papers...'

'But in these tight times we have to think about return on investment—compliments butter no parsnips.'

'Oh, but they do,' Elinor said. 'Compliments in the national press bring customers to the box office. And several reps have folded in the last few years, so the papers pay more attention to the ones that are left.'

'But if people prefer television—videos...'

'That's bottomed out,' said Rose. 'The audience that's left is solid for cinema—young people and film buffs. They renew themselves, too—our average age has gone down, and attendance is up—the old Roxy and Gate audiences come to us.'

'But the reps that folded...'

'They weren't *losing* money, but the owners wanted more return on their capital, and a rep can never yield the *biggest* return on a central urban site...'

'I do assure you we're not talking about *maximizing* profits; and we do appreciate that last year was exceptional. No, we're exploring. These days you've got to find your market, exploit it. For instance, more first-run films?'

Elinor said, 'Then we wouldn't be a rep.'

--

Rose said, 'We'd be competing with the Renoir, and without a complete refit to West End standards of luxury—which is big money—we'd lose.'

'What about increased use of the physical plant?'

'The site's too small to twin the screens,' said Elinor. 'But we're already planning to show four or five films a day instead of three...'

Sefton didn't look impressed. 'And film clubs on Saturday and Sunday mornings, and late shows every night,' said Rose, hastily upgrading a couple of long-term projects into firm proposals. 'We'll need an assistant manager, though—two of us can't cover ninety hours a week—'

'And another projectionist, more ushers, more film rental fees, advertising costs—everything,' Elinor said, catching up with her. 'But it'll work. Here, these are some projections we were going to send you.'

He looked down the page, got out his calculator and punched at it. Finally, almost reluctantly, he said, 'Quite promising. I'll talk it over with Ginny...and write to Andrew, of course. How soon could you start?'

'We're booked through January,' said Elinor. 'But—'

'As soon as we find and train the staff and book films,' said Rose. 'Two months, minimum. February, maybe March.'

'Sounds good.'

He had parked his Rolls Royce on the double yellows, but hadn't got a ticket—yet. A warden was bearing down. Behind her came a student helper bringing Isobel back from a walk. Sefton leaned out of the window to say, 'Perhaps a little outlay on appearances? That sign—you can hardly see it from Gower Street.'

The warden got out her pen; Sefton glided away. Isobel saw Elinor and let out a howl.

'Thank God that didn't happen five minutes ago,' Elinor said, taking Isobel and leaning weak-kneed against Rose. 'I bet Smoothie-chops thinks babies and business don't mix.'

'If he read the stuff we send him, he'd know the council turned us down for a bigger sign.'

They crossed the road for a better look at the Cromer's narrow frontage, sandwiched between Edwardian blocks of flats—three pairs of double doors, just enough wall space for two poster cases, and a modest black marquee overhead, with CROMER CINEMA in sans-serif white.

'A tatty old fleapit,' Rose muttered, seeing it through Sefton's eyes.

'And saving it will take more than a facelift,' Elinor said grimly.

'Maybe brother Sefton's just flexing his muscle for show—look how he caved in once we started laying it on the line. If we can just keep him and Sis happy till Andrew's back...'

'What if he's got Andrew's authority already?'

'Andrew wouldn't sneak off and let Sefton do the dirty work...I don't think.'

'Trouble is, there's absolutely nothing we can do if they *do* decide to sell. Hush, lamb, I know it hurts'—Isobel was teething. 'Yuck, that creep. Maximizing profits, return on investment—I bet he thinks he's one dynamic guy. "Hard times for farmers", then getting into that car.'

Rose grinned. 'My father says when Suffolk farmers say times are hard, it means they have to sell their *second* Rolls Royce. Brrr—let's go in.' As they headed back, she said, 'We should take the initiative. Hand the Wellesfords a package of proposals. Like...um...'

'A restaurant in the basement?'

'The Roxy tried that on the way to folding, remember? It lost money.'

'We could lobby the council to refuse the Wellesfords permission for change of use,' Elinor suggested.

'And have to live with hostile owners ever after?—no way. How about showing ads?'

'Pearl and Dean? I'd go spare watching that junk every time I'm at the front of house.'

'These film clubs I've landed us with, who'll we aim them at?' Rose said musingly. 'D'you think...a children's club on Saturday mornings, so people could dump their children and go down Oxford Street?'

'And nostalgia on Sunday mornings. Pensioners' special: lure them out of the churches. Oh Lord, Rosy-Posy, we've got our work cut out for us.'

Chapter 28

They found an assistant manager and began training him—a enormously tall and gaunt young man from Lambeth named Terry. He and Rose shared the outer office; Elinor would hear them giggling and go join them; or sometimes not. She wasn't in a giggling mood. Isobel had joined Kit at the crèche, but was still teething; and Kit had chicken-pox. Then Isobel got it. They cried each other awake all night most of the month; Elinor was too tired to think. She thought anyhow, incessantly. Start a cinema bookshop in the basement. Take the battle into enemy territory—sell videos. Rent them? Video-viewing booths?

'Videos? How can you even *think* of it?' said Rose, shocked.

Threading through Elinor's harebrained schemes for the Cromer were those vaguer worries. How could she and Tim have had that electrifying talk in the summer, and then—nothing? Little fragments were lodged in her brain like stones in a shoe. Kissing makes me vulnerable. Only adolescents need daily bulletins.

Christmas came and went—Harrogate and Guildford in the snowy cold. Snow and snow fell and stayed all the month of January. There was no past or future, only a present made timeless by the babies. She moved in a flurry of people at work, but felt like a snowman in a snowstorm in a glass ball—alone with her perpetually circling thoughts. Install Dolby sound. Find new places to advertise. Start a film festival. The forbidden fruit of Tim's face.

'I look at you with emotions, and you answer me with words'— Anna Karina in *Pierrot le Fou*.

She felt sulky—Tim's word for the young woman in *Une Femme Douce*. The weather was cold, the pavements were skiddy. Pushing the twin buggy was slow work—when Tim couldn't give her a lift,

211

she took the bus or a taxi. It was a relief not having the long walk with nothing to do but think.

I'm lonely, she thought. But that's crazy. But the words kept sliding into her head.

One day she said it to Maggie: 'It's crazy, but I've been feeling awfully lonely...'

But Maggie had got pricklier again since deciding on Albericht and breaking off with Robin. Her confidences had dwindled, and she was impatient if Elinor showed the least sign of fretting about anything other than the danger to the Cromer. 'Loneliness is the human condition,' she said harshly. 'Don't make mountains out of molehills. You've got a husband and two children—what do you mean, lonely?'

Maggie had once described her mother as: 'Someone who's always one up in misery: My problems are worse than your problems, sort of thing.' She seemed to be getting that way herself. Very well, Elinor thought with an insensible hardening of her heart. You don't want to listen—I won't ask you to.

Chris arrived as Maggie left. 'Channel Four want me to anchor a series on medicine,' she announced. Success suited her. She still wore dark loose clothes, but there was a stylish swirl to her skirts, her boots were smart, and her hair was layered by an expensive hairdresser, not another member of her household. '*And* do a book of the series. *And* I'm still mired in childbirth stuff; *and* I've started something on psychotherapy. It's too much—I'll go berserk.'

'Nonsense, you thrive on it.'

Chris smiled her irregular sardonic smile. 'Too true. Anyhow— how are you doing?'

'Oh, me—fine,' Elinor said as usual, then found herself adding: 'Only...'

'Only?'

The words came out under pressure. 'I'm *lonely*. I never *talk* to anybody, except you and Maggie and Rose—and mothers at the crèche who only talk about children and...'

'Schools, the environment, high fibre, skim milk, aerobics. Or yoga—I meet them in my yoga class.'

Elinor laughed. 'Bull's-eye. But I need—I don't know. Something. It's like living under glass.'

'Sure—"Children are politically and socially isolating." *Quest*, page one.'

'I suppose I thought I'd escape that, going on working, and meeting so many people at work. But I don't talk to customers and follow up old friends the way I used to—there's no time, between those goddamned proposals we're working up for the Wellesfords, and Tim and the children. And when I do have a moment, I want to spend it with them. Maybe it's isolating, but it's what I want.'

'"The nuclear family is reinforced by love as well as economics." *Quest*—I forget what page.'

'Do you remember every word you ever wrote?' Elinor asked teasingly. She felt better for her outburst.

'Just that book—it was written in blood,' said Chris.

'And candle-wax, remember?'

'How come?' said Rose, back from seeing the last house in.

'The Chester Gate squat. Power cuts all winter—'

'And the pigs cut the gas.' Chris shuddered. 'The bad old days when we were pure of heart. Dulwich is deadly, but it beats being *cold* all the time.'

Rose laughed. 'I guess we've all left that scene.'

'*My* politics haven't changed,' said Chris, ruffled.

'My *politics* haven't changed, but what I do about them has. Besides, look at us, hunkered into cushy jobs, which we swore we wouldn't.'

'Not me,' said Elinor. 'I always wanted this job. And it's hard work staying marginal for life.'

'And impossible with children,' said Chris, reversing herself without noticing. 'They cramp your style worse than jobs. You can't camp at Greenham if you're responsible for children. You don't even go on sitting up late talking.'

'Living in couples buggers things up too,' said Rose. 'Remember how we were all going to live as if we weren't in couples even if we were? But you can't. I *live* with Marcus, I can't just leave him out of everything—but some of my friends from those days freak out if I include him.'

213

'Some people don't like doing things with couples because it reminds them that they're not,' Elinor said, thinking of Maggie.

Chris hiked off the desk. 'Okay, I'm off—I've the whole household to feed. M & S's best—why cook if you can afford not to? But my kids and Judy and Vick think it's cheating. They serve regular casseroles on their nights—peel every bloody carrot themselves.'

Four or five shows a day, plus lates, plus morning shows on Saturday and Sunday, meant shorter intervals in which to get patrons in and out, pick up litter from under the seats and check the state of the lavatories; more films to be delivered and checked; more stacks of cans crowding the projection booth and stacked perilously on the stairs; more tickets to be sold, more ushers kept track of, more ordered of everything from paper towels to coffee and cakes. Elinor's office was a three-ring circus, periodically aswirl with ushers handing in stubs, the cashier dumping excess twopences and stocking up with tens, Margaret to say the cans for nine o'clock had arrived, Maggie to see Kit, Mrs Ekins stopping to coo at the babies, Rose or Terry wanting to discuss the package of proposals for the Wellesfords, Lindsay or Hilary arriving to take the children home.

Elinor's spirits rose; she throve on the bustle and gossip. So did the children, who got a lot of attention in their time after the crèche, and lapped it all up: Rose talking nonsense to them and tossing them into the air; Marcus carrying them piggyback; Terry cuddling them in his lap; Mrs Ekins dabbing kisses on their cheeks; Maggie sprawling on the floor in her smart clothes to play with them.

If only Tim would play with them—Elinor sometimes wondered if he knew how. He loved them, she knew that. But he was distant, demanding, fastidious. She couldn't imagine him down on the floor playing horsey.

They were missing out, so was he. She'd try saying something— she hadn't dared while she was in low spirits: it would have come out wrong.

214

She started with Isobel—Isobel needed him more. Kit could turn to Elinor and forget Tim was around. Isobel never forgot, and grew silently agitated if he ignored her for too long.

'Have you noticed the way she follows you with her eyes?' Elinor asked. 'She points like a dog when you come in—and beams like a flower when you pick her up: which she doesn't with me, not like that.'

Tim did not believe he could make a child beam. But after watching Isobel closely for a couple of days he said, 'You're right, she really takes notice of me.'

'Touching, isn't it? But...I don't know about you, but sometimes I'm a little bothered about her. I mean, she's more forward and energetic than Kit, but she's so much less easygoing—sometimes I'd almost say she was tense.'

'Well...' Tim half wanted to pooh-pooh the idea, but he knew what she was talking about.

'I wonder, do you think it would help if I passed her over to you every so often for a dose of personal contact with her hero?' Elinor tried to sound detached and a little sarcastic, so he wouldn't guess how much she wanted him to say yes.

'Why not?' He was flattered—touched, for he loved his dark daughter. He loved his son too, but with more fear: he still felt as if Christopher saw through him.

So every day Elinor found an occasion—other than those when Isobel needed practical attention, about which Tim was always good—and handed her to him to hold: and he held her. Not for long, and a mite gingerly; but he did it.

Isobel liked it, that was certain—there weren't many things about her that Elinor was so sure of. Elinor and Kit were on the same wavelength. Her precious Isobel, her girl-child, whose very pulse she had expected to know like her own, was far more of a stranger. She loved her passionately, but couldn't guess the secrets of her heart; she knew Kit's without trying. Kit held out his arms for cuddling and broke into open joy when he got it. Isobel fretted for it quietly, privately, and received it with silent passion.

'She's loved and petted as much as him,' Elinor said one night over dinner; 'so why does she ask for it so much less...less

215

expectingly? The more you expect, the more you get—I want her to know that.'

'She'll be in for a rude awakening, then,' Tim said shortly. 'The world's a harsh place.' He was uncomfortable with this talk of hugging and petting. Any moment now Elinor would say she wanted it herself.

'Yes, but—' Elinor fell silent. A world of nuclear threat, famine, torture, poverty, injustice, deliberate cruelty and mass extermination *was* a harsh place. But not hopeless. Why else did Tim belong to Amnesty and CND? Why did he cherish the private joys of life—children, love, joinery, walking, textures, falls of light—why raise the great banner of public-private joy that was his music—if not because he hoped?

The more you expect, the more you get. Isobel was getting something from Tim now—it was Kit's turn.

'I wonder if he's jealous of you and Isobel?' she said one day when Kit had had a tantrum. 'D'you think he might need a bit of special attention just for him?'

'Yes indeed,' said Tim, pleased; 'I've thought so myself.'

That night he brought home an alphabet book. The next morning after breakfast he put two cushions on a kitchen chair, set Kit upon them and opened the book to A for apple.

Lordy—that wasn't what she'd meant. And Kit was barely two; he wasn't likely to learn his letters for ages yet.

He took his cue from Tim, though, and tried hard, day after day. Elinor sometimes saw him change from a wriggly giggly baby to a serious child at the exact moment he crossed the kitchen threshold.

He should at least be held for his pains: she'd try to wangle it. 'Those things never stay put,' she said one Sunday morning—one of Kit's cushions had slid out from under, and he was hardly chest-high to the table. 'Why not put him on your knee?'

Tim was not to be caught so easily. He got up without a word, dug in a drawer, secured the cushions to the chair rungs with safety pins and string, and went on soberly teaching his sober son.

That evening Kit toddled up to Tim in the drawing room. Coming to Elinor he would have held out his arms; with Tim he just waited.

Tim looked down. 'Something you want?'

'Play pick-a-book?' It was Kit's name for the alphabet book.

Play? If alphabet lessons were a game, they were one he never won. Did he really enjoy trying and failing beside that exigent taskmaster—or was he trying to *please* Tim?

If so, it worked—Tim beamed and gave him an extra lesson. He didn't touch him, though, except to lift him onto the sofa. Was that enough for Kit? It shouldn't be; the idea went to Elinor's heart.

'I think Kit was wanting affection as much as a lesson,' she said later. 'Maybe if you—'

'He should be learning independence, he's old enough.'

'He's still a baby, he needs—'

'Children sense things, you're always saying that,' he said stiffly; he was horribly hurt to learn that she had been observing him critically. 'Christopher knows how I feel without constant demonstrations.'

Constant! How about occasional? Elinor bit her tongue.

She should have held it altogether, she realised: after her intervention, Tim stood off from both children for days.

Chapter 29

Elinor didn't really want to go north at Easter—she was too edgy about the impending presentation. But Tim wanted to, and it was all arranged: they would stay in Harrogate, not at Swarthgill, and Mrs Scott would look after Isobel during the day while they went walking. Kit was to stay with Maggie. She had already had him overnight several times, and was eager to have him for a whole weekend. 'Don't fool yourself,' she'd told Elinor. 'It's pure selfishness, not generosity.'

'Only you'll ring if he cries for me? More than just when I leave, I mean? He shouldn't, he's so used to other people; but you never know.'

'If he does, you'll hear from me double quick—I'll be so unflattered I'll disown him. Go on, indulge in your unnatural vice.' Walking, she meant. 'And don't fret about the presentation, either. You say you're ready for Sefton and Ginny—'

'Insofar as we'll *ever* be ready to suggest anything so outrageous. Ask them to venture large sums, when they want cash for their piggeries—we must be out of our minds! I'm like *this* with anxiety'—making a ball of her fist; 'I haven't slept properly in weeks.'

But she slept in Harrogate, after a day on the moors with Tim— feeling closer to him there than anywhere, as they moved through the wide bare waste with the same long stride, the country penetrating them, the endless circling horizon, fold upon fold of changing sameness. London seemed far away. She'd half forgotten the presentation by the time they changed out of sodden walking clothes on Monday evening and headed back home through ever-thickening Bank Holiday traffic with Isobel fast asleep in her child seat.

— * —

218

They drew up in Great James Street just before ten. Tim got out and rang Maggie's bell; again; again. Elinor looked up at the first floor windows; the sitting room light wasn't on. She got out and went round the corner; no bedroom and kitchen lights, either. 'They must be at Ockendon Road,' she said; 'I left her a key in case Kit got homesick.'

There were no lights in the front rooms as they drove up. 'She'll be up reading to him,' Elinor said—the children's bedroom was at the back.

But the whole house was silent and dark. Elinor's stomach turned over with alarm. Tim put Isobel on the sofa with a chair as barricade, and without a word they went, one up, the other down, to make a top-to-bottom search. No Maggie; no Kit.

Tim went out back with a torch. Maggie could not possibly be lurking in the garden shed with a toddler on a cold April night, but it was easier to think up crazy possibilities than face grim ones.

'Maybe she's taken him somewhere and lost track of the time,' he said hopefully when he came back.

'Maggie never loses track of time.'

'Then he's had an accident, or she has, or he's ill. I'll start ringing hospitals.'

'Or...'

Tim was already in the music room, digging out *E-K*, muttering, 'Hopkins, Horton, Hospitals...'

Elinor stood stock still, remembering Maggie saying she knew what made women snatch babies from prams. Not hospitals—the police. Tell them to stop a single woman leaving the country with a little boy. No—Maggie wouldn't leave it this late. She's in South America by now with my baby.

Isobel started to grizzle. Elinor picked her up distractedly and went into the music room. Tim said, 'I've tried Great Ormond Street and the Royal Free, they're the nearest to Maggie. UCH next. You be looking through the list—we should fan out geographically.' He looked sick; his back was hunched tight.

No point—she's taken him. But Elinor couldn't make herself say it; couldn't really believe it. Maggie would never do it, if only because it would be bad for Kit. But...

219

Tim hung up, and immediately the telephone rang. He grabbed it. 'Maggie?—Oh hullo, Rose.—*You've* got him? Thank God.—Yes—I'll fetch him.' He hung up. 'Maggie's father—he's dying. Maggie left Christopher with Rose at the Cromer—and told her she'd leave us a note—Rose has been waiting for us to turn up.' Beside himself with relief, he straightened his shoulders and gave Elinor a one-armed hug. His face was alight; even his fuzzy hair seemed to frizz up electrically from his head.

Tim went for Kit, and Elinor put Isobel to bed and unpacked, sagging like overstretched elastic. She should be overjoyed that Kit wasn't in a hospital, a morgue, a Brazilian beach house; but she was too mortified. Maggie kidnap him? What had she been thinking of? Okay, it was reasonable in the abstract—but not about *Maggie*. She wasn't some poor demented creature, she was fiercely sensible and completely sane.

'He's still alive, just,' Maggie said in an exhausted voice when she rang in the morning. 'They've turfed me out while they do unspeakable things. Sorry I had to leave Rose holding the baby, but I couldn't let him die alone. I knew you'd understand.'

Her father died that day. Five days later she called in at the Cromer, still living through what had happened. 'I didn't think I'd even be sad, but death *is* sad, no matter how little you feel for the person. The strangest thing was Kit. At first I thought I'd have to take him with me, you know, then I remembered you'd said the Cromer was open on Bank Holiday Monday, and rang Rose. But it's so hallucinatory, an intensive care unit at night, pools of bright light, machines winking green lights and hissing and glugging and bleeping, patients right out of it but moaning and groaning anyhow; and I'd had *such* a strong picture of having to bring Kit—I could hardly believe he wasn't there. I'd catch myself thinking he must be asleep on my coat in the corner, or running out after the nurses, or on my lap asking why Dad had tubes up his nose. Even now I *remember* him there, though I know he wasn't. But thank God I was in time. I felt bad about sticking up that note and dumping Kit on Rose—but Dad knew me, I was in time for that. A couple of hours later he was in coma.'

'Where was the note?' Elinor asked. 'We never got it.'

'But I left it—oh *Nell*. You must have thought I'd run off with him.'

She couldn't confess it. 'Tim was ringing casualty rooms, actually; and then Rose rang us.'

'Still—bad enough. Nell, Nell, I'm *so* sorry. I taped it to my letterbox, right below the buzzer—I suppose some kids tore it off just for the hell of it.'

'Or hoped it had a key to the flats.'

'No, I'd thought of that, it was just a piece of card with, "Dad dying, Kit with Rose at Cromer, love Maggie." ' She snorted with disgust. 'Oh Nell, I got there and they were doing a *dialysis*. What good they thought it would do—it was so *obvious* he was dying— and he was so *frightened*. Oh Lord—you think because you're in the articulate professional classes the health service won't muck you up, or anyone you care about. I'm even *administering* it—I should be able to stop the juggernaut; but no, you get there and it's all happening.' She wiped her eyes and nose and found a smile. 'Life's a bugger, Nell, and death's no improvement.'

The next day she had news. 'You'll never believe who took my note—Clive. The old man in the ground floor flat saw him—"That blond gentleman who used to come calling on you"—the busy-body. He's often seen him standing outside, since sometime after Christmas.'

'How weird—it's almost a year since you broke it off.'

'What's even weirder—his baby was born in December; it's since then that he's been doing it. I steamed into his office today, and he collapsed in a puddle, said it was an impulse—he didn't have anything in my handwriting. I said if he didn't stop loitering outside my flat, I'd sic the police on him. He knew I meant it, too. So that's that.'

'Unless his obsession's too much for him,' Elinor said, remembering the moment when she saw the misery beneath Clive's mask of composure.

'Oh, he won't jeopardise his career. Still, it'll be a long time before you'll want to let Kit stay with me again.'

221

Elinor had discovered exactly this feeling in herself already, so she was ready for the thrust and the shrewd look. 'Nonsense,' she said, though it wasn't easy to. 'You can have him tonight if you want.'

Bravo, love, Maggie thought, but I won't put you through it. She stood up with a laugh and kissed her. 'Thanks, but I've got an engagement—Albericht the Ample.'

Chapter 30

'The site's too small for another screen,' Elinor had told Sefton Wellesford, but twinning was by far the best way—really the only way—for the Cromer to earn more. An architect friend of Chris's took a look, said, 'There's room for *two* more screens if they're both small,' and sketched them a floor plan: one auditorium in the basement and one in the big space behind the present screen, extending into the dingy yard behind the building. The council's planning department looked at the sketch and intimated—'unofficially you understand'—that they wouldn't oppose the expansion.

Terry didn't wear anything special the day of the presentation—he was a natty dresser anyhow. Elinor came to work in a reasonably smart jacket and a sober grey skirt from Next. Rose wore a boxy brown suit, shiny brown shoes with a medium heel, and a long string of lustrous pearls. 'How do I look?' she demanded.

'Lamb dressed as mutton,' said Terry.

Elinor managed not to laugh—Rose was looking hurt. 'Nonsense, it's perfect. We'll slay 'em. Those real?'—touching the pearls.

'Yup; the suit too—Chanel. Mummy's. The shoes are Saxone's best plastic, though—I couldn't hack Mummy's size 4s.'

Sefton and Ginny said yes to coffee and waited in silence while Terry fetched it and folded his six foot five back into a chair. Sefton turned to him and said, 'Well, suppose we begin.'

Bridling invisibly—the ideas and work were hers and Nell's, didn't Sefton realise?—Rose dusted off the accent and vocabulary that went with the pearls and set off. Three screens—our audience survey—this graph—council—architect—sketch plan. 'Cromer Two would seat a hundred and fifty, Cromer Three, fifty to sixty. Cromer Three would do private screenings and press previews, so it

223

needs to be fairly luxurious, which on a small scale is affordable. It's a sure thing—there's a shortage of small specialised screens in central London. Here's a rough cost breakdown.' Time-scale—tax relief—probable break-even point...extra staff...disruption to Cromer One minimal...

'Cromer Two,' said Elinor as Sefton reached for his calculator, 'Cromer Two would show first-run art-house films. It'll be up against the Renoir, but clever programming should do the trick. Their stock-in-trade is epics of angst, and French bourgeois embalming jobs, whereas we'd focus on the young and sassy—American independents and the like. It should work. If not, we could show cult films till we're in the black, though we'd much rather not. But it's more of a venture than Cromer Three; we won't pretend otherwise. Here are our estimates...'

They both made a point of handing some of the papers to Ginny—who passed them straight on to Sefton. She was listening, though. She had a narrow pursed-up face, well-tended fair hair, and a critical eye. She had dismissed Elinor after a quick inspection. Rose she had paused over, recognising the style as her own—until she noticed her shoes. Terry passed visual muster, but failed the accent test.

'All this would be terribly *expensive*,' she said, directing a glance at the offensive shoes.

Rose said, 'I'm afraid that's inevitable. Next month, when the film clubs start, we'll be working the present plant at capacity. The only way to get more out is to put more in.'

Ginny looked dissatisfied. There was a silence, broken only by the rustle of papers and the tap-tap of Sefton's calculator. Finally he said, 'It *is* expensive. We'll have to look it all over very carefully—and bring Andrew in on things...'

'Quite,' said Ginny, standing up and looking at Terry. He took the hint and helped her into her coat, then followed her out, holding doors. Sefton closed his briefcase and murmured goodbyes for both of them. This time there was a ticket on the Rolls Royce—Ginny was tearing it up.

Time for the first matinée—Elinor and Terry bustled.

It was Rose's day off, but she hadn't left when Elinor got back from letting the house in. 'Is that *all*?' she cried. 'All that hassle, and then—zilch? They didn't even—I don't know what I expected, but...'

'Yeah, some letdown. And it was all over so fast—I thought we'd be *hours*.'

'You sound like Woody Allen's ladies complaining about their hotel—"The food's awful—and you get such small portions." '

Elinor mustered a tiny laugh.

'I quite fancy the idea of Cromer Three,' Terry said, coming back with the stubs.

Rose and Elinor exchanged glances. 'Then it's your baby—if we get it,' Rose said.

'Really? But I'm so new, how can you know if—'

'We know,' they said in chorus. He was incredibly efficient, and engagingly courteous in an old-fashioned way—customers loved it. He would make a better host for private screenings than right-on Rose or offhand Elinor.

'Maybe not programming, just yet, but running,' Rose added: programming wasn't Terry's strongest point, so far.

'I could wear a dinner jacket, like that man at the NFT,' he said rapturously; and they all burst into laughter.

'Don't raid Moss Bros just yet,' said Elinor. 'We'll probably end up as luxury flats—the Wellesford Arms—and you'd be out on the pavement in your glad rags.'

For the first fortnight they thought it was Sefton every time the telephone rang. Then they started saying, 'What's keeping him?' and nervously dreaming up improbable reasons for the delay. 'He's looking for new management—we'll come one day and find ourselves locked out.' 'He's negotiating with Rank to take us over.' 'He's got an architect designing an office block—Wellesford House.' 'He's for us, Ginny's against us.' Ginny wouldn't be *for* them, that they were sure of.

By June they didn't jump when the telephone went; by July they had almost stopped speculating aloud. Every once in a while one of them would say, 'Maybe we should ring *him*,' and the others would say no. Let sleeping Seftons lie. Their hands were quite full enough already. The lates had more customers almost every week, and the Saturday children's morning was building up a head of steam. So far the pensioners preferred church. 'But wait till winter,' Terry said. 'Those pews are *cold*.'

August. No word.

'Of course not—he's on holiday.'

'On his yacht.' They had just run *Some Like It Hot*.

'The small one, I hope: "With all the unrest in the world I don't think anybody should have a yacht that sleeps more than twelve." '

'S'okay, he sold the big one: times are hard.'

September. No word. Tim and Elinor left the children with her parents and flew to Rome for five days. It should have been a week, but Tim had let a fixer talk him into a recording. Elinor muttered darkly when he sprang the news, but didn't storm. She didn't want to spoil their holiday—and didn't want to be away that long herself, with everything still hanging fire.

She brought the office with her. Had Sefton rung? What could she do if they closed the Cromer?—the burning question. Three out-of-work rep managers chasing zero rep-management jobs. Maybe the multiples would want them. But could she stand it— playing *Halloween III* for five weeks?

'Get a job with a distributor,' Tim suggested on the Palatine the first afternoon, going down the dark stairs into the Casa di Livia.

'Are you *crazy*? They're—they're the enemy!'

He burst out laughing. Elinor pouted, then laughed too. The guard frowned, as if their breath might blow the frescoed garlands off the walls.

'Besides, don't think about that—you're here now. Look at that—and that. The grace—and the perspective. Think of the secret of perspective being lost from the fall of Rome till 1400—over a thousand years of primitive art, God help us. Think how fragile art is—the knowledge of it; how easily another dark age could blot out everything *we've* won, let alone—'

'*That's* supposed to cheer me up?' Elinor said sarcastically—but it did.

That night as they began making love she remembered his face glowing when he pointed out the wreathed ribbons on the empress's walls, and with a surge of love made to kiss him. He turned his head aside.

How can it still hurt? he's been doing it for years.

It hurt. Stop, she thought. She didn't want his hands on her, his cock in her. But she didn't say it, didn't know how to, had never said stop, never before this moment wanted to, with him.

Instead, she tried thinking of images that usually made her breath catch with lust—him pushing into her groaning with pleasure; her body splayed out beneath his. No good. She tried imagining things she wished he'd do that he never did: kissing her; sucking her nipples. No good.

Bad fantasy, then...a stranger meeting her eye in the street, walking beside her without a word, touching her arm to direct her indoors, following her upstairs, running his hands up under her skirt, telling her to take off her clothes and lie on the bed with her legs spread, opening his fly, getting out his cock, coming onto her—

No, it was horrid being fucked by a man wearing trousers— fabric scratching your soft cunt-flesh, zip-fastener yanking your pubic hair.

Imagine him taking them off, then. And stop being so picky.

She couldn't concentrate. The fantasy wasn't exciting, it was ridiculous. She was sweaty and disgusted; her feeble flicker of arousal kept guttering out. Finally it caught, and she came—a hot little twitch, one moment nowhere in sight, the next moment over and done with.

Afterwards she felt desolate, at a distance she hardly wanted to close, almost preferring melancholy isolation. For the next couple of days she avoided lovemaking—not the easiest thing on their first real holiday alone since the children.

But he was at his best on holiday—or was it away from the children? He loved the beauty of the world with a gusto that he felt no need to repress, and wanted to share with her; and his delight slowly softened her.

On their last afternoon they went to see Bernini's *St Teresa*, swooning back among her nun's draperies in an ecstasy that was nothing if not sexual. 'Any moment now God's going to lift her skirts,' Elinor whispered.

For a second she thought Tim would scold her for vulgarity. Instead he whispered back, 'When we get back to the hotel, I'm going to lift yours.'

The maid had closed the shutters against the afternoon heat; the room was dim, striped with a few long dusty gleams. Elinor came back from putting in her diaphragm, and Tim pulled her down onto the bed before she could pull off her dress, and lifted the skirt up to her waist—he would have flung it straight up over her head had he not thought that the symbolism might upset her. She caught the tone of his impulse and turned her head into the pillow to make her face invisible, only her body visible.

He came in almost without preliminary, pushing hard, opening her up with each thrust, pivoting, push and push and push, each time touching her cervix, flooding her with passion. Fucking me like a drowning man, she thought with ferocious pleasure. Then he stopped, and she pulled round him, wheedling him into starting again; trying against her own best interests to drive him beyond any bounds. Some odd echo of what they had said in the church was with them—an overtone of profanity, of what the St Teresa represented: a universe pervaded by carnality.

They were bathed in, buoyed up by, tenderness and trust, opened to each other, acutely sensible of every place where their bodies touched, yet almost unconscious of where she ended and he began. Repeatedly they pulled back from the brink, but not far—resigning themselves to each other: impossible giving, impossible restraint. Restraint became impossible, yet went on being possible—the same place at once plateau and precipice: self-denial and inordinacy, giving and withholding, ecstasy and excruciation. In their intent self-immolation they were mystics achieving transport through exercises in physical impossibility—St Teresa, pierced by God's arrows.

After a long time, thinking that a slight shift meant she wanted to come, he whispered, 'What do you want?'

'What do you?'

'I want to give you pleasure.' In another tone he added: 'I want my cock all over you, I want to fill you.'

'I want to fill you,' she remembered afterwards. It wasn't something she ever thought—any more, probably, than he ever thought of wanting to open himself to her. Funny: your desires cascaded in channels worn by the knowledge of what your gender made possible—even if not literally possible: he couldn't actually fill her, or she be endlessly open. Desire was so saturated with emotion and idea—how could you say what was physical and what emotional? Feelings leapt into imagery as soon as born.

Tim, Tim—it was thanks to him that she'd found her way into this fantasy-realm where opposites coexisted and ravishing vague images displaced little fictional ones, or changed them from bad to innocent.

Maybe even her worst fantasies, as well as being dark orgies of humiliation, were also something less unnerving: distorted images—caricatures—of desires too primitive, too irrational, to be held in the imagination at all in their real forms. When she imagined being made to do everything a man wanted, wasn't that less about what the man wanted, and more about her own desire to be forced to do everything *she* wanted? *Everything*; not just what she thought was acceptable—forced to let go her defences and be released from shame and fear; to go beyond where words and reason were any use, to live for nothing but sex.

In real life you couldn't do that—but the imagination was insatiable. In childhood she'd had a fantasy of diving into a room full of lemon snow. The thought still crinkled her tongue with pleasure, though she knew she would only be sticky and sick.

Chapter 31

'For you.' Thoby passed the receiver, shrugging to say he didn't recognise the voice.

'Sheil, yer mum's got pneumonia, she's in Mile End hospital, ward 8C. Thought you'd want to know—visiting her, like. Well, got to go, I'm on night shift these days. Cheers.' He hung up; Sheila hadn't said a word.

He knew my number, then. And never rang. How long never hearing that voice? Twenty years.

She didn't get under the table. She went on helping Thoby put the boys to bed, then got her coat and muffler and said, 'I'm going to see my Mum, she's in hospital.'

'Oh, who was that, then?'

'My Da.'

Thoby couldn't leave the children and go with her. He sat at home skitterheaded with anxiety wondering when she'd come back, or if, and in what state.

She was tense but calm; she'd been less than two hours, 'She's not bad,' she said in response to his questions. 'They're sending her home, they want the bed. I said I'd go look after her at night for a while,—Da's on night shift.'

'Can't they get a nurse? a neighbour?—*anyone* but you?'

'I said I'd go.'

That tone meant: Don't talk about it any more. Thoby shut up.

Sheila hadn't been in the house since her early teens. She expected it to seem smaller and shabbier, but it didn't. It was full of cheap prosperity—freezer, microwave, knitting machine, video. There was a bathroom extension where the coalshed had been, with green fixtures.

Avocado, she thought with an amusement that was Thoby's, then forced it back. She'd left all this behind; now she must take it on again, not repudiate her parents' furnishings for the precious good taste of Hackney. Thoby painted out the brand name on their toaster and soaked the labels off deodorant bottles, for God's sake, so they wouldn't offend his eyes.

She went to and fro, to and fro, from Limehouse to work, from work to Hackney, from Hackney to Limehouse. She slept in her old room. She got used to meeting her father in the morning. There were only two bedrooms; he had to wait for her to get up before going to bed himself. The house wasn't smaller, but he was—or was she just imagining it? On her mother's lower lip, just left of centre, was a huge scabby purple sore like ten cold sores rolled into one.

To and fro, to and fro. She wouldn't let Thoby come, and certainly not the children. He was peripheral; so were they. She had work to do here, sitting by her mother's bed, sleeping in her own old bed with her first cello standing in the corner—why hadn't they sold it?—and her father's pyjamas crumpled on the chair.

She knew the jargon from work, used it herself in Linchpin. Integrate your past into your present, face your anger.

Stop running away, face it. Face—

Had she ever wanted anything in her life so much as when she was her Da's own true love?—resisting, pretending to resist, maybe only resisting because he wanted her to, because it was part of the game that he forced her.

He'd needed to believe that. It meant she was still innocent, that he hadn't corrupted her.

She'd needed to believe it too; it kept her pure in her heart, where she'd known she wasn't.

He'd fancied himself, her Da: getting away with it, cocking a snook at the world. Sometimes he'd made out it was all her doing. 'Ooh, a proper little temptress you are.'

How could she not have responded to a hand that had been insinuating itself inside her knickers since before she knew it had no business being there?

She'd always known. It's our secret, he used to say, just you and me.

231

Too young to know any different, old enough to know better.

Her mother's wheezing got louder—she was trying to sit up. Sheila went over. 'What d'you want, Mum?'

'Cold,' she whispered, making another futile flounder. 'Sorry.'

'That's why I'm here, Mum.' Sheila covered her and went to refill the hot-water bottle. Her mother had crocheted the pink and lilac cover. In the loo—the toilet, we call it in these parts, she reminded herself—the spare roll of lavatory paper was hidden under a doll's crocheted pink and green skirt. Try as she might, she couldn't see it through admiring eyes.

She gave her the hot-water bottle, tucked her in and sat down again by the window, looking out through a chink in the curtains— not the skimpy old bright yellow ones, with brown starbursts; new, lined ones, matching the bedspread, in a sprigged pattern she had no trouble liking; she and Thoby might have chosen it themselves ten years ago, before the country look hit the high street. The hemline of the net curtains went up in the middle like half-lifted stage curtains. Dress circle, front row; the stage empty. The street lights were brighter than the plump moon waxing above the chimneypots. There were a few parlour lights on, and telly flickering; in one bedroom a boy was hunched over a computer. When she lived here, hadn't everybody been in bed by this time?

If he'd been violent, if he'd raped her, she wouldn't have been guilty of desire. The things she'd read about abuse only spoke of pain and rape. But there was worse, there was being led in gently, cunningly, being given pleasure, getting hooked. Then they'd got you by the soul.

Her Da had never hurt her, or hardly ever. 'You okay?' he'd ask. She didn't know the answer, so she said yes. Sometimes he even said, 'Want me to stop, then?' But didn't hear her saying, 'Yes, please.'

She'd wanted to be safe from him, but she'd wanted to make him happy, too, wanted him to love her, wanted him to herself.

That she'd got. She'd been her Da's princess, her Mum had been jealous—but bought her the cello, out of the housekeeping and what she made cleaning and dressmaking, plus a high-interest loan from a local shark.

232

Mum with her head in the sand, Da sending her down the shops to get her out of the way. Sheila would plead to go with her, but he'd say, 'You've your lessons still to do,' or, 'You stay home, miss, and practise that *thing*. Yer Mum paid enough for it.'

Then the Menuhin School; safety—and coming home at half term to find everything different: her all-powerful Da a coarse, hulking, inarticulate middle-aged man, powerless, embarrassed, careful not to brush against her in the passage, as if the School were the Tree of Knowledge, and now she must know she'd been naked.

She'd known before.

Her Da with creases in his cheeks, an out-of-work costermonger, keeping his distance, pathetic, like a statistic. She hadn't wanted to see him that way. She'd wanted, then now always...incompatibles. Safety. But her Da, too. Intensity, enclosure, living in a conspiracy.

She'd left him. He'd needed her and she'd run away. She'd needed him and run away. He'd given her what he could, and she'd rejected it.

Back and forth, back and forth. Her mother's sore was drying up; she could get out of bed and use the commode Sheila borrowed from the Red Cross. In another week she was going downstairs to the loo and back up without huffing and puffing. 'You'd best be stopping at home,' she said. 'The boys will be missing you.'

'Oh, Thoby does for them.' But she took the hint.

Going back to Hackney for good, to Thoby beaming hopefully, she felt a weight of sulkiness settle on her heart. Was he softening her up with tenderness so she'd talk about her ordeal?

He thought she was an innocent victim—remember when she'd first told him, how amazed he was that she hadn't been put off sex for good. Far from it—her Da had made her an addict. But it wasn't the same without the secrecy, the sense of being marked out for sin.

No one must know that, even Thoby. Especially Thoby. *He* was the innocent, with his questions—

'Why don't you talk?' Because if she ever started, she'd never be able to stop. Because she'd say things he mustn't know.

'What do you think?' Half the time she didn't *know* what she thought. Him and his family and their instant opinions.

233

'What do you want?' But she didn't *want* to want things. She'd wanted Da; what he did to her, what she'd done to him. Hadn't wanted, wanted—which?

If she ever did tell Thoby what she wanted, he wouldn't like it. She wanted to practise, watch telly, listen to music, go to a film—anything but talk, or listen. She wanted him to take care of her without expecting things in return. She wanted him not to ask her what she wanted or thought or liked; not to ask her for things she couldn't give. She wanted to be left alone.

Face your anger—what good did it do? She hadn't got rid of it, and she was burnt out. All that passionate effort for nothing.

Not quite nothing. She had learned respect for the refuge her mother found in traditional forms, thoughts, feelings. Her mother loved her husband because he was her husband, and her daughter because she was her daughter. She wasn't self-conscious about it, she just did it. A lot to be said for that. It got you through life; and it was better for children than loving them too needingly. Sheila was afraid of that—dragging the boys' souls out of them with her need.

She had a sense of closure. All this time she had been a little girl, half believing that her nightmares would go away if she grew up and faced them. Well, she'd grown up; and they were still there: the literal nightmares of invasion—of having no boundaries—that still woke her up in a sweat; and the nightmare of what she'd done and been done to, and what it had made of her. She would have to live with them.

Poor Thoby. The truth makes you free, he'd said once, but telling him about Da had made him captive. How could he leave someone who'd had *that* happen?

Was that why she'd told him?

She didn't like the thought. Best not to think. She folded her will tight and got on with life.

The quartet were doing Shostakovich's seventh. 'Funny, nothing's happier than music, but nothing's sadder,' Elinor said over lunch the Sunday before Christmas. 'He never wins through, like Brahms, he's always imprisoned in sadness.'

'Denmark's a prison,' said Thoby.

She nearly said, Russia, then remembered the line in Olivier's *Hamlet*. Whew—nearly made a fool of yourself. 'D'you think it was the times, or would he have been that way no matter what?'

'A bit of both?' said Sheila.

'The times,' said Thoby decidedly.

'It's what he's like,' said Tim. 'While he was writing the Leningrad Symphony, Richard Strauss was over in Hitler's Germany frothing up *Capriccio*.'

Thoby said, 'But is it a difference of temperament or conscience?' and he and Tim hared off onto the question of whether morals and temperament were related or independent. Thoby quoted Wittgenstein and Kant; Tim, Hannah Arendt.

'Any news from the Wellesfords?' Sheila asked through the flying abstractions.

Elinor moved her chair closer to Sheila's. 'None. We don't even talk about it any more, Rose and me, but I don't think we think about anything else. It saps your will, prolonged suspense—Rose says she can't even choose between two pairs of shoes any more.'

'It's so cruel, leaving you without word.'

'Yeah—it feels like that, but probably they just can't imagine how much it matters to us when it's peanuts to them. Andrew will be back in a few months—maybe we'll hear something then. But tell me about your mother—she still weak?'

'Much better—just a little tired, that's all.'

'Give her my best wishes when you see her. I like her—she's got such a nice face.' Elinor smiled, remembering it.

Sheila had a strong impulse to tell Nell...something...a little bit...everything—her lively black eyes were as hypnotic as a gold watch twirling in front of your eyes. Impossible to tell Thoby, but a woman would understand, especially Nell, especially now...

The impulse passed. Nell's job would be saved, or she'd lose it and get another, and the unpleasantness of these months would fade from her memory. What other cloud had ever darkened her sky? How could she understand a past that kept staining the present? She lived on the far side of a glass panel, in a world where everything was happy.

Chapter 32

That wasn't how Elinor saw it. She wouldn't have called herself unhappy—she wasn't used to thinking of herself that way—but the suspense about the Cromer was making her discontented and snappish.

'It's just a job,' Tim said one day, meaning to be comforting.

'How would you like it if you thought you couldn't *play* any more?' she said furiously, and got even crosser when he said it wasn't the same, which it probably wasn't, but even so—

Don't be unreasonable, she kept telling herself. Hold on.

Life was becoming easier, with Kit coming up to three and Isobel to two, but she and Tim still had more to do than they'd once had, and less time to do it in: children changed things. They were still interested in each other's work—Tim told her about music, she told him about movies—but he hardly ever came to films any more, and she hardly ever went to concerts.

She missed music: not just concerts, but the old peaceful mornings listening to him play while she read the *Guardian*. The children's chatter put him out of tune; so the doors between music room and drawing room were closed when he was practising. Most of the time she couldn't listen to the quartet properly, either—you couldn't, while trying to keep four rambunctious children halfway quiet. Sometimes they got so noisy that she had to take them into a bedroom and close the door, and the quartet sounded like nothing more than a distant recording. 'It's okay,' she always said when the players asked if she minded. She did wish they'd think of hiring a sitter every few weeks, but it seemed an outrageously extravagant thing to ask; so she didn't.

She missed the old Sunday walks, too. She and Tim took the children to the Heath or the Marshes most weeks—Tim was keen for them to have more of nature than just plane trees and neat parks. But their dawdle-toddle drove him wild. 'Back in a few minutes,' he would say, then took off at high speed across the grass—and didn't return till it was nearly time to go: Elinor seldom got a turn on her own.

He was also accepting more Sunday matinée engagements, leaving her to take the children out on her own. It was annoying, but she didn't want to tackle him about anything till she knew about the Cromer. She would speak too sharply, be too extreme: her sense of proportion was out of whack.

Growl, grumble, snap. Hadn't she felt this way last winter, too? Better not make a habit of it—the wind might change.

She held on. The months slithered past in a slow blur. January...February—the audit, and a nice profit to report to Sefton and Ginny: who sent a formal acknowledgment.

March. 'Let's ring them in May,' Rose proposed one night—'on the anniversary of the presentation. Give us something to look forward to.'

'A conference call,' said Elinor. 'Three of us to two of them.'

'Ship to shore—brother Sef will be on his yacht.'

'A big one—he's used our profits to trade up.'

The buzzer rang to signal the end of the film, and Elinor went to help let the house out. When she got back, Rose was standing in a complete dither, her hand on the telephone receiver and her round cheeks scarlet. 'Nell, you'll never—I was just coming—'

But here were the ushers, back from going through the auditorium picking up junk before the late film. Elinor steered Rose into the inner office. 'So what's up?'

'Oh Nell, that was Andrew—'

Elinor felt the blood drain from her head. She sat down on her desk.

'He's back—he—they're not going to close us—he says yes, maybe Cromer Three in a year or two, but not Two—'

'Not too what?'

'Not T-w-o. *Deux, dos, due.* He didn't actually *say* Sefton's a greedy prat, but—'

'What *did* he say?'

'Oh—"We've talked it over," and, "We've seen the worst of the recession," and, "You've done so well the past two years," and, "The Cromer Trust is a sacred trust." Mostly he wanted to rap about Canada—his granddaughters and his son's Herefords.'

'But what about Cromer Three?'

'I don't really know, I just listened—he sees the point, and he'll look into it, and how clever and creative we were to think of it.'

'Lucky for us he's so smitten with you.'

'Oh it can't be—'

'I know, I'm teasing, I don't even know what I'm saying. Oh Rosy!'

'Oh Nell!' Rose's face was still blotchy red. 'You know, it's nutty—but I feel sick.'

Elinor didn't, not quite, but she was winded and giddy. 'D'you want me to do the late for you?' she said, just as Tim, come to pick her up, poked his head round the door.

'Nah, I'm—oh Tim, the most—Nell will tell you—got to go: the next house—'

'What's with her?' he said as Rose skittered off trailing dizzy radiance.

'Andrew—the Cromer—he's back—it's all okay, we're safe.'

'Oh *Elinor.*' Tim opened his arms, put them round her, both of them, and squeezed. 'Oh Elinor.'

'Oh Tim—' She burst into tears.

He drew back in alarm. 'What's wrong?'

'Nothing, just so happy, it's...' She stepped closer, hoping he'd hug her again.

'Better get home and let Lindsay go,' he said. 'That damned fool Sefton, putting you through all this. Got everything?'

She slung on her jacket and floated out, giving Rose a quick twirl on her way past the auditorium door. Getting into the car she said, 'This is what they mean, walking on air. How was your concert?'

'So-so. Dull, in fact. But now there's something to celebrate.' He ran his index finger along her thigh.

'Oh *yes*.' Her skin was electric under her jeans where he had touched her, and she was glowing all over from his hug. They smiled at each other happily, and he started the car.

That week was all elation; then they gradually came down to earth. 'This is what it's like after the happy ending,' Terry said. 'The hormones stop pumping, the rest of life comes back on the agenda, and you almost miss the crisis high.'

'Not me,' said Rose.

'Well...' said Elinor, 'I *do* feel deflated. Of all the things we thought could happen—being kicked out, having to revamp everything—the one thing we didn't think of was that *nothing* would.'

But she wasn't tensed up against disaster any more—it was time to deal with things that had been bothering her. The quartet? Forget it. In a year or so the children would be old enough to murder each other behind closed doors while she listened to the music in peace—it wasn't worth making an issue of sitters in the meantime. Tim going off on sub-walks of his own and leaving her with the children? She'd call him back next time it happened, and say it wasn't fair, she wanted to take turns.

She did. He said, 'You're right, sorry, I didn't think of it that way,' and let her go first.

Down from Kenwood House, hands in pockets, imagining him watching her resentfully. But when she turned to wave he was walking in the other direction with the pushchair.

Round the pond, into Ken Wood, trying to enjoy it.

But what she wanted wasn't stretching her legs on her own, it was walking with Tim, alone with Tim the way they used to be. They'd had so little time alone since the children.

Well, that wasn't his fault.

Who said it was? It was inevitable with children.

What was his fault was—

Don't start *that*. The wind might change, remember? You're happy, don't spoil it. Think of the way he hugged you when he heard.

— * —

239

Maggie had had Kit for three days at Christmas, and now Muriel Scott wanted a turn. At Easter she got it: Elinor and Tim dumped both children on her—thank God for doting grandmothers—and had two wonderful days at Swarthgill, out on the moors from breakfast to dinner, walking and walking and walking, happy, at ease.

They spent the last day in Harrogate. Tim was easy there, too—the children had brought that about. As a father, he no longer feared his parents; he was one of them. The old photographs were had out that night, and likenesses exclaimed over; he was part of something solid, a line. Christopher in his turn would become a man capable of begetting a child. Which would make Tim—

A grandfather? With greying hair like his parents', with spectacles for reading music—

He was transfixed by the knowledge that he would die—and probably outlive sexual desire, too, which almost seemed worse; and be tremulous and slow and deaf—unable to play. No, no, better dead without the sweet life of the senses—making love to Elinor, or playing the fiddle, his body leaning with the glide of the bow, his calloused fingertips pressing the strings.

Tim shuddered back into ordinary life. If he had been a drinking man he would have got drunk. Instead, when they went to bed, in spite of being in his parents' house, he made love to Elinor with ferocious, drowning intensity.

He needed to cry out against death; needed saturnalia; and in the aromatic darkness, with his tongue on her cunt and his cock in her mouth, got it. The intimacy of fucking could touch the centre of self and personhood, soul speaking to soul through the preternatural fine-grained responsiveness of body to body, breath in each other's ears like a transpiration of souls, a great rush of self-immolation, self-bestowing, communion; but that rapt breathing distance between head and sexual conjunction was annihilated by what they were doing now—the intimacy was staggering, but the element of spirituality was suppressed. Lovemaking was continually in tension between personal eloquence and surrender to a substructure of being that was not so much two particular people as a woman and a man, and this was at one extreme: the furthest you could go away

240

from the other person's face into a mutuality of darkness, both faces buried in sex; with something primitive about it, orgiastic, a dissolution of self and its defences of personality and frankness into acceptance of bodies at their most carnal.

That night coloured their lovemaking back in London; they entered a phase that emphasised darkness, hiddenness, namelessness: that gave dizzying glimpses into things that were primitive—or perhaps primary, or prior: at the root of desire, more fundamental even than the froth of sexual excitement. As if they had tunnel vision, they returned again and again to particular gestures, slight changes in posture or motion that had emotional effects out of all proportion to the physical difference—a simplicity to what they did, a weightedness. Tim, that wordless man, said, 'Giving you pleasure...' then shook his head helplessly. 'It connects me to *life*.' Elinor walked round in a glow. Nothing could be better than this: she'd thought it so often.

One morning he reached his hand down and began stirring his cock round and round in her mouth, not roughly, but firmly. Momentarily she resented the gesture. Wasn't I doing well enough for you, she thought sarcastically—you need to show me how? But it touched the part of her that wanted to be the medium of his pleasure, to be forced and used. Make me do what you want, she thought. No use trying to tell herself she was upset.

Still holding his cock, he traced the circle of her lips with it, and then, in big, soft, slow circles, her chin, her cheeks, under her nose, round and round, soft, seeking, straying up to her eye sockets and down again; back into her mouth and out again; blurring the distinction between inside and outside; inscribing her face, writing all over it—touching her, literally and figuratively.

Something to do with words, he had once said. With words, with deeds. Concentrate on what I can give, Elinor.

His cock on her face was like fingers reading Braille. He was learning her face by proxy, letting his cock transmit to his fingers information which for some mysterious reason he couldn't let them learn for themselves; kissing her lips with it instead of with his own lips; putting it, instead of his tongue, into her mouth.

241

The moment, the impulse, passed. Time to change, she thought, but was mesmerised; it was he who broke off, pulled her up on top of him and probed her with a quivering sharpness while she lay on his chest, on his belly, almost unconscious with concentration, clenching her fists, repressing groans, until at last she could do nothing but come, shuddering all over, flooded with the massy full-bodied resonance that was missing from purely clitoral intensity—though they were shadings of the same tone, not different in kind: crimson and scarlet, lustre and sparkle, french horn and trumpet, whirlpool and rapids.

Oh yes—tenderness towards him in her heart, to match the *tendresse* in his gesture. *Tendresse, tristesse*, the lovely little cat-faced woman had said to herself in *Une Femme Mariée* and for Elinor *tendresse* was slightly shaded, as tenderness wasn't, with the *tristesse* Godard twinned it with.

But out of bed Tim was as reserved as ever. Sex was isolated from the rest of life, as if it happened in a soundproof booth. For an hour or two they learned each other inside out. Five minutes afterwards, it might never have happened.

She knew he loved her, but at a deeper level only believed it so long as she felt evidence of it on her pulse. After making love she tried to fix each delicate shading of passionate tenderness in her memory, like a camel storing fat in its hump to cross the desert. But sense-memories quickly lost their acute edge; and then she longed for acknowledgment, continuity, daily life sweetened by little caresses and warmths of tone. *Tendresse, tristesse*: tenderness that starts with lovemaking and when it stops, stops.

Chapter 33

In July they left the children with her parents for three days and took Thoby and Sheila to Swarthgill: off to the moors, after an obligatory hour with the Scotts, into a glare of evening sun, past stunted hawthorns and greeny-black gorse bushes. Home, Elinor thought with fierce adoptive passion.

Thoby's interest in vernacular building made him curious about the projecting watershoot stones studding barn walls along the way: were they through stones, were they supposed to keep the walls dry, did they work?

As they left the main road Tim said, 'This is where the Wharfe rises out of Oughtershaw Beck.'

Thoby wanted to stop and look—in another of his eclectic fits of self-education he had tried to understand rivers and their sources. Tim was bursting with impatience, but stopped politely, and they all got out and talked about springs and runoffs and what constituted a river. Elinor was wild to arrive, too; her eyes and Tim's met ruefully.

At last Thoby tore himself away, and they bumped along the track and into frame: the long pure rise of Oughtershaw Moss across the fields; the steep Side; the blur of Swarthgill's little wood; the house. Stop, turn off the engine, step out into country quiet, into the moment when the heart catches up with itself.

Cylindrical bales of hay dotted the field between the house and the beck. 'It still smells of sun,' said Sheila. 'Like bread baking.'

They ate and went outside again, and strolled up the rocky track. It was late. Drifts of ruddy purple hung in the sky. The hay smelt sweet; the air was clear and chilly. In the afterlight things seemed more visible than they really were. Now and then rabbits scuntered flash-tailed up the dusky Side; slowly the whole arc of the sky turned deep starry blue.

'Alluring,' Thoby said, looking across at Oughtershaw Moss. 'Climb it?'

'Oh *no*,' said Tim and Elinor together.

'We did it once,' she explained. 'It was squishy the whole way. But from the top you could see—what were those ridges, Tim?'

'Cosh, Pen-y-Ghent, Ingleborough...'

Cosh. Elinor's memory stirred—the humpbacked bridge, the sudden snowstorm, the one perfect place. 'Cosh Inside—it was beautiful. We tried to go there, but it snowed and we had to turn back. We meant to go again, but we never have.'

'Let's do it this year,' Sheila said. 'Tomorrow, maybe?'

She then forgot about it, but remembered on the last morning and said, 'Could we go to that place of Nell's?'

They packed the car and set off. The warm sunny weather was attracting walkers and motorists into the Dales. They passed a flat tongue of land by the Skirfare where dozens of motorists had set up folding chairs and tables beside their cars for morning coffee.

'The comfort of home, plus scenery,' said Elinor.

'Nature without the nuisance of s-solitude,' Thoby agreed.

'Oh *Thoby*,' said Sheila. 'They're enjoying themselves—you're too hard on people. I don't mean you, Nell,' she added apologetically. 'It's just...Thoby's sometimes so élitist.'

Elinor hardly knew how to reply. 'Oh...' she murmured.

'And there are four of *us*,' said Tim, in whom Sheila's words had struck a chord of fellow-feeling. Elinor was too hard on people—on him. 'Not exactly solitude.'

Thoby said coolly, 'I think it's the height of condescension to pretend—' He stopped and in an easier voice said, 'You're right, Sheila. A closet élitist. I'll come out. Proud to be élitist, in tune with the conservative times.' He hadn't stammered once.

'Well, we'll be safe from trippers where we're going.' Tim said lightly. 'That flat spot catches them like flypaper.'

Sheila was still ruffled. 'Coffee by the side of the road like that, and hampers at Glyndebourne—what's the difference?'

'Not much,' Thoby concurred cheerfully. 'Hateful place, Glyndebourne. Only went once. Wild horses wouldn't drag me again—the gentry in full sneer over the cold pheasant.'

'What did you hear?' Tim asked.

'*L'Incoronazione di Poppea*,' Thoby replied, his accent and intonation so ripely Italian that for a moment Elinor made no sense of the words. 'Twelfth birthday present from me ma. Hot stuff. Beautiful redhead, scanty costumes—scorched the stage. When I hear the words "decline and fall of the Roman Empire", it's her I think of. Wonderful voice, but I was too lustful to notice. Shocked, too. Puritanical age, twelve.'

Tim was wrong about trippers. Two big stolid cars were already parked at Foxup, where the footpath began.

'They'll probably be with us the whole way,' he said gloomily. 'It's not enough of a climb to discourage them.'

Sheila fetched out the knapsacks. Tim passed one to Thoby and quickly slung on the other, though it was Elinor's day for it. She insisted on equal turns, which was fine when they were alone, but mortified him on this trip, for Thoby carried his and Sheila's lunch each day as a matter of course.

'Hey, my turn,' Elinor said.

'I've got it on already.'

'No, you had it yesterday.'

'It's more trouble to take it off than carry it.' He turned away. She tugged at his sleeve. 'No, really, it's *my* turn.'

He glared, willing her to yield. She stared straight back. He knew that look; she would not budge, even if it meant making a fuss in front of people. He shrugged off the knapsack, saying in an undertone, 'If you want to be a martyr...'

Tim must feel he was losing face with Thoby—she was a beast to insist. But why should she pretend she was too weak to carry four sandwiches, two apples and a flask?

They walked along the muddy farm track in silence, keeping their eyes down to avoid cowpats. They were all slightly pessimistic about the excursion. Thoby and Sheila were still peeved at each other, so were Tim and Elinor. Elinor was cross with herself, too, and uncertain whether the others would like Cosh.

Beyond the pasture the track started to rise gently; became firm underfoot; became hard; stony; became a wide stone ledge beside Cosh Beck, worn into hollows and softnesses of outline, fissured by the courses of hundreds of runoffs. In the distance a high semicircle of moor closed the view—Cosh Inside, sweeping round with the course of the beck. In the foreground was the little humpbacked bridge, overhung by tall trees. Grass was growing between the cobbles, and the gate on the far side was mossy. Worries and uncertainties fell from them.

'It was so different that day, all white and whirling,' Elinor said. 'But this is what I remember. The bridge, and that curve luring you on.'

'We met in a snowstorm, Sheila and I,' Thoby said. 'After a chamber group we'd both just joined. It went cold suddenly—started snowing. Sheila didn't have a coat—I put mine over both our heads—shuffle to the tube—Sheila, me, cello, viola. Very cosy.'

'Very awkward,' Sheila said with an embarrassed laugh.

A small dog yapped towards them out of a dip. Two slow-strolling middle-aged couples followed, giving guarded nods as they passed. The women were wearing frocks and high-heeled sandals, the men, town trousers. One of them had a whippet on a lead.

'Not very friendly,' Tim observed, though his own nod had been curt. 'They must be the ones with the cars.'

'No wonder they had to turn back—such unsuitable shoes,' Elinor said.

'Different tribes,' said Thoby. 'Different regional costume. Look at us four—battered boots; baggy old shirts. We're freaks, to them.'

Sheila gave him a grateful glance before walking on ahead with Elinor. He watched her, surprised all over again at the pallor of her smooth hair—over the past couple of years it had gone entirely grey. He was instinctively on Elinor's side of the subdued tiff about the knapsack. Sheila never volunteered to carry theirs, and it wasn't in him to ask her to. Should it be? The knapsack was so light; but the weight wasn't the point. His mind rolled vaguely over questions of early masculine conditioning.

— * —

246

The beck and the stony road curved slowly round into the worn fold of Cosh Inside. Across the beck on the steep hump of Ber Gill sheep were bleating to each other near the field barns. The grass was brilliant green; the sunny blue sky seemed very close. Cumulus clouds rode straight towards them across the high horizon.

'The way they tower up,' Elinor said with a billowy waggle of her hand. 'And such a height of sky above them.'

'Tremendous illusion—seeing right the way up the azimuth,' Thoby agreed.

'Thoby, Thoby,' she exclaimed with happy impatience, suddenly and once for all rid of the idea that he was showing off, 'what in heaven's name is an azimuth—sounds like asthma. Or something you'd measure with that astrolabe thing you once talked about.' She spoke entirely without resentment—in a rush of relief at finally being able to admit ignorance before him without minding. His Italian and French accents weren't showing-off, either. How could he help saying words the way he'd been taught to?

In the very instant of her release from uneasiness, Thoby suddenly half divined that she might all along have been taking him amiss. He wanted to explain that you could indeed measure azimuths with an astrolabe, but refrained.

They ate lunch on a steep little knoll where the beck rounded Ber Gill in a series of broad shallow ledges worn like old stone steps. It was hot; they all rolled up their sleeves. The ledges were nearly dry at this season, but two or three brisk streams plashed eagerly down them, flickering in and out of the shade of a stout ash. Sun-bright water, sun-white stone, sun-baked moor. Like an oasis, Thoby nearly said, then somehow thought he wouldn't. Look the way the stone's faulted, he nearly said, but didn't. He couldn't think of anything safe to say, and ate in uncharacteristic silence. But Elinor's smile when he offered her tea was unmistakably friendly, and he grew easier.

The men went off to pee, then the women; then they all went down to the creamy stone ledges and washed their hands in deep little pools replenished by trickling threads of stream. A few of the pools, full to overbrimming, were spilling over the flat stone of the

247

watercourse in a thin glassy sheet. Elinor remembered her first lunch in Hackney: Thoby and Tim talking about frogs in puddles, intimidating her without meaning to. She was over that, and high time. She felt so benevolent that she let Tim take the knapsack.

They came upon the deserted hamlet of Cosh—a boarded-up Victorian cottage, and the mullioned ruin of an older farmhouse. From a stunted oak nearby hung a primitive swing—a short piece of wood lashed to a rope.

'Recent,' said Thoby, testing it. 'Have a go, anyone?' No one else wanted to. He straddled it and sailed back and forth wearing a look of demented concentration, his long, thin legs stuck straight out ahead of him to clear the irregular ground.

'You look just like Fergus,' said Sheila when he slowed up.

'He'd love it. Euan too. Bring them next time.'

Her heart sank. She didn't want that; there was too much danger on the moors—heights, crevices, bogs, becks. She wouldn't have a moment's peace with them along.

But she knew what Thoby hoped to hear, and said cooperatively, 'Kit and Isobel too—wouldn't it be fun.'

'They're far too young for a walking holiday,' Tim said quickly.

'But they'd like playing round Swarthgill,' said Thoby.

'Yes, Tim, let's start bringing them and staying longer,' Elinor said. 'You loved it at that age—remember telling me about walking through the hayfield?'

How could she sound so enthusiastic? 'It won't be the same with them around,' he said crossly. 'You won't be able to come walking with me.'

'True, but—' Double-take. '*I* won't be able to come walking with *you*?—as if *I'd* always be the one staying with them?'

Taking turns on the Heath was bad enough, but this!—trapped with the children at Swarthgill, with her off walking for hours, and no music or workroom to escape to. 'I'd do my share, Elinor, of course,' he said, masking dismay with impatience. 'Don't turn a trifle into a court case.' Hoping to please her he added: 'Besides, I think of Swarthgill as our place, yours and mine.'

'It's not so private it can't include the children,' she said tartly. He'd been happy enough to bring Sheila and Thoby.

Tim frowned, saying nothing. It was ill bred to quarrel before outsiders. Elinor didn't want to make their friends uncomfortable, either, and held her tongue. But the disagreement was more palpable than they guessed; a small silence pooled round it.

Break it up, Thoby thought, and unwound himself from the swing. 'Come on, Nell, take a spin? Cheap thrills, amazing views. Sheila? Tim?'

They all said no, but the awkwardness was dissipated, and they set off. Elinor, still irritated, fell a little behind. What's wrong with us? she thought—we're usually so happy up here. Her eyes filled with tears, and she stubbed her toe on a knot of grass.

But the day was smiling at her and the terrain was still slowly, steadily rising, becoming more bleak, bare, and wild. The track petered out; Ber Gill faded into moorland. Behind them was the great curve of Cosh Inside, ahead, nothing but hillocks and the sky. The beck meandered to and fro in big S bends up the wide valley floor; it was now narrow enough to cross in one stride.

Elinor, still walking a little behind, admired Tim's arms with their fine web of silky blond hairs glistening in the sun. The hair on Thoby's arms was black and therefore more conspicuous; he had large patches of rough red goose-bumpy skin round his elbows. Her palms prickled at the thought of touching them—would it be like running your hand across the bristles of a hairbrush? His pear-shaped knapsack, containing only his jersey and an empty flask, joggled at every step below his high spare shoulders. Tim's knapsack sat properly on his broad back.

The landscape they were moving through kept reducing itself to ever simpler elements—gentle rises instead of big sweeps; no more trees, walls or field barns, only blue sky and bleached grass, scrubby on the slopes, reedy by the looping beck. If only life could always be this transparent and simple. But how odd that she, who delighted in complex practical activity, was so satisfied by the simplest of actions—walking—and the simplest of sights—grass and sky.

'It's funny,' she said a little shyly to Thoby, 'getting happier and happier, with less and less to see.'

'Isn't it, Nell. Paring down to essentials. Fallacious, really—a highly sophisticated pleasure, this.'

'Or getting in touch with roots—but that's a fallacy too. I've no roots in Yorkshire—in the country at all. I remember reading at university that people haven't always wanted to get close to nature—only since the Industrial Revolution and towns getting so cut off from the country; but we've still got folk-memories of it as a paradise, which it wasn't, it was...'

'Nasty, brutish and short?' Thoby suggested.

Elinor nodded. 'I didn't mind back then, because the country didn't mean that much to me. But now it does, and I don't want such deep feelings to be just sentimentality.'

'Quite. Like the theory that we love our children more now than when we had lots and expected some to die. Offensive notion, don't you think?'

Tim said, 'But that can't be true—look at Rachel and her children. Human nature doesn't—'

'Look, what's that?' said Sheila. They were climbing a little crest, and on the horizon was a long, low escarpment faulted into layers of horizontally fissured rock.

Tim consulted the map. 'Caves, it says. And springs—the source of Cosh Beck.'

Thoby gave an interested, 'Oh,' at the prospect of a source.

Elinor said, 'Caves? I've always wanted to see a cave. One with stalactites and—'

'—stalagmites,' Sheila finished with her.

'I never remember which is which, do you?'

'Stalactites has got a c in it,' Tim said, 'c for ceiling; and stalagmites has got a g for ground. But there won't be any here, or I'd have heard of them. Sorry.'

On they went through long sedgy grass, with a small wind always in their ears, while round them the entire visible world re-defined and re-defined itself every few yards as consisting of less and less; until at the marshy source there was only the low scar, a shallow rise of ground on every side, the thin beck trickling into pools no bigger than mixing bowls, and creamy blue sky without even a cloud in it

250

any more—with nothing but sun-dazzled specks of floating chaff between them and an infinite depth of blue. The caves turned out to be only holes in the scar, no more than two feet high. The beck didn't issue from them, but welled up invisibly from grass-covered crevices in the ground beneath their feet.

'The real source is always out of sight,' Thoby said, disappointed.

'Sounds like a saying from some Oriental religion,' Tim said.

By the caves they were out of the wind. They lay back in the springy grass with the sun beating on their faces, silent with happiness. High ground; grass; water; sunshine: the heart of Yorkshire. There were flowers in the grass—buttercups, dandelions, vetch, harebells.

'Do I hear somebody?' Tim said after a while. It was only a cow, munching over the rise and regarding them with languid interest.

Sheila said, 'No one else will come, it's the back of beyond.'

'The world's end,' said Tim.

'There are other places Which also are the world's end,' Thoby said. 'But this is the nearest...something or other, Now and in England.'

What's that? Elinor wondered lazily, but she was freed from misconstruing his motives and didn't mind not knowing.

Thoby looked at the map, thinking about sources. 'I say,' he presently said, 'this is Cosh Outside.'

'Cosh *In*side,' said Elinor.

'No, *Out*side. Inside was back on the other side of the hamlet.'

'Let me see. Oh, you're right. But how did Outside get to be further in than Inside?'

'Sounds like the story what's-her-name tells, Nana, in *Vivre sa Vie*. Remember, Nell? About the chicken.' The words came into his head in French, but his new-born doubt about how she took his innocent chatter made him translate them. ' "When you take away the outside, there's the inside, and when you take away the inside, there's the soul." '

The soul. The words irritated Tim into breaking up the idyll. 'Three o'clock. It's an hour to the motorway and then three to London.'

251

'Oh...' the others protested, but got up, slapped chaff off their backs and turned their faces away from the quiet source.

'What's on at the Cromer next week, Nell?' Thoby asked after a silent half-mile, by way of beginning to reinsert himself into the world. The beck was still narrow; they were walking beside it, one on each side, now and then hopping across or balancing on stones in the middle.

'Some Bertolucci, and a Garbo season.'

'Ah, Garbo. Incarnation of romantic love. *Ninotchka*—after the big night out, the way she leans back all shining and says, "Bombs will fall, civilisations will perish—but not yet. Give us our little moment." Brings tears to the old eyes every time.'

'Me too,' said Elinor.

Me too, thought Tim; but would never have said so, and was embarrassed that Thoby had.

'I'm sick of hearing about romantic love,' said Sheila, quite crossly for her. 'It's all nonsense. I don't *believe* in it.'

'Neither do I,' Tim said, with the impatience that had been stirring in him since Thoby's quotation about the soul.

'I do,' said Thoby and Elinor together; and looked at each other startled across the brook.

'The basis of things in the real world,' Sheila went on, as if she hadn't heard what had been said, or in what tone of voice, 'is liking and respect, and working to make things tolerable.'

'Exactly,' said Tim.

What a dreadful idea, Elinor thought absentmindedly; but hardly noticed. Elation was almost stifling her. She and Thoby were still on opposite sides of the beck, walking with brisk deliberation—no more hopping from side to side.

She looked at the ground, the water, the view ahead—anywhere but at him: yet saw nothing else. His luminous eyes filled her inner vision. What was he thinking about what had happened? Nothing much? She knew better than that. The same as her, then?—not that she herself knew what that was.

Tim and Sheila were following behind. With an impulse of compunction, she fell back and joined Tim. Sheila moved up beside

252

Thoby, and he put his arm round her—briefly: the uneven footing soon made him drop it. Elinor's stomach knotted—with sadness because Tim so seldom put his arm round her like that; with jealousy because Thoby was touching Sheila.

Many times since marrying Tim she'd looked at other men with sexual interest, but never before with—was it intent? The thin high rectangular set of Thoby's shoulders was poignant. His knapsack still struck her as funny, but her amusement was tender, not distanced. Tim's was the finer figure, but Thoby's had the endearing elegance of a heron or a giraffe.

How could Tim and Sheila not guess?

What was there to guess? What was signified by that simultaneous, 'I do,' that glance of mutual recognition?

Nothing, for the moment, except that she was alive to every breath he drew. About the rest she didn't want to think just yet.

Chapter 34

He rang her the next day at the cinema, and they met on Hampstead Heath two days later.

Elinor had thought about nothing else since Cosh, reinterpreting and recombining all her memories of him, her mind racing incessantly with ways and means and cloudy ethical speculations; but her capacity to think ahead was paralysed. By the time they met she was almost throttled with suspense. He probably does this sort of thing all the time, she thought, approaching him across the grass. She didn't like the idea. But you couldn't ask about the frequency of his adulteries in advance.

Besides, they weren't likely to be legion—Lotharios were made of coarser clay.

Of course for Thoby an affair wouldn't technically be adultery. Not that that made a difference—she and Tim weren't more closely bound by marriage than Thoby and Sheila by living together. Certainly not. But she half felt it in spite of herself.

Thoby watched her come across the grass. Something about her confident gait made him think: She must do this all the time. But it was only a sort of inner joke, almost without anxiety. She wasn't someone who would screw around casually.

'Over there for tea?' he said. 'Sit out on the grass; good for talking.'

No sooner had they sat down and spread out their things than a family sat close by them. Private talk was difficult; the delay made them awkward. Elinor chatted about the Cromer and the children; Thoby's stammer was at its worst. Each of them was thinking: It won't work, how can I get out of this?

They drank up and set off, in a silence that neither of them broke. Eventually they came to some enormous silvery-grey elm logs and sat down. Elinor put her palms flat on the smooth warm wood. Thoby meditated a variety of inane remarks about elms, then turned to look at her and plunged.

'What about us, then?'

She smiled self-consciously. 'What about us, indeed?'

'It's all I've thought about since—'

'Same here. Any conclusions?'

'Not...conclusive ones. Requires consultation, don't you think—democratic process.' He squinted up at the sky. 'What about you?'

'What—undemocratically? But—no. Just that...' She paused, inching her way past a lifetime's conditioning not to speak her desires plainly to men. 'But...I'd like it if...if you would; if it doesn't land us in...'

'Deeper waters than we can navigate.'

'Yes.'

'Trouble is, deep waters are what one wants.'

Her heart gave a hop of pleasure. 'Yes,' she said like a parrot.

He looked at her with delight, her black eyes, her fine black eyebrows, her long neck, her flushed brown cheeks, the little hairs wisping out from her irregular hairline, the endearing way her front teeth were a little crooked—before Cosh he'd seen it as a flaw—and wondered what to say, or do, next, in the middle of the afternoon, in the middle of the Heath. I can kiss her, he thought, and did.

It took her by surprise. Thoby reminded her of her men before Tim, so she had expected prolonged negotiations and agonies of conscience first. For an instant she almost didn't respond, then had to restrain herself from returning his kiss overprofusely, with starved greed.

Kissing only made the question of what to do next more urgent. They separated with a sigh, and he said, 'I tried to think this out ahead of time—practicalities, implications. Got stuck.'

A good sign—he'd be more suave if he did this often. 'Me too. I've not much experience of...' Don't be coy. 'In fact, this is the first.'

'Would Tim be upset?'

'If he knew? Terribly. It would be...' She shook her head. 'Awful. Impossible.'

He'd expected that. His feelings were mixed. He didn't want to deceive Tim, but didn't want to hurt him, either—or face his anger, or lose his friendship or forgo Nell.

'Has he...' Over the years he had fleetingly, abstractly wondered whether either she or Tim had affairs. Now he suddenly very much wanted to know. His new interest in Nell made him more interested in Tim. He wanted to comb Tim for clues about her, and her for clues about Tim.

'I'm pretty sure not,' she replied, guessing that delicacy had made him stop. 'Though of course one never knows for sure'—and Tim wouldn't tell her if he had.

'Would you mind if he did?'

She'd never pictured it concretely. Now she saw Tim's face turned towards another woman's on the pillow, as never towards hers—looking at her, or kissing her, or just breathing her breath; his heavy body pressing open another woman's legs, his cock in another woman's cunt, the intimacy—intolerable. Only for her, that must be.

Looking up, she was startled to find Thoby waiting for her to answer. 'I'd be upset,' she acknowledged. 'Which is pretty unfair. Given...this'—the satiny log, copses tossing bright leaves, a washy blue sky streaming tattered clouds, all nature colluding in their intent.

'True.' He found her sidelong glance captivating. 'But since when has fairness ruled the emotions?'

'Yes, but fairness isn't just a...a cold reasoning afterthought, it's a feeling, too.'

'That's the thing about ethics, don't you think? It's a passion, you live it; you can't just smooth the path for...other passions...by pretending it doesn't exist.'

'Yes, but you can't ignore them either—you've got to balance ethical feeling with...'

'Unethical feeling?' He kept looking into her eyes searchingly, delightingly.

They'd wandered a long way off the immediate question, but for the moment this intimacy of interchange was more important. Thoby thought: This is what I don't get with Sheila. Elinor thought:

Why can't Tim and I talk like this? Their pressing sense of a need that was not simply sexual was in the sigh with which they fell silent and turned towards each other.

The pause lengthened. Almost absently, almost in mere comradeship, he brushed her thigh with the back of his hand; and tumbled abruptly back into sexuality. With another sigh he put his palm full upon her thigh, soaking up its warmth through her skirt, then slid the stuff up and his hand underneath. How had he imagined that because her legs were thin they would be lean and hard like a man's? They were soft, soft, as soft as plush. Insensibly his hand moved further and further up under the tousle he'd made of her skirt; insensibly her thighs opened. There was no one anywhere nearby. The edge of his hand brushed her pants. If he crooked his finger round, he would touch her cunt.

But he didn't. He'd never before in his life sat in a public place with his hand up a woman's skirt, and in the idea of it, though not in the reality, there was something coarse—a caricatured notion of men always heading straight for the genitals—that he didn't want her to associate with him. Her silent stillness wasn't discouraging— it actually seemed to invite an approach direct even to crudity. But she might all the same have reservations running cross-grained to the desire that was curling her toes against the soles of her chappals.

Besides, the further he went, the harder it would be to stop.

Elinor sat stunned by the violence of her feelings. The only image in the part of her mind not entirely given over to the present was of him bending her down with opened thighs onto the green grass; pressing into her; covering her. It wasn't what she rationally wanted to happen in broad daylight on Hampstead Heath—insofar as any shred of her was rational just then; it wasn't even a fantasy, but a sense-image more primitive than wish or fantasy.

No one was near, but there were people in the distance. If they looked, would they be able to see her skirt pushed up, his hand under it? Would they be upset? Might someone recognise them? She didn't care; she did: both. She didn't want to upset strangers; yet it was exciting to think of being seen in this completely sexual state.

257

Two women came into view, not very close, not very far off. Thoby removed his hand; Elinor brushed down her skirt. Each of them thought the other had withdrawn; each was glad not to have been the one responsible for stopping.

Say something, she thought. Where were we? Oh yes, whether Tim and I have had affairs. 'What about you?' she asked. 'Would you mind if Sheila...'

'No,' he said, because it was what he half believed he should feel; then, more honestly, 'Yes.'

'Would she mind about you?

'Less. I...she...'

Sex is problematic for Sheila, was what he suppressed. It would sound like a criticism, which wasn't how he meant it. Sheila needed sex to be a mild pleasure, not extreme or greedy, involving no self-loss—she made very sure of that. She wouldn't have sat here in motionless extremity letting him see the depth and dependence of her response; she was barred from wantonness like Nell's. He didn't want to think about the meaning of the difference.

Elinor's eye fell upon her watch. 'Oh my God, five o'clock.' She stood up abruptly, though she was dying to stay and discuss possessiveness. 'I've got to pick up the children—and we've barely begun talking. But I'll be late.' They hurried across the Heath and into the tube.

As she left the packed train at Russell Square he said, 'Cromer tomorrow, then? I was coming to *Queen Christina* at six-thirty anyhow. I've a meeting, but I can get away by five.'

'Um, but—' The doors were closing; he blew her kisses through the window. Tim never did that; when did he even wave? No, she mustn't use Thoby to make up for anything Tim did or didn't do, it wronged them both, not just...Not just Tim. No use pretending she didn't believe it. She didn't, and she did.

'I didn't have time to say—five today's no better than five yesterday,' she told Thoby when he arrived. 'I pick up the children every day at five-thirty; and then I've got them here.'

'Oh what a tangled web we weave,' he said ruefully. He walked to the crèche with her, then hung round the office until *Queen*

258

Christina began; but they didn't talk about what was on both their minds. Thoby could have discussed Hegel through the children's interruptions, and Elinor, Bresson; affairs of the heart were harder to settle.

They had to sit at a discreet distance. People kept coming in and out—ushers, Rose, Terry, the cashier needing change. Thoby thought of skipping the film for the chance of five minutes' real talk and a kiss or two; but then Maggie dropped in. He gave up.

When Hilary came for the children, Elinor went in for the end of the movie. She couldn't reach Thoby without climbing across half a row of paying customers, so she perched on the jump seat to watch—watch with him, so she felt, through his eyes and ears, though he didn't even know she was there. Such silly speeches—did they make him impatient? Garbo's weren't silly, though—it was as if a different screenwriter had written her lines. Had she ever said a word, made a gesture, that she didn't infuse with grace? John Gilbert's rolling eyes didn't matter, or the ancient retainer weeping into his moustache during the abdication—when Elinor, instead of sneering like a true socialist, wept too.

By the final scene, when Garbo's lover, mortally wounded, died beside the ship which was to have carried them into exile, and she none the less gave the command to sail, Elinor had stopped thinking about Thoby at all. The audacious final crane shot moved seamlessly from a long shot of Garbo walking along the deck, one figure among many; closer, to her standing in the prow with the wind blowing back her hair and velvet cloak; slowly closer and closer to a head and shoulders close-up; and finally into big close-up: her infinitely beautiful, infinitely sad face filling the whole screen. All the poetry of cinema was in that shot.

Thoby came out with the sheepish look of one who has been wiping tears from his eyes. 'That face,' he said, flourishing his handkerchief and blowing his nose.

'Makes up for all the nonsense, doesn't it?'

'Nonsense?'

'Oh, hamming, melodrama, covert authoritarianism.' They were Tim's objections to the film; she'd been watching through his eyes as much as Thoby's.

'One just forgives that, don't you think? Because of her—and the way it's done. It's absurd, but so graceful. Like *Swan Lake*—you don't go for the story'—something Sheila, who was not metaphorically inclined, could never accept. 'You go for the emotions that the story makes a...'

'A shape to hold?' Like *Swan Lake*—you don't go for the story. Exactly. How very satisfying.

Then it was the weekend, and then there were three days when they were never free at the same time. Elinor's reveries after Cosh hadn't included the idea of delay. She could hardly wait to see Thoby alone—at Ockendon Road on Sunday they hadn't had a fraction of a private second before or after the spiky Bartók quartet. After acting merely friendly with him in public, it was hard to imagine that they'd go into a room somewhere and take off their clothes and lie down naked on a bed and make love.

On Friday they met on the Heath, at the same logs. 'We'll have to do better than this,' he said, as they separated themselves with difficulty under the disapproving gaze of a man with a dog.

'But where?'

'An hotel?'

'Too sordid, not to mention expensive.'

'Friend of mine used to meet someone in an hotel. In Muswell Hill. Quite reasonable, he said.'

'Muswell Hill!' She fell about. 'Such a quiet respectable neighbourhood—I didn't know it had hotels.'

'Quiet and respectable, no doubt. But I suppose it is sordid—nothing in the room but a bed, as if it's all you're there for—'

'Which is maybe true,' she interjected with a mischievous look that allured him no end. 'But the bed makes it so formal—'

'All set up: ready, steady, go.'

'But where else is there? I thought about Ockendon Road, because I always know when Tim will be out. But it's his house too'—his more than hers, she still felt. 'I wouldn't feel...'

'And there's often a sitter at the flat till the boys start school. Still, next month the coast is clear.'

'But what if Sheila came home and—'

'Don't worry, I'd tell her we—'

'You mean...she'll *know*?'

'I can't keep it secret, Nell. It's...part of how we live.' She looked so flabbergasted that he added, 'It bothers you—I'm sorry.'

'It's just...' She groped for why. 'Won't she *mind*?'

'I don't think so. There was one time before, and she didn't.'

One time before? Who? When? She said almost at random: 'A bit much, Sheila knowing, and Tim not—three to one, especially when we're together on Sundays.' And how would she face Sheila?

Thoby's black brows knit with perplexity. 'Is that a...a definitive objection?' Their erotic moral glow had disadvantages.

She saw the hole she was digging for herself. 'No—no. Just a reaction.' One time before, she thought. Only one.

'A serious reaction.'

'No no,' she said again. 'Don't take it seriously. You've got to tell Sheila, and I can't tell Tim—that's all there is to it. What's more serious is where to meet. And when. I mean, when are we free at the same time for more than ten seconds? Like now—I've got to go. Again.'

The last time on the Heath they had parted in haste but in hope. This time they were less rushed, but somehow more uncertain of the future. 'We'll work something out, don't worry,' he told her in the tube, brushing her cheek and mouth with a kiss as the doors opened, and reluctantly letting go of her hand.

She nodded and smiled and waved, happy from top to toe, even though she was going crazy with all the delays. Already it was a fortnight since Cosh.

The telephone was ringing when she got in on Saturday. 'Out with the boys,' Thoby said. 'Swimming baths. Then Sheila's turn—be free by five. Come and walk to the crèche with you? Talk a bit. Miss you.'

'Me too.'

He stopped in the outer office; Elinor could hear his cracked hooting laugh, his stammer, his abbreviated sentences. Did they stem from affectation? Shyness? Alone with her he talked more or less ordinarily, and hardly stammered. She pushed aside her paperwork and went to greet him.

At first glance she saw him as she had formerly—a thin man, stooped with laughter, turning towards her with the slightly insubstantial, slightly ridiculous air that his unworldliness gave him—for he was unworldly, though his job was managing money. Then the tenderness that had been for a moment suspended returned. But the impression had an aftertaste almost of disenchantment; she was subliminally uneasy about what it meant to scrutinise him with such a sharp distanced eye.

He and Terry went on chatting. Elinor pretended to join in, feeling irritated—their short time free of the children was slipping away. By the time they left for the crèche they were late and had to rush; no time to discuss times and venues.

'And we'd better not do it at the office, either,' she said, stopping on the crèche steps, 'even in code. Isobel's got this ritual at breakfast, she tells us everything—but everything—that's happened to her in the past twenty-four hours, complete with great chunks of dialogue. She's like a parrot, that child—she doesn't understand half of what she comes out with, but she gets it right.'

'Good ear—she'll make a musician.' He reached for her hand and put a kiss in the palm.

'So Tim says'—melting where she stood. 'We don't listen to the breakfast epic very hard, especially Tim, but you can see the danger.'

'Quite. He might prick up his ears if she comes out with, "Demain à l'Auberge Muswell Hill." ' He loved making Nell laugh, the sound squeaking out around fingers pressed to her mouth. 'Kiss, then we'll collect your parrot from her perch.'

Back at the office they talked across the children's chatter. It was frustrating. Speech had a different meaning without touch; and they had to find words that Isobel could safely repeat to Tim. But they were acutely alive to each other: their likemindedness carried an electric sexual charge.

'See you tomorrow,' he said on the way out. 'Coram populo, but better than nothing.'

262

'Coram what?' Did he mean the street?

'En publique. I'll gaze from afar, sawing my fiddle and think'—he put his mouth to her ear—'unspeakable things.'

'Don't you dare, or I'll flip my wig,' she hissed back, quite loud.

The next morning Isobel's account included: 'And Thoby said, "I'll gaze afar, song my fiddow," and Mummy said, "Dare I'll flip my pig." '

Tim didn't hear a word of it.

Chapter 35

It was pouring with rain, so Tim and Elinor stayed on in Hackney after lunch, listening to a hair-raising *Otello* while the children played with one another and her and Thoby and Sheila. Elinor squirmed at the plot, and felt awkward every time she looked at Thoby, every time she heard his voice, but didn't care. Being in the same room with him made her peaceful and excited, both. It was Tim who finally said, 'We should go, the children need their naps.'

That was not all he had in mind. Back home, they carried the children upstairs, and Elinor soothed them asleep. Tim waited in the bedroom till he heard her come out, then went to the door and with a smile of invitation said, 'It's been a long time.' A most unusually long time—since Swarthgill. But Elinor had had what she implied was a heavy period; and had seemed, and still did, preoccupied and tense—he was never unaware of her moods, however much he protected himself by ignoring them. He had nothing on his conscience, but was she upset with him?

Oh no—she didn't really want to make love; she felt sexually numb from all the suspense about her and Thoby. And would Thoby be ghostlily with them the whole time? But she'd run out of dodges—she returned Tim's smile and went for her diaphragm.

Rain was gusting against the window panes, but the wind whistling along the eaves was warm, and so was the room. Tim was naked in the grey light, looking up at her with that friendly daylight expression that would disappear between one breath and the next.

She kicked off her chappals and pulled off her flowered shift, still damp from the dash between car and house with Isobel; her bra; her pants. It usually excited her to undress in front of him when they were going to make love, but not today. She lay down thinking, This won't work. Kiss me, why don't you? You've kissed me less in six years than Thoby in—

Stop thinking about him.

Tim propped himself up on one elbow and gave her pubic hair an affectionate ruffle—and before she knew it, without any effort, she wanted him as much as ever. Her last fully conscious thought was: Whew. She shut her eyes, opened them to glimpse him hovering above her, smiling secretly, eyes hooded with pleasure. Then he slid down the bed and pushed her leg wide.

For a split second she quailed with nearly instinctive modesty; then wanted to spread herself even wider. His gaze satisfied some fantasy of self-exhibition—not one of her bad fantasies, of being in a porn movie with cameras trained on her cunt, but a stronger, less specific fantasy about opening herself to a man's gaze. A man: Tim himself, Tim a representative of all men—one of the moments when the non-personal element in lovemaking bore down the personal.

Momentarily she remembered her embarrassed excitement at the possibility of being seen while Thoby caressed her. Somewhere within lovemaking there hovered a shadowy irrational fantasy of fucking...everyone in the world? the whole world itself?

Ah—as Tim's tongue touched her clitoris. All sexual joy was liquid, and this was the most fluid of all: liquefaction, heat flowing in the flesh with the miraculous quicksilver roundness of mercury. Quicksilver—no. Silver was a cold colour. Quickgold.

She wriggled round and took his cock in her mouth, savouring its quick responsive tremors and the feel of it along her tongue—vein-ribbed, the biggest vein now and then contracting like a trout purling the surface of a stream; the head softer, spongier, almost smooth, finely grained like a fingertip. So comforting, like...the image that flashed on her mind was Isobel sucking her thumb: that satisfaction so primitive that babies did it in the womb. She smothered a chuckle: Tim mightn't find the comparison amusing—or might; she never knew. Would Thoby?

Thoby, Thoby, stop thinking about—

To escape his ghost she whispered, 'Why is it so wonderful?'—the question Tim sometimes asked her.

265

He raised his head. 'Don't know,' he said in a blurred voice. 'Because...you want men to feast on your body.'

Yes, she thought, yes. But: 'Men?' she said uneasily. It was as if he too had seen Thoby's ghost in the room with them.

He turned his blind face in her general direction. 'Me,' he said. Would she be offended by his nebulous fantasy of being watched by other men waiting their turn with her? He spread her wider with his fingers and burrowed in again purposefully—delving, mining a secret vein.

Curled round and over each other: intimacy, rolled up in a ball together, sucking like babies at the breast. One of his hands rested on her head—a tenderness in the gesture that he never put into words. No—he'd just put it into words. You want men to feast on your body.

Nothing could be better...then why...She went under again, swept off on passion's wave, until, by slow degrees, what they were doing began to seem like sweets without a main course—intense, but insubstantial. Pure intensity wasn't everything. 'Come into me,' she said, breaking off the speechless speech between her mouth and his cock.

He turned her face down and came into her like—like a knife, she thought fleetingly while he fucked her, the soft flesh of her arse and his belly meeting, his cock cleaving her firmly open—the one a foam on the surface of the other—with such force that her cervix went dark with mixed pleasure and pain. Again, again; she could suffer the excruciating delight indefinitely. But the balance tipped towards pain, and she pushed up to make him change.

He sank onto his side, trying to draw her round with him without coming out of her. It didn't work; and there was the usual slippery fumble before he was curled behind her and lodged in her again.

Looking down, she saw his blunt practical hand on her thigh, his parted fingers denting the soft flesh. An erotic sight. They were close, close; he was moving in her with a particular penetrating tenderness. Lying like this she was still passive to his will, but not...not a conquered state...The thought slid away from her; it was too irrational.

266

His movements were growing feverish; each long glide finished with a jerky tremulousness, as if he could barely contain himself. Did he want to come like this, bringing her with his finger? Maybe she'd let him...No, never so satisfying. She stirred, half turning to him, and said, 'Come on top?'

All along her inner arms the warmth of his skin, all along her trunk the soft curly texture of his body hair, his weight between her thighs, on her pubic bone, cushioned and heavy; she was covered all over with warmth, soft warmth, embraced, and at the centre a delicacy, an opening; all of him between her thighs, no barrier.

He stopped abruptly. She was close too, too close to have to worry; and pressed down on him with her palms to tell him. She was rooted in place, the boundaries between them dissolving, his cock part of her, her cunt part of him; no burst of discontinuity between nearly coming and coming—she was nearly there when he came, almost gently, for a long time, and his slow deep seeking motion made her come herself. The words, 'Oh my darling', rose to her lips, and as always she smothered them. 'Oh,' she said instead, and—the limit of her daring—'Oh Tim;' then was annoyed with herself—for how often hadn't she inwardly mocked his stiffly passionate, 'Oh Elinor'?

Afterwards they lay quiet a while, half asleep, his arm round her, her head on his curly chest. Cradled. It gave her new hope every time. Such a thickness of him beneath her head—a bear-man, his solidity a bulwark.

It was so much what she wanted, all of it, this sensually saturated relation, how could she ever want anything else, how could she ever give it up?—not that she intended to.

Thoby came back into her mind as she washed and dressed. Making love to him wouldn't be like this; couldn't be: Tim coming into her—'like a knife', she'd said to herself, but the thought wasn't masochistic. That hot cleaving was no more painful than the sharpness of wild strawberries, or moments in music that pierced her to the heart: in *Come ye Sons of Art* when the two Dellers, father and son, flinging their alto voices, one low, one high, into 'Sound the trumpet', arrived at, 'All the instruments of joy', and sang it and sang it, again and again, their countertenor counterpoint ravishing her like a sexual ecstasy.

Between two women, or two men, sexual acts and impulses could be symmetrical, but between a woman and a man every touch was an exploration of difference: a smooth face brushing a shaven or bearded one; every mutual glance falling upon a myriad of subtle gender distinctions in the proportion of brow, cheek and jaw, the set of skull on neck, the amount of hair in ears and nostrils—and cunt and cock were so different as to make it surprising that their pleasures were seemingly so similar.

But not the same. The word 'lovemaking' emphasised the emotion and mutuality of sex, but clouded its asymmetry. She could make love to Tim, but not fuck him. He fucked her, she *was* fucked, and the physical asymmetry led to asymmetries of fantasy. When he turned her flat on her belly and fucked her, some of the images hovering under whatever democratic superstructure his thoughts had must be of conquest, surely, subjugation, surely, of wresting her body to his use; while within her there hovered images of being cleaved open, crucified with pleasure, a creature of his will. Sometimes she felt like the active one: encircling, gripping, drawing him in—but not when she lay spreadeagled, done to, not doing. In Tim's mind, too, at such moments, part of the deep fantasy must inevitably be an image of her body flung prostrate beneath his own, pierced by it; a body which he could see but not easily be seen by; a body which he could easily hold down if she were to resist; a body in the posture of nuns offering themselves to God, of slaves abasing themselves before their masters: a posture of capitulation, surrender, subjugation.

She shivered with desire at the thought—and flinched from it. Yet what made its meaning dark and dubious was society, not biology; it was fantasy, not reality—exhausted within sex, not played out over the whole of life. Democracy and surrender could be lived in one and the same moment—Tim's conquering and her submissive body were joined in an act of the utmost mutual consent.

Besides, the longed-for surrender wasn't just to another person, but to sex itself: emotion, unconsciousness: 'Something in sex that's not about either of us,' Tim's phrase that often lit the way through her stumbling thoughts. Men too had such longings.

His body, a little while ago, weighing her down. A womb-spasm radiated like red coals.

Why want Thoby, if she had so much with Tim?

Would making love with Thoby be a return to sexual democracy...and the bad fantasies Tim released her from?

Thoby wouldn't weigh her down—that was a safe guess: he was lighter, thinner. She could remember what the weight of a thin man was like—John had been thin.

Was she in love with him? Should she make love to him if she weren't? And if she was...

Would their affair in any way endanger everything she had with Tim? No, of course not. Of course not.

Chapter 36

Thoby groaned with frustration all morning; he had news for
Elinor but didn't dare ring her at home. Then he was stuck in his
regular Tuesday lunch with Prosser, who alternately wolfed steak
and salad and issued instructions which Thoby jotted down, his
pen so busy that he barely had time to lift fork to mouth. Over
coffee he was expected to play court jester to Prosser's sage. He
rather liked the outrageous old egomaniac, but for once it was hard
to be polite, let alone entertaining.

The first two telephone booths he found were out of order. In the
third a young woman was in tears. 'I don't know why I'm going to
all this trouble—you don't even *care* about me!' he heard her cry.

Don't ring, just go there. He did. Elinor was in the outer office,
leaning over a catalogue with Rose and Terry. The sight of her
bright dark face gave him a shock of delight.

'Thoby, what a nice surprise. I've got to go for stamps—want a
walk?' Out in Coram Street she said almost accusingly, 'I thought
you were going to ring.'

'Sorry—was it awkward? think they noticed anything?—but I
had to talk. Haven't got long, though—got to put the touch on a
sugar daddy for the Haydn. Great news—the flat's empty for four
days from Thursday. Sheila's taking the children to Hove. Visiting
my uncle Ezra. Decided yesterday. Fiendish, this illicit affair
business—not being able to ring and tell you. But now...' He trailed
off. She scarcely looked pleased at all. 'What's wrong?' He didn't
really expect there to be anything.

'I don't know. It's...it's been so long, I feel becalmed. As if I can't
imagine anything between us *but* talking on the telephone, and
waiting. And, I've been thinking...'

270

'Dangerous habit.' He was a shade less confident of her, he didn't know why. 'What about?' He hated talking on the trot—he wanted to concentrate on her face, not the pavement and passers-by; and she always walked faster than he liked. Today she was leaving him nearly breathless.

She strode on. Within sight of the sorting office she said again, 'I don't know. Four days...but it's not four really. I can't get off work on Saturday—Terry's holidays. Then the quartet on Sunday—'

'No quartet with Sheila away.'

'But Tim will be home—I couldn't just leave him with the children and go to your place! So it's still only two days. Then nothing. Grabbing an isolated occasion because it's all we can get. We're both so busy, it just goes on like this, nowhere to go, and no time anyhow: and I don't want just a—a fling—there's no point.'

'Of course not.' He was exhilarated and entirely at home. He knew her, he knew her, their minds fitted together like one hand in another. 'I won't settle for that either. I want more—a lot more. This isn't isolated, it's the beginning...Or are you trying to say something else?'

She shook her head, but there was a stiffness in her bearing, a holding away from him; he wasn't sure he believed her. She plunged into the sorting office and got her stamps, and they walked to St George's Gardens in silence and sat on the grass in a dank secluded corner behind a high table-tomb.

'There *is* something wrong,' he said. 'Is it about Sheila knowing and Tim not?'

She didn't answer, and for the moment he didn't press. They had talked and talked every time they met; he could live with a bit of silence when it wasn't fraught like Sheila's.

Their stolen hugs and kisses had become almost more affectionate than passionate—crumbs were too little when they wanted the whole loaf. But a crumb right now—he leaned forward and kissed her, looked round to check that no one could see them, and touched her breast through her blouse. Home, he told her inside his head in an incoherent rush. The centre of the world, your breast in my hand, my fingers slightly sinking into softness, your nipple punctuating my palm.

271

Elinor's thoughts rushed incoherently too. So soon—too soon after making love with Tim. He hadn't touched her like this—so sexually—since...since the Heath. Three weeks ago. She needed a few days to...to...

On Sunday Thoby had played pat-a-cake with Isobel. 'I'll prick it'—clap—'And pat it'—clap—'And mark it with *B*'—big clap—'And put it in the oven for baby and *me*'—up in the air with a squealing Isobel.

'More,' Isobel had cried, her brown face aglow; so he did it again: chant, clap, big lift up. But Tim was watching them absentmindedly from a distance, and Isobel had caught sight of him and got anxious. 'More,' she'd said again, but her heart wasn't in it. Thoby soon noticed; he'd packed the game in, where Tim would have kept it up—if he'd ever begun it—until she was hysterical. Tim did love the children, but Thoby understood them better. She sometimes almost thought he *liked* them more.

She was aware of his hand on her breast, but felt no thrill of touch, no vaguer thrill of exhibitionism, no pleasure of self-giving. Nothing. And nothing when he'd kissed her, or held her hand along Calthorpe Avenue, or appeared in the office, his long mobile face lighting up at the sight of her. Had making love to Tim so concentrated her feelings that nothing was left for Thoby?

He was silent, in a trance, his eyes unfocussed. She wanted to join him; to *feel* something. Casting about for something to release her from stony neutrality, she stumbled into one of her old bad fantasies. She was sitting alone in a box at the opera in a bias-cut satin evening frock. A stranger came in, stood behind her sliding his hands over her breasts through the chilly satin, drew her down into the darkness of the floor of the box, pulled up her dress, fucked her, and left without her ever having seen him.

Like a wish granted by a bad fairy the fantasy flicked her clitoris with heat. But if she needed to imagine strangers to work up any sexual feeling for Thoby...She shivered.

He drew back instantly. 'What is it?'

'Nothing.'

'It *is* Tim, isn't it. Shouldn't we talk about it?'

272

She looked at the rope he was holding out, tempted to grab it. Yes, it's Tim, she'd say. I can't tell him, and I can't lie to him; we'll have to give up the idea. She would sound tender-hearted, high-principled. But the lie stuck in her craw. 'It's not that. It bothers me, but it's a non-issue, really. If we'd had somewhere to go a fortnight ago, the thought of Tim wouldn't have kept me from...'

'Curious use of tenses.'

'Don't criticise my grammar,' she shot out with a return of her old paranoia.

'Your grammar? I *wasn't*.'

'I know, I know, I was just—'

'All I meant was, that you said Tim *wouldn't have* stopped you. But we've got somewhere to go on Thursday, so why didn't you say, "Tim *won't* stop me", not, "Wouldn't have"?'

Whether or not she was in love with him now, she would be once they were lovers—she knew that. So where was the problem? She wanted to run away.

'If it's not Tim, what is it?' Everything was coming unstuck. 'Don't go silent on me like—' He stopped. Like Sheila.

Like Tim, she finished for him, wondering how he knew. But she couldn't explain her panic; didn't understand it herself.

'For God's sake, Nell,' he said into her silence. 'Don't keep me in the dark. Have I said something? Done something? Has Tim guessed?'

She shook her head.

'Then what?'

'I don't know. I don't know.'

A sense of doom was creeping over him. He wanted to know the worst, know it fast. 'It's all up between us—is that what you're saying?' He couldn't believe she'd say yes.

Was she? Possibly...probably...She shrank from it, but his words gave a definite shape to the shadow that had been on her for days. She nodded, staring at her hands.

'But *why*?'

Silence.

'You owe me an answer, Nell.' His voice was crisp, angry.

273

'Because, because, because...' Because I'm afraid of having to resort to fantasy to whip up a sexual response. She couldn't say that—and was it really what was throttling her? Because...

An answer was buzzing somewhere inside her head, but she couldn't hear it. Her throat ached. She had wanted him so much—why not have faith that she'd want him again, and—

And meet him on Thursday to make love? No. She mustn't. Because—

In desperation she said one of the things buzzing round in the top of her mind. 'Because I've no sexual feeling for you.'

No, no, how could she have said that? It wasn't a necessary truth, just an easy one: and cruel—inexcusable. In any case wasn't the real reason, which was—

Inaccessible; her mind stumbled.

All the warmth, the confidence, was erased from his face. I didn't mean it, she wanted to cry. But what did she mean? 'It's not you,' she said pleadingly, 'it's me, I've got jammed up. Maybe you're right, and it *is* Tim—I must be more monogamous than I knew.' No, that wasn't it, either.

Lost, he thought, his hopes curling up at the edges like paper held over the fire. All lost, all his hopes, more than he had known till this moment.

But she had thrust so deep that after one flinching instant he was anaesthetised: and very angry. No sexual feeling for him—why had she led him on, then? The things he'd hoped—that glow of possibility: gone. Her transparent attempt to lighten the blow was galling. 'Th-then of course you can't...proceed,' he said with light deliberate coldness. 'Pity.' He looked at his watch and stood up. 'Got to go.' He hadn't thought he would ever be glad to leave Elinor.

'I'm *sorry*,' she said, getting up too.

'My dear, s-so am I. Still—can't be helped.'

His head was cocked at one angle, his body leaning at another, his voice an offhand croak that she hadn't heard for a month, except in public. He was retreating into his mannerisms at high speed—he couldn't have hit upon a more excruciating reproach. He was so much more than the sum of his affectations that she

274

couldn't bear him to shrink back to what he made of himself for general consumption.

Why so obstinate, anyhow? She would miss him, miss him. They started walking towards the road. 'When will I see you?' she said before she thought.

He shrugged. 'Sunday week—the quartet?'

'Can't we go on meeting as friends? It's so—' She broke off. 'Sorry, that's completely selfish, I just...'

'Don't think so. Courtly love—chaste longing—no hope of reward—bit of a bore, don't you think? Still, you never know—perhaps in a week or two...' He knew better, but it sounded less lovelorn. With a momentary return of an ordinary kindly human note that took the cracked manic edge off his voice and lowered its pitch by three half tones, he said, 'I really do have to be off now—mustn't keep the busy City gent waiting.' Then his persona swaddled him protectively again. He shot his eyebrows up and down a couple of times and squinted up at the sunblue September sky. 'Well. Sorry to rush. I'll be in touch.' He wouldn't be, but they couldn't part without a word of farewell, and none seemed forthcoming from her. 'Not going your way—up to King's Cross, Northern Line to Bank.'

At last she said lamely, 'Okay,' releasing him.

He produced a smile that tweaked up his eyebrows without reaching his eyes, and left as fast as he could while pretending to saunter. At the crossing he glanced back and saw her standing still, looking down.

He walked very fast up Judd Street, hands in pockets and head in the air, then abruptly turned down a narrow opening lined with rubbish bins and stood with his forehead pressed against a brick wall. I've no sexual feeling for you. Had anyone ever had? Not Sheila, not the way he wanted. Because of her past, he'd always thought, but maybe it was because of him. A clown, a lightweight. He knew the impression he made, but how could he change? His mannerisms had once been affectations, but he was at home in them now; he would be naked without them. I've no sexual feeling for you. His for Elinor was irretrievably sexual; he couldn't force it into platonic channels without doing violence to himself. Can't we

275

be friends? No. How dare she ask him to dance attendance on her like a clown?

It hurt. It hurt. He tried to keep staving off pain with anger, but his sense of justice wouldn't let him. He was still angry—she ought to have known her own mind. But she hadn't been deliberately cruel; she too had been in pain.

Friends? Friendship wasn't what he wanted her for—or only part of it. For the past month, slowly, insensibly, a delight, a sense of possibility, had been stealing over him—a fuzzy picture of Elinor and him and his children and hers all living together, without hurting or displacing anyone—without separating his children from either Sheila or him, or Elinor's children from her or Tim—or Tim from Elinor or him from Sheila—though neither Tim nor Sheila had figured in the picture.

Pipe dreams. It would be bloodily painful for the children—for everyone—and he couldn't do it to Sheila. But contained within the fantasy was a sense of hope, of enlargement, which he'd come to depend upon, and certainly hadn't reckoned with losing.

The rubbish bins were foul; a stench of urine rolled up from the wall he was leaning against. Better not stay here weeping; or his eyes would be red when he met the man from the Midland. He mopped them, smoothed his brick-pocked brow and set off again. The revelation of what Elinor could mean to him was drawn across his life like a line across a page.

Chapter 37

The worst thing was the quartet—chatting in artificial tones, avoiding each other's eyes. Both of them would have given anything to get out of it. But Thoby could hardly break up the quartet by dropping out, and Tim and Sheila would think it strange if, after all this time, Elinor backed out of minding the children during it.

She was in a perfectly foul mood for weeks. Garbo on the prowl after her renunciation could be noble, stoic, sad. Not Elinor, who had said no to Thoby under a compulsion she didn't understand, in a manner that gave her nothing to feel noble about. She missed him. Sometimes she felt passionately that she'd made a mistake. Yet she had been obeying an instinct when she said no.

Giving up Thoby made her more impatient with Tim. 'The children need you just as much as your violin students,' she protested one day. 'Isobel sits outside the door like a guard dog while you're teaching; it's pathetic.'

'Don't exaggerate, she goes away after a minute or two. I teach and practise at home—she's got to get used to the fact that she can't have me whenever she wants.'

True, true. His defences were always so reasonable. But—'Why did you want children if you were always going to be too busy to enjoy them?'

'Why does anyone? It's normal.'

'Why did *you*?'

To give them the things I never had, he thought. 'I thought you'd be such a good mother,' he said.

He had not thought beforehand about his own role with the children, beyond unconsciously assuming that he would be the same kind of father his own had been, detached and instructive.

277

The person who would give his children the things he had not had was Elinor, not himself—what did he have to give?

But from that thought he reeled back fast. Everybody wanted children—and he loved his; Elinor had no right to think otherwise.

He had also unconsciously hoped that they would, unlike Elinor, love him uncritically. But Christopher always seemed to be judging him—maybe Isobel was, too. Did they compare him unfavourably with Elinor—Maggie—Rose—Sheila—Thoby—his mother—Elinor's: anyone who made them laugh and squeal? He needed to feel himself approved of. Instead, he felt as if they were all three ranged in critical alliance against him.

Yet for some time a painful desire had been growing in his breast to find a way of being less distant with them. He yearned towards them; he loved to sniff Isobel's sweet shampooey-smelling head when Elinor handed her across to be held—and Kit's, too, when he had occasion to pick him up. Sometimes he even *made* occasion to.

'I'm going to start Christopher on the violin,' he announced one evening in October.

Oh great, Elinor thought sarcastically: more lessons. 'Something you're so good at,' she said—'Won't he compare himself and get discouraged? Why not something simpler, like a recorder?'

He wanted his son to learn his instrument, but she might have a point. 'I've got a nice boxwood offcut, I'll make him one.'

'They're so cheap—you could buy one and spend the time with him, not shut away in the workroom.'

He flinched, but said patiently, 'First I'll make it, *then* I'll teach him.'

He was happy as he whittled the recorder—giving Christopher music: Bach, Mozart, Beethoven, Brahms, Haydn, the springing delight of melody, harmony, counterpoint, of drawing pure, clear notes from sounding wood. From time to time as he worked tears came to his eyes, and he thought, This is what I wanted it to be like. Fatherhood, he meant.

'I've made you a surprise,' he told Kit when it was done, holding it behind his back. 'Something to make music with.'

278

One of the instruments Daddy played, Kit guessed. Not a piano, the workroom wasn't big enough.

'Oh,' he said, frowning, when Tim brought out the satiny-smooth blond pipe. 'I thought it was a violin.' He had never heard adults play the recorder, only children tootling in the crèche. It wasn't a serious instrument, it was childish, like plasticine and crayons. Tim blew him a tune, and he got interested, but the little bird-voiced instrument was infected with his disappointment; he didn't take to it.

Tim was not displeased. Isobel could inherit it: and his work was not wasted if he—and Elinor—had learned what Christopher really wanted. He put the recorder away and bought Kit an exquisite little quarter-size violin, a first book of exercises, and a set of flash cards for learning to read music.

Kit was delighted with the tiny violin. It fascinated Isobel, too. They had to store it out of her reach—she was too young to play with it unsupervised. So was Kit. Part of him understood that it was like teacups or records—fragile and expensive. But those weren't his; this was—Daddy had said so. It was so beautiful; it looked like a cricket bat—a ping-pong paddle—a guitar—a spacecraft—a flat-bottomed boat. A week after he got it, Elinor found him about to float it in the bath.

Every day after breakfast, expectancy rolling off him like sweat, Tim coached Kit for fifteen minutes, and Kit struggled to learn. He had none of Tim's—and Isobel's—slow thorough patience with objects; skills came to him easily or not at all. He wanted to play the violin—but not if all he could get from it was shrieks. But his father wanted him to learn, and he wanted to please his father; so he persisted.

First he must learn to hold the bow pivoted between thumb and middle finger and draw its whole length straight across the E string, keeping his elbow level and his little finger on the stick so that the bow didn't wander. He might have managed that; but he also had to balance one end of the violin on his collarbone and the other between thumb and index finger: always at the same angle, and well up. 'Don't droop,' his father said ten times a session. 'A learner

279

has one arm tired all the time. Keep it high, you'll soon get used to it.'

So much to get right; and all the time loud squawks right by your ear. But now and then Kit got the knack—more and more as the weeks passed. The bow glided straight up and down instead of slithering sideways; and the note stayed even from beginning to end of his stroke.

It was a happy time for Tim. He and his son had something to do together at last; and there was a surreptitious deliciousness in putting his arms round Christopher's warm body and guiding his small, fine-grained hands. He was patient—he, too, had found this stage hard. He drew a little face on his thumb where the bow stick should cross it; broke up the monotony of bow practice by fingering tunes on the string Kit was sawing on; taught him the games his first violin teacher had taught him: how to imitate a crow, a tomcat on the back walls, a hungry kitten—shyly at first, half expecting him to be bored; more easily when he saw how readily he laughed—and showed him how to make the bow glide more smoothly by rubbing it with rosin.

'Look,' he said, holding the translucent amber lump up to the light. 'Beautiful, isn't it? I used to do this when I was a boy, and smell it. It reminded me of Swarthgill.'

Kit put it to his nose. It had a sweet smell, like trees.

'When can I play tunes?' Kit kept asking.

'Soon,' Tim always said. 'When you're ready, the notes will come quickly—they did for me. And you've got to be able to read them.'

In that case, Kit thought, it might be forever. Notes had hard names like semibreve and minim and crotchet, and they rushed up and down ladders and jumped the fence into the next bar for no reason at all. Daddy tried to be as patient about flash-card drill as he was about playing, but he got silently cross. But how could you remember that four black notes with tails were the same as the fat white one?

Nevertheless, one day Tim said, 'You can start on fingering tomorrow.'

'Notes?' Soon he'd be playing beautiful tunes like Daddy.

'That's right.' Tim smiled at Kit's pleasure. 'It'll be fun from now on.' Fingering had come easily to him.

But it didn't to Kit. With one hand you had to bow; with the fingers of the other you had to press the strings in the right places—it was harder than patting your head while rubbing your belly. It took a pent-up concentration he didn't possess; and he was making horrible noises again—back to square one. He was disappointed in himself and the fiddle. He was still eager to please Tim, but was beginning to be humiliated by Tim's ease on the violin. Mastering it sometimes felt almost like a test of his very existence.

But Kit was an easygoing child; his anxiety was within bounds. Music lessons were no worse than other things his parents imposed, like toothbrushing and baths; and he liked doing something with Daddy, and getting caresses in the guise of instruction, which he intuitively knew for what they were. The lessons might have gone on indefinitely.

But in November Tim added a refinement: Kit must learn to tune the strings himself at the start of every lesson.

Try the note, listen to the tuning fork, twist the peg, scrape at the note, listen, twist, scrape, back a little, scrape, a little tighter, scrape...then the next string, and the next, and the next. On and on and on. Kit wasn't dexterous enough; his lurches overshot the note. Day after day he couldn't do it. Day after day Tim finally did it for him—but not until Kit was too demoralised to concentrate properly on learning to make notes. By the end of the lesson, when it was time for flash cards, he could hardly even recognise middle C.

'Hit a hard patch, have you?' Elinor asked him one morning after his lesson—he looked subdued.

Kit nodded.

'What's the hard bit?'

'Everything.'

'But what's hardest?'

'Everything. And tuning.'

'You'll soon get it, I expect.'

'No, I'll never.'

281

She smiled. 'Don't worry, you will. Tim did when he was a little boy not much older than you—and now listen to him.' Down in the music room Tim was limbering up on an étude.

She had touched Kit's sorest spot. He burst into tears.

'There, there, love.' She picked him up. 'What is it?'

I don't know, he thought. He hadn't even known he felt so awful till he started to cry.

'There, there, it'll come with time. After all, you like the violin, don't you?'

Kit shook his head violently—he'd forgotten ever even wanting to play it.

'You don't have to learn it if you don't want, you know,' she said lightly, wiping his eyes and nose.

He brightened, then his face fell. 'Daddy wants me to.'

'Not unless you want to, though.'

Kit knew what he knew, but not in words. His father wanted him to *want* to learn it, to be good at it: better than he could be.

His guarded air bothered Elinor. 'Why not tell him you want to stop for a while, if you're not enjoying it? Or I could tell him for you.'

'Oh no'—anxiously.

'Why not?'

'Daddy would be sad.'

She felt queasy for a moment, then said commonsensically, 'Nonsense, darling.'

'But he *would* be,' Kit said, looking quite frightened.

'Well, I won't if you don't want me to. Promise.'

'Is Kit enjoying violin lessons?' she asked Tim that evening—maybe she could help Kit without giving his secret away.

'Enjoying?'—as if it were no part of the point. Then, suspiciously, 'Does he say he's not?'

'No, no'—hastily. 'But I wonder, learning so early—could it turn him against it altogether?'

'It's not too early—look at all those Suzuki children.'

'But they do it in groups, it's less strain. Actually, why *not* send him to a Suzuki class?'

'I don't want him in mass classes—he'll pick up bad habits without individual attention. And you don't "send him", you go along with him and take the same lessons. Imagine the poor teacher with me in the class pretending to learn the violin.'

'I could go.'

'I want to teach him myself. In time, if he's any good, I'll send him to a teacher.'

She couldn't say more without breaking her promise to Kit.

The next move was Kit's. For a couple of days he turned over the idea that he was free to stop the lessons, then decided to test the water. Untucking the violin from his chin in the middle of a session he said, 'Could I stop, Daddy?'

'Two more minutes, then flash cards.'

'Stop always.'

Tim had been guiding his hand; he dropped it. 'Don't be silly. You shouldn't have asked for a violin if you weren't going to stick to it.'

Kit frowned in bewilderment. Daddy must be right—his parents usually were. But in fact he hadn't asked for it—it had been given to him: and a shadow of what had really happened remained in his memory.

'I don't have to if I don't want to,' he said the next day, looking up from a struggle with the E string. 'Mummy said.'

'Don't have to what?'

'Play the violin.'

Tim scowled. '*Did* she just. Did you tell her you didn't want to?'

Had he? Kit thought about it and shook his head.

'*Do* you want to play it?'

No, Kit thought, I'm tired of it. But Daddy needed him to say yes. He nodded halfheartedly.

Tim knew the real answer already—had half known from the moment Elinor spoke. They had betrayed him, both of them, talking about him behind his back. Christopher did not enjoy the lessons, or his company.

Kit was already cheerful and docile again, but Tim read dislike in every line of his body. That shrinking nod—was the boy afraid of

283

him? He himself was afraid—afraid of what a three-year-old child thought of him. Humiliating—intolerable.

He kept up the lessons for a few days, but the heart had gone out of him. He put off one session for one reason and another for another, then found it convenient to bury himself in the workroom every morning. By Christmas, Kit hadn't had a lesson for three weeks.

'Will you be starting again after the holiday?' Elinor asked.

'No. No time.'

'Not because...' What else could it be? 'Not because of what I said?'

She must have been watching him closely, to ask that. 'Don't be ridiculous—it's because I'm too busy. I'll find him a teacher.'

He was miserable. It was a defeat, and one that comprehended both children, for how could he hope to succeed with Isobel when he had failed with Christopher? His grief was a thorn through his heart. Every time the children looked at him, he was reminded that he had failed in what seemed like one of the simplest of a man's tasks, being a good father. He withdrew into himself and brooded, and his customary weight of unrecognised depression settled round him.

Chapter 38

After Christmas Kit started going to a nursery school near home, and playing with other Ockendon Road children after school—in and out of the neighbours' houses, leaving a trail of scarves, gloves, jumpers, jackets, socks and toys. The student minders, both men, kept forgetting to pick up after him; they preferred coaching football games in the lane behind the house. So Elinor did the rounds in the morning, often stopping for coffee with the mothers of his friends—Carrie, a printmaker who sold her work in Camden Lock; Kate, who had three children under six but said, 'Oh, I don't work;' Helene, who worked part time as a library assistant; and Dundy, a former midwife with a narrow freckled face and a long pale plait, who carried her daughter to the shops on her hip instead of in a pram.

'She's the nicest of them,' Elinor said, telling Maggie about them one evening in March when Maggie had stayed on after Lindsay took the children home. 'Or maybe I mean the happiest—the least divided about what she wants out of life. Or maybe she's just the youngest,' she added with a cynicism that was new to her, 'and in a few years she'll be curdled like the others.'

'Curdled? Looks or minds?'

'A bit of both. Carrie looks as if she'd twang if you plucked her, and Helene's a cross between self-satisfied and dissatisfied. Kate smiles a lot and makes barbed remarks about working mothers—when Isobel had flu she said, "How can you bear leaving her with paid minders?" '

'I've said very much the same thing,' Maggie observed drily.

So she had, and Elinor didn't like it. 'But in the context of our whole friendship,' she temporised: 'Kate's only just *met* me. And

285

they all talk about their husbands as if they're troublesome little boys.'

'Most men are—look at Clive.'

'Albericht?'

'Albericht's an adulterer,' Maggie said bitingly. 'A great big baby who can't survive in a strange town without mamma.'

'Albericht the Adulterer? I liked Albericht the Ample better.'

The look Maggie flashed her was dangerous—so much for feeble pleasantries—but she only said, 'Yes, well...' and changed the subject. 'I keep seeing Tim these days, does he tell you?—the Danish Pastry can't keep away from concerts. Front of the front stalls. Tim and I wave. The Pastry's impressed; thinks musicians sit at the right hand of God.'

'Yes, Tim says he sees you.' Elinor looked at the clock. 'I've got to grab a sandwich before the next house—one of my late-show nights, so Tim doesn't feed me. They've got a killer BLT on the stand now. Join me?'

'Thanks, but I've got half a salmon trout languishing. Other men bring roses; Albericht turns up with large wet raw things—fish, pheasant, filet—then takes me out to dinner, so I'm stuck with them.'

'Consider yourself lucky they're plucked and gutted and all,' said Elinor. 'Remember Ludovic bringing me the rabbit he'd run down with his car?'

'Oh God yes, and you had to skin it—'

'No, he did, I couldn't—'

'And cook and eat it—' Maggie was hooting with laughter.

'And I'd just seen *Repulsion*, endless close-ups of a rotting skinned rabbit. One mouthful and that was *it*. I've never touched rabbit again.'

At least I got her to laugh, Elinor thought when Maggie was gone and the last house was in. A close thing, though—what had got into Maggie, looking so ferocious? Was everybody in a state these days?

She herself was only in a state because Tim was. Or was it the time of year? She'd been low last winter, remember, and the winter before—she shouldn't blame Tim for something that was a function of the earth's tilt.

She shouldn't have said anything about Kit and the violin, anything at all. But how could she *not*? And if a harmless suggestion made him withdraw into himself like a polar bear, what *was* it safe to talk about?

She didn't want to talk about movies. She didn't want to hear about concerts.

When there was no light in his eyes she could see why he thought he was ugly—his face was thick, heavy: thicker now than when they met, though he weighed no more; she could see how he would look at fifty.

Careful—you'll get like those women, discussing their husbands with that tolerant querulousness. She didn't want that. She wanted... she didn't know what. Help in reconciling sexual joy with emotional discontent, or at least understanding how they could coexist.

How was it possible to look at Tim critically, feel distant from him, yet go on responding to him so eagerly in bed? Why didn't it make her feel faintly disgusted with herself or him?

It didn't. But sometimes she made love to him just to feel his arms around her: because it was the only way to get them there.

Maggie, Maggie, she thought longingly. Their friendship had once been based on talking about such things. But it was starvation rations these days. Tonight was the first time in months that Maggie had stayed on after seeing Kit—she'd actually seemed to be avoiding a tête-à-tête ever since the autumn. Elinor had asked her out to dinner several times, and Maggie had kept saying she was engaged. Finally she'd said, 'Oh, all right,' as if yielding to a novel and unwelcome proposition. But she had been cool and snappish all evening, and hadn't suggested another time.

Very well—there were limits. Elinor wouldn't keep running after someone who didn't want her. Friendship with Rose might not be so exhilarating, but it mattered to her—and it was what she had.

Talk to Rose? She seemed so innocent still, so young—she was thirty-three, but looked twenty—like Dundy with her pale plait and crinkly smile.

—*—

287

The remote-control car that Maggie gave Kit for his fourth birthday was the hit of his party. Nobody wanted to play boring old Musical Chairs and Simple Simon; everyone went straight out-doors, in spite of the blustery wind, and spent the afternoon zooming the scarlet Maserati up and down the lane.

Elinor leaned against the wall, listening to Rose tell Helene, Kate, Carrie and Maggie—who was the one who had asked—about the costings Andrew Wellesford was having done for Cromer Three, and wondering what had possessed Tim to invite Thoby and Sheila to Swarthgill for a week in the summer. 'With the boys, of course,' he'd said genially at lunch. Last summer he hadn't wanted his own children there, let alone Euan and Fergus.

'Oh Tim, how nice,' Sheila had said. 'We'd love to.'

Thoby, without even a glance at Elinor, had said, 'Why not?'

She wanted to scream. It would be just awful—but how could she stop it?

Parents took their children home; Tim had to leave for a concert. Maggie stayed behind with Thoby and Sheila to help clean up, then lingered after they left to help put Kit and Isobel to bed and read them a story.

Downstairs she said no to dinner, but accepted a drink, instinctively feeling for a cigarette, then remembering the house rules and desisting with a little annoyed flutter. 'Rose was telling us,' she said, 'me and the ladies of Ockendon Road—I see what you mean, by the way, a tight-assed trio—that Andrew seems all set for Cromer Three. Sounds good. A new auditorium is a specialised investment—you can't make much flogging second-hand cinema seats, I take it—so they won't be in a hurry to turn the site into flats—at least not before they've recouped what they put in.'

'After the scare we had, I'm not going to count chickens till the last fitting's in place,' Elinor said. 'What if Andrew keels over halfway through? Sefton would look at that nice big hole in the basement and think: office foundations.'

'Does Rose mind never getting a cinema of her own?'

'I think that idea faded in the cold light of realising how few reps are left that aren't owner-run, so she'd never get a screen. Besides,

Cromer Three will give us all more scope—and our programming has already moved a bit in her direction. Five shows a day gives us more margin to experiment; and she's got a flair for what people will accept in the avant-garde line—which I certainly don't.'

'It's her taste in men that's beyond me—the hairy wonder, with his second string in Brighton.'

'That's been over for ages, didn't I tell you?—more or less since he started teaching in Camberwell. In fact...' She didn't finish. Given Maggie's sensitivity on the subject of having children, it might be better not to say that Rose and Marcus had been trying for months to conceive.

A pool of silence accumulated. Elinor looked fondly at the dear face—round eyes carefully brown-rimmed, not a speck of liner or mascara out of place; small precisely shaped nose; thin ironic mouth with a soft shine of pinky-brown on it. Maggie's freckled cheeks were still smooth, but there were hollows under her eyes and crowsfeet in the corners, and her short white neck was beginning to wattle under the chin. So was Elinor's own, but signs of mortality bothered her more on Maggie. Stop, she wanted to say to time. Stop.

When Maggie left she felt disconsolate, alone with the sleeping children in the quiet house—like someone mooning over a lost love. Long lost—the friend she wanted back was the Maggie of ten years ago, maybe fifteen. Probably Maggie felt the same. 'I cannot *bear* it, you and your husband and your exactly two children.' That hadn't changed. They were still in some sense each other's dearest friends; but in another sense their friendship was over. Maggie had cut it short because she had to.

Oh God—Swarthgill.

What had come over Thoby—saying, 'Why not?' in his old flippant manner—showing not a flicker of recollection? He must be over it. The thought hurt, even though she, too, was over it. She'd lost the daily sense of being involved with him—with his life, his doings, his concerns—that had lingered half the winter.

But it still took self-command to be around him for a few hours every Sunday—to hide the fact that they had once been more intimate than the others knew, but were now more distant; to exchange a few words in order to seem to be at ease. A week at Swarthgill would be dreadful. Would Tim or Sheila suggest going back to Cosh? Would Thoby just say, 'Why not?'

'I was just passing by,' Thoby said implausibly, teetering on the doorstep the next morning like a scarecrow in the wind and clutching at his forelock. 'Well, yes, love a cup,' following her downstairs. 'Tea, coffee, whichever. Hullo, you'—picking Isobel up. 'And you'—to Kit. 'How's the Maserati?'

Kit fetched it, and the three of them crouched on the kitchen floor and raced it back and forth while Elinor made tea in silence. Why on earth had he come? She was oppressed by the memory of how badly she had treated him, and as an irrational result could barely be polite, as if a smile and a pleasant word would be hypocritical.

After drinking his tea he got up and paced about nervously, then with a gesture as if rolling up a newspaper in his empty hands said, 'About Swarthgill—I saw you look worried—'

'Not really, I—'

'If it's because of me, don't.' He looked straight at her. She'd forgotten how beautiful his eyes were. 'I was shaky last autumn. Fine now.' He stopped rolling the imaginary newspaper and spread his hands in one of his half-ridiculous rhetorical gestures.

'Oh, good,' she said mechanically. He was happy; the stream had closed over the pebble of their involvement as if it had never been.

'But even so, Swarthgill—it'd be awkward. Tim asking out of the blue like that—I couldn't muster an excuse. Got one now, though. Must go and see a Surrealist house. South of France. *Le facteur Cheval*, you know.'

Who? Elinor shook her head. 'And that's okay with Sheila?'

No—she had reverted to disliking going abroad. But he couldn't tell Nell that. 'Saves her from worrying about the boys falling into becks.'

'Just as well, then, I suppose.'

'Thought I should tell you—knew Tim had a Haydn rehearsal— chance to catch you alone. Well—cheer-o.' Now he was holding the imaginary newspaper in one hand and tapping it against his other palm. She wanted to laugh; she wanted him out of the house.

Chapter 39

Tim wasn't playing in a *St Matthew Passion* this year, so on Good Friday they went to one together in St John's Smith Square, where Elinor had sat in the audience through so many concerts watching him on the conductor's left. The orchestral and choral forces were small—it was a period-instrument performance—and the sound that rang through the resonant space was at once precise and ravishingly sensual. She had never so clearly heard how each individual thread ran in relation to all the others; nor so entirely felt the parts meshing into a whole.

Tim was rigid with excitement; he kept nudging her elbow with his fingertip at passages that especially struck him. 'I can't hold out any longer,' he said in the interval; 'I'll have to increase the mortgage, but I'm going to get a baroque fiddle and have some lessons.'

'But you already restring with gut strings for the Academy of Ancient Music and the Haydn.'

'It's not the same. The baroque violin's got a different resonance—can't you hear it?'

She tried to listen for it, but couldn't, not even during '*Erbarme dich*'—Tim's solo with contralto accompaniment, as she thought of it—played tonight by a very young woman whom Tim thought amazing.

'I like you better,' Elinor said loyally afterwards.

'Well you're wrong. She plays the way I only play in my head.'

He was exalted, not downcast; when they got home their lovemaking was steeped in the music, resonant with its passion. He sank into her, pressing rapture out of her in heavy waves; then after a long while pulled her round on top of him and raised and lowered her on his cock, pushing her breath out of her in sharp groans.

She was within a hair's breadth of coming; resisted; resisted; then at last fell willy-nilly off the edge. The pillow smothered her gasp; a moment later she heard a flurry of words that she did not quite catch, except: 'Did you really come?'

'Yes,' she said into his neck, surprised—couldn't he feel it? But it couldn't always be easy to tell whether she was coming or just quivering on the brink—she herself sometimes only knew he'd come when he stopped moving.

'Can you come again?' he whispered when she began pushing down on him again. She hardly ever could, but he kept hoping.

'Nope,' she said into his ear.

'Do you mind if I come?'

She quaked all over him with laughter. 'No—I mean, yes and no.'

'I know what you mean,' he said in the clear daylight voice he sometimes used at such times. For a giddy second she nearly laughed uncontrollably—don't—poor man, too distracting—but it merged into the general tremulousness of all her muscles from going on so long, and subsided of itself.

He lay quite still beneath her for a moment, then with an astonished, 'Oh my God,' pushed his whole body up and his cock deep into her in three quick spasms; then more, longer and slower. She felt it deep inside, an internal convulsion that half set her alight again, but with a fire that quickly died away, not the unquenchable flaring burn of not coming at all. She might come again if she tried, but she didn't want to try. She wanted this quiet aftermath, their bodies still joined in...whatever sex was: a bond, an intimacy, a reach to union with what was outside oneself, different from oneself, yet part of the same creation.

Finally he slid out of her, and she moved sideways and lay in a happy daze with her head on his chest and both arms round him. He let her stay there for a few moments, then moved out from under with a sleepy grunt and stumbled out of bed to wash and pee. Then her turn. He was asleep when she came back. She curled up to him and put her arm round him; he groaned in his sleep and moved away.

— ❋ —

She woke up feeling miserable. *Something's got to change. I can't go on living on sex and thin air.*

A tear ran down her cheek onto the pillow, and another—a slow drip, not a torrent. She wiped them away in silence till they stopped, then reached quietly for a tissue and dabbed her nose rather than blowing it, so as not to wake Tim.

I wish he'd wake up anyhow and ask why I'm crying.

What would I say?

I'm unhappy, I want—

After breakfast they dropped the children in Guildford—'My turn,' Mavis had said, oh the luxury, maybe you never appreciated your mother till she was your children's grandmother—and to have two of them vying to look after them, not to mention Maggie!—and drove up north.

Mavis had made them sandwiches. Tim ate the ham, Elinor the chicken—and from Doncaster onwards had to make him stop every few miles to let her vomit.

'That must be it,' she said each time, 'I'll be fine now'—then: 'Oh no...oh...Tim, could you...?'

By the time they got to Harrogate there was nothing left in her stomach, but she was still vomiting. 'I'm okay really,' she insisted feebly. But she wasn't. She gave in, almost crying with disappointment—she wanted Swarthgill—needed it—and let Muriel Scott put her to bed, while Tim rang to warn her parents off the chicken.

'It's all right—they had the ham for lunch.'

'Thank goodness,' said Muriel. 'Far worse for small children—an attack like this, they'd be in hospital.' She drew the curtains. 'Tim, get Nell the handbell from our room.'

He put it on the bedside table, saying, 'Try to sleep, now. I'll be downstairs—just ring if you—'

'No, you go to Swarthgill,' Elinor said. 'No point us both missing it.'

'Oh, I don't...'

'Really.'

'Go on, Tim, I'll take care of her,' his mother said. Tim went.

293

Twenty-four hours later Elinor was well enough to go down and lie languorously on a sofa. Muriel brought tea and thin slivers of lemon cake. Elinor nibbled, then wolfed; Muriel brought her more.

'How are the children?' she asked. 'Kit as rampant as ever? Remember at Christmas, me telling him yes means yes and no means no, and him saying, "That depends if it's Mummy or Daddy"?'

Elinor laughed. 'That's my Kit—tries to get away with murder, and bobs on the sea of life like a cork. Isobel too—till she gets overwrought and starts thinking yes only means maybe, and no means, "How dare you even ask?" '

'Poor little thing—Tim was like that. Thank goodness he was the youngest, or I'd have wondered what I was doing wrong.'

'Maybe it was *because* he was the youngest? Isobel gets really desperate, trying to keep up with Kit.' Elinor swallowed the last of her tea. She was still hungry, and still thirsty. She poured the milk from the jug into her teacup and drank in one gulp.

'Good sign,' said Muriel—'I'll get you a glassful.' When she came back, Elinor was standing at the french windows gazing at pale light coming and going on daffodils in the grass.

'Here—drink up. And come and sit down. Wishing you were up at Swarthgill? Missing Tim? Pity—next time. Aren't the daffodils splendid? I've got some doubles down at the end—beauties. I'll show you tomorrow.'

'Thank you,' Elinor said politely. She thought double daffodils looked like scrambled eggs.

Missing Tim? Yes, but...

...but it was almost a relief when he wasn't around—not to be always hoping...

Elinor was wrong about one thing—Isobel wasn't desperate about Kit any longer. She was catching up with him, and felt comfortable with him—unless Daddy was around. Kit could still do some things she couldn't, and Daddy liked it when people could do things. He was still cross with Kit about the violin. He should have taught her—she wouldn't have let him down.

'Tim started the violin pretty much off his own bat,' she had heard Mummy tell Terry, 'when he was hardly older than Kit. He just came home and announced he wanted to.' Kit was four and couldn't tie his shoelaces. Isobel could, and she was only nearly three. She would surprise Daddy; he would be so proud.

The little fiddle was on a shelf in the music room. She stood on tiptoe on two volumes of Grove on a chair to reach it, carried it up to her room, took it out of its case, tucked it under her chin, laid the bow across it with a sureness that would have astonished Tim after Kit's slithery fumbles, and drew a quavering but true note out of the A string. The return stroke shrieked, but she wasn't dismayed. Daddy turned the pegs to get the strings in tune. She gave one peg a twist; and the next. When she twisted the third peg, the string snapped.

'Oh, here you are.' Elinor took in the violin and the broken string. 'Isobel, for God's sake!'

The same thought came to both their minds: Tim would be angry and blame—her, thought Isobel, because she'd broken it. Her, thought Elinor, because she should have been watching Isobel.

'What on earth possessed you?' she said. 'You know it's Kit's.'

Isobel looked down. It wasn't Kit's. Things belonged to the person who was cross when you broke them. It was Daddy's.

'Was it one of your games?' Elinor asked, more gently. Things often disappeared upstairs as props for the stories Isobel told herself.

'Not a game,' Isobel said, stung. 'Want to play it. Like Kit. And I *can*.' No, that wasn't quite right. What she meant was that she *could*, if left alone to work it out. But she didn't know how to say it. She burst into tears of frustration.

Mummy scooped her up and hugged her blissfully hard, saying, 'Don't cry, mugwump. It's only a broken string, it happens all the time. Tim does it too.'

Isobel looked up out of the comfortable shoulder in alarm. 'Secret.'

'I can't, pet—the string's got to be replaced. I'll tell him you were trying to play it. He won't be cross.'

If he is cross, she thought, carrying Isobel down snuffling and still rigid, I'll tell him not to show it.

Fat lot of good that would do. Tim would be furious. Poor besotted baby.

Did he need to know? She could put the case back on the shelf and get the string replaced at Beares' without telling him—the kind of subterfuge women traditionally practised on men. She wouldn't stoop to it for herself, but for your children you did things you'd never expected to.

'Tell you what, love—I'll get a new string myself, it can be secret.'

Isobel relaxed at once and snuggled close, and Elinor was glad of her promise, though uneasy about colluding with her to hide something from Tim. She would just do it, not think about it—and hope to heaven that Isobel didn't go and tell him the whole thing in tomorrow morning's instalment of her life story.

The violin was re-strung and safely back in its case; and Isobel hadn't mentioned it at breakfast: episode closed. But Elinor kept remembering Isobel's body stiff with anxiety. Why did she take everything so hard? Why didn't Kit?

She put the question to Tim one night; she was making another effort to share her thoughts about the children with him. 'D'you think we should be treating her more gently than Kit? He's always pushing, so we've got to push back; but Isobel's more often just forgetful than deliberately naughty.'

'Wouldn't it be unfair?' Tim said dubiously.

'You don't treat all your violin students the same—you've said you're gentler with the timid ones.'

'True.' Tim felt like a man in a cartoon with a light bulb going on in his head. He wanted to stop being angry with Christopher for giving up the violin, but did not know how: it had hurt too much, and still did—and he was stiff with Isobel too, because it had not occurred to him to treat her differently. But he was lonely, lonely in his own house, with his own family; lonely for his children. He had lost out with Kit; but perhaps there was still time with Isobel, who from the moment when he arrived at her birth had always seemed

296

more his child. Fathers and daughters, people said. A boy looked to you for an example; a girl simply loved you.

Elinor must not know she had said something that influenced him. Sometimes he felt as if they were locked in battle. If he once admitted she was right about anything, she would rise in triumph over him...and...

He would change gradually, so that she did not notice—when he and Isobel were alone.

In a sense he was never alone with the children. Always there was a critical inner audience—sometimes Elinor, sometimes Thoby, sometimes his mother. The children themselves were part of the audience. Elinor said Isobel was like him. He hoped not. The more like, the sooner she would guess that he only pretended to know what he was doing with her. He was afraid of boring her. He could hardly be very entertaining—a hurried man, always thinking of music. People seemed to find things to say to children; he wanted to learn how. There must be something he and Isobel could do, free of Elinor's scrutiny. She was his last chance.

He turned the question over and over in his mind. He had an obscure desire to present Elinor with a formed and perfected bond between him and Isobel, that would somehow seal and perfect their own bond. Elinor had seemed distant since...since he could not remember when. A long time. To do with him, he sensed, though he could not think why. He wanted to get back to the way they had been before...before...

He could teach Isobel the violin. The cartoon light bulb flashed on; then off, as he remembered what had happened with Kit.

Chapter 40

'Looking for something?' Tim got up and turned down the volume of the tuner.

'Isobel's bedtime book—the big red storybook,' said Hilary.

'I've seen it...yes, here.' The cartoon light bulb lit up, and stayed lit. 'You have a drink and relax. I'm home so little in the evenings—I'll read to her.'

He had forgotten that Kit would be there. Christopher, damn it—but it was a losing battle; half the time now he thought of him as Kit. He won't want me, he thought. But it was too late to retreat—and in fact they both seemed happy to see him. He sat beside Isobel's cot and started the story she asked for.

'Do the voices, Daddy.' Isobel interrupted. 'Hilary does.'

'Don't be silly, Izzy-bizzy,' said Kit from his bed. 'Daddy can't do it like Hilary.'

'Rose can.'

'Rose is a girl too.'

'Terry can,' said Isobel.

'I'll read my way or not at all,' Tim said quickly. Did everyone they knew read aloud better than he did? He was shaking inside himself; he wanted to go away and hide from the hurt of being found wanting. Stubbornly he read the story to the end; then closed the book.

'More,' Isobel said immediately.

He looked at her in surprise, and a certain amount of amusement. 'I thought you didn't like the way I read.'

'Hilary reads us two.'

He glanced at Kit for confirmation. Kit saw his advantage. 'Three.'

Tim looked straight at him. 'Two,' he said firmly, in Elinor's tone of voice, and, in much better heart, read them the story of Chicken-Licken. 'The sky is falling down! The sky is falling down!'

Learn from Elinor, he thought on the way downstairs; imitate her. Was it that easy? Something in him rebelled at the idea of learning how to get on with his children by imitating their mother. But if it worked—

'And Hilary put us to bed and Daddy read us turkey-lurkey,' Isobel told Elinor the next morning at breakfast.

Don't watch me, Tim wanted to say, catching Elinor's pleased look. If she was going to notice every last thing he did, he would not read to them again until some time when she wasn't there.

He looked at his diary when he went up to practise. May was full, and the first week in June, till he got back from tour. But then—here were two free evenings in a row when Elinor was working, and here was another. That should be a start.

He tuned the fiddle, feeling happier about the children than he had in a long time—happy enough to start thinking, as he ran up and down the scale of E flat legato and spiccato, that he should try to make things better between him and Elinor as well. She had so often asked him to talk more; now it was she who was silent. He could hear the silence she had once filled.

Draw her out, he thought; and started that night, on the way home in the car. '*Kiss of the Spider Woman*, I see—how is it doing?'

'Well.'

'And *Mona Lisa*?'

'Full house.'

Her curt answers did not encourage him to go on about films, though it couldn't be him she was annoyed at—she was always cross when audiences flocked to films she thought mediocre. Instead, he found himself telling her about his concert in more detail than it deserved. When they reached Ockendon Road, he parked, opened the door, put one foot out, and on sudden impulse said, in a very slightly enquiring tone, 'You don't chatter as much as you used to.'

She turned to him quickly and said, 'No, I...I...' with a look of such hope that he quailed and got out of the car without waiting for an answer.

Was that that, then—one strangled half-question, and back to silence?

Silence, silence. The children weren't enough; friends weren't enough: talking with friends only pointed up the silence at home. She was a mile off from him—didn't he notice?

Had she ever asked hard enough? She had used his pain as an excuse to avoid pushing: she was too afraid of being turned down. Asking made her as vulnerable as he said kissing made him.

She would try again—when? It was nearly June, and he was going on tour on the eighth. Bustle beforehand, so no chance to talk; catching up with his routine afterwards, so no chance to talk.

Start with something simpler than talk, then: with lovemaking. She knew very clearly what was missing there: the beginning. She wanted to begin by kissing him and being kissed; looking at him and being looked at—tenderly, passionately, in trust, in simplicity.

Such a harmless longing; yet she'd almost suppressed it. She would ask clearly, unmistakably, in words, not gestures: ask for one thing at a time, starting the next time they made love. Look at me, she would say; kiss me. Promise.

'My real birthday was Thursday—I'm three *already*,' Isobel kept telling people at her birthday party. It was on the last Sunday in May, after the quartet's final rehearsal for this year's do.

Maggie didn't come, but sent Isobel a big gift-wrapped package: a doll, with several changes of clothing. Thoby and Sheila gave her a drum. She banged it a few times, then tore open the next present— a recorder from Muriel Scott.

'Plastic,' said Tim in disgust.

Isobel blew it and was entranced; and in a few minutes was playing—Tim and Sheila stared at each other in amazement—the scale of C—then, after a sour-noted fumble or two, the scale of D— 'My God, she's found two sharps!'—then back to C and— 'Arpeggios!'

'What do you expect, "Frère Jacques"?' said Elinor. 'She's playing what she hears you play every day. Besides, she's been doing it on the piano for ages when you're not around.'

'She *has*?' Tim looked at Isobel as if she were a meteorite landed in his back garden, and went for the boxwood recorder—'She needs something better than *that* thing.' Isobel started on—'Frère Jacques'.

'You began too low,' Sheila said when she couldn't find a note lower than C for 'Din dan don'. 'Try here—that's G.' By the time Tim came back, she'd got her into the upper register and shown her how to cross-finger F, and Isobel was shrieking triumphantly through 'Frère Jacques' while Kit whacked the drum.

'Mine,' said Kit, seeing the recorder in Tim's hands.

'I hoped he'd forgotten,' Tim muttered, but handed it over. Kit tried it, but found he didn't sound like Isobel. He went back to the drum—with the recorder tucked down his jeans, where the birthday girl couldn't get her mitts on it.

'You'll have to make her one of her own,' Elinor said.

'Good idea. As soon as I get back.' No, that was when he was going to read them stories. He would buy her one and...no, maybe not teach her anything just yet.

Tim was lying on his back with the pillow doubled behind him. That meant he was awake, though his eyes were shut. Elinor raised herself on one arm, watching his chest rise and fall and his eyelashes now and then quiver with sleepy half-blinks, and thinking it would be nice to make love.

You were going to say something, remember? The next time, she'd promised herself, but then hadn't; so now she really had to.

No, too soon. Next time.

No, next time was right now. She stroked his cheek, her fingers burring on stubble; considered his shoulder, his throat, his face, as if playing a difficult move in a game.

Tim's breathing changed. Without opening his eyes he touched her thigh and slid his hand along it, slowly, caressingly, without a glance or the ghost of a kiss. Straight to business; sex is about genitals.

301

Do something, she thought. But what? His face was sealed against her. She put her head on his chest. He gave it a little push down, not with any force, just indicating something he'd like. No. She wanted a kiss on her mouth, not his cock in it.

But he had a finger on her clitoris and two more stirring in her cunt; it was flowing with sweetness, opening to him. Defeated, in revolt against herself, resenting him and her cowardice and her cunt that obeyed his hand instead of her will, half-yielding to what he wanted, wanting to, not wanting to, she turned round, pivoting on his hand, touched her tongue to his cock, and tried to slide down round it.

Her throat tightened; her mouth dried up completely. She choked and drew back, pretending to fish a hair out of it, fighting a vehement impulse to stop and get up.

Not quite by conscious volition, she found herself in the old fantasy of being blindfolded and naked with several men—free to leave, but not to change their terms, which were: unconditional surrender.

Tim turned from bending his head to her cunt and gave her a quick amused look and a smile that said: hairs in one's mouth, yes, happens to me too. The simplest human solidarity, but enough: she hauled herself out of the pit and back into bed with him. But even when he came into her, her pleasure was out on the surface; her flesh didn't tremble through and through. Come quickly, she thought for the first time ever—let's get it over with.

She tightened round him; he murmured, 'Not so soon,' and moved back.

She set her will against his and pulled in, in, in, knowing he couldn't resist for long. He could bring her afterwards. Coming with him always felt like a thank-offering, a surrender of her whole being; she was too detached from him to want that.

But her body had its own ideas and hurled her into the vortex with him; and though until then her pleasure had been external, her coming was all depth and yielding—helpless rapture quivering down to the soles of her feet like the eddies from a stone flung into a pool. For a moment she was reconciled to him.

302

Then he moved off her, and the only reason they were touching was that she put her head on his shoulder. She ran her fingers over his chest; but he stiffened slightly, and she stopped.

Blindfolded, anonymous—Jesus. She went cold with shame and stopped totting up the take.

Forget it. Do your job. Fifty, sixty, three, four, and two halves—the cashier accepting halfpennies again—

He'd rather fuck you on the front step in broad daylight, she told herself bitterly, than kiss you in the privacy of bed.

She put her head in her hands. She could hear her heart beating; she could hear the silence of a voice not speaking. She felt as if her blood had been drained off and replaced with a transparent and only just life-sustaining fluid. She was surprised she wasn't invisible.

She'd been happy earlier in the year, hadn't she, or the end of last year—where had it gone?

Men's voices in the outer office; it must be Tim, stopping for a word with Terry. Her throat was raw with unshed tears. With an instinct for concealment she started up and went to the small half-unsilvered glass to compose her face. She looked a little hollow-eyed, that was all.

She opened her door and found, not Tim, but Terry's lover Nigel, a young stockbroker with a sculpted lip, a perennially fresh shave, a precise haircut, and a dazzling variety of bespoke striped shirts with white collars and cuffs. A walking definition of Yuppie, as Rose said; but nicer than that, spirited and ingenuous and a stalwart of the Terrence Higgins Trust. She was in no mood for light conversation, but stayed propping up the doorframe anyhow; by the time Tim arrived she was laughing.

On the way home her cheerfulness vanished. Her throat still ached. Do something—*do* something. What?

They needed—she needed—what? To get through this, past it: forward. Now. Tim was on tour from Monday—she couldn't just brood till he got back.

— ✳ —

'D'you you remember,' she said at the end of dinner, laying down her knife and fork—'D'you remember a couple of weeks ago, saying I don't chatter so much?'

'Er—vaguely.'

She waited for him to pick up the dangling thread. He didn't. 'Were you wondering why?'

'I suppose I must have been,' he said with a sinking feeling.

Wasn't he going to say he wanted to know? She'd tell him anyhow. 'Well, part of it is sort of because...because I feel as if you don't want me to talk about...things I want to talk about, and...' She floundered to a halt.

He sighed. 'All right, what is it *this* time?'

His concessions always took her by surprise. She said helplessly, 'Why we don't talk, I suppose. Is this all you want, us the way we are now?'

'All I want: you say that as if it's—nothing.' He got up and rinsed his plate; he felt like a baited bull. Over the running water he said, 'No, it's not all I want. I want...We've been married seven years. Isn't it time you gave up expecting me to babble, and accept me as I am, and stop being dissatisfied with a perfectly normal life? What I want is for you to stop making me feel completely inadequate.'

'*Inadequate*? I didn't know I—'

'It should be obvious that if I avoid talking in certain ways it's because it's too painful. I'm not stupid. I've heard you ask.'

Accept me as I am. I've heard you ask. It's too painful. They'd certainly done what she wanted, talked about something of substance; but it led nowhere except into silence.

THREE

Chapter 41

'Right, I'm off,' Elinor said after breakfast on Saturday, picking up the shopping list. 'There's a lot here—can I leave the children with you?'

'I'd rather not—I want to bring the car round to the back and see what's making that funny noise in the air filter.'

'Okay, I'll take them. Ready to march, you two?'

She cut down the lane to the shops with a child bouncing and tugging at each hand. The sun was suffusing through a skim-milky haze. The air was brisk, but it would be warm later. She wished she had time to take the children to the Heath.

There were a number of light but bulky items on the shopping list, like lavatory paper and light bulbs. Kit volunteered to carry the lavatory paper; even so, Elinor was laden by the time they started for home. In one hand she was holding Kit's hand and two carrier bags, in the other, Isobel's hand and a string bag. Isobel wanted to carry a box of Tampax, but kept dropping it, so Elinor took it back.

They turned into the lane, and there was Tim, a hundred and some yards away, with his head under the bonnet of the car. Elinor's heart fluttered with pleasure at the sight of him. Did his ever do the same?

'Daddy!' Isobel cried joyously, as if she'd been away for days. Wriggling her hand free, she set off at full tilt down the lane. Kit kept his hand in Elinor's. She looked down. He was clutching the packet of lavatory paper and watching Isobel with a look of wry deprecation—the look of someone who had learned better.

Half Elinor's eye was still on Isobel, fifty yards off, seventy-five, a hundred, nearly there, running pell mell, still calling, 'Daddy, Daddy.' Tim's head lifted momentarily; turned back. At that lick she'd be lucky if she reached him without—

Ten feet from the car Isobel stubbed her toe and went sprawling flat on her face.

Elinor nearly dropped her bags and ran. But Kit was holding fast to her hand and dragging his feet, and Isobel, who from the sound of her wails was grazed but not seriously hurt, was a hundred yards away. Tim was on the spot.

He didn't stir. His elbow was out and pumping; he seemed to be tightening something. Didn't he hear the child? Drop the goddamn spanner and pick her up.

Kit gave an oddly resigned sigh, as if something had been confirmed for him. I could have told her there's no point, it said. No point in crying for comfort, none in running in the first place.

Elinor ached to annihilate the distance, pick Isobel up, comfort her. She hurried along, but seemed to be weighted by stones. Isobel was still wailing. Tim went on making that slow, deliberate tightening motion. A familiar note of hysterical abandonment entered Isobel's voice; her shrieks became ear-piercing. Elinor walked faster through air that resisted her.

Kit's sigh. She broke stride; made her feet keep going. Kit could have told Isobel there was no point.

She saw it all, all at once. Cold—cold. Got to leave. Got to.

Time held almost still. No point, there never was. Second by thick palpable second she moved towards Isobel, thinking with utter clarity and utter certainty: Leave. Leave. I'm stifling. The children are stifling. We've got to get away. How have I stood it? I haven't. I'm half dead living with this cold implacable man, and I'm a responsible adult. They've no choice. Don't make them stay in it any longer. Or me.

She was breaking the surface after years underwater. Around her, ahead of her, the air was completely clear, and full of Tim and Isobel and Kit and the car and the lane and Tim eight years ago when they met, and when Kit was born, and when Isobel was born, rushing in just in time—oh if only that moment instead of this had been the note of their lives—and all the time before and after and in between, moment after moment, year after year of slowly withering hope; and at the end of it this instant.

Faster—poor baby.

308

Tim long ago when she twisted her ankle, not hearing her say, 'Hold me.' No, he *had* heard her; he'd said so. Heard—and ignored. Nothing had changed. Her turn to fall then, Isobel's now, and Tim then now always implacably motionless.

Tim turning away from her kiss, over and over, always accidentally; always on purpose. Tim moving away from her even in his sleep.

Kit knew already, Isobel never would. In most things she was cleverer than he, but not about Tim—she needed him more, poor Timlike baby. She would spend her entire childhood running towards him and falling on her face and not getting picked up; the same heartbreaking lesson over and over, slowly, slowly absorbed but never quite learned. No point. No point reaching out to other people. You just fall and lie there abandoned.

They had to get out of that: she, and Isobel—and Kit, who knew better.

Still some distance away, she saw Tim lay down the spanner and turn to Isobel, who just at the sight of his feet stopped screeching and started sobbing instead.

He didn't pick her up in his arms. He stooped, helped her to her feet and took her by the shoulders. 'Be a brave little girl,' Elinor guessed he was saying.

The thought spurred her forward. Time sped up to its usual rate. She covered the last few yards in the flick of an eyelid, plumped down her bags and scooped Isobel into her arms. Isobel burst out wailing again.

After her passage of high resolve across a field of time there was something anti-climactic and muddled about facing Tim across Isobel's dirty raw grazes, with the hot sobbing little body wriggling in her grasp; with Tim looking as if he wanted to say something but didn't know what; with Kit hopping on and off the pavement, elaborately uninterested; with the spanner perched on the bonnet and the bags slumped on the ground. An ordinary domestic scene; the beginning of a final act.

'She gets overexcited,' Tim said, meaning Isobel's headlong rush down the lane as much as her shrieks.

309

'Yes,' she replied, as though nothing had changed. Nothing, everything. She was going to leave him—she, and the heaving bundle in her arms, and the hopping boy off to the side. No point in asking why he hadn't picked Isobel up straightaway, no point in telling him that his future might have been different if he had. No, not true—something else would have tipped the balance pretty soon. Everything in her life with him had tended towards this one overdetermined moment; walking towards him down the lane she'd been walking into frame.

'There, love, hush, we'll go inside and kiss it better,' she told Isobel. To Tim she said, 'She's got gravel in this one, look, on her knee.' An ordinary unaccusing voice, an ordinary comment. 'I'd better wash it. Could you bring in the shopping? Coming, Kit? You can help pull the stuff off the sticking plasters.'

Isobel's hysteria subsided once there were a couple of closed doors between her and Tim. She shrieked a little, reasonably enough, when Elinor scraped bits of gravel out of her knee and palm, and again at the touch of cool water. 'There, there, now, be a brave girl,' Elinor said, vaguely aware of inconsistency—a few moments ago she'd been furious to think that Tim was saying the same thing.

Isobel said bargainingly, 'Kiss it better.'

'Every inch. I'll clean you and kiss you and bandage you up.'

'Clean you and kiss you and bandage you up,' said Kit. It had the rhythm of, 'I'll huff and I'll puff and I'll blow your house in.' 'Clean you and kiss you and bandage you up,' he repeated huff-puffily. 'Clean you and kiss you and bandage you up.' Isobel thought of being insulted, but it was more fun to join in.

Elinor's heart was pounding; she wanted to sit down and think. But there was no escape from domesticity just yet—it was time for lunch. She turned her mind off as if flipping a switch and got food ready as fast as she ever had. Tim came in and helped her. When the children finished eating, he cleaned their hands and faces, and they went out into the garden to play, both rather subdued. Elinor felt giddy. Gravity was only just keeping her in her seat; a slight gust, and she might slowly rise and bump gently about the ceiling.

310

The doorbell rang—the helper who looked after the children on Saturday afternoons. She gulped painfully and got up. 'That'll be Kevin—I'm off.'

'Give you a lift?'

'No, thanks'—quickly. No favours—nothing he wouldn't offer if he knew she was leaving. 'I've...I want to stop in M & S for jeans for Isobel—and it's such a nice day.'

Tim had somehow forgotten she worked on Saturdays; he had been going to suggest a walk on the Heath. He had pictured carrying Isobel on his shoulders—the children seemed to like that. So did he: firm little legs securely in his grip, small hands holding onto his head, not to mention pulling his hair, poking his ears, covering his eyes. He did not want to take them out on his own, though; he needed Elinor there in case they got bored with him.

Even so, he nearly suggested it. He wanted to compensate Isobel for, for...He was not conscious of wanting to make amends for not picking her up in the lane; but she had had a hard fall, and he in particular, for unspecified reasons, should make it up to her with a treat.

It might have saved him—Elinor's resolve might have been overborne by new hope. But the sitter was already there—no point paying him for nothing. The impulse faded, and with it his moment.

Elinor nipped onto a bus, got off at Tavistock Square, went into the garden and sat on a bench as if felled.

Leaving Tim. No, she couldn't think about that concretely yet. She stared ahead of her, thinking about movies, the purply splotches of broken veins on the butcher's cheeks, the jeans she might have bought Isobel—sitting in a state of willed amnesia, refusing to face past, future, present, anything at all. She felt like going to South Molton Street and buying something dashing and expensive, a dress, or shoes.

She got up restlessly and began to walk. Think, she told herself. You've not much time, you've got to act quickly. Think about leaving.

What was filling her wasn't the future, but the past. She walked westward through Bloomsbury, away from the Cromer, eyes on the

311

pavement, seeing nothing and no one, drawn on as if mesmerised by the sight of her feet gliding forward in regular alternation, with the past all around her, from the time she met Tim right up to this morning: things crowding into her mind in great flashes of astonished insight almost faster than she could take them in—as if over the years she'd put everything that upset her about Tim onto hundreds of index cards, all in a random heap; and now they were all falling into place.

Not telling him about the broken string. Isobel rigid with fear, as if Tim were a severe Victorian father.

Offering to tell Tim that Kit wanted to stop the violin; Kit replying, 'Daddy would be sad.' Fathers were supposed to protect their children, not children their fathers.

Isobel playing pat-a-cake with Thoby and growing anxious under Tim's absentminded gaze. He was usually so exacting; she'd thought he was watching to see if she was playing it *well*.

Tim's faintly contemptuous expression as he watched the game. It was beyond his comprehension that Thoby got pleasure, selfish pleasure, from kindling Isobel's delight and building an absurd edifice of giggles and squeals and whoops.

On her side, self-deception, on his, coldness. On her side, a divining of entrails, a reading of hope into accidental moments; on his, a steady, silent consistency of reserve, withdrawal, refusal.

But why? Simply his nature? No, no, for Isobel's was the same, and Elinor refused to believe that her baby was doomed to become as closed off as Tim. Early traumas? Then how could she save her from them? Isobel was more relaxed when Tim wasn't around— more babylike. His unhappy remoteness weighed on her, roused her to a frenzy of need to make him happy. It couldn't be good for her, living in a perpetual ache of yearning for a father who hardly noticed her. But would living away from him be even worse?

Elinor couldn't do that sum, no one could. She must put right what she could, not be paralysed by hypothetical disasters. The lack in Tim existed and would go on existing, and made him incapable of the simplest physical gesture to a fellow creature in pain. He wasn't insensitive; there was nothing fraudulent about the tears that sprang to his eyes in response to music, or about his concern for the poor and oppressed. He could express pity and tenderness for them, and in his art, but not with her or his children. He was too needy himself, too unhappy.

Needy? Unhappy? Tim, whose face shone with music, Tim, whose lovemaking she couldn't yet bear to think she'd be deprived of?

Yes. She connected him to life. He got her to do the work of living for both of them.

Thank God, she thought, moving one foot after the other along Wigmore Street, thank God I'll be able to look him in the face and say, No, I'm not leaving you for another man.

No wonder she had said no to Thoby. She'd been afraid of responding too hungrily to ordinary human warmth and ending up in love with him and him only.

How avidly Tim listened to every detail of her life at the cinema; how little he said about his own social life as a musician—because he had so little. Once she had thought it was because he played with so many different orchestras, and didn't meet the same people week in, week out. But other free-lance musicians had social ties in the musical world. He cut himself off, like...like Margaret the projectionist—the way she tunnelled straight up to the projection booth and stayed aloof from the Cromer's collective life.

He listened with the same avidity when she talked about the children; and focussed it directly on them, too—a plea for love that he didn't dare utter; didn't dare let himself receive. But his need exerted the pull of a gravitational field.

She had forgotten what day-to-day happiness was like. She had come to think that being indispensable to Tim was being happy.

She had thought she could make him happy, but she couldn't. He was a deep, cold well of sulky unhappiness; he couldn't be a father to his children because he was still a child himself.

Talking about their husbands as if they're troublesome little boys, she heard herself say. Most men are, she heard Maggie say. Maybe, maybe not. But that wasn't how she meant it, about Tim.

Isobel flat on her face in the lane, Kit not bothering to run because he already knew better—oh, that was what made her angry. She had in some sense chosen the pain of life with Tim. The children hadn't.

She looked up. Some eerie unfathomable movement of will had guided her steps down Marylebone Lane and across Oxford Street to South Molton Street, beacon of her split-second fancy back in the park.

Two o'clock, and she hadn't told Terry she'd be late. She plunged into Bond Street station and took the tube to Russell Square.

The point wasn't to blame or excuse Tim, but to save Isobel from trying endlessly, her whole childhood long, to win his love by filling his silent insistent demands—for he wouldn't let her, any more than he would meet the simplest of her needs: to be comforted when she fell, hugged when she put out her arms, kissed when she kissed him, acknowledged when she spoke, congratulated when she did well, encouraged when she did badly, scolded when she was naughty—and told in a hundred different ways that she was a delight, a treasure, and gave as much pleasure as she got.

To save Kit. To save herself.

On her desk was a pile of correspondence. She dabbled at it—file this, answer that, take the next out to Terry—and gradually got involved in the job. Only when Kevin arrived with the children did she realise she'd spent nearly three hours not thinking about the future. After that there was no time, until very shortly before Tim came up for her from the Purcell Room.

The quartet's do was tomorrow—could she get out of it? No. The whole afternoon, too, on lunch and talk. Never had she felt less like aimless sociability. After that, thank God, Tim was away on tour. Three days to think, plan, act.

Where could she move to? What about money? The terror of the thought thumped her heart into tumult. Too soon to think about that. Stop.

House prices were—even the tiniest flat—Stop.

Think about it tomorrow. Talk to Maggie. Alone—we can't talk about this in front of the children.

Money, money. She already paid for the helpers and the nursery school, met half of the household bills, and bought the children's clothes and her own; but that took almost her whole salary. The house was Tim's, and the car; he paid the mortgage, and for holidays. Could she rent a flat, feed and clothe the three of them, and pay for gas and electricity, let alone nursery school and mother's helpers? God, think of leaving your husband if it meant going on the dole. No wonder women stayed.

Don't think about it yet. Think about the most immediate hurdle: how to avoid making love tonight and tomorrow. The trouble with hardly ever wanting to get out of lovemaking was not having excuses pat when you needed them.

That problem, at least, was easily solved. She might not have fibs on tap, but she and Tim had developed unspoken, virtually unconscious ways to avoid making love without saying no—fictions of fatigue. By bedtime Elinor was in truth exhausted; all she had to do was exaggerate it a little in a silent playlet of yawns, sighs, stiff movements and instant collapse onto the pillow.

The last time, she thought with dry-eyed melancholy, climbing the steps to Maidie's front door. No more quartet; no more daily intimacy with live music.

'Hello, hello, hi, hello,' she said, threading her way to the coffee past chairs and people. Rose and Marcus. Maidie, polished and commanding like a Georgian doorknocker. Alan's wife and both his daughters. The younger one was nearly through university— she'd been a child of thirteen at Elinor's first do. Lionel Debec with a wild blaze of white in his dark hair—'Like the bride of Frankenstein,' Rose muttered in her ear. Sheila's mother talking to—Elinor's own parents. Her heart lifted at the sight of them. Family. They would...understand? Probably not; but they would stand by, support, rally round: all the things families did.

Thoby was wild as a jackanapes, bobbing round the room with plates of croissants. Alan was pale and grim; he actually looked ill. Only Tim appeared calm—he had more practice at hiding pre-performance nerves. Sheila was quiet and shy like an old-fashioned little girl. Elinor almost expected her to curtsey. Her wide-boned, delicate face was still touchingly young in its frame of grey hair—

she looked far younger than Maggie, though she was three years older.

Maggie not here?—she said she mightn't...Got to get hold of her. Elinor found the telephone. 'Hi, how are you?—Listen, I need to see you; any chance I could come round this evening?—Okay, thanks.'

Two more heads looked in at the door, rather shyly—oh Lord: Nigel, in dove-grey stripes, and Terry. She'd invited them, and they knew no one else. Her responsibility. She threaded her way through the chairs. 'Hi, Terry, hi, Nigel. There's a move to start soon, but there's still time for coffee.'

The quartet started tuning, and the audience found seats—adults on straight chairs in the middle of the room; children, who stayed quiet longer if they were comfortable, in armchairs and sofas that had been pushed to the side. Tim stood up and said, 'Haydn's quartet in F major, opus 3 number 5, Hoboken III, 17—though it may actually be by Hoffstetter, not Haydn at all.' It was the thing he liked least about the do—in his professional life he was not called upon to make announcements.

Elinor's attention leapt forward to tonight—tomorrow—Tuesday—Tim's return on Wednesday. What would she say? She tried to think something out, but thought instead about packing—what? for how long? She couldn't take much—she'd have nowhere to put it. What would they need, she and the children, for...how long before she found a flat—a fortnight? A month?

Through her scurrying thoughts threaded the quartet. She was looking more than listening—at the lovely russet gleam of the bows, the suave bend of the horsehair as it glided across the strings; at Sheila's fingers clambering up and down the fingerboard; at Thoby's hand crouched over the bow; at Alan quite still but for his right arm and the fingers of his left hand; at Tim swaying slightly from side to side. Tim's elbow low, Thoby's high; the cello bow bouncing off the strings in fast passages. The last time.

After the presto Tim cleared his throat and looked at her meaningly. Had he been reading her thoughts? He nodded, unmistakably at her, and for a crazy second she thought he was answering yes.

Oh God. The Haydn serenade, the one he could never hear without tears; the one he'd hummed long ago on the Heath. Over the past months she'd heard them practising the first movement, without recognising what quartet it came from; but not this movement. It was essentially a violin solo with a light pizzicato accompaniment, which the others wouldn't have needed much practice to master. Still, they must have met once or twice when she wasn't around, to put it together. It was a surprise—for her. Tim's nod and look were to remind her of the day on the Heath and give her his serenade, a love-token.

The slow, plangent, incredibly sweet tune poured out of him. No wonder he had crept under the piano and wept to hear it as a child; no wonder tears still always came to his eyes when he listened to it—though not right now: never while playing. 'The tears go into the music,' he'd said once in explanation. His downy cheek; his fuzzy hair; his remote, delicate expression; his body, canted on the chair, bending into his bowing with the weighty grace she knew so well in all its manifestations. Oh Tim. If only that expressiveness weren't otherwise imprisoned in him. It was what she'd loved him for in the first place—that buried nobility, the underground stream that only broke to daylight in music and lovemaking.

She would miss making love with him, miss it, her eyes were full of his beauty. Years ago she had fallen in love with him in Sheila and Thoby's flat, watching him play. Would she ever again be so completely sexually happy? Unbearably sad, unbearably sweet, the serenade wrought on her. Tears came to her eyes. Tim's gift. Lost. She was bolted to her chair by the pain of losing all that was signified by his music; his lovemaking.

Which she must leave his house before having to refuse. He would be back on Wednesday night. Three days. The serenade ended, the next movement began; she went back to organising things feverishly in her head, mentally packing and repacking for different lengths of time—impossible. Where could she go? A refuge by Wednesday. Would Maggie have any ideas?

Everything would be harder. No one to cook. No one to keep an eye on the children while she went to the shops.

317

How much was it all going to *cost*—rent, the children's minders, nursery school, crèche, heating, food, rates, furniture, transportation? No car. No lifts from Tim after work at night; taxis too expensive; and probably a flat down a dark lane miles from the bus or tube. Lugging two children to crèche and nursery school every day on the bus from the nether reaches of Hendon or Walthamstow. She must be crazy.

Housing. Housing. By Wednesday.

Chapter 42

'I'm leaving Tim,' she said straightaway in Maggie's kitchen, to get the worst over with.

'You're not serious.' Maggie looked at Elinor sharply and saw she'd been crying. 'Yes, you are. Here, if you'll hand me the cafetière...' She carried the tray through to the sitting room and sat down. Yet another seemingly happy marriage cracking up. Was there no such thing as married happiness? 'For that jackass Thoby, I suppose,' she said.

'Not "for" anybody,' Elinor said firmly. 'It's not as simple as that.' Thank God she hadn't told Maggie anything about him. She was just guessing—and guessing wrong.

Maggie smoothed her frown with her hand; she was schooling herself out of line-forming habits. She didn't want to hear about this; but clearly she had no choice. She poured the coffee and settled into an attentive attitude.

Elinor's account of nearly eight years of silence, distance and thwarted hope went haltingly; but gained momentum when she got to Isobel's fall. The rest came out easily: her crisis of revelation in the lane, and the knowledge of Tim—of herself—that had been welling up in her ever since yesterday morning.

'So I've got to find somewhere by Wednesday. God knows what or where. In the long term I'll need a two-bedroom flat, *if* I can afford it, but right now just anything that'll hold the three of us. I was wondering if you knew of—'

'In three days? Not likely—it'll take weeks,' Maggie said. If she could just persuade Nell to stay till Tim got back, maybe she wouldn't leave at all. 'Better stay put till you find somewhere.'

'I *can't* stay. At worst I'll have to leave the children there and stay with a friend. Not you, though—I wouldn't want to make it awkward for you with Albericht.'

'Leave them? *Don't* do that, not even overnight. It could be construed as deserting them—you'd strengthen Tim's case for custody.'

'*Custody*?' Hadn't Maggie taken in what she'd been saying about Tim's remoteness from the children? 'He wouldn't want them, that's—'

'You'd be surprised what men suddenly want when their wives walk out. They use children as leverage to get her back—as punishment if nothing else.'

'But I wouldn't be *leaving* them, only at night. I'd pick them up in the morning and take them to the cinema.'

'Listen to me. What counts is where they sleep. And *do* try to keep out of court. To the cinema indeed. No judge is going to like your baroque childcare arrangements. Especially leaving them with minders—all right, mother's helpers—every evening. Daytime wouldn't be so bad, but hardly anybody leaves their children in the evening.'

'I see mine as much as mothers that work nine to five,' Elinor said heatedly.

'It's not me you've got to convince, it's judges and court welfare officers, and they're deeply—*deeply*—conventional.'

'Tim works evenings too, and *he* wouldn't make time for them the way I do—they'd *never* see him.'

'He's a man, courts wouldn't expect so much—the double standard is alive and well. Look, the judge could realise that you'd see the children ten hours a day and Tim only one, but still award him custody in a fit of indignation against working mothers. Don't glower at *me*, Nell, I don't approve of it, but it's the way things are. If you're going to take a step like this, you should know what could happen.'

Elinor subsided. 'I suppose I do know—I've heard enough horror stories about custody cases; but you never get used to the injustice. But I *don't* think he'd try to take them. He wouldn't know what to do with them—and he's not vengeful, either.'

'You can't predict how he'll behave when pushed—you shouldn't leave unless you're prepared to risk losing the children.' Seeing that Elinor was speechless with fright, she followed up her advantage. 'All you've said is what's wrong with Tim. Was anything *your* fault?'

'I didn't say things were his *fault*—'

'I didn't say you did. I said, was anything *your* fault?'

Elinor thought for a moment. 'It's not really a question of fault, it's that we need such different things—Tim too, not just me. He'd have been happier with someone more...repressed and reserved.' The thought of Tim with someone else all these years suddenly made her want to cry. And Tim with someone else in future?—oh *no*.

'Reserve isn't the worst thing in the world—some people see quite a lot of point in it.'

'Not me,' Elinor said dismissively.

Me, thought Maggie, hurt. She tipped out a cigarette and lit it. 'Tim does,' she said, 'and you're married to him, you have children together. You've got to balance your needs against his, and the children's. Why not talk to him? Tell him everything you told me— say you're thinking of leaving if things don't change. But at least give him a chance.'

'I wouldn't get past the second sentence; he'd just walk away.'

'Even if the first sentence was, "I'm leaving unless we talk"?'

'No, he'd talk then, all right, but...'

'Nell, you rush to extremes so fast. You see a fault in Tim and right away you're off for good. Why not a trial separation?'

It sounded so reasonable, but all her instincts were against it. 'You don't understand—something *happened* yesterday. Before then I didn't know how unhappy I was. I kept thinking the problem was in me and the children, not Tim—thinking we'd be happy if only. If only I tried harder; if only I weren't so busy; if only the children were old enough to hold rational conversations with him. Or if only Tim would change. Yesterday in the lane I realised he never would. I suppose I can't blame him—but I can't stand it any more, hoping and never arriving.'

'What it amounts to is, you made a mistake, and Tim's going to pay for it.'

'It's not a question of mistakes'—shortly. 'It's a question of happiness.'

'Dear God, the higher selfishness. We've been arguing about that for the past fifteen years.' Maggie pulled herself up—she would get nowhere with that tone—and said urgently, 'Nell, you've got everything, and you're about to throw it away. Don't *do* it—*please* don't. You don't know what it's like on your own, out here in the cold. You don't *know*. You've been protected all your life. You've got somebody to open lids and move furniture; a safety net between you and the dole; a body in bed at night.'

'I'll have my work and the children.'

'Children don't keep you warm at night. Children don't pay the rent. What if the Wellesfords close the Cromer?—you've already had one scare.'

'I can't stay with Tim in case my job folds.'

'Why not? Thousands of women do. And what would you do if it did?'

'Live on the dole till—'

'You clearly haven't the first idea what it's like living on your own.'

Wearily Elinor said, 'No, but I've seen you doing it, and I've got an imagination.'

Maggie shook her head between her hands. 'You don't *know* how lonely it is. You think you'll survive, but one doesn't.' She looked at the dark stubborn face resisting her with the optimism of inexperience, and her thin-stretched self-control snapped. '*You* certainly won't, you've no schooling in it. You've had a soft life, Nell. You don't suppose you're going to find an unattached man at your age, do you?'

'There *are* men around,' Elinor said, stung out of tact. 'People get divorced—'

'Don't hold your breath waiting for the queue to form. Have you ever looked at the girls men marry the second time round? Hardly out of gymslips. Face facts. Any girl of eighteen, any shop assistant or hairdresser, has more value on the market than you or me.'

'I wouldn't *want* the kind of man who'd rather have a—a—' She wouldn't accept Maggie's terms and say 'a hairdresser'. 'I wouldn't want a man who'd rather have a girl of eighteen just because she's young and nubile and inexperienced, if that's what you mean.'

'You'll stay single, then. Grow up, Nell, you can't afford high-flown sentiments at your age. And don't look so cross. I can't keep quiet when I see you destroying your marriage, your security. Don't jib at the word—it's something real. Life's pretty unbearable at the best of times, don't make it more so. You'll never find another man like Tim. He provides you with a good home—cooks for you, for God's sake. He's kind to the children—'

'I'd rather be alone for the rest of my life than stay with Tim,' Elinor said heatedly. 'And didn't you *hear* what I said about how he treats the children?' Tears stung her eyes; she fought them back.

'Children get beaten, starved to death, sexually abused—*that's* ill treatment, not Tim failing to kiss them every time he sees them. You can't leave him just for that—it's crazy.'

Elinor stood up abruptly. 'Got to use the loo.'

Once there she peed, more out of habit than because she needed to, and leaned on the basin swallowing tears. Value on the market. The higher selfishness. She wiped her eyes and went back.

'You look so tragic,' Maggie said. 'I didn't mean to upset you, but...' She wished she could take back half of what she'd said; she had a feeling she'd gone too far.

It was true; but Elinor was too used to protecting her to say so. 'I know. It's late, I'd better get back.'

Down in the car she leaned her head on the steering wheel and started to cry. Grow up, Nell. Was anything *your* fault?

You've changed, changed, she told Maggie in her head. You used to let me help you, you used to help me, back in the days of John, and before that Ludovic, and...and...

She nearly howled, as if Ludovic and John and Gareth and Mike and the first John were all at this very moment wrenching her with their inordinate griefs and outrageous demands, but were lost to her, too—as they were; as Tim was about to be: her own doing, but none the less lost; and now Maggie. Tears dripped off the end of her

323

nose and fell on the steering column. Tim Tim I can't bear hurting you, mustn't, you me the children too much can't go through with it...oh—oh—how do people live through times like this?

Not 'times like this'; they were never in the plural; they were always unique and neverending.

If she could think that, she was through the worst...for the moment. She tipped the rear-view mirror and looked at her blurred eyes. Her only tissue was already sodden. She blew her nose with it, dried her eyes on the hem of her skirt, and started the car.

Chapter 43

Tim left for Liverpool in the morning and Elinor started ringing estate agents. By mid-morning she had learned that no one had any flats within commuting distance of the Cromer. She tried to ring Rose. No reply. She wandered round the house wondering what was hers and what Tim's, and what to pack—

Somewhere to stay. Everything else paled before that first brutal requisite; she couldn't concentrate on the finer points of cots and clothing.

Still no answer from Rose. Sheila and Thoby? No. She couldn't ask favours of Thoby—and shouldn't anyhow; he and Sheila were Tim's only close friends. If they helped her, Tim would think they were on her side, not his.

Chris, then?

'Dr Haldane's away,' her secretary said.—'Oh, hi, Nell. She's in Montreal with the woman who's filming *Quest*; she'll be back on the twelfth.'

Try Rose again, without any hope of—

Rose answered on the first ring, heard her out and said, 'Stay at mine while you're looking.—No, don't worry about Marcus: he'll be cool. The bed-settee's an instrument of torture, but it's yours, and we'll put the children on mats on the floor.'

'I *can't* impose the children on you—your flat's so tiny—'

'Nonsense, we—'

'No, listen—me only. I'm leaving them here till I find a flat; they'll be better off with only one move.'

'Well, if you're *sure*. Anyhow, it's there if you change your mind. Now—you sound low. You talked to anybody about all this?'

'Only Maggie,' Elinor said wearily. 'And she disapproves.'

'I'm coming over. Terry can open up—I'll ring him.'

Elinor nearly burst into tears. 'Oh Rose, I'd *love* to talk, but aren't you—'

'Don't be daft. I'll be there in half an hour.'

'Right—now tell me,' said Rose, curling up on the end of the bed. They had brought their coffee up to the bedroom so that Elinor could keep an eye on the children, who were playing in their room across the hall.

'I don't know where to start...' Grow up, Nell, the higher selfishness—would Rose think the same as Maggie?

'The beginning?'

'Oh dear, where's that? Breaking up with John and meeting Tim, I suppose, just before I met you. I was so *tired* of being attracted to such tormented men, all those inordinate emotional demands—and I was so pleased that Tim wasn't like that.' Her mouth dropped open. 'Oh my God, Rose—Maggie said was anything my fault—well, that was: trying to have a bit of peace...' She stopped; her throat was tight.

'Never works, does it? So John was the frying pan and Tim was the fire?'

'But don't you see? It means it's all my fault—I *asked* for it. I can't make Tim pay—I made my bed, now I should—'

'Lie in it?' said Rose. 'But why? Much more sensible to get out and remake it.'

Elinor gulped, laughed till she choked; and started heaving with sobs. Rose slid down the bed and put her arms round her, making soothing 'Mmm' sounds and stroking her back. Elinor tried to pull herself together, but tears kept welling up. 'The children,' she said feebly.

Rose flung a pillow at the door. It slammed. 'Okay, you can open the floodgates.'

Elinor put her head in Rose's lap and cried herself out. Eventually the wrenching tears faded into sighs and snuffles, and she sat up, groped for the tissues and mopped herself down.

'Give me,' said Rose, sniffing. There were tear-tracks on her cheeks.

Elinor passed her the box. 'Oh Rosy, I'm sorry inflicting—'

326

'You're *not*. I'm just glad I'm here. Maggie laid a real trip on you, seems to me.'

'And I've *rained* on your jeans!' Elinor got up, checked her face—'Lordy, I look like a statue of woe'—and set the door ajar again. 'The amount I've been crying, I'm just lucky it doesn't show more and upset the children. How I'll explain to them I don't know. Or Tim—oh God.'

'You could practise on me. We didn't get very far, beginning at the beginning—why not try the other end?'

The other end was the long walk down the lane seeing everything she'd hidden from herself for so long. 'Eight years too long,' she said mournfully as she finished her account.

'Better late than never.'

'Maggie thinks I haven't given it a proper chance, though.'

'Not me,' Rose said. 'I'm amazed you hung in there so long.'

'Hope springs eternal, I suppose—there was always *something* feeding it. Like yesterday, him nodding to me about the Haydn serenade. I used to think things like that were the start of a new era—I'd live in hope for *weeks*.'

The telephone. Elinor answered it. 'Oh Maggie, hullo.—Just a second.' She reached for pad and pencil and scribbled. 'Yes—yes—yes...Got it.—Oh I've got somewhere, thanks—Rose's. Okay then. And—thank you.' She hung up, looking dazed. 'I can hardly believe it—Maggie was so fierce yesterday, I didn't even *ask* her; but she's spent this morning scouting for flats: she's got four for me to check out. She said I could stay there, too; but I'd rather stay with you, if it's not too much trouble—'

In love there is no even-handed justice, no reward for long and faithful service—Rose knew she would never occupy Maggie's place in Nell's heart. Nell's affection for her went deep, but that wasn't the same as the friendship of helpless heart's allegiance, with its erotic if not sexual response to a look, a laugh, a tone of voice, a turn of temperament. But it was sweet to be turned to.

'No trouble at all,' she said, very sincerely. She felt like being scathing about Maggie, but made herself say magnanimously, 'It probably just took her some time to come round—she's awfully conservative.'

'Small c. Big C too, but not the way the Conservatives are now.' Hearing the irrepressible scandalised fondness in her voice Elinor said, 'Oh dear;' then, looking at the list in her hand, 'Oh dear,' in a different tone. 'These prices! Maggie says they're as low as I'll get. It's scary.'

'I could lend you a couple of hundred—it's all I've got after the mortgage and supporting my Gucci habit.' Rose still dressed scruffily, but had developed a mania for very soft, very expensive loafers.

'Rose, you're a darling.' Elinor leaned over and kissed her round pink cheek. 'I don't think I'll need it: I rang Dad last night, and he's got more savings than I knew, and offered a loan if I need it. But thank you.'

'At least you won't have to rent for long—you'll be able to buy a flat with your share of this place. Does Tim have the bread to buy you out, or will he have to sell first?'

'This *house*? But it's Tim's. I mean, it's half mine—he changed the deeds. But it's his, really—he already owned it when I met him.'

'You're entitled to it, Nell. Tim hasn't been graciously permitting you to live here. Half your salary goes on childcare—how much of his?'

'Uh, none, but—'

'And where does the other half go? Rates and heating and house repairs and furniture, right?'

'And clothes and food and entertainment—not just the house. Besides, it's not as if he's done anything wrong. He can't help the way he is. I can't take everything away from him at once—me and his children *and* his house. I know you're right, I'll have to, but...' More tears welled up in her eyes. 'Oh what a nuisance'—smearing them away with her fingers. 'You'd think the well was dry by now.'

Rose looked at her hard. 'Still in love with him?'

Elinor hesitated, remembering her pangs at the quartet yesterday—how long ago it seemed. 'No,' she replied at last. 'Saturday in the lane, realising he'd never change—I think I stopped loving him between the time Isobel fell and when he got round to picking her up. But how am I going to *tell* him? I keep planning speeches; but he

328

won't understand, he won't listen. He won't see why not picking Isobel up was the last straw—he won't understand anything.'

Isobel pushed the door open. 'Can me and Kit have biscuits?'

Elinor checked her watch. 'Not biscuits—it's lunchtime.'

'And I'd better get down to the Cromer,' said Rose.

'Have a bite first, and I'll drop you—I've got to take these two to crèche and nursery school, then start looking at the places on Maggie's list.' She took out her hair slides and brushed her hair fiercely. 'Maybe I'll cut it short like yours.'

'I wouldn't. It's so fine and straight—you'd look like a drowned rat.'

'You don't.'

Rose ran her fingers through her curly crest. 'No—I look like a poodle. I keep it short because it grows out in *ringlets*, like Shirley Temple.'

'I could perm mine.'

'Oh *no*—like every other woman in her mid-thirties.'

'Hmph. Come on, Shirley. Let's go eat.'

Chapter 44

'Hullo, waiting up for me?' Tim said, pleased, coming in very late on Wednesday night and finding Elinor still up, sitting in the drawing room with her legs stretched out on the sofa.

'Mmm,' she said, sitting up straight.

He looked round the shadows. Something was different. The room was neater than usual, but it wasn't that. She was quieter than usual, but it wasn't that. A small picture was gone from the wall behind her: her jumble-sale Ravilious. 'Your bather—getting her re-framed?' Without waiting for an answer he added: 'Bedtime?'

'No, I...want to talk.'

He sat down across from her and waited, sliding his fingertips back and forth across each other. Her eye-sockets were deeply shadowed, like the room beyond the spill of the lamp. 'Well?' he said at last.

She took a gulp of breath. 'Tim, I'm leaving you.'

He utterly did not comprehend. 'Don't make bad jokes. Come to bed, I'm tired.'

'I'm not sleeping here tonight.'

This time, in a limited way, he took it in. Leaving him? Not sleeping here? Had she gone mad? His mind leapt to the children. Crazy women did things to them. 'Where are the children?' he asked with deliberate calm.

'Upstairs. I'll come and take them to school tomorrow morning.'

She did not sound unbalanced; his mind whirred out another construction to put upon her words. 'Someone's in trouble— Maggie? Chris?'

Entoiled in misunderstanding already. 'No, I'm—' Should she tell him she was staying with Rose? Men sometimes went mad

330

when you left them—took you hostage; shot you. Not that Tim would. At most he might bang on Rose and Marcus's door at four in the morning.

Anyhow, she'd have to tell him, in case the children needed her.

Later; it wasn't the point right now. Keep calm, keep on track. Start again, from the beginning. 'No, I'm leaving you.'

He nearly said, 'Come off it.' But her voice, so serious, gave him pause. She could not mean it; but she thought she did. Why? Some infatuation. His stomach knotted. 'Who for?'

'Not for anyone.'

He stood up. 'I don't want to talk about this.'

'Tim, we've got to. That's why I'm leaving.'

'What's why? You're not making sense.'

'You not wanting to talk about this—or anything, ever. I've got a hundred things in my head and you don't want to hear any of them.'

He sat down again. He still thought it was just a trick to get him to talk, but had a sick feeling it might be more. His throat hurt. He loosened his tie. 'All right, you're leaving me. Because I don't chatter.' He made it sound ridiculous.

'Not just that.' So much, where should she start? 'We have different...different needs,' she said slowly. 'I need more affection than you can give—more than you can show, I mean. And I need to give you more affection than you let me.'

'You're all over me all the time—when have I ever stopped you?'

'Oh Tim'—helplessly.

'What else? There must be more than that.'

'Remember Isobel's fall on Saturday?' she asked. He looked blank. 'Saturday morning, coming back from shopping. You were working on the car, and Isobel ran to you and fell.' The touch that lit this whole train: did it count for so little in his scheme of things that he didn't even remember it?

At last he said, 'Oh, *that*,' and shook his head in bewilderment. 'That's a reason to leave me? You must be off your head.' Or using the threat to wind the old arguments up another notch—but he did not say that.

331

'You didn't pick her up.'

'So?'

'So...why not?'

Why bring this up in a serious conversation? He said patiently, 'She hadn't broken any bones, and I was doing something. It does her no harm to wait—teaches her not to be a baby.'

'But she *is* a baby, almost. But that's not the point. The point is to stop teaching her sometimes and just comfort her.'

'Don't be childish,' he snapped; then glanced at her with a helpless, enraged sense of having said exactly the wrong thing. 'What else?' he demanded, determined to regain the advantage. Her eyes were black, opaque; they had never had less light in them. Noticing Isobel's recorder under the sofa he got up, put it where she would see it, and sat down again.

He won't understand, she'd wailed to Rose. There was nothing for it but to explain anyhow. 'Remember when Kit wanted to stop the violin?' she began, and haltingly described Kit saying, 'Daddy would be sad,' and his odd little sigh the other day—'He knew there was no point running to you;' Isobel's fear about the broken string and anxiety in his presence; how hurtful she herself found his refusal of non-sexual affection or even comfort—'when Isobel fell, or when I twisted my ankle years ago;' and the muted pain of giving him, year after year, the time he'd asked for, holding on in hope from year to year while the snows of silence slowly buried her alive: then walking along the lane realising he would never change.

Tim listened in stunned silence. They were in the accustomed room, sitting in their accustomed places. Everything looked hyper-real, surprising, as if he had been away from home a long time and half forgotten it. His eye kept straying to the spot where Elinor's print had hung.

'But you never said,' he said when she finally stopped speaking.

'I did. Dozens of times, hundreds of times. Asking you to talk; asking you to...to kiss me; asking you to play with the children.'

'You never said it was that important.'

'I did—and you must have known.'

'You never said you'd *leave* if I didn't...do those things.'

332

'Would it have made any difference?'

'Yes,' he said, without conviction; then: 'What else? There must be more.' But he did not really listen to what she said: it was unbearable. Better to look for weak points, interrupt, protest, justify himself, counter every instance she advanced.

At three o'clock he was still implacably demanding, 'What else?' She was in dead earnest, he knew that now, but he could not believe she would actually leave. He was not in despair; he was aggrieved to the core.

She sighed. 'I've said it all ten times by now.'

It was too dizzying. If he understood her reasons, he might understand why...No. Fair enough, if she had left him in the first few months. But after that, the longer she had stayed, the more it had been implicit that she accepted his limitations. It was monstrous for her to talk about leaving after all this time. He shook his head heavily. 'You keep saying I don't talk, I'm not demonstrative—but you've always said that. Something else must have changed. It can't just be that—it doesn't make sense. You can't break everything up for a—an *idea*. There *must* be something. Another man.'

'There isn't. I swear.'

'Then you must be unbalanced,' he said bitterly. A cold liquid was filling his veins, his lungs, his nostrils, the space behind his eyes where things took place. If he let it seep back into his brain, he would begin to believe this nonsense and be done for. He was tired, deadly tired. Betrayed. No, don't start believing it. He looked at her. She was wan and heavy-eyed. He got a second wind, by making the kind of effort that kept him playing at the top of his form towards the end of a long concert, and said with cunning solicitude, 'You look exhausted. Why not come up and lie down?'

'No, I...' Elinor was nearly asleep in the chair. They had talked each other into exhaustion—for once she had had enough talk with Tim. 'I'll call a taxi.'

He stood up when she did. 'You can't go—I won't let you—you've got to say *why*.'

333

'That's what I've been doing all night.'

He shouted in her face, 'You haven't told me a *thing*—not a goddamn *thing*.'

She moved back a step. Very quietly, as if by dropping her voice she could make him drop his, she said, 'Then you haven't been listening.'

'It's all nonsense, it's all nonsense, it doesn't make *sense*.' He was still shouting.

'What doesn't make sense?' She was asleep on her feet, but she owed him all the time he needed, all the repetition.

'That's the way you talk to the children. Don't be so fucking condescending.'

'I'm *not*,' she said, almost whispering. 'I can only explain if you tell me what you don't understand.'

'I don't understand *anything*—and I don't want you to *explain* anything—I want you to *stop it*!' He bellowed the last words so loud he hurt his throat. 'Stop it and come to bed,' he said in a lower voice.

'You *don't* want me to explain?'

'Explain, explain—Look, I'm tired out, I've had a long day, I've got a recording tomorrow, I can't take any more. If you want to "explain", save it till tomorrow night and let's get some sleep.'

'Okay.' She went through to the music room and rang for a minicab.

Tim was blocking the door to the hall when she came back. 'I'm not letting you go,' he said.

Shaken, she sat down to wait. He was a gentle man, he wouldn't use force on her...would he? Could she be quite sure? She was afraid of the violence of soul that would rise up in her if he so much as gripped her arm with one of those strong hands.

After a short silence he said sullenly, 'If you go, don't think you can come back. I won't let you in—I'll change the locks. You'll never see me again. Or the children.'

Elinor jumped up. 'If you hurt them—' then wanted to bite out her tongue. He wouldn't—and it wasn't what he was threatening.

334

Tim was cut to the quick. Did she think he would hurt his own *children*? 'You're the one that's going to hurt them,' he yelled. 'Dividing their loyalties—confusing them—' His voice cracked. 'You've got to *stay*. Stay and talk. It's what you want—here I am prepared to. You *can't* go now.'

'I can't any more tonight, I'm too tired, and the taxi—'

'You don't *really* want to talk, you just...' His mind was going fuzzy. He tailed off and sat down. It was years since he had been drunk, but this was what it had felt like.

The doorbell. 'I'm going to Rose's,' Elinor said. 'I'll be back in time for the children's breakfast, if you could just get them up.'

'We'll do just fine without you,' he muttered from his seat. 'Though why I should bother with them if you don't...'

The children were playing in the drawing room, washed, clothed and fed, but fretful, when she let herself in. Tim was in the music room with the door open so that he could keep an eye on them. He glanced at her, shut it and went on practising.

'Where were you?' said Kit.

'At Rose's. I told you last night, remember?'

He shook his head. 'Daddy didn't know.'

'Yes he did,' Elinor said, surprised.

'Why didn't he say?'

She couldn't say that he'd been taking his pain out on them. 'Maybe he forgot too—I don't know.'

Either Kit was satisfied or he could smell evasion. He dropped the subject and returned to a Lego castle he and Isobel were building.

Elinor opened the door and into Tim's next pause hissed: 'Kit says you wouldn't say where I was. Don't take this out on them, Tim, for God's sake!'

Without lowering his bow or his voice he said, 'Why not? You are.'

She turned on her heel, angrier with him than she'd ever been. But he would be off to Shepherd's Bush soon; she had to tell him things—plans. She returned to the door and waited for the next break.

It was a long time coming—was he purposely skipping rests? At the first hint of letup she interjected: 'Tim.' She could tell he was furious; his lips were tight. 'Let's keep the children's routine as regular as possible. Hilary will bring them home tonight, same as usual. I'll come after work and say goodnight to them, and stay till you get back. We can talk then if you want. Tomorrow I'll come spend the morning with them again. And so on, till I've found somewhere to live. That okay with you?'

Hilary? Pitying him, despising him. And Rose and that twerp Marcus; and people at the cinema; and Thoby and Sheila and every friend whom she or they as a couple had; and her parents—and, oh God, *his* parents. Was there no end to the humiliation he would have to endure before she came to her senses? Refocussing on his étude, he drew the bow across the strings. A less controlled man would have scraped it; Tim threw out a sweetly faultless sequence at her.

'What is it, darling—monsters?' Elinor said, looking at the drawing Isobel had brought out of the crèche.

'That's you, and that's Daddy.' The figures were at the extreme edges of the paper.

'And what's that coming out of my head?'—great jagged black spokes, most of them aimed into the void between the two figures. Jesus—signs of disturbance already?

'You're brushing your hair,' Isobel said severely.

'Oh so I am.' Whew.

'And Daddy's crying.'

Oh.

Kit was in the office when they got there. Elinor saw the helper out. She had already told Terry she was in the middle of leaving Tim, giving an abbreviated version—nobody's fault; differences of temperament; sudden realisation; flight to Rose's. 'Could you fend off the hordes while I talk to the children?' she asked him, and sat down with them in her office. 'I'm staying at Rose's again tonight,' she began. 'Tomorrow and the next night, too.'

'Why?' said Kit.

'I'm feeling a bit sad, and I need to be alone to think about it. You know what that's like, don't you?'

'Why are you sad?' The question was Kit's, but Isobel's sloe eyes were on her too.

'A lot of things, lovey. Life. It's hard to explain.'

'Davey was sad when his grandmother died.'

'Well I'm not going to die, and neither is Tim—or your grandparents, either. Okay?'

'I didn't think you were, silly. Can we have pizza?'

'Ask properly—and don't call me silly.' A born fox, that boy: give him a half-inch of opening and he took five square miles.

At eleven she went to Ockendon Road...home...to say goodnight to the children. Tim still wasn't back when she came down. She opened the drawing-room curtains so he'd see the light and know she was there, and sat waiting, turning the pages of a picture book, like a guest in someone else's house. His key scratched in the lock just before two. The door slammed; he went straight upstairs. She heard the loo flushing; water running; footsteps; a door banging. She looked round the quiet room, the heavy folds of curtain, the chairs she'd re-webbed, a neat pile of discs by the new CD player, the dark haunch of the piano through the music-room door, Tim's music stand filigreed against the reflections in the back window. Home. She rang for a cab. 'Don't ring the doorbell, there are people asleep—I'll watch for you.'

Tim met her at the front door in the morning and followed her about the house with angry pleas and accusations, heedless of the children, louder and louder. 'Tell me *why*.' 'You can't do this to me.' 'Who are you fucking?' 'You've made a mockery of our whole marriage.' 'You can't go—you're my whole past.'

'Tim, hush, think of the children.'

'*You* think about the children!' He was just not shouting. 'And me, what about me? I'm not doing this to them—*you* are. Not talking, you say—what would I talk about? We've got nothing in common. What do you expect? You put all your energies into the cinema, not our marriage.'

— * —

337

She waited for Tim again that night. He came back very late and went straight to bed. In the morning he met her at the front door again. His eyes were puffy, his skin pasty. 'I know you're fucking somebody,' he said fiercely. 'I'll hire a detective and find out who—'

'It's a waste of money, Tim, there isn't anybody, I told you—'

'I'll sue for divorce—custody of the children. I won't wait for it, either, I'll take them tomorrow. Abroad. Don't you *care*?'

'Of course I care.' Keep calm.

'Well, I don't.' He stomped down the hall and shut himself in the music room.

Don't panic. He won't take them anywhere tomorrow, it's the quartet. He wouldn't take them any other day, either—he'd have to skip concerts. But—custody—'What counts is where the children sleep.' If only she'd listened to Maggie—put them on Rose's floor. He couldn't mean it—couldn't. He never spent any time alone with them if he could help it, he wouldn't start now.

But custody was his best card. If he won them in court, she would have to come back.

There was a shopping list on the kitchen counter. Good Lord—did he expect her to go shopping as usual?

But why not? She set off down the lane with the children. Saturday again. A week since she'd seen Isobel fall and known she had to leave. She marked the day with disoriented sadness. Nothing solid in her life to repose upon. Everything was in flux; not just the large issues, but ordinary, usually predictable things like getting up in the morning, opening the front door of the house, talking to the children, going to bed at night. A week. Had she done the right thing? She didn't know. She'd been so sure—where had that gone? Tim in agony, the children upset, she herself hollow with guilt and pain and muddle—she hadn't known it would be so excruciating.

Had it all been a huge mistake? Should she come back?

A curious constricting pain grabbed the back of her neck and shot down between her shoulder-blades. She tried to massage it out; then instinctively sought relief by muttering aloud: Okay, okay, I'll stick to it.

It worked. Her neck unknotted, and stayed unknotted.

338

When she got back to the house she opened the workroom door and said, 'I'll take the children tomorrow till after the quartet. D'you want them after that?'

'I'll be busy,' Tim shot back with defensive speed, and turned back to the bench. He looked awful.

'Okay,' she said crossly. 'Okay. I'll bring them back in the evening—put them to bed—read them a story...unless you'd like to...'

'No, I'm out,' he growled, making a snap decision. He was being driven out of house and home by this ghost of Elinor, who appeared, did things Elinor normally did, and disappeared again.

Chapter 45

She picked Kit and Isobel up early, to avoid bumping into the other members of the quartet and having to explain things. It was raining. They went to Dulwich to see Chris, then after lunch to the Natural History Museum—on and off buses in the wet. By mid-afternoon the children were tired and fratchy and needed a nap. She could take them to Rose's flat—Rose was at work. No—Marcus would be there with Buffy, who would want to play with them. Peace and quiet and familiar surroundings were what they needed right now. The Cromer.

'This is how fathers with weekend visiting rights must feel—harried from pillar to post,' she told Rose ruefully after settling the children on the daybed.

'You're looking better, though.'

'I am?' Elinor said in surprise; 'I feel...' Awful, she'd been going to say, but it wasn't true. 'You're right—I'm feeling better, too, even camping in the office on my day off.' Something clicked into place in her head: a sort of elation, a sense of well-being. It's all right, she thought. All right.

The children woke up, and she took them to Pizza Express. It was still drizzling, but there was a great rent in the clouds, and an apricot sky showed through, creamy and glowing. Elinor looked at it and felt light, bouncy, gleeful.

At bedtime Isobel said, 'Are you still sad, Mummy?'

'Not now, but some of the time.'

'I want you to stay here.' She looked up appealingly, black eyes troubled, red mouth pouting.

'Daddy's sad too,' said Kit with one of his deep considering frowns.

'Yes—everybody gets sad from time to time.'

340

She kissed them goodnight and went downstairs not knowing whether to laugh or cry: the two of them looking at her with big solemn eyes and making heartrending speeches like the children in *Kramer vs Kramer*-type movies.

'But it really *is* heartrending,' she told Rose at breakfast. 'They want everything to go back to normal, and it won't. D'you think I should explain now?'

'Explain what? They're too young to get it if you say you're leaving Tim, especially when you're still at Ockendon Road so much—they'll only be upset. Wait till you've got somewhere to take them.'

Tim was plaintive when she got to Ockendon Road. When she came back that evening, he was in the workroom and didn't come out. The next morning he stood square in her path in the upstairs hall and said aggressively, 'I've got a right to know what you intend doing.'

The children were playing in their room with the door open. 'Not where they can hear,' she said. 'Downstairs.'

He moved, but only to the top of the stairs. 'Now.'

'Why here? There's a whole big house.'

'I'll talk where I want,' he said truculently. He stumped to the bottom of the stairs, with Elinor following, but wouldn't go into the drawing room.

'So I repeated the same things I've said ten times already,' she told Rose that night. 'And then I looked up and saw Kit standing at the head of the stairs with ears as big as foghorns, and Isobel with *her* ears flapping like bats. Why won't Tim talk behind closed doors— or at night, when they're asleep? He skulked in the workroom again tonight—same as last night.'

'Maybe he's nervous about talking alone, and the children are protection?'

The next morning, Wednesday, Tim said, 'You've been at this a week—isn't that enough? You've made your point. Come back— tonight—and no one need know you've been away: *I* haven't told anybody.'

'I thought you'd tell Thoby and Sheila after the quartet,' Elinor said.

341

'It was called off. Alan's got mononucleosis—'

'Oh, poor man—yes, he looked pretty green at the do.'

'Besides, the less I tell anyone, the less explaining we'll have to do when you come to your senses.'

'Tim, I'm not *going* to "come to my senses". And wouldn't it be a help if you talked to Thoby about it?'

'No!' he said violently. 'I value my privacy. Besides, you mayn't think so, but it's you I talk to. Only you—it's ridiculous, you saying I don't talk. All the past week we've been doing nothing but talk about your grievances.'

'My *grievances*? What do you think I am—a union?' In better days he would have laughed, but of course he didn't.

That night he avoided her again; the next morning he pulled her into the music room. 'Why do you go on with this? It's bad for the children, bad for everyone. Isn't it out of your system yet?'

His voice was aggressive and confident, but he looked miserable. Even now she wanted to do anything, anything, to make him happier; she had to harden her heart. 'Tim, I don't know how to make you see it, but this is really happening. It's not something I'll get over next week or next month; it's for good.'

'But *why*?'

She thought of everything she'd already told him several times over and said in desperate summary, 'Because I'm unhappy. I need to be happy.'

'Oh—happiness,' he said dismissively.

'It's what a person wants from living with someone.'

'Not me. Not principally.'

'Then what *do* you want?'

He thought it over. 'I don't want to be alone.'

'*That's* not enough reason to stay together!'

'It is for me. Nobody wants to be alone.'

'I know, but—'

His control broke. 'Then why are you leaving, if you know, and you haven't got somebody else? I don't understand. I don't *understand*. You *can't* leave.'

'Ssh, Tim, the children are next door.'

342

'Stop "Tim, the children-ing" me,' he said wildly, loudly. 'You tell them God knows what and make it a virtue and then try to shut me up, well I won't stand for it, I'll say what I like, as loud as I like, and I'll speak how I like in front of my own children. I don't want to be alone, and you say you're leaving me, and I'm not going to pretend to be happy about it.' He sat down dejectedly and in a lower tone said, 'I want to know *why* you're leaving. I don't *understand*.'

'Because...because I don't love you any more.' She hadn't said so before; she'd been afraid of hurting him too much all at once.

'What's that got to do with it? I don't love you, you don't love me, but some people try to do something about it, if they're adults.'

She couldn't believe her ears. 'Like what?' she whispered.

'Like what? You're incredible. Go on living together. Respect your marriage. Adjust. Give and take. Your feelings can change, but your responsibility to a family continues. Don't you feel any obligation to show your children how a mature woman should act—a responsible woman?'

'But if you don't love me...' It was a worse blow than she could have predicted, far worse. '*Did* you?'

'Did I what?'

'Love me. Before all this.'

'Good God, is that all you can think about? I don't know what "love" means. This is our marriage, our children; God knows how much harm you're doing them, let alone—'

He leaned forward, screening his eyes with his hand, and began to sob with a harrumphing noise, as if repeatedly clearing his throat. His body shook convulsively. His cheeks got wet, then his chin. Elinor had never seen him cry. She wanted to go over to him, put her arms around him, comfort him; but couldn't. Tenderness was frozen in her. He would shrug her off anyhow, but it wasn't just that. She was cold, physically cold. He didn't love her now; he wouldn't say he'd ever loved her. Had he started crying so he wouldn't have to answer?

A sentence came into her head: 'I'll stay with you if you'll tell me to my face that you love me.' She nearly said it; but he might be desperate enough to take her up on it.

343

'But he wouldn't have,' she told Rose that night. 'He'd have said I was a fool, or told me I should think of the children—anything rather than say those words, even though they're *true*—he does love me—I know it. But I really do think he'd rather lose me than say so. I suppose I should respect him for it, because it's some perverse form of integrity: he doesn't believe in the concept of love, so he won't say it. But it just freezes me.'

'It's not integrity, it's self-protection. It makes him too vulnerable; he daren't.'

'He said that once. About...'—she was embarrassed to admit what she'd let him deprive her of—'about kissing, not love. "Kissing makes me vulnerable. Concentrate on what we've got, not what's missing." And I tried to, God knows I tried.'

'What would freak *me* out,' said Rose, 'is that thing about not wanting to be alone. You want to be happy—he wants company.'

Part of leaving was telling people. 'I've left Tim,' or, 'Tim and I have split up,' to her parents, friends, colleagues, and the children's teachers and minders. The next Saturday morning—a fortnight since Isobel's fall—seemed like a good time to tell the mothers of Kit's friends in the road. Better that they should hear from her than from their children—and she shouldn't just vanish from the road— supposing she ever found a place to vanish *to*—without saying goodbye. Who knows—one of them might even know of a flat.

'Tim's cheating on you?' Helene asked bluntly when Elinor had stumbled out a few limp sentences.

'No—at least I don't—it's—'

'Then is there someone you're...' She lifted a conspiratorial eyebrow.

'No, nothing like that. I just realised I was unhappy.'

'You mean, has Tim been...Does he...' Helene's voice dropped. 'Does he ill-treat you?'

'You mean beat me?' Elinor said, startled, and shook her head.

'Or, you know, verbal violence?'

'No, not at all.' Out of a still-deep loyalty she added, 'There's nothing wrong with Tim, just that his emotional needs are...' Much

344

lower than mine, she thought with brief bitterness. 'Different from mine. I'm...lonely. Unhappy.'

'But that's the state most of us live in,' Helene said indignantly, as if everyone should put up with it because she did.

Kate next. 'You've got to compromise in this life,' Kate told her, quite sharply. 'What would the world be like if we all just went off when we felt like it?'

Dundy next. 'We've got a spare bedroom in the extension, you could stay here while you're looking,' Dundy offered. She was sympathetic, not angry—did that mean she was happily married?

'Thanks a lot, but I shouldn't,' Elinor said, touched. 'Tim wouldn't believe I was gone for good if I only moved across the road.'

Now Carrie. 'Shouldn't you be thinking of the children?' Carrie said.

'I'd be afraid of infecting them with my own unhappiness if I stayed.'

'You won't if you put up a good front.'

'But children can sense things—it affects them—'

'I haven't been exactly happy with Jack since before Emily was born, if you must know, that's eleven years, nearly twelve, and it hasn't affected Josie or Emily one bit. Do what I did. Take a month off, go on a cruise—you'll be able to go on for another ten years.'

Trying to find a reply, Elinor found herself stifling a yawn. 'Oh dear, I'm so sorry—I haven't been getting much sleep,' she said, and got up to make her escape.

At the door Carrie said, 'Think what they'll gain from a stable childhood—wait till they're eighteen. For their sake.'

Till Isobel was eighteen—fifteen years of unhappiness and pretence? Impossible. How could Carrie do it—how could any of them? Take breaks to make your marriage endurable, as if it were a boring job. Why stop at a cruise? A lover would be cheaper, and more fun.

Maybe that's what Carrie meant; maybe it was what she'd done.

You've got to compromise, Kate had said—and in minor matters it was true: you had to put up with early-morning crossness, each other's families, tuneless whistles, tapped fingers, slurped soup,

345

tempers, depressions, panics. But those weren't central issues, or not for Elinor. Happiness was. About that she couldn't compromise.

Stay for the children's sake. But was that why those women stayed, or because they'd rather be unhappy than poor and lonely, living on their own with young children and only part-time work?

She was so lucky; thank God she'd kept on working.

She found Kit sleeping in a bunched huddle when she went to say goodnight, with his duvet pulled over his head—he'd probably had a nightmare. Isobel had kicked her duvet to the bottom of the cot; she had one arm flung up boldly and one knee raised, as if leading a charge.

Think what they'll gain—stay for their sake.

No; and not only because the children would be better off seeing less of Tim. She would give her life for them if necessary—plunge into a burning house regardless of risk, instinctively. But not her happiness. There were sacrifices you didn't make even for them. Feminism might not solve anything, but it could help. Put yourself, it said, on at least an equal footing. Your children were as important as you in the scheme of things, but not *more* important.

Stay till they're eighteen, Carrie had said. Were children really more pain-proof by then than at two, six, ten? Probably—though things could happen at any age—five, twenty, thirty—to make you lose your confidence and stop believing you'd float if you went beyond your depth.

But she couldn't stay with Tim now, knowing he would never change. Make love to him without hope, without love?—impossible.

No—it *was* possible, she *could* do it. And Carrie was right: the children might suffer less. But she would be unhappy, and eventually so would Tim be—unhappy with her, not just in himself. Maybe they wouldn't quarrel; it would be one of those quiet, civilised unhappy marriages. But that kind harmed children, too. How did they learn to look for love and happiness in adult life if they didn't see it at home?

346

'It hasn't affected Emily or Josie one bit,' Carrie had said. But what about when her daughters grew up and had children of their own—would she want them to stay in unhappy marriages for *their* sakes? Surely not—but she was setting a bad example. For your children's sake as well as your own, you had to try to live the way you would want them to.

She kissed Isobel and Kit and left. Back at Rose and Marcus's flat, sinking bumpily towards sleep on the astoundingly uncomfortable bed-settee, she thought about hard choices. When Isobel grew up and had children, would she want her to plunge into a burning building to save them? No no no—but...yes. Would she want her to give them a happier childhood by staying unhappily married? No.

What she wanted to give her children was the confidence to know that the water would hold them up if they went beyond their depth—though not that the air would hold them up if they stepped off a cliff. And of course you had to teach them to swim first.

Maggie heard of another flat that was just right, and Elinor pinned her hopes to it; but it fell through. June ended; July began. She lived from day to day in a precarious indeterminacy that, as it continued, began to seem almost like a new stability. Her crying fits were over; she was buoyed up by the odd elation that had started the night of the apricot sky. One day Tim threatened; another he promised to change; another he heaped abuse on her; another he told her he couldn't live without her. He refused to believe she was gone; he refused to tell anyone she'd left. It was profoundly unsettling to have one of the most clear-cut actions of her life treated as a fiction. His misery hurt her; she was used to alleviating it, not causing it. But every time she thought of going back, the pain in her neck returned.

Another flat turned up—a mean little place off Green Lanes, but it had what passed for two bedrooms; and it was close to a bus route that went past the end of Ockendon Road and down to King's Cross—easy walking distance of the Cromer; one tube stop in bad weather. It was for sale, not rent. Elinor hadn't wanted to buy a flat unless she liked it; but property prices were going up every month, almost every day. Rose and Maggie both advised her to buy now, while she could still, just, afford to break into the spiral, then look for a nicer place at her leisure. Tim refused to discuss money at all. She consulted a lawyer, learned that since Ockendon Road was in their joint names she could use it as security, made an offer, persuaded the estate agent that her salary would cover the mortgage until she got her share of the house from Tim, arranged to rent the flat, which was empty, until contracts were exchanged, negotiated a staggering overdraft to cover most of the deposit, borrowed the rest from her father, took a deep breath, signed the agreement confirming the sale subject to contract, filed for divorce on her lawyer's advice so as to force Tim to reach a financial agreement about Ockendon Road and maintenance for the children, neither of which he would discuss, then in one massive weekend's effort, while her parents looked after the children, moved her things out of Ockendon Road into the flat, helped by Rose, Marcus, Terry and Nigel, who had an HGV licence and hired a monster lorry, which looked big enough to take the entire house but got filled to the top with just a quarter of its contents, and in a final great burst of energy had the children's bedroom ready by the time Mavis and Walter brought them back on Monday night. It was only five and a half weeks since she had decided to leave.

Chapter 46

The wind went out of her sails once she'd got the children to bed. It was her first evening really alone—while staying with Rose and Marcus, she'd always had company. She sat in the cramped sitting room in a clutter of boxes staring at the windows, feeling vulnerable. Anyone in the houses opposite could see her, but she couldn't even make herself get up and pin up sheets for curtains.

Alone. All alone. Had she really left Tim because he wouldn't talk?—because he didn't pick Isobel up in the lane? There was no one to talk to here. And if she climbed on a chair to pin up a sheet and fell and cracked her head, she would just lie there. This was what the neighbours meant: better unhappy than alone and entirely responsible for herself and the children.

No—think how lucky you are. You earn enough to support you and them. Tim's not trying to take them away. You've got loyal friends. Ring one of them right now, you'll have company in half an hour.

But the problem wasn't company tonight, it was living alone. A body in the bed at night.

She crept to the bodyless bed, slept ten hours, woke up exhausted. The zip had gone out of her. It was all she could do to be reasonably cheerful with the children. She got them to nursery school and the crèche, went to work, yawned all the way to bedtime, slept ten hours again, woke up exhausted again. Where was that sense of well-being? She was lonely. Looking at her face in the glass, she saw hollow eyes, sallow cheeks. Thirty-six. Practically middle-aged. Nobody would ever want her again.

'Cromer Cinema—oh Maggie, hi. How were the Greek islands?'
'Aegean. How's the single state?'

349

'Grim,' Elinor said tersely.

Maggie missed the beat.

'Aren't you going to say I told you so?'

'No, I'll just think it. How's Kit?'

'Missing Tim, otherwise okay.'

'Missing Tim—aren't you letting him *see* him?'

After counting to ten Elinor was still seeing red. 'I,' she said through her teeth, 'have tried till I'm blue in the face to—'

'Nell—'

'—to get Tim to see the children. He says he'll see them when I come back home. Now if that's all—'

'Nell, Nell, I'm *sorry*—I'm a complete idiot.' Maggie waited for a forgiving noise. 'Please?'

'Okay'—grudgingly.

'Now—they need their father: what are we going to do about this? Shall I see if I can talk some sense into him?'

'Okay'—less grudgingly. Then, with a sigh of release: 'Oh Maggie, if you *could*. He hangs up on me.'

He didn't hang up on Maggie. She asked him to come to dinner after his concert the next night, and let him rant about Elinor till one in the morning, listening so attentively that he thought she completely agreed with him.

'What worries me,' she finally said, 'is the effect on the children.'

'That's what I keep telling her, but she's utterly irresponsible.'

Maggie made a noise of disagreement, but didn't argue. 'Do you see much difference in them?'

'I haven't seen them since she moved—I won't negotiate to see my own children.'

Maggie looked as if she quite saw that. 'But shouldn't you anyhow—for their sake? They must be missing you terribly. Would you like me to help arrange something?'

'If you want to, fine,' he said. He had seen where she was heading, and let her lead him there. He doubted whether the children missed him, but he missed them—but had not known how to change his line with Elinor without losing face.

Maggie rang Elinor in the morning, then Tim, then Elinor, then Tim, then Elinor. 'We've got a deal. You take the children to him on

Saturdays at six, he'll bring them back Monday morning. He'll have them one week-night too, if he's free. And I deserve the middleman of the year award.'

The first time Elinor took the children to Ockendon Road, Tim whisked them in and shut the door in her face. Bringing them back to Green Lanes, he rang her bell and shot off down the steps as soon as she answered it.

The following Saturday he did the same whisk-and-slam; on Monday he again rang and fled.

'Wait—we've got to—' Elinor called out. But he was gone.

'How can he have the children on a week-night if he won't even speak to me?' she sputtered to Rose.

'Give him time—he's hurt. Maybe he'd find the telephone easier than face to face? Or you could get Maggie on to him again.'

But two nights and a day with the children exhausted Tim; he could not face a week-night as well. Back in May—a century ago—he had suddenly seen that entertaining them could be easy, but the insight had got lost after Elinor left. He was terrified of boring them; he crammed their Sundays with outings: films, the swimming baths, the Heath. Even Sunday morning had to be filled: the quartet was still off—which did have the advantage that he did not have to say anything to Thoby and Sheila. With luck Elinor would come back before Alan recovered, and they need never know.

'I'm busy every evening this week,' he told Elinor irritably when she rang.

'I'll bring them on Saturday, then.'

'I'm playing on Saturday night—make it Sunday.'

Damn it, she thought, you're weaselling out of it already. I work on Saturday nights too, as you very well know. One of us has to pay for a sitter—why not you? But she remembered what Rose had said. He'd been hurt—give him time. 'Okay—ten Sunday morning. Is Alan still—'

'Yes.'

'Have you told Sheila and—'

'None of your business.' He hung up.

Sooner or later she would have to tell them if Tim didn't—they were her friends too.

—✳—

'A night this week for the children?' she asked over the telephone a week later—he'd done his whisk-slam-flee act again this weekend.

'Not this week, and not next. I'm going away. Salzburg, the Austrian Alps, Rome. I'm going to find someone to have fun with.'

She hung up in a fury. Son of a bitch. In the afterglow of their time in Rome two years ago he'd promised to keep two weeks free this summer, one week for Swarthgill, one for Salzburg and the Austrian Alps. Now—going without her—well of course, but he said he couldn't live without her, so why bother with holidays?—and Rome too, where they...

Someone to have fun with. Someone female—and guess what kind of fun. She hated him, hated him—how could he—

She tried punching a pillow—Chris said it was therapeutic. It wasn't. She seethed for a while, then in a spirit she tried to tell herself wasn't tit for tat rang Sheila and Thoby. No reply.

Of course not. School's out; they're looking at Surrealist houses.

'Blast Tim anyhow,' she fumed to Rose the next day. 'I wanted them to know before they went away—it'll seem bloody odd nobody telling them for practically three months. It was wasted delicacy giving Tim a chance to talk to them first—his whole existence is founded on not talking to anybody about anything to do with himself. All he wants is to have *fun*.'

'You should be taking your holiday, too,' Rose said. She was concerned about Nell. 'If you're too broke to travel, do things here. See London. I bet you've never been to the Tower, Parliament, Madame Tussaud's, the Lloyd's building—'

'They'll be full of tourists.'

'It wouldn't stop you abroad. But if you want to slither round them, get a Pevsner and see all of Wren or, uh...'

'Hawksmoor,' said Elinor. 'There was a stage when Thoby talked of nothing but Hawksmoor and Sir John Soane. "Fascinating deformations of space, Nell—strange foreshortenings." I went and had a look at St George's Bloomsbury, but I couldn't see what he was talking about.'

'So take a busman's holiday—go to the movies.'

'Oh Rose, I don't know. I've been miserable ever since I've been in the flat. It's so *sad*, the whole thing—Tim, me, the children—all

352

feeling worse than we did before I left—so what's the point? I had to leave, I still feel that; but...'

'You've been psyched up for weeks—all that high drama, adrenalin pumping, go, go, go, no time to think. Now the pressure's off—you've gone flat. Go look at some deformed spaces—or there's Buster Keaton at the NFT.'

'Someone to have fun with.' If Tim had wanted his words to work on her, he'd succeeded. Every day in every spare moment she burned with sexual memories. Every night in bed they seized her and kept her awake until she gave in and made herself come, then couldn't sleep for a racing heart. Lust for him scorched her; she remembered, again and again, him sinking into her—a sense-image so unadorned that she was surprised the man in it was so specifically Tim. But it was.

She tried a church or two; she tried a Buster Keaton or two—they couldn't compete.

Go back, then?—quick, before he finds someone else?

If I could, I'd go back just to fuck him, she thought.

Another few days of the long empty August passed. Gradually her fever for Tim slacked off; so did the depression she'd been in since moving to Green Lanes. Her step was bouncier; she felt buoyant again, and started glancing with a warm and speculative eye at personable men—beautiful Italian youths with layer-cut black hair and godlike profiles, lounging in for a Rosi season with pale cashmere sweaters slung round their shoulders, wafting arrogance like expensive aftershave; a man in a lift in Wardour Street with a look of easygoing mischief that stung her sexually, though they only exchanged a few words about whether the lift was the kind that remembered more than one call.

Maybe she should have given him more of a signal...maybe she'd forgotten how...maybe she'd had the jitters? After eight years of monogamy making love with someone new would be like going off the high diving board.

It was so strange, this shoal of her life—like the intermission in a blockbuster. Part One over; what did Part Two hold? Not celibacy: the man in the lift had looked at her with interest; and there were others. Thank God her job took her into the world—how did women at home with children meet men?

But permanent attachments were another matter—she'd known that when she left. She remembered Chris saying once, 'There are so few nice men anyhow; and if they're in their thirties and unattached, either they're undersexed, or they're gay, or they're trouble.'

Everybody but her was on holiday, everybody. She drifted on fluctuating waves of optimism and sadness. Do something, she told herself, take control of your life. A decisive action. Break Tim's sexual hold, have a light disengaged affair—she consciously avoided the word 'casual'—with someone you like.

Someone she liked—a minimal requirement, surely; but she could hear Maggie's hollow laughter. And the August faces at the cinema were too young or too old. Men in their thirties and forties were away on holiday with their happy families.

Chapter 47

Tim bypassed Salzburg and spent his Austrian week walking as high and far as he could, in a torpor of misery, tiring himself out, keeping the ghost of Elinor behind him where he couldn't see her. But in Rome, going alone to places they had seen together, he came face to face with her, and stopped being able to believe that she was staying away only to blackmail him into changing his behaviour— and found himself alone in the world.

Drastic fantasies invaded him. Sue her, beat her up, kill himself, abduct the children, kidnap her, rape her...

Invite himself into her flat, overpower her—

Tie her up? He would bruise her. Rape her? She would be dry; he would hurt her. He could not bear the thought. He wanted to force her will, not violate her body.

Pick up a Roman beauty and fuck her silly, then tell Elinor about it. But he had no desire to. All through their marriage the richness of their sexual life had kept his eye ripe for other women, though he had been monogamous by instinct and in practice. Now, when he needed that eye of lust, it was gone.

Back in London he took the plunge, bought a baroque violin, and threw himself into practising. It helped; but grief flooded back as soon as he lowered his bow. He had never been so unhappy in his life. Time the great healer—what a laugh. Twelve weeks since Elinor left, and he still hardly got through each day. He went to bed as early as he could, slept a few hours; woke at four or five in the morning and immediately began to count the hours to sleep. His stomach was in a tight knot; he had no appetite. Perhaps if he wasted away she would have pity on him.

The weekend came, and with it Isobel and Kit, overjoyed to see him. He was glad to see them, too, but it soon wore off. He was

355

planning things to say to Elinor, to do. Invite yourself into her flat and refuse to leave till she sees sense. Ring her up and plead. A hunger strike. A letter. Tell her you love her—why not?—it's true. Promise to—to—

How could he promise to do what she wanted when he didn't understand what it was?

Did Maggie? He rang and asked her to Sunday dinner.

Kit had hardly seen his fairy godmother all summer; he was excited when he answered the door. Maggie hugged him and gave him a slithery green rubber snake to scare Isobel with. But Isobel wasn't scared; and Maggie was less fun than usual. She sat in Mummy's chair at dinner, and concentrated on Daddy.

After dinner Daddy put them straight to bed, but Kit got up and tiptoed to the stairs to listen. They were talking about Mummy. She should come back, Maggie said. Yes, thought Kit. He liked their funny little room in the flat, but it wasn't an adventure any more, it was everyday life. But everyday life should be Mummy and Daddy together at home in Ockendon Road.

The voices dropped. Kit went back to bed and told Isobel what he'd heard.

Isobel shut her eyes tight. Sometimes she thought Daddy had sent them all away because she'd broken the violin string. I'll never do it again, she promised silently, if you'll just let us come back.

Maybe Mummy and Kit could stay in Green Lanes, and she could be all on her own with Daddy. Her and Daddy, her and Mummy and Daddy, her and Mummy and Daddy and Kit...

'Haven't you had enough of this?' Tim said when he brought the children back, standing in the doorway with a fog of misery on his face. 'It was *awful* on holiday without you. Nobody else is the same.'

'There was somebody?' she said before she could stop herself.

He looked at her hopelessly. It was worse without her than he knew how to tell her. 'No,' he said reluctantly. 'I wanted to, but...I keep thinking about you.'

Me too, she thought, looking at him; waiting for a sign. It was too late, she knew it was. Tim couldn't change; and she'd seen too much about him to go back, fallen too far out of love. But he might have won her back on the spot if he'd said: I need you, I love you.

He said what he had come to say. 'Maggie says we should see a couples therapist. I rang the Tavistock; we've got an appointment the thirty-first at ten-thirty.'

'Oh *Tim*. No. It won't do any—'

'How do you know if you don't try? Maggie says they don't just try to patch things up; if they think it's hopeless, they say so.'

'It never works, Tim, you said so yourself—everybody we know that's been down the marriage guidance has got divorced anyhow.'

Shaking his head as if he didn't remember, he said, 'Maggie thinks you're having some kind of breakdown—she thinks you *should* see someone.'

'Maggie can go fuck herself,' she said violently. Behind her Kit's voice rose to a shriek. 'I've got to go, they're murdering each other.'

'No, wait—you'll come to the Tavistock next week?'

'For heaven's sake, Tim, no. It's no use.'

'I should think you'd try for the children, if not me. They don't understand—people say things. Yesterday the man in the cake shop asked Isobel were the buns a nice treat for her mother. She looked at me to say something—but what *could* I say?'

'Try: "No, it's for us three,"' Elinor suggested impatiently. The children had stopped wrangling; could they hear every word?

'That's not the point, the point is what you're doing to them.'

'Tim, the world doesn't consist of nuclear families that we're the only deviation from. They know lots of other children with divorced parents at nursery school and the crèche. Don't make it harder for them. Of course they want us to be together. But we're not, and we're not going to be. What if I were dead? People would say the same things in shops, and it wouldn't be my fault for not being there.'

'If you were dead, at least I'd know where I was,' he shot back, and left.

Fizzing with irritation, Elinor picked up the children's weekend bag and went into the sitting room, where Isobel had started

357

straight in on her long-term project, building a Lego garage for the Maserati.

'Mummy, make Kit stop helping me,' she said immediately.

Kit stopped of his own accord, though, and went up to Elinor and said, 'My Daddy is a good kind man.'

'Yes, of course.'

'And a good father. And takes good care of us.'

What's this? Those weren't Kit's own words—or his tone of voice—that was... 'Did Tim tell you to say that?'

'He says you'd come back to our house if you knew.'

'Kit, love, no. I know you want me to, but I can't.' Idiotic man, didn't he know better than to use the children as intermediaries?

'Why not?'

She gave the answer she always gave—he'd asked a dozen times. 'Because I've stopped loving Tim; and I'd be unhappy living with him when I don't love him.'

You always say that, Kit thought, but I don't *understand*. A question had been in his head for weeks, under more and more pressure. It popped, and the words came out. 'Will you ever stop loving *me*?'

'Oh darling, no, I'll always love you. Both of you.' Isobel was ostentatiously busy with her garage. 'Grownups sometimes stop loving each other, but mothers...parents, I mean'—she shouldn't leave Tim out of it—'don't stop loving their children.'

'Why not?'

'I, uh, I don't know.' Why didn't somebody write a book for separated parents—ready-made answers to their children's impossible questions? 'Maybe because the two of you were once very tiny and couldn't do anything by yourselves, and so I...so Tim and I, had to do everything for you. And before that you were inside me, and part of me—'

'I wasn't inside Daddy.'

'But he felt you inside me, and your heart beating; and he saw you both being born.' It wasn't getting through; Kit's Tim-like gaze was baffled. 'Do you think you'd ever stop loving me?' she asked at a venture.

Kit thought about it. 'No.'

'Well, it's the same with me. For the same reason.'

'What reason?'

'God, I don't know,' she said in exasperation. 'It just *is*.'

Kit glared at her, but understood. Checking the corners of his mind for scraps of undelivered message, he found none, and went back to plague Isobel with his jerry-building.

Elinor bit her lip with vexation. Blast the man. Couples therapy, fiddlesticks. She had a mind to ring and tell Maggie a thing or two. Meddling where she hasn't been asked—taking Tim's side against her—

Not coming to see her—talking to Tim, not her...Maggie, Maggie. She shouldn't grudge it if it helped him—but it was hard.

'Hullo, Tim, it's Sheila, we're back. What about the quartet—is Alan better?'

'I, er, yes.' Without Elinor there would be no one to look after the four children. What could they do—hire a babysitter? It was yet another problem she had landed him with—though it paled to nothing beside the bitter news he had digested this morning in a letter from his lawyer. Elinor half-owned the house; unless he could buy her out—which he could not, especially after lashing out on the baroque fiddle—he would have to sell it. She had deserted him, now she was robbing him of his home.

'How was your summer?' Sheila went on. 'And how's Nell?'

'I don't know.' It had to be said. 'She's not here. She's moved to a flat.'

Sheila felt the foundations of her life tremble very slightly. 'And...the children?'

'With Elinor. Do you want her number?'

'Oh—if you would; thank you.' She scribbled. 'Thanks, Tim. And...I'm so sorry. Er, how are you?'

'Fine, thank you. See you Sunday.' He hung up.

Thoby raised his eyebrows questioningly.

Sheila said, 'Nell's not with Tim any more.'

'What do you mean?' He stood up in agitation. 'He kicked her out? She walked out?'

'He didn't say.'

'Why didn't you ask?'

'We could ask on Sunday. Or I could ring Nell—he gave me her number.'

'I don't care—whatever you want.'

Sheila picked up the receiver. He went into the kitchen and stood gripping the edge of the counter. Her soft voice didn't carry; ravenous curiosity drove him back.

'Oh, do you think so?' she was saying. 'Oh, did she.—And Kit?— Did you?—Oh yes, curtains never do.'

She hung up. 'They've split up,' she said. 'Nell's living in Green Lanes. I'd better put it in the address book.'

Fear, elation, hope, despair, doubt surged through him simultaneously; he turned away to hide his naked face. 'Split up? Why? Whose idea, his or hers?'

'Hers, I think—but I didn't make sense of it. No fault of Tim's, she said, just differences.' Why did Thoby look so angry—was he hurt? 'She'd have told us before,' she explained, 'only she was giving Tim a chance to tell us first, because he knew us first. And then we were away. I don't understand, though. I thought they were so happy!'

'Man in the picture, did you gather?' he asked, rummaging in his briefcase.

'She didn't say so, I don't know.'

He shrugged as if losing interest. If she were living with someone, she'd surely have told Sheila. Surely, surely. Then—

Don't be a fool. No sexual feeling for you, remember?

He was in no danger of forgetting; he ran on that thorn at least once a day.

So. She had left Tim, but it couldn't be anything to do with him. With what, then? Differences. What kind?

His thoughts were so full of her; yet how little he knew her. Nothing she had said last summer had remotely suggested that this was in the offing. He must find out from her own lips why she'd left and how she was and whether she needed anything.

Hope stung him awake half the night like a falling dream; and in the morning he woke very early thinking: Is there a chance? He had to know, had to see her. Their eyes meeting across Cosh Beck; her thighs parting under his hand on the Heath; her tongue in his mouth in the office—she hadn't *always* had no sexual feeling for him.

By late afternoon he was worn out with speculation and only wanted to go home to Sheila's silence and the boys' noise and the Proms on the radio. But he went to the Cromer anyhow.

Terry came up behind him in the foyer with a couple of Pizza Express boxes. 'Looking for Nell? Here, this one's for her and the daring duo.'

Six o'clock, of course, the children; he'd forgotten. A fantasy of impassioned speeches and fervent embraces shrivelled in his mind.

She was kneeling on the floor with them, working at a jigsaw puzzle, her dark hair falling forward in untidy wings from her hair slides. She looked up and said, 'Oh! I thought...I thought it was Terry and the pizza...'

'Me and the pizza.' Was she confused, embarrassed? If so, was it a good or a bad sign? He said no to a slice of pizza, but accepted the olives the children made her remove from theirs. He wasn't hungry, but it was something to do.

'So,' she said after a few bites. 'How are you?'

'Fine.' The domestic details of forks and napkins and picnics on the floor had composed him; there was relief in postponing the risk of another rejection. 'Why I've come...' is to say I love you. Not that. Be businesslike. 'Is to ask what can I—Sheila and I—do to help?'

Elinor fought back inordinate disappointment. 'Oh Thoby, thank you *so* much—but things are mostly under control by now.'

'I'd like to hear what's happened, though—unless it upsets you to—'

'No, no...' His cool tones: nothing could lie behind them. 'Only...' If she told him the details now, he would go away with no more reason to call on her, and that would be that. 'Only, talking with these two; they're riveted by the subject, and they start demanding, oh, you know—'

361

'Explanations of things that haven't got one—I see the point,' said Thoby, himself suddenly realising that he needed an excuse to meet her again. 'When would suit?'

'Sunday afternoon? Tim has them then.'

'Daddy's got a television,' said Isobel.

'And a video,' said Kit. 'We saw *Star Wars*.'

'I thought Tim didn't like television.'

'Apparently it's just me that doesn't.' Remembering Thoby's friendship with Tim, Elinor didn't repeat Rose's comment: 'Saves him from having to talk to the children.'

He looked at his diary and shook his head reluctantly. 'We've someone coming to tea Sunday, and people to dinner.'

We, he said. We've someone coming. Did that mean he wanted to bring Sheila next time? 'What about Monday, then—come to dinner.' From sheer despair she nearly added, 'The two of you,' but bit her tongue in time. If she did, he'd *have* to bring Sheila. Give him a chance.

Her voice was so cool—was she inviting them both? Like her, he saw in the nick of time that it would be fatal to ask. 'Fine, but not you cooking. Out. You okay for a sitter? Good. Diwana in Drummond Street?' He heard his own frenetic staccato, but couldn't slow up. 'What time?—Fine.'

He left in a hurry, dithery with hope—he couldn't be with her and not feel it. He would come alone on Monday night. Sheila wouldn't think it was strange...but he might just say he thought Nell needed to talk one to one.

Chapter 48

'So. Tell me,' he said over the bhel puri.

Only Maggie and Rose knew about the years of silence, and Isobel's fall. It wasn't fair to criticise Tim to all and sundry—what Elinor told other people was simply that the two of them were so different that she couldn't make a go of it. Thoby wasn't all and sundry, but he was Tim's friend, so she gave him the short version.

'And?' he said when she finished.

'And?'

'Narrative full of tactful gaps.'

'I thought Tim might talk to you—you're the only one he would.'

'He w-won't.' He believed it—he and Tim had never exchanged a personal word. He also meant: I don't want him to; I want you to. 'Tim and I—friends for a long time; but not close.'

She stopped resisting. The story came smoother with re-telling: silence, absence, coldness; years of thwarted hope; the fall in the lane; Tim's despairing refusal to believe she was gone for good.

Nothing she said about Tim surprised him, yet he was dumb with surprise. Silence, thwarted hope—the conditions of his own life with Sheila. He had even made the same mistake of assuming that musical expressiveness implied emotional expressiveness, though in his case the illusion had been shorter lived.

Whenever Elinor paused, they looked at each other, and away. He knew what he was thinking. What was she? The air felt electric. Were they both talking and eating and falling silent in a field of force, or was he generating one all by himself?

'You're different, you know,' he said, mopping up the last of his *dal*. 'Easier. Jollier.'

'That's strange: I've been pretty low—fending off Tim, knowing I've done the right thing, but wondering all the same.' There were tears stuck somewhere behind her eyes, from talking about her and Tim.

'Still. You even look different—bouncier.'

She laughed with sudden recognition. 'You're right—living with Tim, I was always a little subdued.' She leaned on her chin in a sort of exhilarated suspense. 'Funny, I lost my sense of proportion sometime in the summer, but it's back now. I'm where I decided I had to be, me and the children, and it's okay. But if only I'd woken up sooner—years ago. It would have been so much easier for Tim. Kit and Isobel, too. But then I wouldn't have had them—Kit and Isobel—so...'

'Don't blame yourself, Nell. People do stick, it's the natural impulse. Things have to get badly messed up for them *not* to—you keep hoping...' But he didn't want to muddy the clear pool of concentration between them by talking about him and Sheila.

A silence fell. He thought: We've been talking all evening about not talking, and now we're doing it ourselves. But there were silences and silences. Looking at the queue for tables, he said, 'We've still tons to talk about, but I suppose we'd better move on.' To her flat, he would have added, but would she think he was trying to rush her into bed? 'What about a pub?'

Elinor thought: What about my flat? But would he think she meant: Come home and sleep with me? Just a few months ago he'd come to Ockendon Road and told her she didn't bother him any longer. Was he here simply as a concerned friend?

Still, she'd risk it—she hated pubs. 'So noisy and smoky, pubs,' she said in her most practical voice. 'Come back to mine, then I can pay Hilary off—I'm counting pennies these days, living on one income instead of two.' Oops—would he think that was a hint about the bill?

He made no attempt to pay her half. She was relieved, but faintly wished he'd offered anyhow. She didn't want men to hold doors for her, either, but was sometimes miffed if they didn't. Caught between generations: if you were brought up one way and came to another as an adult, there were always recusant corners of consciousness.

They strolled in the direction of Thoby's car. The evening air was almost warm, and the sky still greenish, crayonned with long purple streaks. 'Like the first night at Swarthgill. Remember that walk, Nell?'

'Do I!'

The warmth of her tone drove caution from his head. 'I remember another walk, too—to Cosh.'

'Me too.' She was barely audible.

They stopped with one consent, halfway across Hampstead Lane railway bridge. His heart was bursting its bounds. Looking down at the glimmering rails he said, 'What you said that day in the square—'

'I know, I'm sorry, it wasn't—' She tried to summon up explanations. Her mouth was dry.

'*Why* did you say it?' he burst out angrily. 'And why begin if you didn't mean to go on—why lead me on?' It wasn't the carefully worded question he'd meant to ask.

She craned over the high parapet, elated—he wouldn't be so angry if he were simply a friend. 'I was afraid,' she said, finding her tongue. 'Of the contrast between you and Tim. Of learning too much about what was wrong with my marriage, wanting to get out. Afraid...afraid of feeling too—' How could she say it? But she owed him the forthrightness. She put her head down and got it out: 'Afraid of falling in love with you too much, so it was only you, not Tim.' She turned and started walking again.

A few paces took them to his car. He started up; turned the wheel to pull out; stopped at an angle. He needed it spelt out. 'What you said that day, about having no—no feeling for me. Is it still true?'

'No. It never was. Only that one moment.'

'Oh Nell.' He let in the clutch and shot into the middle of the road. 'Damn—didn't mean to do that.'

'But—' she began.

'Now there's a car behind me. Wants my place, too. Easier to go—sorry.'

He peered round the flat while she was paying Hilary, making polite noises—but she was right, it was mean and poky. Once they

365

were alone, he sat down in her third-hand armchair and said, ' "But", you started to say. But what?'

She sat on the end of the sofa. Their knees were nearly touching. 'It's not really "but", it's more "not yet".'

He raised his eyebrows, ready to turn into Thoby the clown. 'You've got doubts?'

'No, but it's too soon. I didn't leave Tim because of my feelings for you; but he'll never believe that if we, uh, get involved right now.'

'Does he have to know?'

'Funny, that was my line last year, about Sheila.'

'Situation's different. You're not living with Tim, you've no obligation to put him in the picture.'

'He'd find out—the children would say they'd seen you here—'

'Unless I only come while they're with him.'

'I'd feel funny about that: having him take care of them while I...'

'And if he does find out—so what?' Infuriating woman. It was like grasping at a ghost who had materialised for a few minutes and was now busily evanescing—the Eurydice of Green Lanes. 'He'll be poleaxed whenever it happens, whether it's me or someone else.'

'Oh but so much worse if it's you. He'd never forgive you; he'd never forgive me.'

'I can cope.' Fine feelings were all very well, but Elinor's were always threatening to come between them.

She thought him unfeeling. 'I don't know if *I* could. And it's not the only thing. I don't know if I can cope with...with being part of yours and Sheila's life. And...' She couldn't say the thought that had riven her: him and Sheila together, while she was alone, thinking about him.

'Is that a polite way of saying no?'

'No, just: Not yet. I know it's not fair—'

'I'll say.' Why did she have to look so damned determined? 'How long? A month? Three months? Four, five, six, a year?'

She was used to Tim's silent obstinacy, not to argument. 'I don't know,' she said sulkily.

366

They stared at each other, both furious; then something clicked in his mind. He took a long breath, whistled it out. 'You're right, I'm too impatient. I shouldn't try to force your pace.'

She blinked. 'What d'you mean?'

'What I said. I'm sorry I tried to push. Tell me when you're ready—I'll wait.'

It was like leaning into a wind that suddenly dies. 'I don't understand—how can you just completely reverse yourself?'

'It's called living in the world,' he said cheerfully. 'One of us had to give way—I decided it would be me.'

'Oh. Thank you.' She wasn't altogether sure she was pleased.

'That's settled, then.' He stood up. Cheer came harder than he was letting on; he'd better leave before he started pleading.

'But I want to see you,' she said feebly, then was appalled—it was what she'd said last year after turning him down.

He heard the echo too, but ignored it. 'You will. Uncle Thoby the cheerful eunuch, visiting the children, same as if I were on the up and up. Cinema—less risk of hanky-panky. I'll bring the b-boys.' He'd been handsome and impassioned; now he was quirking his shoulders, tilting his countenance quizzically, throwing his eyebrows on high—the whole ragbag of tics.

'I don't want you to be a cheerful eunuch.'

'Grumpy eunuch?'

'Not a eunuch at all.'

'Ah, then—' he pantomimed a lunge.

She drew back involuntarily. He blinked, hurt, and she gave an embarrassed laugh and touched his hand. 'I'm sorry, you just—I just...Maybe I'm not ready. I'm still sort of...grieving, maybe.'

'Well,' he said, his face slowly clearing.

'Well...' she replied. Yesterday at the cinema, this evening at the restaurant, they had exchanged chaste cheek-brushing pecks that symbolised distance as much as closeness. That wouldn't do now. But would they kiss or wouldn't they, and if so, how, and what would it mean, and what might it turn into?

They would: she would. She came close and put her arm on his shoulder, her hand on the back of his neck, her mouth to his, softly, meaning to be gentle, ambiguous, except that her mouth opened as

367

of its own accord, and their tongues met. He pulled her closer; she met him with a serpentine movement, pressing forward and yielding.

The air was thick with the crackle of burning bridges. They were both thinking: Yes, like this, now. Thoby, against his will, also thought: No, not like this—too awful if she regrets it afterwards. And there wasn't enough time—Sheila would be waiting up. They moved their mouths fractionally apart to draw breath, and he made himself loose his hands and unmould his body from hers, till all that held them together was her fingers still touching the back of his neck. Her eyes were wide open; in them he read comprehension and disappointment. And relief?

'Well,' he said inanely, hating to leave, knowing he must; and without his conscious volition found himself on the other side of the door.

He capered down the stairs and had to restrain himself from driving home in hoops and loops and zigzags. The intimacy of their wrangle—the way they'd instantly got beyond politeness: something would sooner or later happen, patience, wait, yes he would, however long she needed, understand her plight, not make it harder, not ask for more. Poor Nell, lovely Nell, Nell of my life, Elly-nelly-nelinor.

Chapter 49

He went to see her at the cinema on Tuesday, Wednesday, Thursday and Friday, at the convenient just-after-work hour when her children were there as chaperones, and played with them while he told her the pent-up thoughts of the last day—the last year—the last ten years—and listened greedily to everything she told him. It was easy to edit for the children's ears—you could say almost anything if you used a neutral tone that didn't catch their attention; and didn't make assignations that Isobel might disclose to Tim in her oral epic.

On Saturday afternoon he brought Euan and Fergus, and the four children played noisily and happily for a while, then noisily and unhappily. He apologised for his boys as he carted them off, though it was really Kit and Isobel who had become difficult—Kit needling Isobel; both of them jealous of any attention paid to Euan or Fergus.

They hadn't been that way before the summer. Maybe what Nell said was true, and they'd be better off in the long run not living with Tim; but right now they were more disturbed than she seemed to see. But would you ever leave if you fully faced how unhappy you'd make your children?

Sunday, Monday—her days off. He had said he would see her only at the cinema, so he didn't suggest meeting her elsewhere. She was with him all the time anyhow. On Sunday morning at the quartet he played the viola, and thought of her. In the afternoon he took his children for a walk, and thought of her. In the evening he talked with friends who came to dinner, and thought of her. On Monday he worked, and thought of her.

This business of sleeping with two people was the devil, even before it began. Honesty, real honesty, went by the board. When—

if—he slept with Nell, he would tell Sheila—but he wouldn't say that he thought of her all the time. Perhaps only complete and willing monogamy, never even looking at or wanting another woman, could keep one in good faith. But he couldn't not want Nell; it was unimaginable. She had what he missed in Sheila: force, play, depth of response.

He mustn't think like that, constantly comparing them, or he'd end up criticising Sheila to Elinor, telling her the secrets Sheila didn't want anyone to know—which wouldn't be cricket.

By five o'clock on Monday he had been communing with Elinor's ghost for thirty-six hours, and was desperate to talk to the real person. He broke down and rang her at home to invite himself round. 'The children are there, aren't they?—Good—makes your flat as public as the cinema.'

Elinor was bathing the children; Kit was wriggling and ducking from the flannel. 'Kit, hold *still*,' she said. 'You've got to have your ears washed. Same as last night, same as tomorrow night. You won't get out of it just because Thoby's here—you're just prolonging the misery.'

Thoby squatted by the tub and made them squeal by scooping up water and pouring it down their backs. In a neutral voice he said, 'Peculiar, seeing our friend'—Tim. 'He knows that Sheila and I know you've left, but he only talks about music and holidays. Unnerving.' His desire for open speech grew stronger. 'But not for Sheila.' He felt a slippage of his will. 'She quite sees why he doesn't say anything.' He slid further down the slope: 'More comfortable for us, too, she says.' And further: 'She's always happier politely looking in the other direction.' Seeing how far he'd gone, he busied himself with sailing Isobel's boat to and fro between her hand and his.

Elinor was obscurely moved to side with Sheila. 'I was listening to a Bach cello suite on the radio, the one she sometimes plays after Sunday lunch. Okay, sweetie, up and out'—to Kit, lifting him into the towel. 'Pierre Fournier—a bit disappointing after Sheila.'

'*Sheila?*'

Elinor stood her ground; Tim had taught her not to be over-impressed with mere skill. 'Technically she's not as good, of course; but her phrasing, her feeling—'

'Don't you know the Casals recordings?' he said in surprise. 'She uses his phrasing, bar for bar, that's where the feeling comes from. Isobel out too? Come on, little one, boat into dry dock. Put-put-putter-putt-whoosh, and now it's time, and *up* we go.'

Isobel wriggled triumphantly in his towelling grasp, entranced by having bagged fascinating Thoby while Kit had to make do with boring old Mummy. Kit read the wriggle and said, 'My turn.'

'No!' said Isobel, clinging.

'*My* turn.'

'Be quiet, both of you,' Elinor said with repressed vehemence. Why did they have to quarrel in front of Thoby?

He solved the wrangle by keeping Isobel in one arm and lifting Kit up into the other. He carried them into the living room, put them down on the sofa and played this little piggy with all their twenty toes at once, then licked his chops and rolled his eyes and muttered darkly about toe pie and toe sausages and breaded toes and toes in blankets and toe fu until they shrieked with delighted terror.

'Truth is, Nell,' he said in a lull, suddenly finding it intolerable that she should credit Sheila with Casals-like depths, 'Sheila's utterly musically unoriginal.' He wanted to add bitterly: Music is all we've had in common for years, and even that's imitated. Whoops—back on the slippery slope, and sliding fast. He made himself say instead: 'Not fair, though. Casals' shadow—hard for cellists. Here, pass the pyjamas, I'll do Isobella.'

Isobel insisted on having Thoby carry her, then changed her mind and reached for Elinor. He picked up Kit, put him in his bed and kissed them both goodnight. Time to go. He was desperate to stay: to go on talking; hear her read the children to sleep; make love to her. He planted a chaste kiss on her cheek and left.

He went home, helped put his own children to bed, ate, then couldn't sit still. Sheila was in front of the television. He muttered something about needing a breath of air and went out to ring Elinor

371

from a call box to say he wished he hadn't spoken that way about Sheila. Halfway through the first sentence he got cut off.

He rang back; got cut off again; found another call box, rang back.

This time the line was crackling. 'This is useless,' he shouted. 'I'll go up to Highgate and ring from Maidie's.'

'That's ridiculous,' she shouted back, 'that long trip just for a telephone call—'

'But I want to talk—'

'Don't go to Highgate, come here.'

His heart instantly filled the entire volume of the call box. 'But we agreed—because you—'

'I've changed my mind,' she said. 'It's impossible like this. After you went...'

'Me too. All week.'

'Me too.'

He saw a snag. 'Trouble is, it's nearly nine; I'd have to be back—'

'Even so.'

'And the children—if they come looking for you and find me too...'

'I should stay chaste till they're grown up?'

'I'll be there.'

Go home, say the old stumps need stirring and you think you'll walk to Highgate and say hullo to Maidie; lope to the tube; sprint for a train and make it; sprint for a connecting train and miss; arrive puffed and wild-eyed on Nell's's doorstep and in a fit of nerves almost turn and run off; but stay; ring the bell; go in.

'I should never have used the word "eunuch",' he groaned. 'Fatal.'

'It doesn't matter,' she said for the tenth time. 'First times are often like this. Especially after all the delay.'

'You say such kind things.'

'True things.'

'Kind, too.' He'd been stealing glances at his watch for some time. 'Trouble is, I've got to go soon. Now, practically.'

'Next time will be better, you'll see.'

'Hope so. Couldn't be worse, could it?' He hugged her harder.

372

'It's all wrong, having to leave with things like this.'

'I know.'

'I want it to have been right *this* time.'

'I know.'

'Makes it no better, does it, me reproaching myself so that you've got to make soothing feminine responses.'

He'd noticed, had he? She chuckled.

Her breath on his neck, her arms round him, her hands on his back. 'I don't want to go. Even if nothing changed all night, I want to stay.'

'Me too.' She didn't want him to go, didn't want to return to bed alone and lie alone with a chill along her body where his warmth had been. If he stayed, maybe they'd fall asleep and wake up later and it would all work. This way, his sense of failure would loom and gloom between them next time. *Men*, she thought; then made an inward apology to the god of reason. Not 'men', just every man she had been involved with. Each of them had been impotent once in a while, even Tim; and in each the ritual of attempts repeated long after she could tell they were in vain, accompanied and followed by self-reproaches requiring lengthy reassurances, had been remarkably similar, more so than anything else about their sexual being. Even self-aware, ironical Thoby could act as if one setback were the end of the world.

He was the first, though, who in those circumstances had ever thought of making *her* come—rolling off her with a groan and a trail of apologies after one of his fruitless attempts, ruffling her pubic hair, sliding his middle finger onto her clitoris, and saying, to overcome her polite reluctance, 'Just because I can't is no reason why you shouldn't.'

They dressed in a slightly furtive hurry, as if they didn't yet have a right to the sight of each other's bodies, and stood in the little hall kissing goodbye by borrowed light from the bedroom.

'It'll be *all right* next time,' she said forcefully as he unwound himself.

He shrugged a few tatters of manhood round himself and said, 'I know.' Maybe if he said so, it would be true.

— * —

373

The next time was eleven the next night, after Elinor finished work. Time was short; Thoby had told Sheila he was seeing a friend and would be home by one. But that didn't stop them.

It went a little better—he wasn't impotent. But he was nervous and overwrought; scarcely had he entered her when he came in a rush of pleasure instantly overwritten by contrition. 'Sorry,' he said. 'Sorry.'

I didn't mean, I don't usually, he wanted to add, but, feeling her quiver beneath him, hyper-alive, hyper-responsive, thought of a better use for his tongue and went down on her, scattering apologetic kisses on the way. Her particular taste was still new enough to surprise him by its difference from Sheila's. Through one ear he could hear her pant, hold her breath, pant; in the other, pressed by her trembling thigh, he heard his own blood coursing, and had the illusion of feeling her whole body breathe, like hearing the sea in a conch. Hold off, stay like this, he wanted to say; he felt like a sleepy child at the breast.

'Next time, it really *will* be all right,' he said, kissing her in the hall with a kiss that smelt of her. 'Everything's gone wrong already— what else could?'

'Plenty. The children will wake up.'

'The time after, the roof will leak.'

'The time after *that*, Tim will ring just when...'

'The next time I'll get stuck in the tube.'

'So then you'll come by car, and it'll break down.'

'And the next time...an earthquake?' He shrugged—not very funny.

She was inspired to add: 'Not to be confused with, "Did the earth move for you?" '

Thoby felt much better. 'Friday night too soon to start the disasters rolling?'

'Late show Friday—no, wait, I'll ask Terry to sub for me—he owes me one. But I'll have to do the second evening house, so you'll still be home late. Won't Sheila notice?'

'I've got to tell her about us now, so at least she'll know why.'

374

'Oh my—I forgot. You *sure* she won't mind?'

'Dead sure,' he said with more confidence than he felt. 'I told you, she didn't the last time.'

How could that be possible? Perhaps Sheila had hidden it: he'd intimated that she was reserved. 'The last time—did Sheila know her?'

'No, but she's...' Too afraid of passion to be sexually jealous, he thought. 'She's not a sexually jealous person,' he said, 'she just needs to know she's safe.' That was why he wouldn't see Nell again until Friday. Tomorrow was for telling Sheila, and Thursday for showing her he was in no hurry to rush off to someone else: that he still wanted to be with her; that she still came first.

'But I'll miss you,' he said as Elinor kissed him goodnight. 'I'll come to the Cromer on my way home every day—and ring—but I'll miss—this.'

'Me too. And—' Tell Sheila...she wanted to say: but tell her what? Tell her I'm not betraying her. But she was; she knew it.

Sheila said nothing when he told her. Nothing, not a word. She looked upset; but sat quite still, looking at her hands. She hardly seemed to be breathing. Her knees and ankles were pressed tight together; her hair was falling forward over her cheeks. It touched him intensely, the grey of her hair. It only made her more beautiful—black had been too harsh a contrast with her soft light eyes and skin—and it seemed like a symbol, though one he couldn't understand, of the pain she lived in.

Why don't you say something? he thought. If he got up and left the room right now, would she ever bring the subject up again, or would it sink into the general silence?

Finally she said, 'Are you going to leave?'

The same question as last time; the same answer. 'You, for Nell? Of course not. I love you.' And her.

After another silence she said, 'Poor Tim. How does he feel about it?'

'Don't think he knows yet.'

'Are you going to tell him?'

375

'I wasn't intending to, no'—drily.

'Nell should, then—somebody should. It'll be awful, him coming here on Sunday—playing—lunch—us knowing and him not.'

Thoby was startled by the echo of his talks with Elinor over a year ago. 'They're not living together,' he suggested; 'it's not his business any more.'

'That's no reason. They're still married—somebody's got to *tell* him.'

'Not me. And I don't really think you should—'

'*Me*? I couldn't. But somebody should.'

She said nothing more. Her silence weighed on him more heavily after what Elinor had said about Tim's. On Thursday he said, 'I was thinking of seeing Nell tomorrow night.'

Sheila nodded as if it were a long-established routine.

'But not if it's a problem for you...'

She shook her head.

'Would you rather I didn't?'

'No, I don't mind.'

Yet he could sense her cowering inside her skin, pained.

Poor Tim, Sheila kept thinking—she'd instinctively sided with him ever since learning that Elinor had gone. He was the deserted one; she'd known him longer; and though she was drawn to Elinor's warmth, she had more fellow-feeling for Tim's reserve.

Besides, Nell hadn't talked to her, she'd talked to Thoby...But that was only because he had gone to see Nell, and she hadn't.

She could have gone—maybe she should have. It would have been an act of friendship that might have made it impossible for Nell to think of sleeping with Thoby. But Sheila hadn't even wanted to see her, far less talk. People who left their marriages had a decisiveness, a violence, that she admired, but shrank from. Elinor's act seemed to put her almost in a different species.

Sheila had survived her childhood by severing her sexual feelings from the vulnerable core of her being. If she was sexually jealous of Thoby, she didn't know about it: no images of him and Elinor in bed rose to torment her. But she did imagine him delighting in

376

Nell's liveliness, independence, this-worldliness, ease with people, confidence with children, readiness to talk. Admiring Nell; preferring Nell.

She too had always admired her, wistfully, from something of a distance, as if admiring a painting. Now the painting was on its own. Would Thoby walk into the frame, leaving her behind? She was in suppressed pain. He and the children were her family; he sheltered her. She didn't love him passionately, but she did love him—but resented his extravagant emotional demands: his eyes burning on her face when they made love; his voice sighing in her ear, 'My love,' as if trying to extract something from her, a vow, a fervour. Why did he need wild flights of passion; why not leave her to herself and keep himself to himself and let them both get on with their lives within the safety of the bond they'd made?

If he left, would he take the boys? No, she needed them. No, he would have to take them—they would fall down the stairs, burn themselves. No, how could she live without them? But without him to amuse them they would be bored—would hate her—would wish she were Nell...

The quartet—she would lose it—how could she sit beside him and play if he were living with Nell?

What about money? She earned a lot less than him.

Nell earned a lot less than Tim, too—how was she managing? Would Thoby, his love transferred, transfer his income too? Could the boys and she live on nothing but what the Falcon paid her?

Chapter 50

The telephone was ringing when Elinor opened the cinema on Thursday.

'Fergus is off school—I can't come to the Cromer today—flu—I'm home with him.'

'Did you tell Sheila?' she asked; 'How did she...'

'Hard to say. Bothered, I think, but she didn't say much. She wanted to know if—if Tim knew.' He was aware of saying even less than Sheila had said, but didn't know where loyalty lay. He wished Nell would insist upon the whole truth—yet what was it?

Elinor felt sore, but held her tongue. She wanted to know all about his life with Sheila, but she must respect the limits he drew. Was Sheila jealous? Angry at Thoby? At her? Had she hurt her—a woman and a friend? A bit late to think of that.

The other telephone started ringing. 'Damn,' she said. 'A customer—got to go. See you at mine, then, tomorrow night?'

'If Fergus is better. Can't bugger off to pastures green and leave Sheila holding the baby—wouldn't be fair.'

She had to agree. 'D'you think this is the start of all those things we said would go wrong?'

'Better not be. I want to *see* you. In bed. Soon. Now.'

'Me too.'

'I'll ring later. Kisses—'bye.'

The other line stopped as she hung up, but the telephone she'd just been using started up again. 'It's me,' said Rose. 'I'll be late. Guess what, the most amazing thing, you'll never believe. Try guessing, just try.'

'You've got a screen.'

'Nah, you're cold.'

'You've met Rivette? Godard?'

378

'Still cold.'

'Rose, you're not pregnant?'

'Bingo!'

'Oh Rose, terrific. When's it due?'

'Thirteenth of May.'

'Fantastic, Isobel was only a fortnight later. It'll be such fun— rerunning history. I do envy you—unless you're feeling off, God forbid?'

'All I'm feeling is spacey. In orbit. Nell, when you found out, did you want to look at—at baby clothes?'

Elinor burst into laughter. 'No, dear, I didn't, but if that's what you feel like—'

Her smile faded after Rose rang off. She wanted—she wanted— another child? Thoby's? Not in her rational mind she didn't, but that wasn't where desire was formed. 'Oh dear,' she said to herself, and went out to tell Terry the news.

'What's tonight's plague?' Thoby asked as he came in on Friday night.

'Plague?'

'Locusts, boils...' Death of the firstborn, no, he wouldn't say that. 'Floods, telephone calls.'

'Tonight's the children waking up, isn't it?'

They did, too—or Kit did, fighting out of a nightmare when she and Thoby had just begun to make love.

'It's an omen,' he said. 'We're doomed.'

She went in to Kit and lifted him onto her lap. He clung tight, heaving with strangled gulps. In the daytime he was so much happier than Isobel; why were his nightmares worse? He soon drooped to sleep again, and let her put him down. Children were so impossibly beautiful—his long fair lashes flattened upon his lower lids; his fine-grained skin splotched brilliant pink where his cheek had been pressing her shoulder. He half-woke in fright each time she tried to leave; so she lay down beside him for a few minutes, trying not to think about how awful it would be if Thoby's erection didn't come back.

But it did, easily, almost casually, as if there'd never been a problem. 'In five minutes Tim will ring, I hope you realise,' he said into her breast.

She giggled. 'And in ten the roof will leak.' He sounded happy, at ease—more so than she, who kept remembering that things had gone wrong twice running. His hands on her, hers on him, the whole length of their bodies touching, caressing banter giving way to fragmentary endearments; to sighs; to silences: she was both inside it and outside.

She judged her readiness by how much she wanted to be ready, but wasn't wet enough; he stuck at the rim of her cunt. She pushed, but got him no deeper.

'No hurry,' he said.

But she was in a hurry—to make it all work, so that next time he'd be confident, and she'd be able to relax. Saying, 'I need...' she reached for the moisturiser and put a dollop on her cunt.

She smoothed the last bit onto his cock. 'Ah,' he said, losing a last trace of rueful detachment. 'Ah,' he said again, sliding into her on a wave of supersmoothness.

'Oh,' she groaned, yielding, as to force majeure, suppressing from her voice the note that would sound like protest—that was a sort of protest. She was setting the pace herself; but no amount of real or artificial lubrication, no gentle slowness of entry, no mental preparedness nor sheer desire to fuck ever quite overcame her momentary resistance. She tightened against him, then gave way like grass flattening beneath a wind; sank triumphantly down around him; lifted up; sank again.

They were over the reef of the first moments. She stretched out her legs around his and lay on his chest, propping herself on her elbows. His face was flushed, his mouth parted in an O, his breath quick; yet there was something serene about him, an equilibrium. He was looking at her from far back in his eyes. She couldn't go on meeting them, or keep her own open at all. She shut them, recalled Tim's averted gaze, and hoped Thoby didn't mind hers. Probably not—she remembered someone in her past saying, 'Men keep their eyes open, women don't.'

Somewhere she was still alert to the chance that things might go awry—too alert. Would she come? Could she? Should she pretend? It might make it easier for him—perhaps for both of them next time.

If she didn't come, he'd feel he had failed her—she didn't want that.

But...

His fevered tranquillity communicated itself to her. Her thoughts fragmented; stopped. Sensation bore her down out of her head; she was possessed by the always-amazing sense of being absolutely centred in the centre of her body. She'd been there for some time, but she'd been too anxious to recognise it. Nearly there, she thought, and with a momentary return of anxiety tried to make it happen, but only fell further off; then was really there, before he was.

'Oh my darling,' she heard in her ear, and he came into her after-pangs, prolonging them into a slowly dying cadence.

Nearly together. When it just happened, really there was nothing like it. Did Thoby make a habit of it—or had he been holding on desperately?

He hugged her so hard that she coughed; his cock popped out of her, slip-plop—a quick, neat, absurd movement. She laughed, lifted off him and snuggled into his arms. In a moment he was asleep.

He started to snore; the noise woke him. 'Made it,' he said, sitting up. 'Third time lucky.'

Elinor smiled, though she was distanced by the words, and remembered Simone de Beauvoir's thing about men wanting to separate themselves after making love, women wanting to stay connected. But why?

Ask Thoby. Not now, though—he's got to go. But the sense of freedom to talk—about that or anything else—elated her so much that she got through the parting without feeling melancholy at all.

'Oh my darling,' she remembered as she fell asleep, and smiled happily.

Sheila just nodded when Thoby said he was thinking of seeing Elinor on Sunday evening. But it was Euan's turn for flu. On

Saturday night he woke up with diarrhoea and vomiting, and they were awake most of the night taking him to the loo, washing him down, soothing him betweentimes.

'It's not *fair*, leaving me alone with them,' Sheila said angrily in the morning. 'What if he was *dying*?'

'He wasn't.'

'What if he was?' she insisted.

'I'll make it Monday, then—if Euan's better.'

'What if he's not?'

'Then I won't go. What is this, Sheila—are you trying to say you don't want me to go?'

'Oh no.' She sat down to her cello. 'Why don't we go over the start of the Schumann? They'll be here soon.'

'Shouldn't we talk about this?'

She shook her head, struck the tuning fork and drew a dark note out of the A string. He wanted to dash her music stand to the ground and snatch the bow from her hand; but sat down in defeat and got out his viola.

At eight on Monday evening he rang Elinor again. 'Euan's still a bit off—I said I'd sit with him a while before coming.'

He got there at ten. 'Sorry—couldn't just...can't stay long, either—promised—'

'Then Sheila *is* upset.' Elinor sat down on the sofa and cast him up a stricken look.

'Yes, but she won't *say* so. Only about the children.'

Her mouth turned down at the corners. She folded her hands palm upwards, and in a small voice said, 'I wish—I wish—it's been *days*. I'm sorry, I shouldn't—I'll try—'

It hadn't occurred to him that she'd be disappointed too. 'Oh Nell, oh my love,' he said, gazing down at her with his forehead ruckled.

The words pierced her. It was the wrong moment; she was too wrought up to be happy. Yet she was happy—and wrought up: feelings spiralling round each other till she felt wound round like a maypole. Sit down, she thought, so I can kiss you. As if he had heard her, he did. She put her arms round his neck, kissed him and breathed in his ear, 'My love.'

'I'm sorry—I wanted it so, too,' he whispered, giddy with her words.

Hearing it cheered her up. 'At least it's not all happening inside my head any more.'

He disentangled himself and looked at her.

'I mean, we're talking about it, not *not* talking. I was always talking to Tim inside my head, but he wouldn't let me talk *to* him.'

'I've been talking to *you* all day in my head; but...' His loyalty to Sheila suffered another slippage. 'But when I'm with you—it's complicated. It's all wrong—I haven't—because of Sheila—but you make me think—' He reached a decision. 'There's no point coming here and replicating my misery at home.' It was out.

'Misery? I thought—I thought you two were happy.'

'I thought you and Tim were, till you told me. One assumes it about other people, don't you think?'

'Do you want me not to ask about it?'

'Oh I want you to! But—' But he'd begun; impossible to stop. 'She won't *talk* to me,' he burst out. 'Everything you said about Tim—you don't *know* how much I recognised. Even the part about the children. She loves the boys so much, but she's terrified she'll somehow harm them—or make them hate her.'

'Hate *Sheila*?'

'I know—it comes from—she was...sexually abused, it's called these days. By her father. "Sexual abuse victim"—dreadful word. Like "drug addict"—reduces people to psychologies.'

Elinor, stunned and curious, wanted to ask what exactly Sheila's father had done, but the question was too obviously prurient. 'How old was she—how long did it go on for?' she ventured.

'From the time she was about four, till the Menuhin School—her chance to get away. From then on she worked to wipe out the past: practise the cello—lose her accent—educate herself into the safe middle class. She thought middle-class men never molested their children. When I met her, she'd never told anyone—she only told me a bit at a time. It's so complicated, Nell. You'd think she'd have gone off sex altogether, but far from it. But it's always in conflict

383

with fear—disgust. She can't be happy with sex, or without it; so she *makes* herself like it: but at a price: bed is the only place where she can show affection—or let me give it. There are these sexual moments; then she cuts herself off.'

'Hasn't it got any better?'

'Worse. She only used to be that way in patches. Now it's nothing *but* patches. She's got so many ways of avoiding talking—works every waking hour, for one. She doesn't want me to talk about my interests; she doesn't want to talk about her own. As soon as the children are in bed she practises; then she turns on the telly and watches *anything*. It's unbearable. I thought she'd change in time—security, the power of love, all that. But she hasn't. So *I've* tried to change—need less—accept the way she is.'

'Shouldn't she try to meet you part way?'

'She doesn't think so—she thinks I should be content with what can be shared without words. But I want to be living *with* someone—living *together*, not just under the same roof—a love relation. God knows I've *tried* to want less—and tone myself down. My enthusiasm overwhelms her—so does yours and Tim's. We like so many different things—she's afraid to.'

'Afraid? But she's far braver than me—going round rough parts of Southwark visiting pensioners—'

'That's because it's for other people. Sometimes she spends all day organising coach trips, home helps, funerals; then comes home and can't make herself go to the corner shop. I don't mind doing those things for her—what I mind is the silence. The children give me a lot; and that helps—but it doesn't stop me from needing what I don't get with Sheila.'

'But what does *she* want—with you, I mean?'

'A quiet life,' he said bitterly. 'The traditional kind—couples who get on with things and don't expect to remain romantically in love, if they ever were.'

' "I don't *believe* in romantic love." That's what she said at Cosh.'

'And we said, "I do;" and I started wanting more again. Started wanting you—but not *just* you. More love. More happiness. More companionship.'

'They *do* have a lot in common, Sheila and Tim...'

384

They looked at each other across a sudden silence, both wishing that Tim and Sheila could get together and leave them free for each other. They knew it wouldn't happen; and Thoby was uncertain whether he even wanted it to. Their eyes still met with the heat of their unspoken declaration; it was one of those moments that justify life, of flare, surge, gathering, perfect vulnerability to experience, perfect happiness. Yet what was he doing letting himself be carried onto the high flood of love and affirmation? There was a line running from his coracle rocking on the deep to the far-off shore of Sheila and children. Was he ready to cut it? Did he want to? Oh yes, he wanted, wanted, this: life that sprang from and included this: eyes' and hearts' exchange of being.

But Sheila. Pity, love, loyalty, children, inextinguishable hope. He stirred, took one hand out of Elinor's, checked his watch. 'Damn, it's late. Got to go—Sheila will be...And I'd better spend a couple of evenings at home. What about Friday evening?'

The natural sequel to talk like this was lovemaking and more talk, not nothing for four whole days. She swallowed disappointment; something like anger, something like jealousy. 'Late show Friday. And I can't ask Terry again.'

'God, I forgot, you're working. If only your hours weren't so cockeyed, we'd have some evenings together. What about Friday morning? I can rearrange things, take time off.'

'The children will be here.'

'To talk, I meant. I almost want to talk more than make love—which is saying a lot.'

Damn it, she thought, turning away from the door. Her hours *were* out of synch with his—with most people's. But she had two full days a week free; the real reason they couldn't have more time together was that he lived with Sheila. She remembered Maggie saying, 'It's all in their control, all. Your whole emotional life depends on when they can get away from their wives. If you want to see them, you fit in. You learn not to say, "Can you come tomorrow?" because they hardly ever can, and it's too painful—for them, having to refuse; for you, being refused.' No, she mustn't think like that. He had said, 'My love': hold onto that.

She lay awake remembering everything he had said, with vague hopes shimmering at the edges of her consciousness. She was nearly asleep when she thought: He didn't say one word about leaving Sheila, not even, 'If only I could.'

Sheila had been so wounded by life—how could he?

Chapter 51

Tim arranged for the mother's help to stay late on Saturday so that he could see Maggie after his concert. He had got into the habit of visiting her every week or so to talk about Elinor. Always about Elinor, as never *to* her, on and on, while Maggie sat with her feet up, leaning forward to tap her cigarette or refill their glasses, her smoke wreathing round him and settling on his chest. She drank more than he was used to drinking, but he nearly kept up with her: like someone reinventing the wheel he had found that whisky made it easier to talk.

'How can she do this to the children?' was all he had been able to say, stumblingly, at first. 'As if a marriage is nothing. As if a family is nothing.'

Then it had started coming more easily. 'If she'd *said*, I'd have— I'd have—why didn't she *tell* me? How was I to know?'

Then, like an ice-jam breaking: 'She says I'm cold, but I'm not, it was just my manner; and now I'm trying to break through. I tell her I can change, but that's not enough for her. I promise everything and it's not enough. I'm talking now, talking about my feelings, that's what she wants.'

Misery alone would not have driven him to volubility—on his first visits he had had a wild hope of getting Elinor back by learning how to talk the way she wanted. But talking had made him see the point of talking; he had come to need the release of speech. Tonight he said, 'I've changed—*you* can tell, can't you?'

'Oh yes—'

'But she says it's too late. How can she not even try? It's not *fair*.'

'Later,' he said the next morning when Isobel tried to start telling him everything that had happened to her all week: he had enough

387

on his hands, feeding the children and preparing lunch. Then came the quartet, and lunch, and then he had arranged for the children to play across the road. But at dinner there was no avoiding the *roman fleuve*. He let it wash over him, until he half-heard something that made no sense.

'What was that?'

'Thoby lives at our house now.'

'Don't be silly.'

'He *does*. He goes to sleep in Mummy's bed.'

Tim gulped for breath. 'Is that true?' he asked Kit.

Kit was less certain of where Thoby was living. 'Sometimes.'

Elinor and Thoby? *Thoby*? What—how could she—how could he—since when? All along, obviously; that explained it all. The children had finished eating. He swept them up to the drawing room, stuffed *Star Wars* into the video machine to keep them quiet and withdrew to the music room. He had to leave the door ajar to keep an eye on them, but they knew better than to interrupt him there.

Violence accumulated in his mouth, backing down his throat, fuming into his nostrils. Slut, whore, bitch. He locked his mouth shut. His tongue moved, his clamped lips twitched. If he opened them, those words would spew out. The children would hear.

Her children, who cares?

His too.

Poor innocents. Thoby there when they wake up at night. Exposed to Elinor's adultery. Adultery. She's not divorced *yet*! I'll cross-sue—Thoby co-respondent—

While he lay alone upstairs in the bed they had shared, she was—

Throw out the desecrated bed; burn it. Send her the ashes. In a funeral urn. He swallowed a gulp of black laughter.

Thoby in this very room, this morning, grinning like a popinjay above his viola—crowing over him, the bastard. How dare he enter the house of the man he had wronged—play as if nothing had changed—eat food that should have choked him?

No more quartet. I won't sit in the same room as that—

Sheila smiling too, innocently. Poor Sheila. Betrayed. How could Thoby—Don't be naive. Men do it all the time. Women too. Just because I never—ridiculous ideas about fidelity—why didn't I— lovely women in orchestras, audiences—plenty of chances. Tears bathed his eyes. He had not *wanted* anyone but Elinor.

She was taking everything away, everything. Herself, children, house, friends, quartet. He would miss the quartet—more than ever now that there was so little else in his life. If she had a jot of decency, she would have left him that. The world was full of men—why Thoby?

He would not *let* her take it away. He would face them down, show her—

Face Thoby, laughing at him, triumphing?

She had once called Thoby a comic scarecrow—how could she sleep with him? She must be desperate. He despised her, sleeping with a scarecrow out of desperation. He had not stooped so low.

Thoby on a bed; Elinor beside him, sucking his cock. The picture was fuzzy in the middle but clear enough: his wife sucking off a thin naked man with Thoby's face. He shuddered with nausea. An even blurrier image: Elinor with legs spread wide and arms thrown back on the pillows as if utterly open to the will of the thin man on top of her; her hips slowly rocking, her cunt pulling in, loosing, pulling in—he well knew that posture, that ceaseless small-scale move- ment, like the sea. Well knew. But no longer. Oh Elinor. How can I *live* without you, how can I go on day to day, week to week, and you not here?

Tears dropped on his tie. You've driven me to this. Alone in a darkening room with, instead of music, the zap of galactic missiles next door, and the maddening blue flicker on the ceiling. Play something; drown it out.

He had not the heart. It was the first time music had ever failed him. Six months ago if someone had asked him which he would choose if he had to, music or Elinor, he would have said music. But without her, his lost Eurydice—

Orpheus when he lost Eurydice sang. Don't let her unman you completely; play.

389

His chin sank on the fiddle, his fingers curled to the bow; but lift it out of his lap he could not. He did not even try. It was the bottom, the worst, the moment when after three and a half months of disbelief he began to believe that she meant it. She had gone; she would not come back. Elinor. Che farò senza Eurydice? He lifted the bow and played the melody in a whisper, a thin thread, hearing the words in his head, then stopped, overcome.

He had all week to decide about the quartet. He thought of asking Maggie's advice, but was too humiliated to speak to her. Had she known about Thoby? He did not want to set eyes on Elinor—he hired a sitter to receive the children when she brought them to Ockendon Road on Saturday, then cleared out in good time himself, drove on automatic pilot to the South Bank, and wandered over Waterloo Bridge to Trafalgar Square and into the National Gallery. It was full of pictures of naked women and their lovers. They were all so fat. He preferred Elinor. Only the Cranach Eve was anything like her.

Eve, Eurydice, Elinor—how could you? My wife, still my wife, my only—Che farò? In front of the children. He would—he would—

I won't go, he thought that night, putting the children to bed, but woke up in the morning thinking: Don't let her take *everything* away; and went, a little late so that there was no time for small talk: just hand the children over to the sitter, set up his stand, take out his violin, say are we ready—not quite meeting Thoby's eye—and play.

It was easier than he had expected. He had dreaded seeing nuances of scorn, but Thoby was transparently well-meaning— cheerful and bird-chirpy, bobbing and turning his head with his quizzical frown; his, 'Don't you think, Tim?'; his air of being about to say something just off the subject. Impossible, while actually in his company, to imagine him malicious, triumphant.

Playing was all right, but afterwards he was throttled with embarrassment. He found an excuse not to stay for lunch and left at the same time as Alan.

'He knows,' said Sheila, looking through the window at his rigid back.

— ✳ —

He drove home, fed the children, stuffed their things into a bag, added a few toys, his shaving kit, a change of underwear and his walking boots, grabbed his fiddle and briefcase of music, shoved the lot into the car, told the children, 'We're going for a drive,' buckled them into the child seats and set off, heading for the A1. To visit his mother. No. To Swarthgill. They had never seen it, poor children.

Tomorrow night she would start ringing when he didn't bring them back—brr-brr, brr-brr in the empty house; she would grow alarmed—ring Thoby and Sheila—the neighbours—the mother's helps—go to Ockendon Road and let herself in with the keys she'd forgotten to give back—run up and down searching—look for clues to where he had gone—finally stand breathless—at a loss—terrified: like the night when they couldn't find Maggie and Kit.

Good. She had kept him in the dark about Thoby—he would pay her out in a coin she understood. They were his children too; he had a right to take them to Swarthgill. Anywhere.

Cars, people and houses kept Isobel and Kit entertained until the A1; then they grew restless. Trees, fields, cattle—see one, you've seen them all. Tim tried getting them to keep count of horses, but there were too few; of lorries, but there were too many—they couldn't count high enough. Isobel got very cross and said Kit was cheating.

'I'm *not*. You're just too little.'

The worst insult. Strapped in the child seat, she couldn't tear him limb from limb, but she hit him with one furious fist. He hit back.

'Stop it, you two!'

'He said—'

'*She* started it!'

'He—'

'If I hear another word—' Tim moved into the middle lane and slowed down to sixty. He was passing one lorry; another began overtaking him. Ground between millstones: thunder outside the car, yells within. There was a car not very far ahead of him in the middle lane. Slow up, keep a gap—and mind the car moving up fast

391

behind him—closing in; sitting on his tail; flashing him. Tap the brakes in warning; again; again; put them on slowly and steadily.

The car on his tail swerved out into the wake of the overtaking lorry. He pulled out behind it and drew in close, flicking his high beam on and off in retaliation. The children were still shrieking.

A BMW appeared out of nowhere; flashed him. Damned if I'll pull in—it's utterly obvious, nobody can go any faster till the lorry pulls in. Blast Kit, blast Isobel; they could hardly scream louder if he *did* crash—

If—their bodies flung—bones at angles—blood running from noses, ears—crushed...He broke into a sweat and pulled back into the middle lane.

'Children,' he said in a level voice, barely audible over their racket. 'Children, stop it *now*.'

'But she—'

'*Now*. Not another word; or I'll pull off and belt you both.'

The idiom was unknown to them—he had never hit them and was not going to start now. But the tone meant business. They stopped. He crept up to seventy and glided carefully along. A sign appeared, 'Service Area'; he followed it.

Oh God, a Happy Eater. The name, the sign, set his teeth on edge. Too late to drive on, though—the children were already agitating for chips, Coke, crisps.

'Absolutely not,' he said, letting them out and taking their hands. 'Milk or juice, and a biscuit.'

'Hot dog? Hamburger?'

'Hamburger,' he conceded. His fault for bringing them here.

Shepherding them through the door, he nearly stumbled into three people dressed as chickens. Yellow legs; yellow hands; towering beaked heads—what world or underworld had they—

He took in their jangling charity boxes, their mild English faces tilted back for a better view from under their beak-masks, their soft country voices asking for contributions in an embarrassed mutter, and felt a fool; but cross. If they had alarmed even him, what about the children?

The children were entranced. 'Look, Daddy,' Isobel whispered when they were past. 'Chickens.'

Has she ever seen a real chicken? Probably not—only Chicken-Licken in the book. Six-foot-high chickens. Did it matter?

Not to Isobel, not to Kit. Only to him; and what was wrong was not the scale, but that three adults were soliciting for charity in a motorway café wearing beaks and giant yellow stretch baby pyjamas in hopes of getting more contributions dressed as chickens than as human beings. It was a wonder they hadn't been told to cheep.

The food and décor were exactly what he had expected. The milk was UHT; he had his coffee black, and nothing to eat. The children tucked into hamburgers and sticky buns, offering him bites. He declined, trying not to shudder.

'I need to pee,' Kit said on the way out.

'All right, I'll take you. Isobel, you wait right here.'

'Me too,' said Isobel.

He was nonplussed. Elinor could take Kit into the Ladies; but could he take Isobel into the Men's—a row of urinals; men with their cocks out, surprised in mid-stream? Hot-faced, he picked her up, told Kit to follow smartish and marched in, meeting no one's eye, and into a cubicle. It was filthy. Out, into another: three in a space meant for one. He wiped the seat for Isobel, lifted it for Kit, lowered it again for himself and peed sitting down, so that the strong smell would not rise straight into their noses. Flush, pick Isobel up, march out.

'We're supposed to wash our hands,' said Kit.

Tim kept going. In the foyer he put Isobel down—reluctantly. It was a comfort holding her close, his beautiful dark daughter.

'We're supposed to wash our hands,' Kit said again.

'Later.'

'I want to now.' He'd dribbled pee onto his fingers. A month ago he wouldn't have cared, but his nursery school was promoting 'good toilet manners', and the message had got through to him very thoroughly.

'All right, come on. Isobel, wait here.'

393

For a miracle, she did not insist on coming along. When they got back he saw why. She was mesmerised by the chickens—who had stopped shaking their boxes and were chatting together, canny and amused: human beings, not chickens.

At the next exit he turned round and headed back for London, thinking subdued thoughts, with the children asleep behind him. It had been a rotten idea anyhow. Underneath his inward rant he had known that. It was hard enough keeping them entertained in London; what would he do with them at Swarthgill? They were too young for long walks; and even indoors he couldn't have left them alone for a single moment—every room had an open fire. And he was performing Tuesday; he couldn't skip that. And what if Elinor had called the police—or his parents? He should have thought of that. They would have driven over from Harrogate and found him skulking like a five-year-old—the shame...

He would show her, though. She was not worth losing sleep over. No more promises and threats; no more pleas over the telephone. She would be sorry when it was too late.

After the children were in bed, he tried repeatedly to ring Maggie. She wasn't in. He went to bed early, and slept the whole night through for the first time since June.

'For you.' Rose waved the receiver at Elinor, who was perched on her desk. 'Maggie.'

'Okay, I'll take it inside.'

She came back in a few minutes, looking sick. 'Tim knows about Thoby—he—I'm not a fit mother, exposing them to—to Thoby and me in bed—as if I *would*!—and he, he, he—' Her teeth were chattering.

'Sit down, Nell. Wait a moment.' Rose fetched tea from the foyer. 'Drink some. Now. What's he done?'

'He rang Maggie and told her he'd started to—go away with them—snatch them—'

'Holy shit—what stopped him?'

'He decided they need me, Maggie says. Though if I'm so unfit— Funny, the children did say they drove to a Happy Eater and saw

394

some people in chicken costumes. I wondered what had come over Tim; but I never thought...'

'Where was he going, did Maggie say?'

'She did *not*—and I couldn't ask. She kept saying how hard it was for her, telling me at all. "A conflict of loyalties—I'm Tim's friend too," ' Elinor quoted bitterly.

Rose surprised herself by saying: 'Still, she told you, right?—she knows where her *first* loyalties are. How come Tim told her, anyhow?'

'He goes to see her practically every week to talk about me. God knows he needs someone to talk to; I just wish it wasn't her.' Maggie in the enemy's camp, ranged against her—it didn't bear thinking about. 'The marriage guidance—that was her notion. Not *my* idea of first loyalties.'

'You're killing the messenger that brings the bad news,' Rose said gently.

'I'm *not*, I'm—' Elinor looked into her mug. 'You're right. I'm sore because...because Maggie and I used to be better friends than this, and I'm jealous of Tim, because he can talk to her now and I can't.'

Oh my dear, Rose said to her silently, oh my dear. The miseries of imperfectly requited love—hers for Nell; and Nell's for Maggie, ever since Maggie had...changed...or been changed by unhappiness—or whatever it was.

'Maggie doesn't think he'll do it again, and I don't want to seem too paranoid, but—' Elinor smiled shakily.

'You could keep the children with you this weekend.'

'But what about next weekend, and the next—when will I think it's safe? It's been hard work, getting him to take them every week. If I start cancelling, so will he; then they'll never see him. I'd never have a moment alone with Thoby, either.'

Rose's faith in Nell was somehow shaken. Did she want Tim to take the children just so she could have more time with Thoby? 'But one of the reasons you left was to get them out of Tim's orbit.'

'No—so they'd see less of him, not nothing. They love him, after all—and he loves them, too; he's just lousy at showing it. I don't know, Rose, I don't know. *I'm* happier away from Tim, and Kit may be; but Isobel isn't. She misses him all week; then all weekend she's got him, but she misses me. So she's never happy. Sometimes I wish he'd move to Edinburgh or America—too far to see them regularly. But then they'd really feel abandoned.'

Chapter 52

The doorbell had to be Tim, no one else would call after eleven. Maggie was tempted to stay put. She quite enjoyed his visits, now that she no longer had to hypnotise him out of silence; but he always stayed and stayed—he didn't have to get up early, and forgot she did. He had been bitter enough before learning about Thoby, and now he'd be worse, far worse—rank with grief and rage, damning Elinor one moment, wanting her back the next. Maggie always contradicted his wild accusations, but felt disloyal even listening to them.

But she went to the door. He'd have seen her sitting-room light— you couldn't let a man down after leading him to think you were there for him.

Tim was too sad for angry abuse. He told Maggie about sitting in the music room unable to play, knowing Elinor was gone for good; but he almost didn't want to talk—not talk compulsively about Elinor. He was getting a bit tired of it. Silences fell—of his making, of Maggie's—that weren't like his old silences with Elinor, which had been tense with resistance to demands he had feared being unable to meet. Maggie didn't make those demands. He felt different—more weighted, yet lighter. The weight felt like resignation, the lightness like release from anger. He was still angry, still sad—yet there was this lightness; and this weightedness that was more like gravity, more like a thoroughbass, than like the stone he had carried in his heart since June.

One drink too many. He was sleepy, and yawned. Noticing that she too was yawning, he stood up and stretched and said, 'I'd better be going.'

Tiredly at the door he tried to summon up a smile, and instead leaned forward to kiss her cheek—in simple gratitude, though with the more complicated subterranean motives of paying Elinor out by canoodling with *her* best friend, as she had with his, and of showing her in his head—and Maggie too—that he wasn't in fact a monster of coldness.

Whisky had undermined his inhibitions. Maggie's little face, leaning up to meet him, was warm and alive. His mouth brushed very close to hers. Without premeditation he moved to kiss it. Their mouths touched, then with a movement that either of them might have started, though in fact it was he who did, they moved closer and tentatively embraced. He'd forgotten all about paying Elinor back.

He had talked to Maggie as never to Elinor; now he was kissing her as he never had Elinor. That didn't occur to him, but it did to Maggie, in a tumult of emotions sweeping her all at once. Guilt for kissing her best friend's husband. Satisfaction at getting his sexual attention away from Nell, however momentarily. Triumph at receiving the kiss Nell had pined for in vain. An intuition that she would get more kisses from him if they went on—either he'd broken through some barrier, or it had only been there with Nell. Lust, simple lust, that made her want to wrap her arms tighter round him and let it sweep her away.

But she was deeply monogamous, and still involved with Albericht—who would sooner or later be posted somewhere else; whom she loved, damn his eyes, though with an exhausted hopelessness that made it possible for her to think about Tim. An end was coming.

But not yet. She drew back, and when Tim made to follow put her hands on his chest to keep him at a distance.

'Why not?' he asked.

'You still belong to Nell.'

'No I don't, she's thrown me away.'

'You feel as if you do, that's what counts.'

True. 'And if I didn't?' It suddenly mattered to him that this intensely desirable woman should want him.

She considered various replies. 'That would be another matter.'

He took the implication. She was attracted; were he free of Elinor's shadow, she might be interested. It was the first good reason he'd come across to try moving into the light. That would show her—Elinor, not Maggie.

He caught the thought and had the grace to be ashamed of it—for Maggie's sake, not Elinor's. He took in her captivating face, all planes and quirks and high-chinned gallantry. Pinning it up in his mind as a badge of possibility, he said, 'I suppose I'd better be going. I'll ring you next week, come round maybe. I'm free Tuesday—'

'Albericht, Tuesday.'

He looked at his diary. 'Friday, then?'

'Fine. But—as friends, not...'

'I understand.'

He went away cheerful for the first time since Elinor left. The next morning the stone was back on his heart, but seemed a little less heavy. He had something to look forward to next week besides two moments of seeing Elinor, once when she brought the children, once when he took them back.

Maggie went to bed with a beating heart and didn't sleep for a long time. She hadn't thought of Tim for herself at all when he first started coming to see her—and not only because of Albericht. She'd been hoping Nell would go back to him. But once Tim told her about the affair with Thoby, she had begun to think about...she knew not exactly what. Tendrils of possibility.

About a single man in whose wings she might find shelter.

About Kit—being his stepmother, seeing him every weekend, loving him as much as she wanted, helping Tim understand him...and Isobel...away from Nell's critical eye. He needed tactful encouragement, not the impatience of someone to whom dealing with children came easily.

About the solidity of a house after all her years in a flat. If she sold hers and came in with Tim, he wouldn't have to sell his house.

About (tremulously, distantly, not daring to peep very close) having children herself—plenty of women did at her age these days.

About a body in bed at night. Someone to share a life with.

Not just any body: a man she had always found attractive; a man of strong sexuality, who was yet monogamous—that was essential. She'd been the other woman too often; she couldn't bear to be a wronged wife, criticised to other women as men criticised their wives to her.

She lay awake other nights in the next few weeks, after other visits from Tim. It was what she wanted, she was more and more certain. It would work, too—she'd make it work. Her demands on him would be fewer than Nell's, and easier. She needed personal talk, but that was what friends were for; she'd never needed, or even much wanted, to pour out her heart to men she was involved with.

It was extreme need that had driven Tim to start turning himself inside out with self-revelation; once he was less miserable, he would lapse back into silence. Not completely, though—she would contrive to keep lines of communication open. A little address was needed—the feminine arts Nell wouldn't condescend to employ.

Tim was luckier than many people: music, his chief means of release from himself, was available to him every day. Still, he was a fundamentally unhappy man; Maggie had no illusion that she could make him happy—not the way Nell, say, was happy. But she herself was one of the unhappy ones; she understood him better, would make him a better companion—and he her. His depressive temperament had made Nell miserable, but for her it would be like looking into a mirror. They might even cheer each other up.

She could have Tim right now; she wanted him right now. But every instinct warned her that it was too soon. She had to play a very cautious, very skilful game in order to get him for the long term, and in a halfway decent condition—not always half-hankering after Nell. She remembered Nell saying it took you two years to recover from being left. Tim had been alone for only four months. He was still raw with pain and longing; still changing every week under the pressure of grief and anger; faithful to Elinor even when she was faithless to him.

She wouldn't wait two years—if she didn't take him sooner, he would find someone who would. But he needed another few months.

And she had to decide about Albericht.

But Albericht was already receding into a dream. Sometimes when she turned to him to say something she was startled because his face wasn't Tim's.

The night of the great storm Elinor started awake to a great clatter. The children, she thought, jumping out of bed. They were safe in bed asleep, unperturbed by bang howl bump clink tap whup crash.

The wind was whistling along the gardens at the back, pushing trees relentlessly in one direction, not tossing them to and fro. Slates whizzed off roofs and shattered cold frames, extension rooflights, a lean-to greenhouse. At the front the wind rushed groaning down the narrow street like a river funnelled into a gorge. Rubbish-bin lids flew by, and slates and branches, borne along on the river of wind. An invisible hand wrenched off a length of cast-iron guttering and hurled it javelin-like down through the roof of a car. Scaffolding crashed helter-skelter like spillikins. A bicycle was dragged along riderless and dashed against a basement window. A traffic cone. Sand whirling up from building sites. Papers. A flapping blue polythene tarpaulin. Leaves thick as bats streaming out of a cave. Branches from trees bigger than any in the road.

Other people were up too, watching from other darkened windows. Elinor was excited and lonely. Were Thoby and Sheila up too, looking out together, arms round each other for warmth and solidarity? Was Tim watching it alone? Her arms felt empty. Thoby, she thought. Tim, she thought, and pushed the thought away.

In the morning she went to the Heath with the children to inspect the damage. A lot of other people were doing the same thing, mournfully, yet half exhilarated by nature's brute destructive power.

On Parliament Hill Euan and Fergus ran up to them. Elinor looked round for Thoby, and saw instead Sheila, climbing towards her on a long diagonal, squinting into the sun. They hadn't met since the quartet's do in June. Elinor sketched a wave. Did Sheila see her? Would she change direction when she did?

Sheila waved back. When she was close enough she said, 'Dreadful, isn't it,' meaning the trees; and kept the conversation to the storm. The children wanted to go to the pond. Elinor and Sheila followed, exchanging pleasantries. Sheila seemed at ease; she even mentioned Thoby. Elinor blushed at his name like a criminal with a guilty secret; but had a hard time thinking of anything to say that didn't include it. He was what they had in common, after knowing each other for years. The bond of their long moment of women's intimacy at Isobel's birth was wordless, nameless, primitive; it couldn't, unlike some kinds of shared experience—jobs, friends, pastimes—be summoned up to cover differences of temperament.

It wasn't the first time she had walked beside Sheila trying to think of something to say. Friends could walk in comfortable silence. But you needed to be friends already, or the silence rattled. They hadn't got there before; they certainly wouldn't now.

'Dreadful sight, Nell,' Thoby said the next evening in bed. 'So many uprooted trees—like pathetic fallacies.'

'What's a pathetic fallacy?'

'Where you think nature's reflecting your mood.'

She laughed. 'I don't feel like an uprooted tree.' But she did, a bit: uprooted from life with Tim; not yet rooted in a new one.

'Sometimes I feel like a banyan,' he said, 'but without the central trunk. No middle, just aerial roots touching down here and there. Fingers without a hand.'

'*Les Yeux Sans Visage*,' said Elinor. Two could make obscure references.

But it was no use trying to one-up Thoby; he just wanted to know about a film with such an intriguing title.

402

'It's Franju—a minor new wave horror flick, stylishly lit—very black and white. A plastic surgeon disfigures his daughter's face in a crash, so he kills another girl to graft her a new one.'

'What happens?'

'Oh Thoby, it's not worth wasting words over. The skin grafts don't take, so he keeps on killing.'

But she had to sit up and tell him the whole plot, meanwhile thinking: an uprooted tree—and Thoby the banyan with the missing middle not the one to re-plant her. Touching down here and there: with Sheila; with her; centred—where?

'What I like about you,' he said, 'you tell me stories.'

'Just film plots.'

'Lovely film plots. My Scheherezade.'

'A story a day keeps the executioner at bay.'

'I love you.'

Her heart gave a bound. 'Me too, you.' First times. My love, he'd said last month, and often since; now, at this odd moment, came the declaration in full. She looked down at her hand on his chest, over his heart, where love was supposed to reside, and thought: I'll remember this forever.

When he said it again the next week, her heart bounded again, but more complicatedly. She'd been thinking. 'And Sheila?' she asked recklessly. She had to know.

He wished she hadn't asked. 'S-Sheila too. Not the same. Old loyalty—children...' Tactless—Nell looked hurt. But he didn't want to pick and choose his words here: he had enough of censorship in his life with Sheila. 'Knowing her so long, you see,' he tried to explain. 'So much history—so much effort. Not loving her would be like not loving oneself.'

'You mean like "Nelly, I *am* Heathcliff"?' Elinor asked, pleased even in her distress to be for once the one who was quoting.

'Not at all. That's the way I feel about *you*.'

She looked at him, slowly comprehending her triumph. That's the way I feel about you. Identity, fusion, hearts silently reading each other while tongues busily chatter. That identity, that

403

simultaneity, spread out across the whole field of life, not, as when she was living with Tim, restricted to making love—which was a special case—and walks in Yorkshire: spread out across laughter, talk, fierce disagreement; across silences that were light, not heavy with self-suppression—silences of concentration upon something else, not of avoidance.

In spite of what he'd just said about Sheila, she almost expected his next words to be something about leaving her; but they weren't.

Chapter 53

Thoby didn't know what to do or think; he didn't know what he wanted. Nell, Sheila, his children. Nell more than Sheila. As the weeks slid down into the trough of December that much was clear. His long patience with Sheila was slipping. The silences he had borne with a semblance of good humour were becoming intolerable. He came home after work hoping she'd be out; if she was there, he busied himself with the boys or the viola. He hadn't practised so much in years; his playing improved by leaps and bounds.

How could you live with someone whose presence was a dead weight on your heart? He was barely polite to her half the time.

Yet he still loved her.

They spent Christmas in Highgate, then left the children with his great-uncle Ezra and went to Paris for a holiday that had been arranged since the summer. He was dreading it, but it went well— the longer he was away from Elinor, the less irritated he was with Sheila. She still loved Paris; they had a good time looking at buildings and pictures and vistas together, and eating wonderful food, though Sheila would only eat one dinner in two, keeping what she saved to give to a shelter for the homeless that she'd nosed out on the first day; keeping him silent company while he ate. It drove him barmy, but he respected it.

A good time. Placidity, balance, taking the good with the bad, accepting limits: a classical ideal. You could find a good life by hewing to that, clear-eyed; disciplining your nervous excitable taste for romantic extremes.

But an hour with Nell put paid to the equilibrium he thought he'd achieved in Paris.

405

That was surely decisive.

Yet the children: they needed him. The way time stopped when he was with them.

Yet the dead weight on his heart. He was morose all week, and even gloomy with Elinor their next time together.

'What are you thinking?' she eventually asked.

He always loved it when she asked that question—Sheila never did—but the true answer had often been one which something—confusion, loyalty, uncertainty—stopped him from giving. The confusion was still there, but he couldn't find another layer of thought to tell her about instead. Perhaps he didn't want to. 'I'm thinking about wanting to be with you.'

'You are.'

'All the time. For always.'

She'd wanted to hear it so much; but not in that reluctant voice. She couldn't make herself say, 'Me too.' She just looked, waited.

He said, 'Remember the first thing I asked you when we met on the Heath after Cosh?'

'Where to have tea?' She didn't know if her tone was dry or bemused.

'After that. Sitting on a log. I said, "What about us?" It's still the question. I think about it all the time. Leaving. Living with you, if you'd have me. But Sheila. But the children. I've got as much place in their lives as she does; they'd miss me much more than yours miss Tim. And me them. And how would she cope with them without me—how would she cope with anything?'

'She's always seemed so good with the boys.'

'She is. But that's not how she feels. I need *you*, Nell. I need your passion, I need your affection. I've never felt anything so strongly. But you can see the fix I'm in. Sheila depends on me utterly—how could I leave her? It would be like abandoning a child you're responsible for.'

That question had been staring at Elinor for months. 'Surely there'd be other men attracted to her?' she asked, clutching at straws.

406

'Oh she wouldn't be alone for long. That allure—men fall for her in droves. Streets lined with corpses. But she'd be thrown upon marginality again.'

'Meaning?'—with a touch of impatience.

'The way she was when I met her. Affairs with married men— fleeing deep attachments. Thinking she was doomed to be always a mistress.'

'Like Maggie.'

'No, you say Maggie wants to be married. Sheila was terrified of living with anyone—thought she was incapable of it. If I left her, that'd prove it. She'd go right back into her shell, dug in further than ever.'

'Allure,' Elinor said rather bitterly. 'It's what Tim said about Vivian. And Maggie. *And* Sheila. It makes me feel like the girl next door. A good kid, but no allure.'

'Three unhappy women. Don't envy them, Nell.'

But she noticed he didn't say *she* was alluring.

You can see the fix I'm in—how could I leave her? It was like running on sharp spikes.

Could he leave? 'People do stick,' he'd said in the Diwana over bhel puri; 'Things have to get badly messed up for them *not* to.'

How badly?

Yet she felt amazingly happy. I need you; I've never felt anything so strongly. Could it be this simple? Probably not.

She was saturated with thoughts of him, but never saw enough of him; their hours barely overlapped. She was free in the morning— but had the children. He was free in the evening—but had his children, and Sheila. She worked on Saturday, he on Monday; and the quartet took up half of Sunday. They snatched what moments they could.

He was temperamentally elusive, too—seldom sure what he'd be doing at any given time a week off; and reluctant to be fixed down to a time or a place. Elinor didn't want to chase him with a butterfly net, but hated never knowing such a simple thing as when they'd next meet. He would drop in at the office and enjoy himself all the more for having come on the spur of the moment; while she...enjoyed it too, but rather the less for not having had a chance to look forward to it.

If we were together, she thought fifty times a day: and forty-nine times a day stopped herself. 'People do stick.' For all his airy spontaneity there was something dogged about him, patient, like a horse in harness: something she recognised—it was how she'd felt before leaving Tim. It wasn't a good thing to bow patiently beneath the yoke of life, unless you had no other choice. But did he?

If he left at all, it would be in his own time. She couldn't have left Tim before she was ready—not even if Thoby had been waiting for her.

Was Thoby ready? Maybe yes, maybe no. She couldn't afford to hope; couldn't help hoping. He wanted to live with her—but couldn't even manage a weekend in the country with her. He slipped elver-like between her fingers.

'I've got to tell Nell,' Maggie told Tim soon after they began.

'She'll learn soon enough without your help.'

'Precisely. I don't want her learning the way you did—Isobel rattling it out.'

'Why not? It's how she let me find out. It's not as if she'll be interested—she doesn't give a damn about me.'

Maggie had her own ideas about that, but only said, 'It's just a courtesy.'

'I don't want the two of you...talking about me.'

She knew what he meant. 'We won't,' she promised.

Tim had to be content with that—but wasn't. He no longer wanted Elinor back—his desires and hopes were focussed on Maggie. But he blamed Elinor, deeply blamed her, for not giving him a chance to change. She had humiliated him—rejected him. He could not bear the sight of her; her eyes withered him. He wished he need never come within their orbit; but had to, twice a week, when they exchanged the children. That would be the advantage of sole custody—avoiding having to see someone who'd rejected you.

—※—

Maggie had to wait till Elinor finished on the telephone. 'Listen, I've something to tell you, that may be...a surprise,' she said in rather a rush.

'Fire away.' Elinor's mind was still half on the runaround she'd just been given. No thirty-five millimetre print, though she'd been promised one; sixteen, take it or leave it.

'It's about Tim...Tim and me. We're—'

A door blew shut in Elinor's mind. Blood mounted to her head. Her husband; her best friend—indecent. Obscene.

Maggie, reading the signs, looked down at her hands and gave her time to recover by murmuring, 'It's just since last week—after Kit's birthday. I didn't know if you'd...mind, but I—we—thought you should know. I hope it's...not a shock...'

Elinor tried to smile. 'No, just a surprise, though it shouldn't be—you and Tim always...' Fancied each other. 'Liked each other.' Her mouth felt thick.

Noise in the outer office: the sitter with the children.

'Maggie!' said Isobel, and climbed straight onto her elegant grey lap.

Kit gave her a kiss and said, 'We're going to Coram's Fields—you too?'

Maggie glanced at Elinor, and Elinor said, 'Do,' though another kind of jealousy was piercing her. The children had ignored her and gone to Maggie—both of them. When had Isobel started getting on Maggie's lap—when had Maggie started encouraging it? How much was she seeing the children at the weekends? Was she trying to win them away?

Of course not. Believe in her friendship.

Would Maggie and Tim try to get custody of them—a couple, with a house, against a single woman in a flat?

No, and for the same reason: friendship. Besides, why should Maggie try to take over Kit and Isobel? She could have children of her own.

Maggie—children—with Tim? Her womb contracted with pain.

'Actually I've got to get home,' Maggie said, sensing that Elinor was still in tumult.

'Walk with us, then, it's on your way,' said Elinor, not very graciously.

Maggie did, lengthening her pace as of old, click-click in her high-heeled shoes, while Elinor shortened hers. They and the children walked four abreast, all holding hands. Elinor and Maggie said almost nothing—Elinor was too raw, Maggie too aware of rocks and reefs.

Isobel started singing 'Row, row, row your boat'; she'd just learned it at the crèche. 'Merrily, merrily, merrily, merrily,' Kit joined in. Elinor's eyes met Maggie's over the children's heads, and Maggie asked, 'D'you think they're too young to sing it as a round?'

'I don't know. You could...' Elinor looked away. 'You could ask Tim.' She was holding Isobel's hand, and Isobel Kit's, and Kit Maggie's: a chain conducting faint vibrations of good will from Maggie's end to hers; and perhaps back again.

At Coram's Fields they exchanged another quick half-shy look, and Maggie's uncertain expression softened into a smile of regret for gulfs old and new still gaping between them. Oh my dear, Elinor thought. So much loss; and what remedy? Though still tight with unfair irrational misery, she managed to say: 'I hope it's...If you're happy, then—I'm glad,' in case it should ever be true.

It was like swallowing ground glass. She had a bad evening and a worse night. Poor Tim, she tried thinking—this is how he must have felt about me and Thoby, only worse. It was no help. I can't stand it, she thought, digging her nails into her palms. Tim, the past, years of my life, my children's father—cut off. No retreat.

Some time in the small hours she thought: But would I do the same again—leave Tim?

Yes.

Thoby or no Thoby?

Yes.

Well, then?

Sweet reason was no help. She remembered, in her flesh, concretely, Tim's hand brushing the soft responsive skin of her inner thigh.

410

Another moving image: Tim sitting on the edge of the bed, her kneeling in front of him, sucking him—his hands cradling her head; his legs open round her body, enclosing it, while she worshipped the god of pleasure embodied in him—paying tribute not to Tim in particular but to all men. Something in sex that's not about either of us.

She'd seen a print like that in a book once: a pillar with a smiling bearded head of Priapus set on top and an erect cock jutting out of the side, and a girl with wreaths of flowers, smiling too, stooping to garland the god's cock in thanksgiving for the pleasure he gave her.

With Thoby she had less access to that non-personal greed. His glowing tender gaze was so suffused with personal tenderness that he never entirely receded from being Thoby to being a man who was also Thoby.

Loss, gain. Thoby flowed, he overflowed, with tenderness—little caresses; kisses tucked here and there on her face and body; words like dear, darling, sweetheart; telephone calls 'just to hear your voice'; his hands on her breasts, his tongue in her mouth, his eyes widening with pleasure. What had been missing with Tim; what she'd wanted: the personal.

But with Thoby she didn't feel so taken over, so possessed. She wanted everything between them to be better than between her and Tim, but everything wasn't. Sex, in particular, though emotionally richer, was less saturated with carnality—like bread, not caviar: nourishing, but less vehemently stimulating. He feedeth my soul.

Did democracy, tenderness, by their very nature exclude insolent wild greed?

The meanings of what she and Thoby did were different, even when the physical gestures were the same. After that one astonishing moment long ago on the Heath, there was nothing in their sexual relation like the time in Rome when Tim flung up her skirt after seeing the St Teresa statue, and they both knew that his impulse had been to cover her face with it—a shared wantonness.

She had loved Tim, and he her, but he had refused to say so or act so, except sexually. Their sexual bond had been real when much else of what she'd imagined they had in common had been a figment of her hopes. She'd never wanted to believe that; she'd wanted sex to express something more central than itself; hadn't wanted their love to amount to nothing more than being good in bed together.

But to be as sexually happy as that was no trivial thing; it wasn't 'just sex'. It had been an expression of...of she didn't know what: things too primary for analysis. In the absence of so much else, their erotic bond hadn't been enough to sustain her; but it had been one of the great goods of her life.

In a day or two she found that she could, after all, live with the idea of Maggie and Tim, so long as she didn't try to imagine what it might emotionally or sexually consist of. Okay then, keep your mind to yourself.

When she delivered the children on Saturday, Tim met her at the door with his usual hard angry stare. She wanted to say something to mark the change in his life—not let him intimidate her into silence.

'Maggie came to see me,' she said, wondering if Maggie were inside.

He reddened. She had no right to mention it. He did not want her greasy curious fingermarks over his private life. He shut her up the only way he could think of, by stepping inside and slamming the door.

Her turn to go red; to think: He'll never change; to fume down the steps. But it was okay. Her doubts had vanished once she was face to face with him. She had stopped loving him. His heavy, handsome face no longer made her melt; she no longer shrank at his anger. The break had been made.

Winter dragged on well into spring. A low ceaseless wind that seemed not to have stopped since the great storm blew grit about the streets and worked its way inside the lighter-weight clothes which it was impossible not to want to wear by the middle of April—the end of April—the beginning of May.

In the middle of May Rose had a daughter and named her Roseanna—'I like my name, so she's getting it with knobs on.' Elinor held Roseanna longingly and thought about Thoby and babies and her age and how little time there would be even if he ever did leave Sheila; and quite lost track of whether she really wanted more children. There were ways and ways of wanting.

What she certainly wanted was more of Thoby. Much more. Will he, won't he? Sometimes it took all her energy not to ask him. She was possessed by waiting: for summer; for Thoby.

Chapter 54

Sheila's secretary invited her and the boys to stay in an aunt's cottage in Sussex over the Whitsun long weekend. Sheila accepted, so Thoby felt free to suggest an outing to Elinor. 'Somewhere in the country—two nights and two days together.'

'Yorkshire? No—jolly awkward if we met Tim and Maggie there—they're taking the children up.' Maggie on the moors would be a sight to see: like Dietrich teetering into the desert after Gary Cooper on her three-inch heels in *Morocco*.

'Big county.'

'Still, I'd be tense every time I saw another couple.'

'Know Norfolk? Wonderful churches. Salt marshes. Remote villages. Sense of space. Castle Acre—romantic ruin.'

They were looking for a bed and breakfast, but stopped on impulse at an inn that looked simple and ungentrified—no olde-Englishe on the sign; no horse brasses and warming pans in the bar. The bedroom could have done with gentrification; it was cold and smelt of mildew, and the bed had nylon sheets.

'At least it's not quaint,' said Elinor.

'Or light'—the walls were dark green, the bedspread and curtains brown.

'Or bright'—the ceiling light was twenty-five watts and twelve feet in the air, the bedside lamp a dimness behind a burgundy shade.

'Or modern. Untouched since the war, don't you think?'

'Or convenient—did you see where the loo was? A mile along the corridor.'

'Or friendly, with Madame Defarge at the desk. *Tale of Two Cities*,' he added so that she wouldn't have to ask.

'I know'—a touch huffy; then, with a grin: 'I saw the movie.'

414

But there was a big lumpy double bed; what else did they need? And breakfast the next morning was good—cooked, not Continental, with fried bread, for which Elinor had a passion. She ate Thoby's too.

They drove from church to church, village to village, then in the afternoon went for a long walk, very happy. Footpaths by young green fields; high plumed clouds in the creamy blue; horse chestnuts weighty with candles that from a distance were massy, dense, but close up dissolved into airy froths of little delicate flowers, all frilly spurs and points. 'The chestnut casts his flambeaux,' said Thoby on a white-flecked footpath.

'Housman,' Elinor said before he could.

He looked at her surprised, but said nothing: he was learning.

'Surprised I knew?'

'Not at all.'

'Liar.' Then, confessing: 'Maggie used to quote that every spring.'

The sun was bright again through the curtains the next morning, and the room was hot, though not from the sun; the ancient radiator was on flat out. They pushed off the mound of blankets. Thoby was still too hot, and lay outside the sheets; Elinor kept the top one over her. He sat up on one elbow, looking at her face, her swathed form. The light was catching the down on her cheek, just below the lower lid. He touched it, and she put a kiss in the middle of his palm, looking up at him between his parted fingers, her brown eyes starred with light. 'My love,' she said.

'My love.' His heart moved towards her; he wished they could stay here forever, in the caul of their two perfect days. He bent over her, kissing her, and almost without knowing what he was doing let his hand drift down over her sheet-shrouded body: shoulder, arm, breast, then smoothly and more purposefully down to her ribcage, down to her belly, down, making a careful detour·round her cunt, to her thighs, that opened under his touch, and back up again, belly, sides, breasts, shoulders, arms, up, down, his hand firm, smooth, moulding the sheet over her.

415

She tried to slide her hand out of the swaddlings towards his cock, but he tucked her back in; and she yielded. Her breasts warmed at his touch under the cool sheet; it was like the cloths that sculptors put over unfinished clay statues. She was his Galatea, he was moulding her into life, pure love in his hand on her body, in his eyes on her face, in his mouth on her cheek.

He slid his hand over her cunt and along it, through the cloth—landing a frustrating fraction too low, though she didn't break the trance to tell him—but wouldn't let her hand free to touch him. He looked at her with delight; then pulled up the sheet from her side and delved under.

The flat of his tongue over her clitoris like a palm; then he burrowed up the bed towards her head to kiss her, his mouth salty from her cunt, and came into her, and she melted into the steady state of transfixion that was like nothing else.

They were borne on a flood tide. For a while, buoyed on a halcyon wave of love, pure love, they stemmed it; but it was moving through them with its own force. 'Oh my love,' she heard in her ear as she came, in a great ingathering; and felt him open to her on an arc like a shot arrow.

'From fucking to fried bread,' Thoby murmured, watching her tuck in at breakfast. 'Shortest route from the sublime to the ridiculous.'

Then they were out in the world again, nosing round ruined abbeys, peering up at the angel roof at North Creake and through the manor-house gate at West Barsham. At intervals all morning Elinor remembered, with an inward gasp, his body reverberating like a bowstring when he came.

They ate their sandwiches leaning against an early English arch in a priory ruins—Thoby quoted Wordsworth—then drove north to walk on the salt marshes.

Inland it had been sunny and calm, but at Overy Staithe a piercing wind was levelling at them from the sea, and sea and sky and shaley sand were the same bleak indefinite whitish-grey. Thoby bounded about like a retriever, bringing her flowers, sedges, shells and bits of rock and pointing out ringed plovers, oystercatchers, redshank, cormorants, curlews, avocets, and three species of tern.

She knew nothing about birds and liked them big and decorative. How could he be bothered to distinguish among terns?

It was heavy walking, worse than Oughtershaw Moss, without the compensation of height, breadth or scope. The dunes oppressed her, and the trail of litter along the path, and the trickle of people who didn't look as if they liked where they were any better than she did, and the sea far off beyond the ragged dunes, and knowing that once they were there Thoby would want to walk for miles along the coast, telling her the names of more birds and rare sedges. Salt marshes were horrid. Her trainers were full of sand. Our last afternoon wasted, she thought; but nodded, smiled, agreed that this or that was 'good'—Thoby's word for pretty, beautiful, entertaining, interesting: 'Good, isn't it, Nell?' of a hammer-beam roof, a bit of seaweed, a funerary inscription—and asked questions to hide her sulky distaste for one of his favourite landscapes.

'Is that—' he said suddenly, seeing a woman's smooth grey head rise from behind a distant dune. 'No. Thank goodness. Thought it was Sheila.'

'Isn't she in Sussex?'

'One hopes.'

They reached the sea and started along the shore. The footing was better on the damp sand; but the wind was sharper. There were shells and rope and seaweed along the tide-line, and a blue washing-up-liquid bottle, and cigarette packets. 'Thank goodness—thought it was Sheila.' Well? Who was she to mind that, when she'd been afraid of meeting Tim in Yorkshire?

His hand moulding her through the cool sheets. Did he ever do that, exactly that, to Sheila? More to the point, would he do it now?

Jealousy, rank jealousy, stop it.

They could be so happy together—look at yesterday; look at this morning—and he wasn't happy with Sheila. But he wouldn't leave, she was sure of it. Everything would keep him there, everything but her: his children—the ties of shared history—Sheila's lovableness—Sheila's life-wound—Sheila's beauty, hardly dimmed by time's touch, only mellowed, more poignant, more touchingly vulnerable. He might say he was unhappy; he might *be* unhappy; but he made love to Sheila and liked it, whatever the constraints—perhaps liked it more than making love to her, just as she, in her heart of hearts, knew that she and Tim had been more to each other sexually than, for all their love, she and Thoby were. She didn't intend to ask if she was right. She could just about bear thinking so without knowing; but if he said yes, she might rise up in wrath and rend their relation from end to end.

Unfair, unfair, remembering Tim as she did.

But that's in the past. Sheila's not. Tonight when he gets home will he fuck her, after fucking me this morning? She walked on, head down, hands jammed in her pockets. Her eyes were smarting, but dry; every time tears rose, the level wind blew them away.

Think how happy you were this morning, she told herself; and yesterday. But that was the whole trouble. It wasn't because of Sheila that she was miserable, or the dreary old salt marshes; it was because so much happiness was unbearable when they'd be back in their separate lives in a few hours. Being with him like this just made her want more more more—Thoby playing with the children; Thoby in her bed all night; Thoby getting up before her in the morning to go to his job; Thoby there at night when she got home from hers—

He won't leave; he won't leave.

Could she stand it, in the long run?

Thoby could tell she was miserable; it made him miserable, too, in spite of hovering sandwich terns and rustling sedge. His life—decisions—Elinor—Sheila—Euan—Fergus; what could he do about it all? He almost wished she were the sort of person who made ultimatums; or even that Sheila were. All this good behaviour: too civilised by half. But that was what he was—and Nell—and Sheila. They were stuck with it. And he with Sheila, and his life. And Nell with him—until she couldn't stand it. He wanted them to go on for ever, but he knew better. Affairs ended.

They should be talking, not plodding along in isolated misery; but wind and sea and seabirds made it difficult.

Turn back then. It took him some while to act on the thought, for part of him stubbornly wanted to keep going to the last tip of land. He was annoyed at her for not seeing the salt marshes as he did. But

418

finally he gave up. 'Cold wind,' he said apologetically. 'Should have stopped earlier. You're tired.'

'Not very.'

'Bored?'

'No—you?'

'Not a bit. What's good about being with you, Nell—even if I *am* bored, it's with what's going on, not you.'

'Me too,' she said, recognition breaking through her unhappiness; and they exchanged a look of delight. His eyes were so beautiful, even scrunched up against the wind. She wanted to keep looking at him, talking to him; but they'd reached the embankment and had to walk single file against a steady stream of late-afternoon last-chancers.

'Should we go straight back?' he asked at the car.

'To London? Oh no—something else first.' Something to prolong the fragile illusion that they lived like this, together.

They stopped at Castle Acre, off the main road, up through the town and along and down to the priory, with fat clouds of cow parsley lining the road.

It was late. The ticket booth was closed, but you could still get in. A couple entered ahead of them; a number of people were straggling out. They walked slowly round the ruin, staring up at the great crumbling west front with its tiers of Norman arches. Thoby talked about revetments and ashlared pilasters and the medieval economy. The sky was pink and blue through the big vacant Perpendicular window. Elinor was intensely happy again, looking at his black-browed emphatic face, listening to his light voice crack at the edges. For certain, this man would never bore her. Even when he was boring her to distraction with his chatter about rocks, she was riveted by him himself, the bedrock of his being, over which there played the spume of particular subjects, some interesting, some not. Happy.

They sat down on a low ledge warm from the day's sun and looked out at the intensely English scene: long summer-afternoon light, green ripening fields with a faint haze glimmering as if exhaled by the crops, here a well-tended ecclesiastical ruin, in the distance a church tower among trees. Happy. But as they sat in momentary silence she was suddenly afraid, she didn't know of what exactly. That things would run down; that eventually there would have been too many times like the hour on the salt marsh; and more pain than happiness between them. The sea wind reached its chilly fingers inland and touched her spine. Tears came to her eyes. She blinked; they spilled. She turned her head away. If she hid them, maybe she could find her way back to being happy again.

'What's wrong, Nell?' he said quietly.

'Why should anything be wrong?' she managed to say without sniffing.

'Your breathing changed. You're crying.'

'I'm not.' Sniff. But she was. She abandoned hope of refurbishing the day. 'I was thinking, What if this ends.'

'You mean all this?'—gesturing at the landscape. 'World War Three, as in? Or...'

'Or us.'

'But we'll go on for ever. I can't imagine not.' If he said it fervently enough, they might both believe it so faithfully that it would stay true.

'Me neither. But it might end. I might, myself. End it, I mean. Us, I mean, not me'—though he'd hardly think she was thinking of suicide. She sniffed and rummaged for a tissue. 'The thing is...the trouble is...' Her tongue wavered between sentences. 'Saying anything about you and me and this situation, anything negative—I can't; because it'll sound like putting pressure on you, which I—' She couldn't honestly say she didn't want to. 'Which I'm not trying to.'

'I know, but you've got to say it anyhow; we can't just not talk about it. Come on'—when she just nodded mutely, wiping her bright-red nose with sodden tissue—'tell me. Why would you end it?' He knew the answer already, but he had to get her talking.

'Because there's no future in it, and—and—I want there to be.'

'Can't you just *carpe diem*?' he asked gloomily.

'No, I want a life with you, not snatched moments. And—'

Sheila wanted the same thing—what could he do? 'And...?' he prompted.

420

'I want...' It was a moment for telling the truth. 'I want to come first.'

'You do,' was out of his mouth before he could think how it betrayed Sheila.

A jolt of joy went through her; but she said: 'No—equal first at most; that's not what I want. I'm not asking you to do anything, just saying what it's like for me, on the outside. I don't know how long I can exist conditionally—waiting, wondering. You've got a life—a life and a half—I've got bits of one. I don't want to get like Maggie—bitter about living on the fringes of married men's lives.'

'I know, I understand—but for me—I can't—and I don't know when—or if. I keep thinking and thinking and getting nowhere. When I'm with you, it seems easy. But when I'm with Sheila—the idea of actually saying, "I want to leave you"—hurting her that much, deliberately—I can't. I mean, I don't know if I can—what would make me do it. You must think I'm a coward.'

'No. It's not...' She stopped to cope with welling tears of despair. 'To...not to...If you want to do something, and don't because it'll hurt someone, that's not cowardice.'

'But you did.'

'I'd reached my limit. You...haven't.' If he couldn't bear to hurt Sheila, did he think she'd been cruel to Tim? Well—she had been: had nerved herself, made herself hard, done it. It had seemed necessary, but that didn't make it less cruel. 'The only thing I wonder...if you live at such a distance from each other, are you sure Sheila would be hurt—might it actually be a relief, you saying it first?' That was the furthest she could go in the way of incitement.

'I—no, it's not symmetrical like that.'

A silence fell between them like a shadow. She sniffed; sniffed again; found another tissue. The only other people still about, the couple who had come in ahead of them, passed in front of them, looking up at the arcading, and headed towards the exit.

Thoby reached out his hand to hers. She seemed about to snatch it away, then didn't. It lay inert beneath his. He pressed it, withdrew. A tinge of blue was gradually infusing the haze above the fields. What did he want? He didn't know. Not to be sitting here paralysed with misery, unable to straighten his shoulders. But

421

better this than the level plain of his life before Nell. Thoby the equable zany: not enough. He knew what he wanted. The impossible. To live with Nell without leaving Sheila; to hold, help, protect Sheila without having to live with her.

She stirred and stood up, shivering, and rubbed the gooseflesh on her forearms. 'I don't know,' she said. 'I don't know.'

He looked unhappily up at her. Her eyelids were damp and crumpled, her cheeks sallow, her nose red. Best to face the worst head on. 'You saying this is the end?'

'No!' End, when they were so happy? Yet she was so unhappy. Ridiculous, such contraries. 'No,' she said more temperately. 'No, I don't want to end. I want to go on.' But...

The unspoken word hovered on the air.

They went back to the car, both wretched. Thoby looked at the one-inch map and said, as he'd been saying all weekend—it was something he had in common with Tim—'We don't have to retrace our steps, there's an unnumbered road. With a ford.'

The road was so narrow that may and cow parsley tickled the car's sides and set them sneezing. Down they went, gently down, beside the stream now. Branches reached in and grabbed at their hair. Insensibly they cheered up.

Round a shallow corner the stream broadened into a pool. The metalled lane came to an end a few feet above it, in front of a rusty fence that was there to keep cars from driving straight over the edge. A steep dirt track branched down to the watersplash. They got out and had a look, but the ford was too deep for the car. Carts could have done it; perhaps tractors still did.

The long light was dusky pink. They leaned on the fence in silence like farmers leaning on a gate, and watched the stream eddy and purl like bull's-eyes in crown glass. Round them were fields deepening to evening, the distant abbey empurpled, long-legged insects on the water, the smell of hay and water, the stream running hidden between bushy banks into the pool and away again through the sallows.

The water was sliding rapidly. You could gaze right down to the brown sharp-edged pebbles on the bottom, but it was easier to focus on the clear purling surface. Every few minutes a brown trout jumped, catching insects, or just touched the surface with a little plicking noise. The trout were almost invisible, flickering between the stream-bed and the air, except when late sunbeams, rippling deep into the water, criss-crossed them with pale snake-bandings.

'Like Cosh,' Thoby said.

It wasn't a bit like Cosh, but she knew what he meant: deep country, and a Cosh-like isolation and quiet—though there was more noise if you listened: a motorbike up in Castle Acre; a lorry somewhere; the distant drone of cars on the A-road; the sky-high whine of a jet aiming for Lakenheath. Other than that there were no sounds but water purling, birds chattering, leaves rustling, and plick, plick of trout surfacing.

The summer light slowly faded. Their nerves were peeled naked and their hearts turned towards each other, but they said nothing beyond, 'Look,' or, 'There's another.'

It had been late in the day, late, to realise that Tim could never give her what she needed. As Chris said, there were fewer nice men around than women; and most of them were married or otherwise attached—like Thoby. Late. She'd exposed herself to a life of extremes and loneliness.

Would she do it again—still—now that she was beginning to know the cost? Sometimes a foreboding shook her; but usually the answer was yes. On her own with two children wasn't where she'd have chosen to be at the age of thirty-seven—but it was better than being unhappy with Tim.

She loved Thoby; she wasn't about to break off with him just because he stayed with Sheila—or not yet; or not so long as her desire and will had anything to do with the matter. She'd stick as long as she could; and that would be a long time. Perhaps for ever—but she doubted it. Their relation had a provisional curl round the edges. Half a life wouldn't be enough for her if she met someone who could be centred upon her, whom she could live with.

Oh but she didn't want to think that. Lose the black-browed man beside her, hunched over the fence high-shouldered and brooding,

423

every sense alert to her and the fading day and the glassy stream? Unthinkable.

Trout jumping, the hazy abbey fading into landscape, the sky ashes of roses. How could she be so happy and unhappy in the same breath? Emotions leapt in her like trout quickening the surface; till in spite of her better judgment she almost wanted to invest the moment with a significance, a finality, to say, this is it. But there was no finality in her heart, or in the moment, only continuity. The stream ran invisible towards them, pooled out, ran away again under the bushes.

In most lives, in hers, there was no one moment to which all things drew and from which all emerged, no moment of climax. There was only this moment, and this, and this, with certain rare ones casting an obscure refulgence backwards and forwards. Cosh was one such; and Thoby saying, 'What about us?' on the Heath— and Isobel falling in the lane. That was perhaps the nearest thing in her life to a single decisive moment with a dénouement, though it had led not to great clarifications, simplifications, resolutions, but to a new set of not entirely satisfactory conditions; new struggles within the meshes and complexities and muddles of ordinary life.

It was all right. If happiness was to be hard won, and as often as not threaded with pain, at least it came, in the form of trout leaping below the glass of a disused ford; Thoby bending above her with pure love in the dim morning light and moulding her body beneath the sheets; Isobel's olive face peaceful in sleep; Kit rollicking towards her banging the drum while Isobel followed shrieking on her recorder; the memory of Tim paying her his body's tribute; Rose's Roseanna pulling her heart out of her with unfulfillable longing; Maggie's eyes meeting hers over the children's heads; Thoby's eyes meeting hers over Cosh Beck, or meeting them now.

A Selected List of Fiction Available from Mandarin

While every effort is made to keep prices low, it is sometimes necessary to increase prices at short notice. Mandarin Paperbacks reserves the right to show new retail prices on covers which may differ from those previously advertised in the text or elsewhere.

The prices shown below were correct at the time of going to press.

☐ 7493 0780 3	**The Hanging Tree**	Allan Massie	£5.99
☐ 7493 1224 6	**How I Met My Wife**	Nicholas Coleridge	£5.99
☐ 7493 1064 2	**Of Love and Asthma**	Ferdinand Mount	£5.99
☐ 7493 1368 4	**Persistent Rumours**	Lee Langley	£4.99
☐ 7493 1068 5	**Goodness**	Tim Parks	£4.99
☐ 7493 1492 3	**Making the Angels Weep**	Helen Flint	£5.99
☐ 7493 1364 1	**High on the Hog**	Fraser Harrison	£4.99
☐ 7493 1394 3	**What's Eating Gilbert Grape**	Peter Hedges	£5.99
☐ 7493 1216 5	**The Fringe Orphan**	Rachel Morris	£4.99
☐ 7493 1510 5	**Evenings at Mongini's**	Rusell Lucas	£5.99
☐ 7493 1509 1	**Fair Sex**	Sarah Foot	£5.99

All these books are available at your bookshop or newsagent, or can be ordered direct from the address below. Just tick the titles you want and fill in the form below.

Cash Sales Department, PO Box 5, Rushden, Northants NN10 6YX.
Fax: 0933 410321 : Phone 0933 410511.

Please send cheque, payable to 'Reed Book Services Ltd.', or postal order for purchase price quoted and allow the following for postage and packing:

£1.00 for the first book, 50p for the second; **FREE POSTAGE AND PACKING FOR THREE BOOKS OR MORE PER ORDER.**

NAME (Block letters) ....

ADDRESS ....

....

☐ I enclose my remittance for ....

☐ I wish to pay by Access/Visa Card Number

Expiry Date

Signature ....

Please quote our reference: MAND